PRAISE FOR
THE STORM CROW

"*The Storm Crow* is a fantastic debut. Written with both power and charm, it showcases some of my favorite worldbuilding ever in a YA fantasy and has nuanced, wonderful characters and relationships. Dragon fans should get ready for their next favorite creature. I loved this."

> —Jessica Cluess, author of *A Shadow Bright and Burning*

"*The Storm Crow* is everything we love about YA fantasy, with an enchanting world and original magic that keeps the story fresh. Clashing kingdoms, thrilling action, and an imperfect heroine make this book a must-read. This soaring debut was a delight."

> —Adrienne Young, *New York Times*
> bestselling author of *Sky in the Deep*

"Josephson's debut displays ambitious worldbuilding and an engaging premise involving the magical crows, which affect everything from storms to healing; Anthia's battle with depression is portrayed with frank authenticity, and features well-developed LGBTQ characters."

> —*Publishers Weekly*

ALSO BY KALYN JOSEPHSON

The Storm Crow

THE CROW RIDER

KALYN JOSEPHSON

sourcebooks
fire

The Kingdoms of
KYTHRA

THE

The Seamounts

The River Ren

Underwater
Volcanoes

Verian Hills

ILLUC

PORT
MARANOCK

SORDELL

The
AMBRIELS

The Etris Forest

SEAHALLA

The ARDRAH
SEA

ELAIR

MYCAIR

EDIR

The Kessel
Woods

ELARIS

ARIS

CARDAIL

BHODAIRE

ISAIR

FENDAIL

KERIS

N

The Cut

VASHKA

ROVI

WITHDRAWN

The Andia River

Remnants of the Kovan Forest

A

ALRON

JINDAE

IRA

oss Bay

The EASTERN WASTELANDS

Tyross Mountains

TRENDELL

STAIR

Calase Mountains

TERIN

ESELIN

To my Guillotine Queens:
it's all in the execution.

Published by Sourcebooks Fire, an imprint of Sourcebooks
P.O. Box 4410, Naperville, Illinois 60567-4410
(630) 961-3900
sourcebooks.com

The Library of Congress has cataloged the hardcover edition as follows:
Names: Josephson, Kalyn, author.
Title: Crow rider / Kalyn Josephson.
Description: Naperville, IL : Sourcebooks Fire, [2020] | Sequel to: Storm crow. |
    Audience: Ages 12-18. | Audience: Grades 10-12. | Summary: Thia yearns to
    trust her crow, Res, his unstable magic, and herself enough to lead the rebellion
    against the Illucian empire and become the crow rider she was meant to be.
Identifiers: LCCN 2019059018
Subjects: CYAC: Fantasy. | Princesses--Fiction. | Crows--Fiction. | Magic--Fiction.
Classification: LCC PZ7.1.J786 Cro 2020 | DDC [Fic]--dc23
LC record available at https://lccn.loc.gov/2019059018

Source of Production: Versa Press, East Peoria, Illinois, United States
Date of Production: April 2021
Run Number: 5021412

Printed and bound in the United States of America.
VP 10 9 8 7 6 5 4 3 2 1

ONE

The ocean had always reminded me of the sky.

Both were vast, ancient domains that we could never hope to control, and each time we entered them, we placed our lives in the hands of something that could crush us.

Something about that thrilled me.

I stood at the bow of the *Aizel* dressed in my flying leathers and a thick green cloak the ship's captain, Samra, had reluctantly lent me. Salt air nipped at my face, the wind running long fingers through my curls and lifting them to dance like ribbons.

A shadow rippled across the water ahead of the ship. I lifted a hand, feeling the brush of feathers a moment before Resyries landed on the railing before me. Wings outstretched against the wind, the crow balanced effortlessly, the gossamer shine of his dark feathers blending into the blue predawn light. The connection between us thrummed with quiet contentment, something neither of us had had much of in recent days.

After our flight from Illucia, we'd headed to the Ambriel Islands but had decided to skirt around them rather than make land, since the islands were likely full of Illucian soldiers searching for us. Their queen was not going to let me escape so easily. Not when I was the only one who could hatch the crow eggs she'd stolen from Rhodaire. Not to mention I was technically still betrothed to her son.

I winced at the thought of Ericen. Unexpectedly, we'd become friends during my time in Illucia. The fingerless leather gloves I wore each day had been a present from him, a symbol of strength when I'd needed it most. But the prince was loyal to his kingdom. Loyal to his mother.

"I have to let him go, Res," I said into the wind. So why couldn't I?

Res trilled softly, sensing my melancholy mood. Nearly a month old now, he was almost big enough to ride, a thought that both thrilled and terrified me. I was days away from reaching a goal I'd been working toward my entire life, but I couldn't separate it from what else it meant: war was coming, and we were ill-prepared.

I crossed my arms against the chill wind. "This is all such a mess. Caliza doesn't even know about the eggs Razel took, let alone that we've escaped and are heading for Trendell. She's probably worried sick." I had a letter prepared for her but hadn't yet been able to send it.

It pained me to think of her worrying, though she'd never let her distress show. It'd always been that way. Her the sturdy land, me the wild air, our mother the ever-changing sea.

What would she think of her daughters now?

Res turned, leaning his head toward me. I placed a hand on his beak, and for a moment, there was only us. A girl, a crow, and the vastness of the empty sea. I gathered that feeling of serenity and tucked it away inside myself. Whatever came next, I wanted to remember this moment of peace.

A thin line of sunlight cut a red slash across the horizon, softening quickly into the warm orange of a candle flame. It illuminated a distant coastline like the spine of a slumbering beast.

Rhodaire.

Our route had taken us far out to sea in a wide arc, consuming two weeks and most of our supplies but hopefully throwing Razel off our trail. All that mattered was that we still had enough time to reach Trendell before Belin's Day, when the other kingdoms had agreed to meet and hear out my pleas for an alliance against Illucia.

In a couple of weeks, we would either stand united against the empire or fall divided beneath their blades.

The deck creaked, and Caylus appeared at my side. Every inch of him was pulled tight, from the rigidity of his broad shoulders to the steel in his green eyes. Words had never been his strength, but our proximity to the Ambriels had only made him more withdrawn.

The sea breeze caught my hair again, lifting and tossing my dark curls as a slow, heavy unease curled in my chest, thick with guilt. It was my fault Caylus had been torn from yet another home. My fault Kiva lay injured in bed, her sword arm now useless. My fault everyone on this ship was now a target for a cruel queen.

I wanted to be a leader, to be the sort of person people wanted to follow. So far, I'd only made things worse.

I slipped my hand into his. "What are you thinking about?" I asked. It was one of his favorite questions. He might be shier than a spring flower in winter, but he did like to talk to me, and I liked to listen.

"Crows," he said with a hint of a smile. "Magic." The smile faded. "War."

I squeezed his hand. "I know I said it before, but I understand if you don't want to do this. It isn't your fight." Though the idea of doing this without Caylus at my side hurt more than I wanted to admit. He was a steady rock, a comforting reflection. We understood each other, and in a way, we'd help rebuild each other.

But that didn't make this his war.

He bit his lip, but before he could respond, footsteps made us both turn. Samra stood in the center of the deck, her unruly black curls pulled up in a tight bun, her good eye sharp as freshly cut glass. "We need to talk."

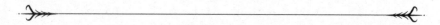

In the warmth of Samra's small office, Caylus and I sat in two handcrafted chairs opposite the captain's own. Loath to be left out of anything, Res had crowded in behind, though he was as tall as Caylus and twice as big around. He dropped his head onto my shoulder as if it might make him smaller.

I was keenly aware of Kiva's absence. Her shoulder had healed quite a bit in the last couple of weeks, but the pain tonic the ship's healer, Luan, had her on made her sleepy. She often wasn't up until late in the afternoon.

A pot of tea steamed in the center of the great oak desk, a matching set of carved antlers supporting the tabletop. The office was simple, almost bare, save for a narrow shelf lined with trinkets and books. A worn flag bearing the ship's namesake, an aizel—a snow-white, horned cat—sat beside tiny wooden ships painted pure black, colorful bits of rope tied in complicated knots, and small sandstone figurines of seahorses and miniature krakens.

Two weeks on her ship had done little to warm Samra to me, though I was starting to doubt "warm" could ever describe her. The captain was gruffer than a jagged cliff. If she weren't the leader of the Ambriellan rebels and didn't share my goal, I'd have expected her to have thrown us overboard by now, if only because Res's talons had left more than one scratch on her ship, not to mention the wind, rain, and lightning.

His control over his magic had grown considerably, though he still had far to go. Not for the first time I wished Estrel was here. She'd taught me everything I knew. I felt like a pale imitation trying to do the same for Res, but I had to try. His mastery over basic winds and rain could only take us so far. We needed lightning and thunder, powerful gales and torrential downpours.

We needed a storm.

Samra didn't sit as she poured light golden tea into handleless mugs smaller than my palm. The steam carried the flowery scent of chamomile as she passed each of us a cup with the solemnity of an Ambriellan priestess handing out prayer candles.

"We're approaching the Rhodairen port of Cardail," she began, long brown fingers curling around her mug. "We'll stop there to resupply and then strike out for Trendell. It should take us just over a week, which will put us in Eselin several days before Belin's Day."

A quiet excitement swelled inside me. Cardail wasn't Aris, but it was still Rhodaire, and not too long ago, I'd thought I'd never see it again. Res let out a low trill as my emotions seeped down the bond.

"You're going to love it," I told him. "We have the best bakeries."

I shot a glance at Caylus, expecting him to protest, but his distant gaze was set on the small round window at Samra's back overlooking the sea. I'd hoped some distance between us and the islands would return the curious, absentminded boy I knew, but he hadn't even shown much interest in Res's training the last few days.

"The point of this stop isn't to indulge the crow's sugar addiction," Samra growled, ignoring Res's squawk of disagreement. "We get in, get what we need, and get out. Cardail is too close to the Illucian-occupied area of Rhodaire to risk staying for long."

Illucian-occupied area of Rhodaire. How could five words

turn my blood to ice so easily? My hand tightened around the warmth of the mug. Surrounded by endless water, it was easy to feel disconnected from the truth waiting for us on land: an army sat on Rhodaire's doorstep, and it was poised to attack.

I started to object, but Samra talked over me.

"On that note, any of you making the trip onto land will do so cloaked and hooded." She downed the last of her tea as if it were a shot of Ambriellan whiskey. "I don't want word getting back about my connection to you."

Samra might head the Ambriellan rebellion, but she was also the daughter of the kingdom's council leader, and that council was pledged to Illucia. It was her pretense as a loyal servant of the empire that made her such an effective rebel, and being seen harboring fugitives wouldn't just mean the end of her façade but potentially her family's lives, something she'd made quite clear when she agreed to take us to Trendell.

"That also means no crow," she said.

Res lifted his head with a snap of his beak, a spark of lightning buzzing at the tip. The captain stared flatly back at him.

"You do draw a bit of attention," I said reluctantly. He straightened, rolling back his shoulders as if to say "as I should." It lasted all of a second before he perked up, head tilted as if listening.

A moment later, the door burst open, and Kiva appeared in the doorway, pale, sweating, and clutching her injured shoulder.

"Come quick. Something's wrong."

TWO

C ardail was on fire.

Or at least, it had been. Thick plumes of smoke rose
from the charred remains of the town, great swaths of black cutting through the town like the aftermath of fiery talons. Jagged
holes gaped in the place of windows, and broken doors hung off
hinges. The street along the seaside was eerily empty. A graveyard of splintered wood and torn sails was all that remained of
the ships once docked in the bay.

It looked like Aris after Ronoch.

"What happened?" Caylus asked.

"I'd wager fire, but I s'pose lightning could have done it." The
voice of the ship's lookout, Talon, floated down from the rigging
above. "Your crow doesn't sleep fly, does he? Either way, that
town's right charred through. Like a Duren's Day cuttlefish."

"Enlightening, Talon," Kiva intoned. "Your skills are wasted on this ship."

He winked and flashed her a grin.

"It was Razel." The Illucian queen's name was a bite of steel in my mouth. "We thought she might attack Rhodaire to draw me out."

"We don't know anything yet." Samra regarded the town with folded arms and an impassive gaze. "Let's not jump to conclusions."

Kiva snorted. "A Rhodairen town along the coast to Aris from Illucia was set on *fire*. Seems like a pretty clear message to me."

I eyed the ship wreckage, memories of fire and smoke threatening to claw their way out. Res trilled softly and nudged my head with his beak. My hand reflexively found his feathers, seeking his warm reassurance.

"Can you navigate through the debris?" I asked Samra.

She looked at me as if I'd asked whether she knew Res had feathers and didn't answer. Around us, the crew was already in motion, adjusting sails and ropes. Caylus peeled off to join them, something he'd often done during our time at sea. Apparently, children in the Ambriels were trained to sail the same way Rhodairens learned the crows and Illucians the sword. It seemed to soothe him, if only for a while.

Kiva swayed slightly at my side. I put a steadying hand on her uninjured shoulder. "You should go back to bed."

"And let you and bird brain go into the mysterious smoking town without me? Not happening." She flashed me a smile that was half grimace.

Res clipped his beak in annoyance, releasing a puff of wind

that fluttered Kiva's braid. I rolled my eyes. Where Caylus and Res got on wonderfully—likely a result of the copious amount of treats he fed the crow—Kiva had never been much of an animal person. That and she was literally incapable of not insulting everyone she met.

It took several minutes for the crew to steer through the wreckage and bring the ship safely into port. When the gangplank lowered, Samra led me, Res, Kiva, and Caylus down onto the dock.

"I thought I said no crow," Samra said.

"That was before we found the place ransacked," I sniped back. Her constant orders were starting to grate on me. We were supposed to be in a partnership, but Samra seemed to think I was one of her crew. It didn't help that she had a way of seizing control of a conversation, making me feel like I needed to defer to her. How was I supposed to convince her to ally with Rhodaire, to think of me as an equal, if she treated me like a child?

The captain spared me a brief scowl before charging on ahead. She slid a thin mask over her face, the same half-black, half-white one she'd been wearing when I first met her in Caylus's workshop. Anyone who saw Res would know us in a heartbeat, but she'd remain anonymous.

We moved together through the deserted streets, picking our way through overturned crates and the smoldering remains of goods and scattered belongings. A child's stuffed crow lay singed and still smoking in an empty doorway, an overturned cart of woven rugs that had been slashed to ribbons across from it. Shattered glass mixed with ash, and the scorched leaves of trees turned to blackened skeletons.

I took every step with my breath trapped in my throat, waiting for the all-too-familiar sight of gleaming bone and melted skin.

Kiva's boot caught a stone and she lurched forward. Before I could react, Res was there, his outstretched wing guiding her back to her feet. She shot me a look, daring me to comment, but I didn't have the spirit for mirth any longer. Not as the slow reality of what had happened sank in.

"Where is everyone?" she asked. "You don't think Razel ki—"

"No." I refused to think it. These people were not dead. If Razel had attacked to draw me out, if my escape had led to these people living through what I had… "No," I said again.

Caylus slowed beside a pile of debris. He knelt and reached for a strip of blue cloth. My first thought was Illucia, but the shade was wrong. It wasn't the royal hue they bore but a bright, sea-blue ice.

And the sight of it turned him to stone.

Just as I started to ask, rocks clattered in an alley to our side. I whirled as a thin form leapt into view, bow drawn and aimed at Kiva.

"No!" I leapt toward her at the same moment the string resounded with a snap.

I waited for the thud of metal in flesh and the wave of pain, but it didn't come. My eyes had closed involuntarily, and I slowly peeled them open.

The arrow hovered inches from my face.

It dropped to the ground with a clatter, taking my breath with it. I nearly wilted, but Kiva seized my arm. Res's eyes glowed bright silver.

He'd done it again.

In Illucia, Res had shown signs of magic beyond his expected storm abilities. Somehow, he'd wielded a shadow crow's power to hide and shook the earth with the magic of an earth crow.

Now he'd stopped the arrow like a battle crow.

"H-How?" the shooter stuttered. His thin voice stilled me. He was only a boy. Ten, maybe eleven at the most. The bow was too big for him, the quiver sagging loose at his hip. He fumbled for another arrow but dropped it, nearly losing hold of the bow in his attempt to catch it. With a curse, he turned to flee—and ran straight into Samra.

She caught him by the forearms, hardly seeming to notice his struggle. "Explain yourself."

"Let him go!" My voice cracked as I surged forward. Samra frowned, and I straightened beneath her dark gaze. "He's a Rhodairen citizen, a *child*, and I said to let him go."

She watched me with that same unreadable look, holding on a moment longer as if to test me. Then she slowly unfurled her fingers.

The boy stumbled back, rubbing at his wrists. "Please don't hurt me," he begged. "I thought you were them."

"We're not going to hurt you," I said softly.

His umber eyes were round with fear. Then they settled on something over my shoulder, and he let out the smallest gasp. "A crow!"

Res straightened, puffing out his feathers and lifting his head.

The boy's eyes somehow grew wider. "But that means you're—" His mouth fell open as the realization of who I was clicked into place. "Saints, my sister's not going to believe this! She said the rumor the princess found an egg was a lie! I told her it wasn't. I told her! Oh, what's his name? What kind of crow is he? Can I pet him?" The words flew from the boy's mouth almost faster than he could form them, the near arrow mishap already forgotten.

I grinned. "Resyries. Storm. And yes, I think he'd like that."

The boy shot forward as fast as the arrow he'd fired and threw his arms around Res, burying his face in his feathers. The crow's wings curled around him in a protective arc.

"Storm," Samra said slowly, as if testing the word for weakness. "Then how did he stop that arrow?"

"That's not all he did." Kiva's voice came quietly, tentatively. She was staring down at her injured arm with a careful, uncertain awe. Slowly, she rolled it forward and then back without a hint of pain.

"Thia, I think he healed me."

The boy's name was Jaycyth—Jay for short—and the bow belonged to his mother. She was a soldier who'd been called up for reinforcements when the Illucian threat appeared on our border. He lived in Cardail with his older sister, his father, two hounds named Stick and Stone, and a frog called Toad.

All this he told us before we even turned the corner at the end of the street.

"I don't think he needs to breathe," Kiva muttered to me at one point.

Jay also told us his family ran the town inn, which was

where the rest of the villagers had taken refuge, wanting to put distance between themselves and the coast. He was supposed to be gathering fruit from the orchard when he spotted our sails.

We turned another corner, revealing a small courtyard bustling with people and animals before a squat, two-story building with a sign that read *The Edgewood Inn*. Sure enough, the line of a small wood rose behind it, casting a shadow over the people hauling buckets of water from the well at the square's center and lining up to receive food from a vendor roasting spiced chicken.

It felt good to see Rhodairen faces, to hear Rhodairen voices. A smile spread across my lips, remaining plastered there the deeper into town we went, the familiarity of my people like a warm winter coat.

"Jaycyth!" A deep voice barely preceded a thick-chested man as he broke through the crowd. "Where in the Saints' name have you been? I told you to come straight back."

Jay burst forward, seizing his father's shirt and tugging. "Look who I found!"

I moved aside, letting Res step forward from the shadows of the alley. A gasp sounded across the courtyard, an excited murmur swelling through the crowd alongside shouts of "A crow!" and "The princess!"

I stepped forward. "You must be Jay's father."

My words broke the man's stare, and he dropped quickly to one knee. The action rippled through the square as person after person knelt. It struck me in a way I couldn't quite explain. It wasn't just the formality of it, something we rarely adhered to in the capital where the royal family's presence was as likely in the local tavern as the grand hall. No, it was the looks on their faces as they took in first me, then the crow at my side. The way their bent backs straightened and the edge of exhaustion in their eyes softened into something warmer.

Into hope.

"Please, stand," I called across the square. They listened, rising as one. "My name is Anthia Cerralté, princess of Rhodaire. You may have heard the rumors that I discovered a crow egg and took it with me into the heart of Illucia. Well, you can see now those rumors are true."

A murmur coursed through the crowd. Jay jumped excitedly, still clutching his father's shirt.

"With the help of Resyries's magic, we will protect Rhodaire. For now, I'll offer you whatever help I can." I looked from person to person as I spoke, meeting their tired eyes. "Will someone tell me what happened here?"

"Mercenaries," said Jay's father. "They came in on ships from the north. There were Illucian soldiers with them but only a handful. Most of them were Ambriellan."

Caylus stepped forward, proffering the bit of blue cloth he'd found in the rubble. "Did their ships have a kingfisher on their flag?"

Jay's father nodded, and Caylus paled. Samra let out a low string of curses.

"What?" I asked.

Caylus's hand closed about the cloth so tightly, his knuckles flared white. "Malkin."

The man who'd stolen so many years of his life, the one

who'd forced him to work and to fight until it'd destroyed him physically and mentally.

He was working with Razel.

I wanted nothing more than to wrap my arms around Caylus and hold him, but I felt the weight of a hundred pairs of expectant, hopeful eyes.

"What did they want?" I asked, though I feared the answer.

Jay's father shook his head. "They didn't say. They didn't really hurt anyone even. Just ransacked the town, piling everything they could out into the streets and setting it alight. It was strange, really. Even the fires were odd. It was like they just sprang up fully formed, and they ate through stone. I've never seen anything like it."

I had. It was just like Ronoch. The fires had come swift and fierce as the blaze of a fire crow, searing through everything like paper. We'd found oil on the stones and in the rookeries, but even that seemed inadequate to explain how fast the fires had spread and how hot they'd burned.

"We aren't the first though," he continued, folding his arms. "Enair burned a couple days ago, just the same way. Like a—"

"Like a signal," I finished quietly. A signal for me. Razel didn't know where I was, and she intended to draw me out. What better way than setting fire to towns along the coast, knowing I'd eventually have to make land to resupply? Even if I didn't see the smoke or find a burnt town, word would spread.

"Which way did they go?" Kiva asked. "We'll hunt the bastards down."

"Not with my ship you won't," Samra said. "I agreed to take you to Trendell, not to hunt down that night-cursed spider."

I rounded on her. "They're not going to stop! They'll keep burning towns unless we stop them."

"And give Razel exactly what she wants? You're playing straight into her hands."

Frustration tore through me, and I forced a deep breath. "Razel thinks she can control me. She thinks I'll come running to protect my people only to end up cowering in fear at the fire around me. But I won't. She's underestimated me, and I'm going to make her pay for it."

"It's only a matter of time before Malkin starts hurting people," Caylus said, eyes trained on the strip of cloth clutched between his fingers. "If only for his own sick entertainment."

Cold fury prickled down my spine. "I'll show them what happens when they attack my home." The connection between Res and me thrummed to life as I spoke, rising with my words. I faced the gathered crowd as a sudden wind gusted through the street. "Queen Razel wants to scare us. She thinks I'm weak. That Rhodaire is weak. She's wrong."

Res let out a low call, and thunder boomed in the gray sky. The wind rose, swirling slowly at first before gathering into a steady gale. It caught the smoke and the ash and carried it away, out past the shore and over the sea, leaving behind a clear, cobalt sky.

Kiva grinned up at it as someone in the crowd called out, throwing up their fist. More echoed them, a cheer filling the air.

Samra watched me with dark eyes, her frustration practically palpable.

This wasn't over.

THREE

Although we'd planned to load up on supplies in Cardail, we ended up leaving most of what we had with the villagers instead. Isair, the next town down the coast, was slightly larger and would be better suited for restocking anyway. Less than a day's sail for a normal ship, it'd take us only a few hours with the aid of Res's wind. He perched at the stern of the ship, wings spread, guiding a current gently into our sails until the ship all but flew across the water.

I studied the faint outline of the pale, key-shaped scar on my palm. When I'd asked Res about the other powers, he'd sent only confused, questioning pulses back along the connection. Whatever he'd done to stop that arrow and heal Kiva, it hadn't been under his control, but I had no doubt it was the same reason I'd been able to reach into a roaring fire and still retain the use of my hand.

The idea of what he could be thrilled me. A storm crow was a force to be reckoned with, but a crow that could use all eight abilities?

Razel wouldn't know what hit her.

I scanned the deck, expecting to find Caylus working with the crew, but found only a grizzled, sharp-faced man watching me. Onis. He was one of the oldest crew members, second only to the ship's cook, Darya, and he hadn't done anything but glower at Res and me since we'd boarded back in Port Maranock.

When I caught his eye, his fingers went for the colorful Ambriellan knots at his belt, his lips moving in a quiet prayer.

Kiva appeared before me with a furrowed look of annoyance.

"Make it go away," she demanded.

I blinked at her. A moment later, a tiny kitten trotted up and sat down beside her. I grinned as Aroch licked one snow-white paw.

"He's only following you because he knows you don't like him."

"He's a cat."

"Exactly." I patted her on the shoulder. "Watch Res for me, will you?" Before she could object, I slipped past her and inside the ship, seeking out Caylus's cabin. The door was open, and I found him leaning against the wall. He peered out the small window, lost in thought, his arms crossed as if to hold himself together.

"See anything interesting?" I asked.

He startled and I winced. It was so hard *not* to sneak up on him when he was like this.

"Is something wrong?" he asked as if he hadn't heard my question. Knowing him, he hadn't.

I stepped into the room and leaned back against the wall with my hands tucked behind me. "I don't know. Is there?"

He bit his lip, averting his gaze. This wasn't the first time he'd chosen silence in the face of my questions. Caylus had always been reserved, but since we'd left Illucia, I'd found him retreating into his thoughts more often than not. Pulling him out had become harder and harder.

I took in the nervous tap of his fingers against his ribs, the way he leaned harder against the wall as if it could be a shield. Discovering Malkin's involvement had shaken him.

I thought of the conversation we hadn't finished that morning.

"You can stay on the ship," I said softly.

"No." The iron of his answer shocked me. He pushed off the wall, forcing his arms down to his sides. For a moment, I saw the boy who'd stepped between Ericen and me on the bridge, the fighter he must have been under Malkin's control. "I have to face this. If I can't—" He shook his head. "What am I even doing here?"

I pushed off the wall, crossing the small room to take one of his large hands in both of my own.

"You're here because you're a good person," I told him. "Because when I was in trouble, you helped me, and I will forever be grateful for that. Now it's my turn to help you." I squeezed his hand. "You don't have to face Malkin alone."

His agitation settled, his fingers closing around mine. He didn't say anything, but he didn't have to. This comfortable silence was a space we inhabited together. Safe, content. We'd built it sitting in his workshop night after night, but it'd gotten lost in the vastness of the sea. I clung to it now, hoping it would be enough.

We reached Isair just before sunset. The town was blessedly free of smoke and flames, but a massive, richly ornamented ship took up most the harbor, its railings etched with gold like delicate embroidery. A while flag snapped in the wind, bearing a bright blue kingfisher.

Malkin was here.

The fading sunlight illuminated a broad boulevard running along the coastline in either direction. Several piers branched out into the sea, each as empty as Cardail's had been. No one bothered us as we docked. No one called out.

We'd decided to leave Res on the ship until we needed him, since his presence would make scouting the situation unseen near impossible. With my black gold bow strapped to my chest and a full quiver of arrows, I led Kiva, Caylus, and Samra off the ship and into the darkening town, Samra donning her black-and-white mask to hide her identity.

As one of Rhodaire's main port towns, I'd visited Isair once as a child on our way back from the Ambriels. Then, music had flowed along the docks in an endless stream, threaded with bouts of laughter, and Estrel and I had eaten what felt like a hundred orange cakes.

Now it resembled a tapestry stripped of its dye, bleak and lifeless.

Malkin might not have set it on fire yet, but his people had already begun their work. Piles of belongings littered the streets before homes with broken doors and shattered windows. People had clearly been forced from their homes. From what I remembered, the city was a maze of stone and alleys, the streets oriented as if drawn by a child's scribbling hand. Where would Malkin have corralled everyone?

We moved down a broad central street that opened to an empty crossroads. A towering statue dominated the center. Draped in white-flowered delladon vines, a fresh crown of woven ivy sat atop its head.

A Sella.

I slowed, surveying the ancient being. Tall and thin with long hair and too-sharp cheekbones, it was easy to imagine how many had once seen these creatures as gods.

Kiva stepped up beside me. "I'd have expected this in Seahalla but not here."

"It's strange," I replied. "I didn't think anyone in Rhodaire thought of the Sellas as anything more than long-dead legends. Is it only in Aris we've stopped believing?"

"It's only in Aris your mother was able to crush what remained of that belief," Samra said. Her voice felt even more condemning from behind that mask. "She closed the last Sella temple in Aris."

"But why?" I asked.

The captain's lips pressed into a thin line, but she simply turned back the way we'd been heading. "Let's go. We're wasting time. Malkin could light this place up at any moment."

As I turned my back, I couldn't shake the feeling that the statue's gaze went with me.

As we exited the square, voices sounded, and we ducked into an alley. Caylus peered cautiously around the edge before pulling back.

"Malkin's guards," he said softly. "I recognize them."

"Great. Let's say hi." Kiva patted the sword she'd borrowed from one of the crew, Sinvarra still lost to Shearen, the Vykryn soldier who'd taken the black gold blade from her.

"Or—" Caylus's voice caught. He gritted his teeth. "I could turn myself in."

I gaped. "What? No."

The voices grew louder, one saying something jeering to the other. They carried a torch with them, the light dancing along the far wall.

"They'll take me to Malkin," Caylus said. "It's the fastest way to find out where he is."

"And to get yourself killed," Kiva said at the same time as Samra said, "It makes logical sense."

They glowered at each other. I ignored them, reaching for Caylus to object, but he was already moving. He stepped into the road.

The voices cut off. The light stilled.

"Caylus?" asked a female voice. "What in Duren's name are you doing here?"

"It doesn't matter what he's doing here," said the other guard. "Malkin is going to be thrilled. Come here, boy."

Caylus stepped reflexively back, and the firelight illuminated his face. Fear blazed behind his green eyes. Then hands closed around his wrists and arms, dragging him forward. I lurched after him, but Samra seized me, holding me back. I bit back a curse as the sounds of scuffle faded along with the light. Only then did she release me.

Res's curiosity plucked along the bond, checking that all was okay. I sent back a reassuring pulse I didn't truly feel.

We crept out after them, catching sight of the two guards towing Caylus around the corner ahead. Grateful for the descending cloak of night, we followed as far behind as we dared, taking turn after turn deeper into the heart of the town. Gradually, our surroundings grew more familiar. I recognized the sloping road they'd just turned onto ahead, the tightly knit buildings lining it a little taller than the rest. It led to a massive square outside the home of the town's leader.

The shuffling of feet and murmur of voices rose ahead of us. As we neared the turn, Kiva threw back an arm to stop us.

"Illucian soldiers," she whispered. "Two of them, guarding the back of the crowd."

"Dammit." We were going to lose Caylus to the crowd. I surveyed the area around us, then looked up toward the shop at our back. There'd been a festival in town the day we'd come, and people had thrown petals down from the rooftops, symbolizing falling feathers. Which meant—

"This way," I said.

The shop door had been kicked open, revealing shelves of folded cloth and bolts hung up for display. I made for the stairs in the back, the others following me up two flights before emerging onto the roof.

A strange scene unfolded in the square. The townspeople had been herded into it, the four main roads in thick with people, soldiers at their backs. Some were Illucian, others Ambriellans dressed in clothing of kingfisher blue and pearl. Still, there was something strange about the crowd's docility. Retired riders lived in this town. Soldiers. How had such a small force corralled them?

I searched the crowd for Caylus, spotting him only as their slow forward progress disturbed the tide of people.

At the front of the square sat a makeshift throne of aged driftwood. A man in his early thirties occupied it, a massive tapestry depicting the kingfisher symbol hanging at his back. A mix of Illucian soldiers and Ambriellan mercenaries surrounded him.

"Did he...make a throne?" Kiva asked.

"Malkin's a theatrical son of a bitch," Samra replied.

Malkin Drexel had silken copper hair that curled across his forehead above a black coral circlet, hung across his brow like a crown. Cool gray eyes stared down at something before him, alight with satisfaction.

A young Rhodairen man was on his knees before Malkin. He'd been stripped of his shirt, and his back gleamed savage red from the whip marks lining it.

I snarled, snatching my bow from my back and nocking an arrow before Samra stepped in front of me.

"We need a plan," she said.

"I'm going to put an arrow in his eye," I said. "That's the plan."

"Don't be a fool."

"I'm getting tired of you ordering me around."

"Normally, I'm all for a good fight," Kiva cut in, "but Malkin's seen Caylus."

I sidestepped Samra. The two soldiers had pulled Caylus through to the front of the crowd.

Malkin's full lips spread into a smile worthy of a fox. I wanted to break his jaw.

"Caylus Zander," he said, his voice saccharine. Dangerous.

Caylus didn't respond.

Malkin rose. A long blade at his hip shifted as his hand settled on the ornate hilt, white as bone and inlaid with swirls of gold and black coral. He descended the dais, slowly, purposefully, each step a statement of power, of control. He stopped before Caylus, and my fingers went to my bowstring.

Malkin reached out, taking Caylus's chin in his hand. A shudder rolled through Caylus's shoulders, his muscles going taut as Malkin tilted his face up, then to the side, as if inspecting wares for purchase.

When he let go, Caylus let his head drop. His chest rose and fell in quick bursts, and my mind raced back to the night he'd told me what Malkin had done to him. The torture, mental and physical, that he'd endured at this man's hands for so many years.

Seeing them together now, I knew he hadn't told me everything.

My mind worked quickly. Even if I put an arrow in Malkin's chest, the guards might turn on the crowd, and Caylus was in the center of it.

"You owe me a great deal of money," Malkin said. His voice, his movements—they were all gentle, like sharp teeth grazing softly along bare skin. "Perhaps you'd like the chance to fight for it? We were just getting ready to organize some…entertainment." His eyes slid to the bloodied man on his knees.

Still, Caylus said nothing. How much of what Malkin said even registered?

Malkin tilted his head. "If you win, I'll grant your freedom. If you lose…" He crouched before Caylus, leaning forward to whisper something in his ear. Caylus jerked back, the two guards on either side of him forced to brace themselves to keep him still. Malkin's fingers brushed Caylus's cheek in a soft caress before he stood, a satisfied smile spreading across his lips. As if the reaction was all he'd wanted.

Malkin waved a hand. One of the guards pulled out a knife, shearing Caylus's shirt from his body in one cut and leaving a glaring red line in its wake.

Corded lines crisscrossed Caylus's back, their pale white stark against what little golden skin remained untouched. Someone had whipped him, savagely and more than once. Most of the scars were old, but a few were still the thick rises of wounds healed in recent weeks, likely dealt days before Caylus escaped to Illucia.

My stomach churned. But it wasn't the scars that made my throat close and my breath catch. It was the way Caylus's shoulders sagged, the way his head hung. Quiet. Withdrawn.

Defeated.

Fire danced along my skin, hot and sharp. Res's concern flared along the bond.

"Thia—" Samra began.

An arrow flew a breath from Malkin's face, thudding hard into the throne behind. I'd nocked another one before it even struck.

The hum of voices died. A hundred pairs of eyes swung toward me, Malkin's included.

"Let him go," I ordered.

His gaze slid over me in the slow movement of a knife skinning an animal.

"A friend of yours, Caylus?" he asked. "Not the Rhodairen princess I've heard so much about?"

I aimed the arrow straight at Malkin's heart. "You have one chance to leave my people be. Board your ship, leave Isair, and never set foot on Rhodairen soil again."

Malkin tilted his head. "And in exchange?"

"She doesn't put an arrow in your heart," Kiva growled.

"How magnanimous of you," Malkin said with a laugh. "But I think you'll find you're greatly outnumbered."

I reached along the connection to Res. A flutter of power echoed back. The moonlit sky began to darken, and a quiet wind poured through the streets.

"Some of those soldiers have bows," Kiva warned.

I nodded. The cloud cover deepened.

Malkin looked up, his smile fading as the sky grew thick and charged. Whispers spread through the crowd, and the archers nocked their arrows, searching the sky.

I felt Res before I saw him. A flash of lightning lit the sky, illuminating his black form against the clouds. People shouted and soldiers cursed. A bowstring snapped, but the arrow careened off course, knocked aside by the wind.

Res shot upward, rising out of the range of arrows and beyond the clouds.

"Tell Razel," I called above the rising winds, "that if she wants me, she can come get me herself."

Then the rain began. It fell in patches, first over Malkin's clearing, then over the Illucian soldiers at the edges of the crowd.

To ice.

The drops hardened into razor-sharp hail. The first of the mercenaries screamed as the ice shredded through cloth and skin. Malkin threw up a shielding arm, but the hail drew lines of red in his golden skin.

The movement shocked Caylus back to himself. He seized the Rhodairen man, dragging him back into the crowd as the mercenaries bolted. The crowd parted as the soldiers fled, Malkin screaming after them to stop, the hail chasing them like a swarm of angry wasps.

Bring down the throne.

A piercing call echoed over the voices of the crowd and yelling soldiers. Light crackled in the sky. Then a bolt erupted, striking the throne. Splintered wood shot in all directions, a fire rising from wood. Fueled by Res's magic, the flames flared higher, snapping at Malkin with vicious teeth.

Malkin stumbled away. Lightning struck again, hitting the ground a few feet away from him. Then he bolted.

The crowd cheered as the hail and wind chased the fleeing mercenaries and soldiers back toward the coast. I followed,
leaping easily to the next of the closely packed buildings. Kiva
followed, leaving a cursing Samra behind.

The main road emptied onto the boulevard that ran along
the bay. Kiva and I ran to the edge of the final building, Res
hidden in the clouds above.

Malkin's men had already boarded the ship and were moving
as quickly as they could to get out to sea. I saw a flash of copper
hair as Malkin dove into the captain's quarters, barricading himself against the hail.

In the midst of the chaos, a tall, slender figure stood at the
bowsprit of the ship. Cloaked and hooded, I caught only a flash
of gold before Res's wind swept down, shoving the ship roughly
out to sea. It rocked and bowed, the churning waves turning it
about.

Res broke free of the clouds, keeping well out of arrow range
as he banked in low, wide circles.

Make sure it can't come back.

As the ship grew smaller on the horizon, the unruly waves
tossing it left and right, the hail tore down once more, turning
the ship's sails to ribbons.

I smirked at the fading sight.

Then something moved at the corner of my eye.

I spun, bow raised, and came face-to-face with Ericen.

FOUR

Everything stopped.

I stared at the prince, and he stared back, his black Vykryn uniform transforming him into a shadow in the night.

And then my mind caught up, and I was lifting my bow, and his hand was reaching for one of the swords strapped to his back.

But I was quicker.

I lashed out with my bow, striking the back of his sword hand with the upper limb. He hissed and leapt away to put space between us.

He threw up his hands. "I'm not here to fight you, Thia."

The slight rasp in his voice pulled at something in my chest. A reminder that I'd cared about him. That maybe I still did. "Then walk away."

"I can't. I need—"

I didn't wait for him to finish, slashing again with my bow.

He dodged, hand returning to his sword. "Listen to me, Thia."

"I've done enough of that already."

I'd listened, and I'd believed him. But I understood now. Ericen might be a better person than his mother. He might not believe in the ways of his people that led them to wage war and conquer nations, to spill blood in the name of their god.

But he was still the prince of Illucia, and he would not betray that.

The air stilled. My hand tightened on my bow. His eyes traced the line of one of my leather-gloved hands—the glove he'd given me. Then I moved. Quick as a wingbeat, he drew a sword from the sheath on his back. I nocked an arrow, drew, and loosed just as his sword knocked my bow aside. The arrow grazed his arm, but he didn't slow, sweeping the flat side of his sword toward my ankles.

Kiva's sword caught the blow. She followed through, throwing Ericen back. He moved with the blow, easily keeping his balance.

"Thia, wait—"

I slashed again, not giving him time to speak. He deflected it, then shot forward inside my reach. I tried to twist away, but he caught my wrist and swung me hard into the wall beside the door.

My breath left my lungs in a whoosh of air, but I clung tight to my bow, even as he pinned my wrist into the wall. I felt the heat of his body against mine, a flare of energy in the chill night air. Felt the rise and fall of his chest in time with my own, his gaze locked onto mine.

"You can be more than what she made you," I whispered.

He recoiled. Kiva's footfalls were the only warning he had before she slammed into him, throwing him aside.

Regaining his footing, he backed away, sword pointed down, other hand raised in a show of peace. "Listen to me. I came as soon as I learned about my mother's plans with the fires. I didn't want you to walk into a trap."

"Funny," Kiva growled. "This feels a lot like a trap."

He ignored her. "Please, Thia." His blue eyes were bright in the light of the moon, beseeching. "I need to talk to you. There's something bigger going on here. Bigger than Illucia and Rhodaire."

You have no idea. Illucia didn't know about the rebellion forming against them from the ruins of the nations they'd decimated.

"After you escaped, I went back to the throne room. Auma and the monks were gone."

Kiva flinched at the mention of Auma's name.

"My mother was furious. The things she was saying—" He cut off, hesitating.

"What?"

"They didn't make any sense."

"*You're* not making any sense, Ericen," I growled.

"I'm trying to help you." He stepped forward as if to press the sincerity of his words into us.

I stared at him expectantly.

His jaw worked. "She said something about the Sellas."

I stilled. "What about them?"

"She wasn't making any sense," he repeated, shaking his head. "She was talking about them like—like they were still alive."

"That's ridiculous," I said even as a chill trailed down my spine.

"I'm just telling you what I heard."

"Why should we believe a word you say?" Kiva asked.

Ericen looked at me. "Because I couldn't do it. I couldn't choose her over you."

I stepped back, stunned. The night we'd escaped from Sordell, Ericen had been right there. He could have called the guards, could have sent Vykryn riding after us a wingbeat behind, but he hadn't. He'd let us go.

Ericen lowered his hands to his sides. "You were right about her, Thia. About everything. I always knew you were, but I was too much of a coward to act on it."

I swallowed against my dry throat, unsettled by the earnest look behind his eyes. He'd lied to me before. In Rhodaire, he'd convinced me he was every bit the cruel Illucian prince I'd expected, and I'd believed it. He was too good at telling me what I wanted to hear.

Who was to say he wasn't pretending now?

But what did he gain—what did Razel gain—by his coming here alone to spin a wild tale?

Slowly, he sheathed his sword. "I made a mistake. I get that.

But I thought you of all people would understand how hard it is to have your entire life turned upside down. For everything to change."

My grip tightened on my bow. After Ronoch, normal had seemed so far away, the word had lost meaning. That lost feeling was akin to drowning, trapped beneath the dark waters with no idea which way was up.

"You asked me to leave everything I ever knew behind." Ericen's voice roughened. "I thought I couldn't do it, but I was wrong. You showed me that I could."

"And you showed us that you're a traitorous bastard," Kiva replied. She angled her sword toward his throat. "I don't believe a word he's saying, Thia."

But I wanted to. I wanted to more than anything, and that scared me.

Ericen didn't look away from me, even as Kiva's sword hovered inches from his throat. The idea of her running him through bothered me a lot more than I wanted it to. He held my gaze unflinchingly, a familiar glint in them. A challenge. To trust him?

The rooftop door banged open.

Another dark figure erupted onto the roof brandishing a black gold sword. I barely got my bow around to block the upward strike. The force of it knocked my bow from my hands, sending it skittering across the rooftop.

Kiva pivoted to intercept the second attack, forcing them back. I retreated, Kiva between me and the now grinning Vykryn. Shearen looked every bit as vicious as he had when he'd tormented me in Sordell.

"You made for a wonderful distraction, Eri," the blond boy said.

My stomach dropped. Ericen had been stalling. Everything he'd said was a lie.

The prince stepped forward, lips parting as if to say something, but he swallowed the words down even as his eyes begged me to understand.

"This was far more than I expected to find." Shearen hefted Sinvarra, grinning at the growl Kiva emitted. "You'll be returning with us, Princess. Ericen?"

The prince drew his sword, his eyes promising apologies even as he lifted the blade.

A resounding screech barely preceded Res's diving form. Rising from the dive, he landed, talons extended, on the rooftop ledge, wings flared wide. In a powerful stroke, he brought them together, releasing a wind that forced Shearen and Ericen back a step.

Kiva moved, striking Sinvarra from Shearen's hands. She swept the sword up through her forward momentum and rose with the point directed straight at Shearen's neck. Ericen fell still, eyes wide at the balancing crow. Was that...awe? I'd known Ericen had an interest in the crows. He'd tried to ask me about them more than once, and I'd refused to answer. But I'd always thought it was a fascination with their power. Not this... reverence.

"This seems familiar." Kiva grinned and pressed the sword point a little deeper into Shearen's skin.

He hissed.

"I should slit your throat," she said.

"No!" Ericen lurched forward but stilled when Kiva tilted the blade further.

"Ericen," Shearen growled, but he fell silent at a sharp look from the prince. The last I'd seen the two of them, they'd been at each other's throats. Now Shearen was taking orders without complaint? What had happened these last couple of weeks?

I hurried across the roof to snatch up my bow, nocking an arrow and aiming it at the prince. "Leave."

"Thia—"

"Be thankful I'm allowing you to go unharmed," I said, ignoring Kiva's sidelong gaze that asked why in the Saints' name I was doing just that. But I couldn't explain it to her. I barely understood it myself.

Despite everything that'd happened, I couldn't bring myself to think of Ericen as my enemy again.

Ericen grabbed Shearen's arm, forcing him toward the door. Even up against a crow, Shearen looked loath to surrender. But as Ericen shoved him through the door, the prince glanced back at me, and I swore he looked relieved. Then they were through the door and down the stairs.

I leaned over the building edge. Two massive black Illucian warhorses waited at the mouth of the alley below. Shearen and Ericen emerged, swiftly mounting and kicking their horses into a canter.

Make sure they clear town, I told Res.

He leapt into the air, circling us once before taking off after the horses as they made for the boulevard that curved out onto the traveling road.

"Come on," I said to Kiva. "Let's go check on the others."

With the help of the town's leader, Samra had seen to the townspeople. By the time we returned, they'd already organized cleanup crews and started guiding the remaining crowd back to their homes.

As Kiva left me to get a report from a nearby soldier, Samra stepped up, blocking my path. She'd yet to remove her mask. "You let him go."

I frowned. "Malkin? What did you want me to do, kill him?"

Her gaze cut toward me. "You're at war. You're forging an alliance against one of the greatest military mights this world has ever seen. You can't scare it with a little rain and wind. Eventually, you and that crow are going to have to spill blood." She didn't wait for me to respond before pushing on through the dispersing crowd.

I let her go, unsettled. My mother probably would have captured them and had them executed or killed them before they could escape. I hadn't wanted to risk Res when forcing them out was an option, but it was more than that.

This was the first time I'd ever asked him to hurt someone. The first time we might have killed or seriously injured someone. But Samra was right. Eventually, we would have to.

I continued through the crowd, seeking Caylus. I didn't

make it far. It seemed every single person wanted to speak to me. They bowed and thanked me, pressing tokens of thanks and luck into my hands that I respectfully returned, promising them their safety was enough.

Then a curvaceous, thick-muscled woman stepped into my path, a broad smile on her kind face. I let out an involuntary gasp of recognition. "Jenara!"

The retired rider wrapped me in a hug so warm and tight, I never wanted her to let go. It'd been months since I'd seen her, first the day of the town festival, when I'd watched her crow make animals out of water, and then again in the capital for each yearly hatch night. She'd been there on Ronoch, and she bore the tiny speck-like scars of falling embers.

"Thia," she said in a voice of warm honey. She pulled back, holding me at arm's length. "Saints keep me, it's good to see you."

"It's good to see you too," I said with a grin.

"That was some impressive work by your crow." She nodded to where Res had just landed on a nearby building, his bright silver eyes searching the crowd with a familiar hunger. The connection between us prickled with a feeling I knew well: *food food food.*

"Even for a storm crow, the directional control of the water and the transition to ice was incredible. Especially at his age."

"I'm starting to think there might be a reason behind that," I replied. She lifted a brow, and I hurried to explain the odd occurrences with Res's powers, ending with my theory that somehow, he might have access to the other crow powers.

"Fascinating," she said, rubbing her chin. "Why don't you

and I put it to the test in the morning? I'll help you train him as if he were a water crow, and we'll see what he can do."

I grinned. "That'd be perfect." We shook hands, and I scanned the crowd. "You haven't seen a tall Ambriellan boy anywhere, have you?"

"The one that viper pulled in front of the crowd? He's in the town hall building." She gestured at the structure behind her.

"Thanks."

We parted ways and I made for the hall, asking Res to keep an eye on things outside.

There was something familiar about the building, its layers rising up toward a point, the edges carved in delicate swirling designs. One of the big double doors had been pinned open, but the other bore the proud, massive shape of an aizel, its coat carved about it like melting clouds of mist.

Black metal hooks that would have once held lanterns to light worshippers' way jutted out periodically. A shiver prickled my skin.

This had once been a Sella temple.

Ericen's warning pulled at me, but I shoved it aside. I couldn't trust him.

The doors opened into a narrow hall with rooms shooting off on either side. People bustled about, and I pulled one aside to ask after Caylus. They directed me to one of the small side rooms, where I found a healer finishing up tending to the cut from the guard's blade.

The healer bowed to me as I entered. Caylus didn't even look at me. He sat on a small workbench, eyes trained on the floor.

"Can I have a moment with him?" I asked the healer. The girl nodded and slipped from the room, closing the door behind her.

Caylus's hands tightened about the edge of the table, and I knew he did it to keep them from shaking. A flush filled his cheeks.

"What is it?" I asked softly.

He shook his head, bringing his hands to his face. "Malkin," he whispered. His fingers curled in as he dragged them along his face and behind his neck, lacing them tightly. His elbows pressed together like a cocoon to hide in. "You shouldn't have to fight my battles for me." His voice came out hoarse. "No one should. But I—I just..."

His words scraped at raw memories. Hiding under the covers. Craving darkness, solitude, quiet. A place where I couldn't fail, and I couldn't lose. Even now, I worried I'd slip, my past my constant shadow.

I stepped closer. Gently, I wrapped my fingers around his wrists, his skin warm to my touch, and pulled his hands from his face.

It felt like reaching for a drowning man.

"I understand, Caylus," I said gently. "I know what it is to feel useless. Powerless. Weak. But you are none of those things. Sometimes, we need a little help. That's what I'm here for. To help fight those battles."

Finally, he looked at me, and what I saw in the depths of his eyes trapped my breath in my throat. From the day I'd met him, Caylus had always been quiet, a little nervous and a little awkward. He didn't trust easily, and he'd always seemed uneasy, like he expected the world to crumble around him at any moment.

He was broken, and it was Malkin's fault.

My skin warmed, a trace of heat rising from my stomach to my throat like a tendril of smoke from a growing fire. Suddenly, I regretted my decision to let him go free. He hadn't deserved my mercy.

Malkin had done this, and he went unpunished because of Illucia. Because of Razel. She'd destroyed so much more than I'd realized, hurt so many people.

Caliza. Kiva. Caylus. Auma. Samra.

Even Ericen.

I wrapped one of Caylus's large hands in both of mine and silently made myself a promise. Before all this was over, I would make Malkin Drexel regret ever laying a finger on Caylus.

And I would tear Razel down.

His lips parted, then closed, then pressed into a firm line.

"There's a story about an Ambriellan sailor," he began at last, "who sailed the world alone. When he didn't return, his friends assumed he'd died. Then one day, a merchant ship came across his boat, floating off the Illucian coast. When they asked him whether he was lost, he said he was. When they offered to give him directions, he said he knew the way home."

As he spoke, his fingers flexed in and out, the white scars stark against his golden skin. "'Well then,' the ship's captain asked, 'how can you be lost?' And the man replied, 'Because no matter where I am, it's never where I should be.' And when the captain asked him where that was, the man said, 'I don't know. I can't find it.'

Unable to help, the merchants left him there. They say to this day you can spot the sailor's dinghy floating in the mist, still searching."

Maybe it'd been his detached tone as he told it, or maybe it was the way he stared at the wall before him, but the story left me uneasy, the room crowded with his words.

"That's not a very happy story," I said.

"No, it's not. But I understand him, the sailor. If you don't know what you're looking for, you'll spend your whole life searching for it."

My throat felt dry. "What are you looking for, Caylus?"

He leaned his head back against the wall. "I don't know."

The words settled heavily. When I first met Caylus in Illucia, he'd only just escaped Malkin weeks before. His wounds, both physical and invisible, had been so raw. Just like mine. Together, we'd helped each other heal.

And seeing Malkin again had ripped his wounds right back open.

Caylus's hand fell over mine, and only then did I realized I'd curled it into a fist. "I just—" The words caught in his throat. "I just need some time to think."

I felt myself nodding, and though I knew he wanted time alone, I couldn't quite make myself leave. It felt like abandoning him.

"I'm here for you if you need me," I said.

"I know." He smiled, and it settled the unease inside me. Maybe I was overreacting. Maybe he really did just need some time to process everything. But as I stood to go, crossing the short gap from bed to door, I couldn't shake the feeling that the distance opening between us might never be closed again.

FIVE

We returned to the ship with plans for Jenara to meet us the next morning. Kiva, Res, and I ate dinner with the rest of the crew in the mess hall as we did every night, but Caylus stayed locked in his room, and I reluctantly let him be.

Like every night before, as the conversation dwindled and people reclined in their benches, full of hearty stew and thick, warm bread, someone stood to tell a story.

Myths and legends were the kingdom's domain, and I'd heard many of the tales the sailors told before, famous as they were among the nearby kingdoms.

The storyteller was an older woman, threads of gray lining her wheat-colored hair and laugh lines framing her kind green eyes. I recognized her as the ship's cook, Darya. She held a pint of ale in one hand, the other held up for silence, which was quickly given.

"Any requests?" she asked, her voice strong but soft.

I leaned forward. "Do you know any stories about the Sellas?" I asked, ignoring Kiva's incredulous look. There was no harm in investigating what Ericen had said. "Real ones, not the fairy tales in the books."

Darya laughed. "Who says because they are fairy tales they are not real?" The question prickled at the back of my neck. "True enough, there's little history of the Sellas left behind. No books that are more than stories, few artifacts that have not crumbled into dust. In many places, they've been all but forgotten, almost as though someone erased every mention, every memory, until they faded into obscurity. And yet we all agree they were here once. They did exist."

Behind me, someone made a low humming sound of excitement, and I realized the story had already begun. With Kiva on one side of me and Res on the other, I settled back to listen.

"So what happened?" Darya asked. "Once, people worshipped the Sellas like gods. We paid homage to them for their protection from the land's wild magic, for gifts of power beyond our belief, and for the benevolence with which they let us live freely. Or at least, so one story goes."

As she spoke, Darya wound her way through the mess hall, the slow rock of her voice hypnotizing every gaze. It wrapped me up like a wool blanket, carrying me away in the story.

"Others say the Sellas were hungry and cruel, saturated with power and with nowhere to use it but on weak, powerless humans. They extorted us for their protection at the same time as they tormented us."

She paused in the center of the room. "War broke out between humans and Sella, led by the crows of Rhodaire, and we proved far more capable than our gods expected. An unsteady truce was reached.

"Now," she said quietly, her voice taking on a curious edge, "what came next is up for some debate. Some say the Sellas, their pride wounded from defeat, sought to destroy the humans who had bested them. Others say the Rhodairen riders intended to ensure they'd never face a Sella threat again. But they all agree that in the end, the kingdoms banded together and slaughtered the Sellas."

A strange unease cut through me. There was an uncomfortable parallel between her story and the future I hurtled toward. An alliance forged in the face of an unbeatable foe and the promise of blood to be spilled.

"When the Sellas died," Darya continued, "the magic died with them. It retreated from the land, as did all the creatures it'd once sustained, from the aizel to the South Sea serpents. But it hit Sellador worst of all, turning the land to dust and desert. And so the Eastern Wastelands were born, their border now guarded by remnants of long-ago magic."

Silence settled in the wake of her words, as if everyone feared to break the spell she'd woven. Across the room, Onis watched me with bright, almost feverish eyes, a talisman clasped in his hands.

I leaned forward, startling Res awake with a flutter of feathers and shattering the trance. "How can we be sure they're all dead?" I asked, and a chorus of chuckles sounded back that I ignored. "What if some of them survived?"

Darya smiled sharply. "Perhaps they did. Perhaps they've been lying in wait to get revenge on the humans who turned against them. Or then again, perhaps this is all just another fairy tale."

I lay staring up at the bunk above me, where Kiva's snores emanated in waves. I couldn't put my mind to rest.

It was full of Darya's story, Caylus's pain, and Res's strange magic. And it was full of the look in Ericen's eyes. The guilt, the determination, the battle between the two as fluctuating as the sea.

Giving up on sleep, I rolled out of bed and wrapped a cloak about myself. Res slept soundly in a pile of blankets as I emerged into the hall and climbed the stairs to the main deck. The chill night air cooled my hot skin, each breath laced with the briny scent of the sea. The waxing moon hung heavy in the cloudless sky, bathing the deck in silver light and illuminating a figure near the bowsprit.

I recognized the wiry build and stiff posture of the ship's captain and joined Samra wordlessly, staring out at the black waters of the open ocean. For a while, the only sound came from the snap of the sails and the break of water against the hull.

We'd hardly spoken since Kiva and I had abandoned her on the rooftop. It struck me that in my attempts not to be ordered about by her, I'd blatantly shoved aside her own concerns about being seen working with me, something that put her family in danger. I'd been so concerned with being a leader that I'd forgotten one of the most important parts of leadership was listening to those around me.

But if I couldn't get Samra to agree with even my simplest decisions, how was I going to convince her to ally her rebels with Rhodaire? My response had been to force my decisions, but that only made her dig her heels in deeper, creating a chasm between us.

Maybe leading didn't mean just making decisions and enforcing them. That was what Razel would have done. What my mother would have done. Maybe leading meant being the kind of person people *wanted* to follow.

I took a deep breath. "I'm sorry about today. I shouldn't have forced all this without you on board. I should have listened."

At first, I didn't think she would respond. Despite her decision to help us, I knew Samra didn't like me much. She resented me for my mother's decision not to help the Ambriels. I understood. My bitterness at my mother had only grown in recent weeks.

I tried again. "Your father—"

"I don't give a damn about my father," Samra said with deadly quiet. "He can rot in the night's depths for all I care."

"But your family—"

"I didn't mean him." Her hands tightened into fists at her sides, then relaxed all at once. "I was twenty-one when Illucia attacked five years ago." Her voice had a slight rasp to it, as if the words were still too raw to speak. "My mother was a soldier. She died early in the fighting. My father is the leader of the high council, or what little remains of it. When Razel's army took Seahalla, she forced the council to submit to her."

It was an easy image to conjure, a line of leaders on their knees before the Illucian queen. Razel liked to exert control, and she liked to force people into submission when they stood against her.

"When they came to our house, my father refused," Samra continued. "Even though he was already loyal to the bastards. He thought he could extort them for more money and power." She spit the words out like sand. "My older brother and I were there when they came. They slit my brother's throat."

The words pierced ice cold, and I wrapped my arms about myself for warmth. Another family member dead at Razel's command. In her lust for power.

An ember of fury flickered to life in my stomach. Lately, it never seemed to leave. Everything I saw around me, every thought I had of Illucia or Razel—it all lit a fire inside me. I let it burn.

"I broke the jaw of the soldier nearest me." She flexed her hand as if remembering the sting of bone against her knuckles. "They blinded me in one eye in retribution."

Samra didn't stumble over the words. Didn't shift her weight or clench her hands or betray any hint of the turmoil inside her. She relayed the events like a general reporting the dead—grave, reverent, colder than the sea spray misting against my skin.

"My father submitted of course. My younger brother and sister were in Trendell at the time. They unknowingly returned home only to be used as more leverage against him."

"It's them you wanted to protect," I said quietly.

She didn't reply, but her silence was as good as a confirmation.

A soft breeze lifted her dark curls and pulled at the ends of my braid, prickling like frosted teeth at my skin. The ember in my stomach blazed hotter.

"I'm going to stop her." My voice trembled with rage. "I'm going to make her pay for what she's done."

The captain shifted her dark eyes to me. "Careful of what promises you make. The Night Captain doesn't take kindly to liars."

I shivered. I'd heard stories of the Night Captain as a child, mostly from my mother on the rare occasions when she spent the evening telling me stories, but two weeks of nights on Samra's ship had given me a new appreciation for the legend, which spoke of flaming ships left burning in the night after Diah's crew was done with them. Apparently, even mentioning her name was considered ill luck. The night was her domain, and uttering her name on a lone ship with nothing but miles of vast ocean in every direction risked invoking her power.

I held Samra's gaze. "I give you my word."

She studied me, her eyes obsidian in the moonlight. Then her gaze softened, and the barest hint of a smile pulled at her lips. "Perhaps you're not so bad after all, for a Rhodairen."

The unspoken meaning behind her words rang louder than the crash of the sea: *perhaps you are not your mother.*

Perhaps you are better.

"Did Caylus ever tell you how we met?" Samra's voice pulled me from my thoughts. I shook my head, and she continued, "Most of the fighters that come to Malkin's court are free. Caylus was one of the few in his debt whom he forced to fight. Though at the time, I didn't know anyone was, or I'd never have gone there.

"After Illucia claimed the Ambriels, I started joining the fights. I had trained all my life, and throwing myself into those fights was the only thing that kept me from killing every Illucian soldier I saw."

Her jaw tightened. "One day, I learned who Caylus was from a girl who claimed to be his sister. When he fought, I saw the way he receded into himself, as if he became someone else entirely in order to do what he had to. He hates fighting, and because of that, he won't be able to make this journey with you. He's spent too long fighting. Given too much of his life to it. If you go down this path, he won't walk it with you."

My cheeks flushed with a frustration I didn't fully understand. "You don't know that. He's here, isn't he?"

He'd left behind his new life, his workshop and his bakery, all to help me escape, to fight. Without him, I never would have made it out of Illucia.

She shook her head. "He cares about you. Maybe he even loves you, and it has brought him this far. But whatever bond the two of you forged sitting in that workshop of his wasn't made to go to war. You run toward a fight. Caylus has been forced into them again and again, and he is one wrong blow away from breaking."

"You don't know what you're talking about." Even as I spoke, a sliver of doubt prickled at my insides. What if she was right?

Could our connection survive the landscape of blood and steel and pain we would soon face?

"Maybe." She turned away, gaze settling once more on the sea. "But it's what I think."

The wind picked up, whistling through the masts and rattling a distant chain. I turned back for the warmth and safety of the bunks below.

SIX

E xhaustion had settled deep into my bones by the next
morning. I'd spent the rest of the night lying in bed, unable
to sleep, and now each step felt like a gust of wind pushed back
at me. It was a familiar sensation, a heavy, slow feeling that had
haunted me for months. Some small part of me had hoped it had
gone for good, but in truth, I'd known it might always be there,
ready to drag me down the moment I waded too deep into my
self-doubt, into my dark, acrid memories, into the knowledge of
what I faced.

I'd done all those things in the long hours of dawn. Now my
mind swam with thoughts I couldn't control, couldn't banish.
Would Caylus abandon me? Would Ericen catch us and drag
me back to Illucia? Would Trendell ally with Rhodaire?

Never mind that Res had just used his powers successfully for the first time against our enemy. Never mind Kiva's arm was healed and she had Sinvarra back.

The feeling never cared about the stuff I should be happy about. It was like the sea or the wind or the rain; it simply was, and I had to deal with it.

The whine of slicing metal snapped my train of thought. I whirled out of the way as Kiva brought Sinvarra down in a broad stroke and leapt back, my boots clattering against the solid wood of the main deck. The cacophony of sounds all around us flooded back, centering me in the moment.

Kiva grinned, sword poised for another strike. My heart hammered. The black gold blade had been wrapped to dull its edge, and Kiva would have softened the blow, but it still would have hurt. I needed to pay attention—it wouldn't be long before sparring became war. I had to be prepared.

The eyes of the crew strayed from their tasks to watch us, and Talon, the ship's lookout, shouted unhelpful advice from the crow's nest.

"Charge her!" he called. "Take her legs out!"

The sun heated my flying leathers, and sweat beaded on my brow. Kiva's skin was flushed pink, her jaw set. She lunged again. I dodged, stepping inside her guard and twisting. I seized her sword wrist and threw an elbow back into her stomach. She wheezed, releasing the sword like I'd expected—and then her arms came around me in a great bear hug, pinning my arms to my side and leaving me trapped.

"Hit her in the chin!" Talon called. "The chin!"

"Shut. Up," I wheezed.

Kiva laughed and, after a moment of my struggling, finally released me. "You're fun to spar with when you're distracted," she said. "I get to stomp you without trying."

"I'm going to put seaweed in your bed," I grumbled back.

"Are the two of you done?" Samra called from the quarter-deck. Aroch perched on her shoulder. "You've been taking up my deck space for long enough."

I waved in acknowledgment and approached the shadowed area below where Res perched on the quarterdeck rail. He had his wings half lifted, the breeze fluttering his feathers. He balanced easily as he experimented with the feel of the wind.

For one long breath, I let my dark thoughts rise. Ericen would catch us and kill him. I wouldn't be strong enough to be Res's rider. One crow wouldn't be enough to stop Illucia. He'd be the last of his kind, the other eggs forever out of my reach.

With a heavy exhale, I shoved the rising tide of emotion back down, where it settled into a molten pool of lead in the pit of my stomach. The feeling might never leave, but I'd learned how to fight this battle. I'd learned that I could.

I am more.

"Rider ahead!" Talon called a moment before Jenara ascended the gangplank. She wore her old riding leathers, a sight that brought me closer to tears than I wanted to admit. It'd been a long time since I'd seen another rider wearing them.

Res fluttered down before her, something small and green clasped delicately in his beak. He dropped it proudly before Jenara.

"Is that for me?" She scooped the item up, revealing a grass-colored rope knotted in the shape of a leaf.

"Is that one of my talismans?" Samra leaned over the deck railing. "Your crow's a damned thief!"

I grinned sheepishly, holding up a piece of black coral Res had given me that morning. "I was going to give this back at dinner."

Samra grumbled something under her breath as Kiva snickered, sheathing Sinvarra. "What, nothing for me?" she asked.

Res eyed her sidelong, then leapt from the ship, disappearing over the edge. He soared upward a moment later, circling back around to Kiva. But rather than land, he simply opened his beak atop her and doused her in water.

I swallowed a laugh, but a low chortle burst from Jenara.

"Saints! Stupid chicken." Kiva shook the water from her arms and stomped over to where she'd left a cup of water, only to find Aroch there lapping it up. She threw up her hands. "He's in league with the bird!"

Res let out a cackling noise much like a laugh and circled back to land before Jenara. She patted him gently on the neck. "I'm ready whenever you two are."

We waited while Jenara retrieved two buckets, one filled with seawater, the other empty, and set them before Res.

"This is one of the most basic water crow training exercises," she explained. "The goal is to move the water from one place to another."

A painful familiarity flared at Jenara's instruction, pulling free memories of my lessons with Estrel. She should have been the one helping me train, the one at my side. I'd thought it more than once while working on Res's storm magic with Caylus, but I felt it even more keenly now, standing next to another rider clothed in flying leathers.

I turned the feelings aside and looked to Res. "All you."

He squared up, lifting his head. Then he gave a low, whimpering caw and flopped pitifully to the deck, his wings spread limp as if unable to hold them up for need of food.

"Impressive," Jenara mused.

I groaned. "Caylus isn't here to give in to your begging." I winced at the own truth of my words. This was usually the part where I griped at Res and Caylus bribed him with scones and cookies. But he hadn't come out for breakfast, and I worried he wasn't eating.

Res croaked softly.

"He isn't coming," I replied just as quietly.

Res eyed me, plucking at the cord as if to ferret out the lie before slowly clambering back to his feet. He hopped to the bucket full of water, leaning close to inspect it, then tapped it once with his beak, making it ripple.

"Focus on the size of the water," Jenara told him. "Imagine its weight and substance. Think of it as a single entity."

Res lowered his head, focusing on the water. Energy surged along our bond. I hovered over his shoulder, holding my breath.

The water beveled, rising up the sides. I nearly squealed in delight. Then whatever control Res had over it evaporated, and it sloshed back into place.

"You did it!" I exclaimed.

He cawed triumphantly, lifting his head.

"Sort of," Kiva muttered from the shade of the quarterdeck. She'd commandeered a new glass of water, and Aroch now sat on one of her broad shoulders, a fate to which she seemed resigned.

Jenara chuckled. "It wasn't bad for a first try. Let's keep going."

We spent most of the afternoon on the task, trying again and again until Res finally managed to move the bulk of the water from one bucket to the other. Then we switched to moving different-sized globs of it, which proved far more difficult. By the time the sun had begun to set, Res was exhausted, hungry, and looked about ready to heft the water bucket over the side of the ship.

"That's enough for today," Jenara said, scratching Res's neck. He leaned into it, nearly knocking her over. "It's a shame you can't stay longer."

I nodded. "We have a few days to spare, but it's probably best we don't linger where Razel can easily find us."

"Well, in that case, take this." She handed me a folded paper from her pocket. I opened it to reveal a detailed training routine for Res to follow. She flipped the paper over in my hands, pointing to a corner where she'd written a list of towns and names, some of which I recognized. They were all retired riders.

"Friends of mine live in these towns. They're all on your way to Trendell, and they each rode a different kind of crow in their day. Stop by if you can and see if they can help you with Res."

"I can't thank you enough," I said, tucking the paper safely into my pocket.

She smiled warmly. "It's you we should be thanking. It's no easy task you have ahead of you. Take care of yourself. Both of you." She clapped me on the shoulder again, then enveloped me in another hug, saying in a low voice, "And make Razel pay for what she's done."

"I will."

After posting a letter to Caliza to let her know I was safe and to update her on the fires, surviving crow eggs, and our upcoming itinerary, we set sail from Isair early that evening, half the town pouring out onto the promenade to see us out.

It took a little convincing to get Samra to agree that stopping in the other towns was for the best, but in the end, she accepted that Res needed the training. With just over a week of travel remaining and nearly two weeks before Belin's Day, we could spare a few hours in each town for me to track down the riders and get their help starting Res on training regimens for the other powers.

It felt good to have an immediately actionable plan. Something to keep me busy through the days of travel and distract me from the immensity of what waited ahead. It didn't stop that heavy feeling from seeking me out, but it helped.

When Caylus didn't come to dinner again, I carried a bowl of stew and plate of bread to his room, my mind so engrossed in the latest Sella tale Darya had spun that I almost missed the sounds echoing from within. A sharp, heavy thudding. Rhythmic and bone deep, it made me shudder. I turned the handle and pushed open the door.

A dim sona lamp shadowed Caylus's broad form. His back was toward me, his shirt gone, baring the crisscross of angry red and white lines. He'd pinned a pillow to the wall before him and wrapped his hands in strips of cloth, but neither had stopped his knuckles from scraping raw and staining both fabrics a bright, vicious red.

He drove his fists into the pillowed wall again and again, the strike of bone against wood turning my stomach. Caylus didn't even flinch. How used to pain did someone have to be before bloodying their knuckles against a wall over and over again had no effect?

"Stop." The word came out as a whisper, lost beneath his strikes. I swallowed hard, finding my voice. "Caylus, stop!"

He froze, arm half-extended, bloody knuckles metallic in the dim sona light. For a moment, he simply stood there, his shoulders heaving with his wild breathing, every muscle coiled like a knotted chain. Then he faced me, and the hollowness in his eyes nearly broke me. Tears tracked down his cheeks, his jaw a tight line.

I didn't know what to do.

"Why?" I asked hoarsely.

He squeezed his eyes shut, shaking his head. Trembling, I set the bowl on the small desk and closed the distance between us. I reached for one of his damaged hands, still curled into an impossibly tight fist. He shuddered.

He's spent too long fighting. Given too much of his life to it.

Samra's voice beat a dangerous tattoo in my head.

Caylus has been forced into them again and again, and he is one wrong blow away from breaking.

An uncomfortable thought sprouted in my head. He didn't want to fight, but he would for me.

He didn't want to be here, but he came for me.

My hands looked so small beside his. I curled my fingers around his hand, cupping it like an injured bird. "I don't expect you to fight for me, Caylus," I said. His eyes widened, but I pressed on before he could argue. "You've done so much for me already. More than I had any right to ask, and I'm so sorry for what it's cost you. I know how hard this is for you, and I know it isn't what you want. You don't have to do this."

"You don't understand," he breathed, voice jagged. He stumbled through his words, not with his usual nerves but with an energy barely contained. "I want—I—" He stopped. Tried again. "There's something wrong with me, Thia." The words were half confession, half prayer, and they spilled out of him. "When I first met you in the Colorfalls, and then when we went looking for Malkin, it was like some other part of me took over. I *wanted* to fight. I wanted to drive my fist into your opponent's face until only blood remained."

I drew in a sharp breath. He didn't notice, his eyes trapped on some spot over my shoulder without truly seeing.

"There's this—this *hole* inside me that I fall into when I'm fighting, and I lose myself to it. I don't know how to stop when I'm inside there. I don't know how—how to find myself."

What are you looking for, Caylus?

I don't know.

"It becomes my purpose," he said. "I want to help you. I want to stop Malkin and Razel before they destroy anyone else's world like they destroyed mine. But I don't want to fall into that hole again. I don't want that to be my purpose."

Malkin had made fighting Caylus's life. He'd made it his survival, his everything. And no matter how much ocean we put between the Ambriels and us, those chains still bound him.

I still held Caylus's hand, trapped between my own as if letting it go meant letting him go, as if he'd simply fade away.

"Your past doesn't have to be your future." Ever so gently, I pressed my fingers to the place where his nails dug into his palm. Carefully, I straightened one finger, and then the next, until the fist was gone, leaving bloody crescents in its wake.

He stared down at his damaged hand, his fingers trembling in my grasp. He tried more than once to talk before the words finally came. "Have you ever felt like no matter what you do, there's no putting the pieces of yourself back together?"

"Every day."

He swallowed, nodding. Caylus knew all about the pain that had plagued me for months, that still did. Hatching Res didn't erase the loss of so much. Some cracks couldn't be mended; they only became a part of you instead, forever places that left you unsteady.

"It feels impossible," he said. "Like trying to repair shattered glass."

"You should know better than anyone that's not impossible." I placed my hand palm to palm with his, his skin rough with calluses and scars. Each one told a sad, dark tale. "If you melt it down, you can re-form it into anything. Even something new."

His fingers curled about my palm, his touch tentative. "You make it sound so easy."

"It's not," I admitted. After months of struggling to put my own pieces back together, I knew how hard a process it was, how many cracks still ran through me. "But it's easier when you have people to help you. I will always be here to help you, Caylus."

I lifted my free hand but paused, my fingers hovering above his face. I didn't know what stopped me touching him. The gesture suddenly felt too intimate, the boy before me at once foreign and familiar. But not touching him felt like drawing a line, one I wasn't sure I wanted to.

The distance that had opened between us sat like an invisible hand against my chest, pushing me back.

In the end, I let my hand drop, feeling oddly betrayed by myself. I stepped back to find him looking at me in confusion, his head tilted like it did when faced with a problem he couldn't solve.

"What?" I asked.

He bit his lip. "You feel it too, don't you?"

I shook my head, though a part of me knew exactly what he meant. This distance between us was made of more than fear and painful questions. More than my fire to fight and his desire to be something more than what Malkin had made him.

What had grown between us in his workshop had been a friendship unlike any I'd had before. Kiva was my life, my blood, but Caylus had been there for me during a time of my life I never thought I'd see. He'd helped me hatch Res, raise him, and train him. Our connection had grown from a shared sense of curiosity and a need for healing.

But I didn't love him. Not in the way I'd hoped. And looking into his gentle face, I knew he felt the same way.

"I care about you so much, Caylus," I said softly. "You gave me peace in a place that threatened to break me, and I owe you everything for that. Without you, I may never have figured out how to hatch the egg, and your friendship means more to me than I can ever say."

He waited, green eyes dark in the fading dusk.

I forced my voice steady. "But the feelings I used to have for you, that I thought I might always have for you, they aren't there anymore."

Caylus's hand trembled in mine. He bit his lip, started to speak, stopped, and then did it all again in a pattern of uncertainty I'd grown to know so well.

"I...don't feel that way either," he said.

A relieved smile pulled at my lips. "I'm so glad you're here, Caylus. I really am. You make me feel calm, something I'm not very good at being, and I need that. And I will always be thankful for everything that you've done for Rhodaire and me. I can never repay you. But I think…" I hesitated.

"That we're a little too different?" he offered, and I was surprised by the accuracy of that situation. He'd never been the most perceptive of people, but he'd always been aware of me, of what I wanted and needed. He was a better friend than I could have asked for.

"Yes," I said. "But I also think our lives are meant for different paths."

I'd railed against Samra's warning, but now I saw what she did.

I saw a boy who had been knocked down too many times to count but who had always stood back up. I saw a brilliant mind that wanted nothing more than to learn and grow and discover new things, even if it meant losing himself in them. I saw a friend.

Caylus ran a hand through his perpetually unruly hair, unsuccessfully attempting to get it to lay flat. "To be honest with you," he said softly, "I've started to realize... Well, I'm not sure." He paused, folding his arms almost protectively about himself. "I don't know if I'll ever feel that way."

I raised an eyebrow, listening.

"I really care about you, just not in *that* way. Not romantically. I've never felt that way toward someone, and..." He trailed off. "Well, I don't know. Sometimes I feel like I followed what was expected of me instead of what I wanted. And I'm not sure I want to be in a relationship like that." He shrugged his broad shoulders. "I'm still figuring it out."

I nodded in understanding. "I'm here if you ever need to talk about it."

Caylus smiled, squeezing my hand. "I'll still be here for you too. I'm coming to Trendell one way or another. I've always wanted to visit Eselin anyways. Did you know they have a university that's open to the public? It's free too. Anyone can walk in and sit in the lectures."

"Thank you. Having you with me means more than I can say." I squeezed his hand gently, lifting it. "You should get Luan to look at your hands. And come join us for training tomorrow. Res is so much more compliant when you're around."

"I think that's the scones," he muttered, and I glowered at him. "Right, no scones."

I snorted, even as something inside me threatened to break. This was the way things were meant to be between us: easygoing, comfortable, quiet. But none of those were what waited for us in the coming weeks.

"Are you going to be okay?" I asked.

He smiled. "Eventually."

I nodded. Sometimes eventually was all we could ask for.

SEVEN

I returned to my cabin to find Kiva sitting on the floor diligently cleaning Sinvarra. Aroch lay curled in her lap, and from the thin red claw marks on her forearms, I suspected this was the outcome of a long struggle. Res splayed across half the floor, trilling softly in his sleep.

Kiva's lips pressed into a firm line as we entered. "I know that look," she said. "What are you blaming yourself for now?"

I dropped onto the edge of the bed. "Nothi—" A cloth struck me in the face before I could finish. Shoving it aside, I glared down at her and tossed it back. She caught it, running it along Sinvarra's gold-veined midnight surface.

"Fine," I grumbled. "Each day brings us closer to the possibility that the other kingdoms will reject us, I'm worried about being a leader for Rhodaire, Caylus and I broke up, and now Ericen—" Kiva groaned, but I pressed on. "I felt wrong leaving him in Sordell, and I feel wrong leaving him now."

"We can't trust him," she said, echoing so many conversations we'd had before.

"He didn't have to warn me."

"It's part of his game. He was stalling for time until he had backup."

I hated that I didn't know, hated that I couldn't tell.

Kiva stopped polishing the sword abruptly. "Wait a second. Did you say you and Caylus broke up?"

I groaned and flopped back onto my bed. By the time I finished telling Kiva everything that'd happened, I'd snuggled under the covers and lay staring at the bunk above me.

"I feel like I'm dragging him into his worst nightmare," I finished.

Kiva sighed softly. "You can't save everyone, Thia," she said. "It isn't your job."

I looked back at her, her expression uncharacteristically soft. A thousand feelings bubbled to the surface: the need to prove myself capable, to be strong. To handle things myself for once. To be a leader. And with that, the fear that I would fail, only to slip back into that heavy darkness.

I fought them all back down, offering her a quick smile that she wouldn't believe for a second.

"Maybe." I turned onto my other side as a familiar feeling crept onto my shoulders. Drawing a deep breath, I let it out slowly, imagining the weight sliding away like a snake. But the unease remained, always there, always waiting for me to slip. For me to lie down and not want to get back up.

Refusing to give the feeling purchase, I rolled back to the other side and perched on the edge of the bed. I felt jittery and restless, surrounded by questions without answers.

My fingers curled around the bed frame. "What do you think about what Ericen said about the Sellas?"

Kiva snorted. "More lies. Like I said, he was just trying to stall you."

"With talk of long-dead magical beings?" I shook my head. "He could have said anything. Why bring up the Sellas?"

Setting aside her cleaning cloth, Kiva slid Sinvarra back into its sheath with a sigh. "What are you thinking?"

It felt like a ridiculous idea, but I couldn't shake it. "There's still so much of the Sellas in Rhodaire. The statues, the temple. We tore them all down in Aris, but in Isair, it was like—" I hesitated, feeling foolish. "Like some people still believe they exist."

Doubt riddled Kiva's face. "More likely they just never got around to tearing them down. Breaking stuff takes effort too, you know."

I rolled my eyes. "There's something going on, and I intend to find out what." I stood, making for the door.

"Where are you going?" Kiva called.

"To get some answers."

I nearly walked straight into Onis as he emerged from Samra's office. He reeled back, a hand going for his talismans.

"Sorry," I said reflexively, then instantly wished I hadn't when all he did was scowl at me. "Do we have a problem?" I asked.

His nostrils flared. "My problem is you and that night-cursed crow. Rhodaire's always been too quick to meddle in magic. Now that beast is doing more than he should, and you're raising talk of the Sellas? Duren protect us from your foolishness." He waved his hand across his face in a gesture I'd seen some of the other crew make.

I stared at him. Religion had never been my strong suit, but I was pretty sure he'd just warded himself against me.

Onis leaned closer, his voice dropping to a growl. "Your ancestors may have worshipped the Sellas, but we knew better in the Ambriels. Nothing waits for those who meddle with those creatures but death!"

With that, he swept past me, muttering to himself about reckless Rhodairens.

Frowning after him, I yanked Samra's door open. She sat at her desk, a pile of papers before her, fingers rubbing her scarred eye gently.

"Are you causing trouble with my crew?" she asked, clearly having heard everything.

"What? No. He's causing trouble with me."

She leaned back, lacing her fingers and pushing out to stretch them. "Onis is an ornery one, but he's a good sailor and he's served me well. Just ignore his superstitious nonsense."

I refrained from pointing out the talismans on her shelves; that wasn't what I'd come for. "Can I borrow your copy of *Saints and Sellas*?"

She raised an eyebrow. "Why?"

"Curiosity," I replied. "I haven't read it in a long time."

Samra's expression remained impassive, but I could feel her weighing me. Then she shrugged. I hurried forward, carefully extricating the book from the shelf and retreating for the door before she could change her mind.

Back in my room, I pored over the book well into the night. The stories were different than I remembered, darker and more vicious. Humans who angered the Sellas died painful deaths or else were subjugated to far worse fates—maimed or blinded, cursed or trapped in the Wandering Wood for eternity.

The book painted a picture of the Sellas that was both beautiful and cruel. They were as graceful as they were deadly, as magnanimous as they were ambivalent, content to grant humans gifts and then snatch them away when we inevitably corrupted them.

It was that piece that fascinated me, the idea that the Sellas granted people magic. Every story followed a human granted magical abilities, and each one ended the same. When the human inexorably used the magic for war and destruction, the Sella always knew, for by giving the human magic, it created a connection between them. In the end, the human died a bloody death.

There was something there though. Something familiar.

"A connection," I muttered to Res. "Like the bond between us."

A sleepy tug echoed back at me across the connection, tinged with irritation. Apparently, Res didn't appreciate my late-night conversation.

An idea sparked. "A magic line!"

"A what?" Kiva grumbled from above.

I winced. "Nothing, sorry. Go back to sleep." The bunk above shifted, and a moment later, Kiva's heavy snores filled the room again.

I'd learned about magic lines from an abandoned journal in a forgotten library back in Aris. The scholar had believed that magic was passed down from generation to generation, like hair color or height. It was a connection, like the one that bonded Res and me.

Was this what happened when a crow chose a rider? It created a magic line between them? It would explain why riders often came from the same families. The crow's magic must influence the person's physiology somehow, creating the magic line, which was then passed down from parent to child.

It was a theory Caylus had had too.

The bond between rider and crow was something we only partially understood. When a crow hatched, it usually imprinted on the first person it saw. It was for this reason that new riders would take their chosen egg to one of the many hatching alcoves at the top of the royal rookery at the start of the process.

When Res had struggled to access his magic back at Caylus's apartment, Lady Kerova had told me to push on the bond. The result had been disastrous. I'd helped Res release his magic, but he'd lost control, revealing his presence to Razel's spy. But it suggested that the bond was a conduit for more than just emotions and thoughts.

Could it also be a channel for power?

Sleep tugged at my eyelids. Kiva and Res had the right idea. The book had yielded interesting possibilities, but who was to say they meant anything? They were just stories, after all. Who knew whether I was just molding them to fit my own purposes?

I needed more information.

EIGHT

Our next stop was Keris, a bustling fishing village nestled in a small cove. According to Jenara's list, I'd find a retired battle crow rider here named Lazarayev. They weren't hard to find either. It took all of a flash of Res's wings before we had a crowd around us and someone had volunteered to go fetch the old rider.

Flashing Res about was another thing Samra and I had come to an agreement on. I refused to hide any longer, since that was exactly what had led Razel to start attacking Rhodairen towns. It'd be a few days before word reached her of what we'd done in Isair, and by then, we'd have already moved through several towns, following a path that looked very much like we were returning to Aris.

The crowd parted for a middle-aged person with the long, pale blond hair common among the Korovi and a thin, wiry body. I'd met Laz once in Rhodaire, the day I'd wandered into a blacksmith's shop in the Turren wing, entranced by the black gold weapons on display.

Laz bowed to me, and I returned the gesture, a smile tugging at my lips. "It's good to see you again, Laz. Jenara said you might be able to help me with battle crow training."

"And you, Princess," they replied. "I'd be honored to help, though I have to say I'd heard rumor it was a storm crow you hatched."

"About that."

After leading Laz onto the ship and filling them in on the strangeness of Res's powers, they wasted no time in devising a training plan for us. The most fundamental battle crow power was the ability to harden their feathers into metal, something Res struggled with.

"It's as much mental as it is physical," Laz explained. "You have to see your feathers as the metal you wish them to become."

Res clicked his beak, closing his eyes. A moment later, they flew open, and he spun to face the door to the crew's quarters as it creaked open. Caylus appeared, his auburn curls catching the first rays of sunlight. I perked up, at once glad to see him outside and suddenly nervous. For a quick, uncertain moment, we just looked at each other. Then I spotted the handful of cooked chicken in his hand, and he smiled sheepishly as if to say, "Not scones!"

Res hopped over to Caylus, cawing excitedly. A knot

loosened in my chest, though it refused to let go entirely. He was okay. We were okay.

"You can't give him treats before he's done anything!" I said exasperatedly as Res gobbled down the chicken.

Caylus tilted his head, looking perplexed. "He's hungry," he said as if we hadn't had this exact conversation ten times before. All Res had to do was feign an injured wing or sway wearily on the spot, and Caylus would feed him whatever he wanted.

"You're just doing this to annoy me now, aren't you?"

Res let out an indignant squawk, and Caylus simply blinked at me.

"Ugh, never mind," I muttered, marching up to where Res was sniffing Caylus's hand for missed chicken. "Caylus, this is Laz. Laz, meet the boy who derails all my training sessions."

Laz waved.

Caylus's eyes brightened, no doubt at the prospect of seeing more crow magic. This was the boy I knew.

"What are you working on?" he asked.

"Battle crow magic."

Caylus's eyes rolled toward the sky in the telltale sign he'd retreated into some private thought as Laz peppered Res with a few more instructions, but as the crow squeezed his eyes shut, feathers fluttering, nothing happened. He let out an exasperated huff.

"You know the way you manifest the clouds?" Caylus asked, drawing Res's eye. "Try to do the same with your feathers. Manifest the metal."

Res's concentration trundled down the line. His wings

twitched, his feathers shifting. Then they flickered. I smothered a gasp with a hand. They flickered again, then settled into a deep, shining gray.

Metal.

Res let out a triumphant caw, lifting his wings. I yelped, leaping back as he nearly knocked me to the ground. Caylus caught me with a steadying hand.

"Watch it with those things!" I snapped.

Res chirruped, but Laz nodded gravely. "An important point. Battle crows have incredible strength, especially when armored up. Getting hit with a metallic limb is a far cry from a feathered wing. It takes practice to get accustomed to the additional weight, and even more to control your body in this state. I recommend remaining armored up for long stretches of time while you go about daily activities."

"You heard them," I told Res. "Full metal mode for the rest of the day."

We spent the rest of the afternoon with Laz, during which Res even managed to release a couple of metal feathers as projectiles. Thankfully, Samra wasn't around to see the holes.

Talon pulled one out of the mainmast and peered into the hollow inside. "I'd've thought it'd be the whole feather," he remarked.

"That would make flying very difficult," I replied. "It's just an outer metal layer they release."

"Huh." He stuck the feather in his pocket. I rolled my eyes.

At the end of the training session, Laz wrote down a suggested schedule like Jenara had, leaving us with instructions and advice.

"I wish you the best with your training," they said as I escorted them back to the dock. "I hope when this is over, you'll come see me in Keris."

I smiled. "Deal."

When I turned back to the ship, Caylus stuffed his hands behind his back, but not before I caught a glimpse of something that looked suspiciously like a scone.

The next few days followed a similar pattern. We stopped in each town on Jenara's list, seeking out the riders there and requesting their aid. Some were familiar faces, some new, and each one imparted invaluable advice for Res's new powers.

Seveila, a retired fire crow rider, taught him how to create and extinguish flames, the latter turning out to be much more difficult. Gavilan taught him the peace of mind and patience required to heal with a sun crow's skills. He struggled with the earth crow lessons from Esos, ending up with a long list of training activities to practice, something we did with every moment of free time we had.

Caylus's help was invaluable. He had a way of rooting out what was stumping Res and helping him look at it in a new light. The riders understood the powers and the training, but Caylus and Res had had a connection from the beginning. Granted, it was built on cookies and scones, but between Caylus's sugary motivations, the riders' experience, and my bond with Res, we made steady progress.

Most of the crew watched with rapt fascination. Except Onis. I couldn't walk past the grizzled sailor without him clutching his talismans and muttering prayers under his breath, but he didn't confront me again like he had outside Samra's office.

On the seventh day of our journey and with the town of Fendail and its shadow crow rider behind us, Res and I prepared for our final stop in our journey: Rosstair, home of the wind crow rider and also one of the kingdom's most well-known flight training courses. It was barely a day's ride from Aris, and we often funneled new recruits out to it for monthlong intensive flight training.

I scratched the top of Res's head. "We should take a break from the other magics and work on your next level of storm magic."

A low rumble in his throat mirrored the vibration of hunger he sent down the bond. He nudged me with his beak, and I pushed him away gently.

"You just had breakfast," I groaned.

"What's the next level?" Talon asked from where he clung to nearby rigging. His feet were hooked in, and he leaned back in it like a sling, his bright red hair a beacon against the blue sky.

I withdrew a piece of paper I'd scribbled a training plan on weeks ago. "Every crow has a different training program tuned to their type of magic." I showed him the paper. "They're broken down into beginner, intermediate, and advanced techniques. Res can pretty much do everything in the beginner and intermediate one, so it's time to start working on the next set."

Talon skimmed the list. "I heard you tell Kiva he's done a lot of this stuff already." He pointed at the advanced section.

I snorted. "He's *messed up* a lot of this stuff already. It's not just about exhibiting the power; it's about controlling it."

Res trilled in disagreement, opening and closing his wings in short bursts.

"Well, prove it," I replied. "Create a storm cloud. One storm cloud."

Our bond thrummed, Res's magic rising. The light caught the silver in his eyes, and the space around him seemed to thicken and charge. The air just above Res blurred, as if obscured by a rolling fog. It condensed, darkening into a single, puffy rain cloud.

A wave of satisfaction slid down the link, and Res flapped his wings as if to say *told you so*.

The cloud shifted, sliding through the air. Before I realized what he was doing, he'd moved it over my head. A moment later, a torrential rain poured from the cloud.

It'd barely struck me before I sprang forward with a screech. Res dodged me, flapping his wings in a burst of strength that sent him fluttering a good five feet away. Laughter rocked down the cord as he beat his wings in amusement.

"Bloody chicken," I hissed.

Talon's distant laugh echoed. "Crow one, princess zero."

I huffed. It was supposed to be crow and princess versus everyone else.

"The minute he can safely control lightning bolts, I'm frying you," I called back, to which Talon only cackled.

"Can't he just transport us to Trendell?" He snapped his fingers. "Now that he's all shadow crowy and all."

"He's barely had any training," I told him. "I'm not getting stuck in between places, but if you'd like to volunteer, be my guest." Talon grinned, and I added, "Besides, even the most powerful shadow crows couldn't transport an entire ship. The most I ever heard of them taking were two people. Most of them could only transport themselves. I'd be surprised if Res can teleport anyone else."

"Boo." Talon swung idly in the riggings. "Ooh, I know! Let's find an old Sella road instead. My ma said they connect the whole continent."

"If those roads ever existed, they disappeared with the Sellas," I said. The only time I'd ever even heard of them was when my mother told me stories from *Saints and Sellas*. The book last night had mentioned them more than once. "Anyways, what do you care? You're a sailor. Don't you like sailing?"

"Of course. But I'd like teleporting through shadows even more."

"Well, you'll just have to settle for lightning."

Res snapped his beak, and a burst of thunder echoed in the cloudless sky. Talon yelped with surprise, nearly losing his balance on the rigging. I laughed, and he joined me, swinging down from his perch to chase after Res. The crow sprang away, landing by me with a flutter of his wings. I spun on him, and he chirped in surprise, barely managing to avoid my embrace.

With a snap of his wings, Res sent us both tumbling to the deck in a flurry of wind.

"Oi, that's gotta be cheating," Talon said with a groan.

Flat on my back, I simply laughed, and then again when Res appeared above me, looking far too proud of himself.

"Yeah, yeah, you win." I pushed his beak away, and he huffed.

Caylus appeared above me, a wry smile on his face. He offered me a hand up, and I took it, hauling myself to my feet. He nodded to something over my shoulder.

"We're here."

I spun about.

A sprawling, white stone city sat nestled in the rolling hills like a pocket of sea foam, glistening in the noonday sun.

Rosstair.

It was time for Res and me to fly.

NINE

I'd always loved Rosstair.

One of Rhodaire's biggest shipping cities, it had a massive promenade lining the coast. The sloping city culminated in a wide boulevard filled with warehouses, some of which had been repurposed into collections of pubs and stores, including one of my favorite bakeries.

It was also where the flight training school had been built, right over the thin Fera River that trickled down from the hills the city rested on.

All of that I expected as the *Aizel* docked in port.

The army of green and silver soldiers, I did not.

"What in the Saints' name?" Kiva surveyed the gathered ranks with an uneasy hand upon Sinvarra.

Samra stepped up beside me. "Is this not normal in a city of this size? We are quite close to Aris."

"It would be if they knew we were coming." I reached along the cord to Res. It wasn't that I thought Rhodairen soldiers were a threat. It was that after all Razel had done, any strange situation made me wary. Had she somehow infiltrated the city? Were the soldiers a distraction?

"Who's that?" Caylus pointed to where the crowd had just parted, letting through a tall, willowy woman with dark, curling hair unbound to her waist. One hand held up her skirts, and the other trapped her circlet to her head against the sea wind. She forgot both when she saw me.

"Caliza!" I bolted down the gangplank and into my sister's open arms.

She enveloped me, holding so tight, the bracelet on her wrist dug sharply into my back. But I didn't care. I never wanted her to let go.

"Thia." Her voice strained. I held her tighter.

When we pulled back at last, there were tears in her eyes. Something tugged in my chest, and my eyes burned. She held my face in her hands, her fingers trembling. "Oh, I'm so glad you're home." She pulled me into her arms once more.

Home.

Then something was forcing its way between us. I stepped back as Res stuck his beak in the narrow gap between our bodies, sniffing Caliza.

She yelped, stumbling back, and stared openmouthed. "Thia, he's beautiful." She started to reach out a hesitant hand but pulled it back. She'd never been comfortable around the crows. But no sooner had she begun to retreat than Res tucked his head under her hand, trilling gently.

Caliza gasped. Then her hand settled and she let out a small laugh, which slowly grew. "Thank the Saints," she whispered. "Thank the Saints."

After receiving my letter with our itinerary, Caliza had thought it prudent to check in with me in person. And, she admitted after Kiva's incessant needling, she'd missed me. In return, I told her about our training with the other riders, introduced Samra and Caylus, and rehashed our encounter with the mercenaries in Isair.

All this we exchanged over cups of ice-cold talcé in the lobby of the flight training complex. The building had been built almost entirely of frosted glass imported from Jindae, the seams a dark, satiny metal. I knew from experience that the door to the left led to a barrack, the one to the right to the armory. Between them sat an expansive training ground.

The whole thing had been repurposed to train troops after Ronoch, but I could still see the remnants of the flight course through the sheer back wall.

The sight of it sent a shiver through me.

Caylus stood before the wall, inspecting either the glass or the grounds beyond it and muttering to Res. The crow pretended to listen but kept leaning closer to Caylus's talcé glass, which dangled forgotten in his hand.

Samra had gone to oversee restocking the *Aizel*, and Kiva stood talking to some new recruits off near the armory. Most of the active-duty soldiers had been pulled up for battle, leaving the complex eerily quiet and empty.

When I asked about the state of the kingdom, Caliza informed me that Razel had retaliated when I left Illucia. Her troops had pushed all the way to Edir.

Caliza expected they'd have to give up the ground as soon as Edir was evacuated and push south to Elaris. The town was well suited to battle, having been developed as a midway point in the kingdom to serve both as a transport for supplies out to the border as well as an easily defensible base after the last war with Illucia had resulted in heavy damage to Aris.

She bit her lip as she finished speaking, fingers worrying at a few strands of hair.

"What is it?" I asked.

Her gaze jumped to Caylus, then Kiva, and she stood, offering me her hand. "There's something else I need to tell you."

I took her hand, allowing her to lead me into the barrack building and into the privacy of a small office with only a simple desk, chair, and bookshelf. A thick, creeping dread unfurled inside me at the hesitance in Caliza's expression. The last time she'd looked at me like that, she had told me she'd engaged me to Ericen.

"Maybe you should sit down," she said.

I crossed my arms. "Just say it, Caliza."

She took a deep breath.

"Estrel is alive."

Distantly, I was aware I'd stopped breathing, but the knowledge felt so far away. Everything felt so far away, as if I were looking at the world from below water a hundred feet deep.

"I don't understand," I said.

Estrel was alive.

She was alive, and she'd kept it from me.

Estrel had been horribly burned in Ronoch, then vanished from the healer's ward in the days after. When she hadn't come back, I'd known something must have happened to her. It was the only reason she wouldn't have contacted me. The only reason she would have left me alone.

Then Caliza said she was dead, and everything made sense. Except she wasn't dead, and now nothing made sense.

She'd left me with no mother, a sister I hadn't understood, and scars that wouldn't go away no matter how many nights I prayed. She'd let me believe she was dead long enough for the wound to scar over, but only just. Long enough that hearing this news tore it open once more.

My knees struck the ground, but I didn't feel it. Someone moved at my side, and Caliza was there, wrapping her long arms around me as I buried my face in my hands and cried. Res tugged on the cord, sensing my pain. When I didn't respond, he pulled harder. It felt like someone was trying to tear my heart out, but it was already gone.

The door at our back slammed open, and Res leapt in. When he couldn't identify an immediate threat, he let out a low, whining caw, nudging my back with his beak. I reached out, burying my fingers in his feathers.

When at last I could breathe normally again, my chest felt hollow. As I pulled away from Caliza, sitting back into little more than a heap, familiarity settled. I knew this feeling. This heavy emptiness, as if there were nothing real inside to hold me steady, but a thousand shackles pulled me down, down, down.

Res shifted forward, his wings spread, and flopped across my lap in a mess of feathers and soft coos. He simply lay there in the silence, his mere existence a false promise of new chances.

No matter how many chances I had, this was always where I would find myself: broken.

Eventually, I stopped shaking. I shifted, my limbs stiff and sore, until my back was pressed against the wall. Res moved with me, our bond thrumming with his calming energy, and I latched on to it. It was like being washed out to sea, carried farther and farther out by each retreating wave.

I looked to Caliza. "How?"

Caliza sat back against the wall beside me. "She came to Aris on the night you left Sordell. She didn't say where she's been or why she left, only that she'd heard about the engagement. I told her you'd be in Eselin by Belin's Day, and she left for Trendell that night."

"How is that possible?" I croaked.

"I don't know," she said softly. "I thought she was dead."

I traced the scars on my left hand with a finger, memories of the searing bite of fire and acrid smell of burning flesh pressing in. The world wobbled, my stomach rising into my throat, and I clenched my hands so tight, my nails dug into my palms, forcing deep breaths until everything settled.

Whatever reason Estrel had for abandoning me, it would never be enough.

Someone knocked gently on the door. Caylus stood there, his broad shoulders taking up much of the frame, a cup of steaming tea in hand.

I almost laughed. Of course he'd found tea. In a kingdom that never drank it, in a military complex he'd never once set foot in, he still managed to find a cup.

Caliza squeezed my arm and stood, leaving me with Caylus, who took her place beside me. He handed me the tea, and I held fast to its warmth, sitting in the comfortable silence Caylus always brought with him.

This had always been how it'd been between us.

He took my hand in his like I'd done for him, and I felt the rough lines of his many scars, the places where his body had broken alongside so many other things. But I also felt the calluses he'd earned from his workshop, the small burns that came from baking muffins in the morning or absentmindedly touching a still-steaming teakettle.

He'd begun to rebuild his life, to rebuild himself. Piece by piece. Day by day. Like I had. Like I still did. This feeling was a part of me, but it wasn't all of me. I couldn't just will it away, but I could learn to work through it, and I had. With the help of my friends and family, I had.

Maybe together, we could actually do it.

I am more.

More than this feeling of darkness. More than the urge to give up. More than my pain and my past.

I let out a soft breath. Estrel was alive.

It still didn't feel real, even as my insides felt as though they'd been carved out with a jagged knife. Somewhere, deep beneath the pain and confusion that had threaded through me, relief flickered. She was alive.

Alive, and waiting for me in Trendell.

TEN

A re you sure you're okay?" Kiva asked again as I emerged from the barrack office dressed in my flying leathers.

I gave her a flat look, but I couldn't really blame her. She'd been there for me through a lot the last few months, and she knew me better than anyone.

"Honestly, not completely, no," I replied. "But I will be, and for now, that's enough."

Once, the news about Estrel would have towed me beneath the current. Now, with Kiva here, with Caliza and Caylus and Res, with all that I'd worked through in the last few months, I knew I had the support to find my way through this too.

Res hopped along beside me, trilling excitedly. He kept "accidentally" buffeting Kiva with his feathers and urging me on with the tip of his beak. I latched on to the elation thrumming through our bond and let it fill me as we entered the main lobby.

Caliza waited with a bridle and leather saddle bundled in her arms and a smile on her face. "I'm so happy I get to see this!"

"What?" Kiva asked. "An adolescent duck falling on its face?"

Res snapped his beak, the only warning Kiva had before her shadow reached out to trip her. I caught her before she could fall, grinning. "Don't pick fights with the magical crow, Kiva."

She glowered at Res, who puffed up in response.

I waved away the mild alarm on Caliza's face. "Come on. Let's go outside."

The main training courtyard looked little like I remembered it. What had once been designed for flight and crow training had been transformed into something vaguely reminiscent of the training grounds in the castle at Sordell. Sparring rings, sword practice stations, and archery targets all filled the arena. But remnants of the complex's old purpose still persisted. A line of massive hoops hung suspended overhead for practicing aerial spins, massive T-shaped perches below them for landing, and the crowning jewel of the training complex: the drop wall.

A massive stone slab four times the height of the nearest building, it'd been formed by earth crows ages ago for flight practice. Steps zigzagged across its flat face, a platform jutting out at each switchback so crows could practice at increasing heights. Normally, a fledging would start by attempting various types of flights on their own, but Res had long ago learned the feel of the wind. Now he just had to account for me.

I took the bridle from Caliza, spinning eagerly to Res. He let out a loud caw, stepping back.

I sighed. "If I lean left and you go right, we're both in trouble. When we get more comfortable with each other, we can go without it."

Res eyed me as if he were considering the multitude of heights he could drop me from.

I lifted the bridle. "Is it okay?"

Something like a dramatic sigh grumbled down the link, but in the end, Res lowered his head, allowing me to slip the bridle around his head and beak before securing the saddle on his back. My hands quivered as I worked, and he squawked when I pulled the girth too tight. I winced. "Sorry."

Res and I walked along the grounds for several minutes, letting him get used to the feel of the leather against his feathers and readjusting anything that wasn't comfortable for him. Then we climbed onto the highest platform, well away from the edge. Though it seemed the riskiest, starting so high, it was actually the safest way. It gave Res plenty of time to adjust to my weight and correct for it.

Nearly a hundred feet below us, Caylus, Kiva, and Caliza waited.

I looked to Res. "Ready?"

He straightened, puffing out his chest and lifting his head.

I grinned and, with my heart hammering, slid a foot into a stirrup. With a familiar ease, I swung onto his back, settling lightly into the saddle.

Everything stilled. I forgot the whisper of the wind through the trees, forgot the warm caress of the afternoon heat, forgot even the war looming on the horizon.

In that moment, there was only me, and there was Res.

Our bond thrummed. I closed my eyes, letting the feeling fill me. Slowly, the touch of the wind came back, the brush of sunlight against my skin like warm fingers.

Kiva let out a loud cheer, and the rightness of the moment filled me in a rising tide.

After so much loss, after so much pain and blood and death, we were both still here. Resyries was here.

And I was a rider.

I laughed once, loud and sharp. Res flared out his wings, releasing a piercing call. I leaned forward, keeping my weight centered, my knees clear of his wing joints, a thousand of Estrel's past refrains echoing in my mind: *Trust your crow to do the flying. Lean with them. Don't lead them. You must move as one.*

Go. I sent the word down the connection in a flutter. Res leapt, clearing the platform with ease, his wings two massive shadows stretched wide. They caught the current, holding us steady.

I let out a whoop as Res glided smoothly through the air. The wind poured over me in a caress, an old friend I never thought I'd know again. Res's joy swept through our bond, filling me in rushing waves. It rebounded inside me, paralleling my own, two emotions made one.

I felt the wind brush through his feathers as if they were mine, felt his wings stretch and press against its power. He shifted beneath me, tilting and readjusting, compensating for my presence. But he didn't falter, not once.

Rosstair stretched out before us like the white sands of an Ambriellan shore. Distant figures stopped to stare, hands lifting to point. Indistinct voices echoed with excitement. I relished being so high up, where the weight of the world dropped away and all that remained was this flight, this moment.

The familiar feel of the wind threading through my hair and nipping at my skin made me feel lighter than I had in months. As we flew in lazy circles, the gentle rise and fall of Res's body with each wingbeat lulling me into serenity, I closed my eyes and simply let that feeling fill me.

For the first time in a long time, everything felt okay.

Until Res landed. I forgot to keep my weight back, and he went tumbling headfirst into the moist earth. I toppled over his head, landing on my back in a rush of expelled air and staring up at a very disgruntled-looking crow.

The moment the breath returned to my lungs, I laughed.

Kiva appeared with a grin above me. "I could have sworn the goal was to stay on the bird."

Res swatted her with a wing, and she laughed, offering me a hand that I took. Caliza arrived in a panic, but upon finding me okay, she pressed a hand to her lips. "That was the most amazing thing I've ever seen," she said.

I grinned.

By sunset, Res and I were both sore and exhausted. We'd run through a series of exercises from varying heights, practicing takeoffs, landings, turns, and banks. Once, we'd narrowly avoided running into the drop wall, and another time, he'd flown so close to the trees outside the complex a branch had almost snagged the reins, but we made it through without any broken limbs or feathers.

The first time we dove, I nearly shrieked. Res barely snapped out his wings in time, and it unbalanced him, leading to another tumbling landing. The next time was better, and the next after that, almost passable. I guided him with my knees, helping him learn when to open his wings.

The retired wind crow rider Jenara had told me about joined us partway through the day, but with Res's wind experience through his storm magic, there was little he could offer besides techniques for fine-tuning Res's summoning and control when a storm wasn't already present.

After, we gathered for a quiet dinner in the complex's mess hall, Caylus tossing Res pieces of chicken while Kiva broke down our escape from Illucia for Caliza bit by harrowing bit until I pointed out that she'd turned as pale as her napkin.

The simple normalcy of dinner with my family and friends stood in stark contrast to the looming future. We were out of time. Come morning, we would leave for Trendell, and I wished so badly Caliza could go with me. But Rhodaire needed her in Aris. Even this trip down to see me had been a luxury we could hardly afford, though I couldn't express how much I'd needed it.

My world had felt so very far away from me for so long. I was happy to have a piece of it back, if only for a little while.

As Caylus and Kiva cleared the table, Res hopping along

beside them for any scraps, Caliza pulled me aside into the empty lobby.

"Are you ready for the alliance meeting?" she asked, fingers already seeking her hair. She wound the strands around and around.

"I have to be, don't I?" I folded my arms, locking my anxiety inside. "If I can't convince them, Rhodaire will fall."

Caliza regarded me with assessing eyes. "You don't believe you can do it, do you? Why not?"

I started to respond, then stopped. My fears had always felt like shadows waiting to be given shape. If I spoke them, they'd tear free from the darkness and suffocate me. It was so much easier to keep them close. To hold them tight.

But that had only ever made them stronger.

"I don't know how to do this," I said. "I'm not a leader, and I don't have any experience with politics. I'm not you, Caliza."

Her fingers stilled in her hair. Tentatively, she reached for me, sliding her hand into mine. I let her. Our relationship had always been a volatile thing. So often, we'd wanted the same thing—to excel at our chosen paths, to earn our mother's respect, to protect Rhodaire—but we'd gone about it such different ways.

Where I had turned to the crows, Caliza had become the perfect princess, then queen, and we'd struggled to understand each other's decisions. It wasn't until after Ronoch, after our mother's death, that we'd realized she was not what had held us together but what had forced us apart.

We'd had to learn to be sisters again. We were still learning.

"You walked into one of the most dangerous kingdoms in the world and faced one of the cruelest, most conniving people I've ever met, and you survived." Her voice was the low rush of a river, gaining momentum. "You hatched a crow beneath her very nose, organized the beginnings of an alliance unlike anyone has ever seen, and turned the heart of the Illucian prince himself."

Her hand tightened on mine, and I let her pull it to her chest, holding it as gently as a tiny bird.

"You might not be a politician, Thia, but you've proven you don't need to be. I told you once before and I'll tell you again: you are a tempest of lightning and thunder, and people cannot look away from you. There is a strength to you that lifts others up, and that's what this world needs right now. Not another politician. You."

She smiled, the action crinkling the corners of her eyes, and at once I saw our mother in that smile, and also someone else. I saw myself. I saw myself the way Caliza saw me. Powerful. Unyielding. Strong. Because I saw the same things in her.

"You give me strength, and you will do the same for them." She pulled me close, and for a while, I just let her hold me, safe in the embrace of someone who I knew loved and believed in me.

Who made me believe in myself.

Her voice softened as she spoke again. "Be prepared when you see Estrel. Ronoch damaged her deeply. She lost everything that night too." She hesitated. "Try to remember that if you can."

We said goodbye to Caliza early the next morning with a promise to send a letter when we arrived in Eselin, then rejoined Samra and the crew on the *Aizel*.

It was a fine Rhodairen autumn day, sunny with a fading chill, and it buoyed the rising hope inside me as we embarked amid a crowd of cheering people.

I slid onto Res's back, and we leapt from the side of the ship, sailing low over the water before soaring up above the crowd. Res called out, releasing a final thunderclap of goodbye, before we circled back to the ship.

"Show-off," Kiva muttered as I dismounted.

I grinned. "It makes them happy."

"And it gives them hope," Caylus added.

"I wish it could do the same for him," I murmured with a flick of my eyes toward Onis. The scraggly crewman stood tying off a length of rope, eyeing Res indiscreetly with a sour look.

Kiva clapped me on the back. "Forget him."

As I turned, the ship's healer, Luan, approached me. She proffered a letter. "One of the crowd asked me to give this to you, Princess."

I took it with a frown. "Who?"

"Someone who'd been paid to deliver it. Apparently, it's been chasing you through the towns you've visited." She shrugged one slender shoulder and retreated.

I tore the letter open with growing apprehension.

My mother knows where you're going.

I stilled. Ericen.

My head snapped up, and I searched the retreating shoreline for him, but the milling crowd had dispersed into a frenzy of movement, and the white stone buildings were already growing smaller. If he'd ever been here, he was gone now. I returned to the letter's crisp writing.

Shearen overheard some of your crew discussing it in Isair. I'm sorry, Thia. I didn't know he'd followed me, and I had to keep up appearances once he was there. I convinced him afterward that I'd wanted to capture you myself, but I'm not sure my mother believed me. She suspects me, but I intend to stay with her to help you any way I can from this side.

I know you don't trust me, but I'm on your side. I'm sorry it took me so long to say it.

Take care of yourself,

Ericen

The letter crumpled in my closed fist.

A few moments later, Kiva, Samra, and I stood deliberating the letter in Samra's office.

Aroch had clambered onto Kiva's shoulders the moment she'd entered and refused to budge. "I don't believe him," Kiva said.

"Surprise," I muttered, and she batted my shoulder. I held up my hands. "I know, I know. I trust too easily and all that. But what if he's not lying? What if we're sailing into a trap?"

"He's the trap!" Kiva exclaimed. "Razel's probably hoping we'll abandon whatever we're planning or turn aside for Aris or somewhere else predictable."

"Or he's genuinely remorseful for what happened and trying to help us."

"What part of *he betrayed you* don't you remember?"

"The part where he *let* us escape!"

Samra stood abruptly, interrupting our debate. "There's nothing to debate here. Whether the prince's warning is true or not, we have to get to Eselin. We'll just have to deal with whatever we find there."

Her words cooled my annoyance with a sharp chill.

Whatever we found, it wouldn't be good.

The trip to Eselin was charted to take just over three days, two at sea and a final day and a half inland to the capital. Res and I spent the first one flying every chance we could. We'd ditched the bridle and begun practicing using his magic while in flight, something that thrilled Caylus but only inspired more muttered curses from Onis.

On the second day, Caylus pulled me aside to show me some drawings he'd done with modifications he suggested to the saddle make it more lightweight, flexible, and comfortable. He also had a list of critiques. Apparently, if Res adjusted the angles of certain turns, he could gain more momentum through them, thereby conserving energy. Caylus had even drawn diagrams with a series of numbers and arrows I didn't understand but that he promised were very important.

He'd barely finished speaking before I was back in the saddle, putting it to the test.

It was out on one of those flights that I noticed the clouds. Thick and steely gray, they gathered on the horizon with alarming speed, carried by a rising wind.

Res and I banked back toward the ship, which we'd left a few miles behind with an aim to test his endurance on long flights. By the time we alighted on the deck, Samra was already shouting orders to her crew, the storm visible from the ship.

"Can Res do something?" she asked as I joined her at the quarterdeck.

"We should be able to turn aside the worst of it," I replied. "But full-blown storms usually take more than one crow to control. You should still take whatever precautions you normally would."

As the crew prepared the ship, Caylus aiding them, Res and I joined Kiva at the bowsprit to face down the impending storm.

"It's strangely fitting, isn't it?" she asked.

"I love a good storm as much as the next person, but I could have done without this one." The timing of it felt portentous. I glanced up at the snapping flag of the *Aizel*, a slither of unease unfurling.

The wind came first, tugging at the tied-up sails and lashing waves against the hull. Then the storm enveloped us. What had been a metallic mass of gray clouds when I first spotted it had darkened into something black and raging, as if the very sky warned us to turn back. Rain began to fall in a curtain, and thunder boomed.

Then light split the sky open.

Keep that off us as best you can, I told Res, keeping my thoughts calm even as my nerves jittered. There was a stark difference between a crow controlling a storm they created and controlling one formed by nature. A real storm had a life to it, almost a soul.

And it didn't like to be contained.

A bolt struck the water off the left side, spraying water into the air. The wind tore a sail free with a vicious howl. The crew rushed to tie it back down, but the wind had it in its grip.

Calm the wind.

Res's eyes glowed a soft silver as power emanated down the cord. A moment later, the wind curtailed and quieted, allowing the crew to secure the sail. No sooner had they than the gale came screaming back, almost throwing Talon off his feet.

"Saints!" Kiva seized my arm with one hand and the ship railing with the other. The wind broke, but only just, and then thunder echoed. Rain lashed the deck, stinging my face and arms, and the sea pitched higher and higher.

Res screeched as a bolt of lightning forked to the side,

deflected by his power. The thunder pounded like a drum, the sky flashing with light.

"He's making it worse, Captain!" a voice called above the storm. Onis had seized Samra's arm on the deck below. "Or else he's incurred its wrath. I've never seen the like of this!"

The wind snapped Samra's response away, and I gritted my teeth against the urge to yell at Onis. The storm needed my whole attention.

Yet before I could turn away, light sparked in the sky above them. Instinct took over, and I screamed for Res. His wings flared wide as the bolt struck, singeing the very air.

And somehow, he caught it.

The lightning bolt held fully formed above Onis's and Samra's heads. It twitched, fizzing in and out of shape like light diffusing through a crystal as Res struggled to hold it. Heat and light radiated off the bolt, casting the stunned faces of the crew in a ghastly glow.

Then Res thrust the bolt aside with a snap of his wings.

It struck the mainmast. Wood splintered in every direction, and the yard snapped, the sail tumbling and tangling into the netting and ropes below. The mast groaned and swayed in the heavy wind, listing hard to the side.

"Slow its fall!" I screamed at Res.

His earth crow power caught the mast a moment before it crashed into the deck, nearly crushing a crew member who'd scrambled away too slowly.

"That night-cursed demon nearly killed us all!" Onis cried.

"He just saved your life!" I yelled back.

Onis scowled. "This storm is his doing to start with. I—"

"Enough!" Samra's voice roared above the storm. "Onis, back to your post. Talon, Caylus, tie the mast down. Thia, get us through this Duren-forsaken storm!"

We fell into motion at her orders. I focused on helping Res control the storm. The lightning had already calmed, the rain's rhythm slowing. Res helped quiet the remaining elements, slowing the wind and pushing aside the final bouts of rain.

As the last of the dark clouds faded to silver, they parted, letting through slivers of incandescent sunlight. It flooded the deck in gold, shimmering in the water.

The ship fell silent as the water stilled. An entire ship's worth of eyes settled on Res and me.

Then Talon let out a low whistle. "Remind me not to make the crow angry."

Under Caylus's instruction and with Res's aid, the crew was able to repair the mast and jerry-rig it into functioning. Caylus seemed happy to have a new project, and Samra was happy to let him handle it, even as she grumbled over every little scratch and nick the ship had taken. The sails were patched, the deck cleaned of water and debris.

When the work was done and the afternoon light waning, I sought out Onis. Our trip together was nearly at an end, but he was one of Samra's crew, which meant he was a rebel. If he was going to fight with us, he couldn't treat Res like a rabid dog.

He stood by the repaired mainmast, eyeing me as if I were a pit of desert snakes. His fingers played with the frayed ropes of the knots at his belt, worn from his constant touch. I started toward him, and he abruptly peeled off, heading for the crew quarters. Scowling, I followed.

When he reached the bottom of the short flight of stairs, he spun on me. "Stop following me, girl!"

"We need to talk," I replied, lifting my head. "And my name isn't girl. It's Princess Anthia Cerralté."

Onis shifted his jaw as if working a loose tooth. "You're not my princess."

"No. I'm just the person trying to organize an alliance to free your kingdom from a vicious ruler. Or don't you care about any of that?"

"It isn't you I have any problem with! It's that night-cursed creature." His fingers sought his talismans. "You Rhodairens always put so much stock in your magic, but you never thought about where it came from. I've seen you reading those stories. Anything born of the Sellas is evil!"

"Res isn't evil!" I forced my voice back down. "He's trying to help. He saved your life."

Onis sneered. "That storm probably came for him to begin with."

"You don't know what you're talking about."

He waved a dismissive hand. Before I could press him more, a sharp crack sounded from above. A moment later, something snapped and the ship shuddered.

Onis and I bolted up the stairs, bursting onto a frenzied

deck. Sailors shouted, Samra's voice cutting above them all as she dealt out orders. And there, stuck through the middle of the deck like a massive spear, was the top of the main mainmast.

"I thought Caylus fixed the damn thing!" Kiva appeared at my side.

So had I. But apparently the damage from the storm had been too much. The topmost sail had been brought down with the wood, tearing through the mainmast.

I frowned. The mainsail was useless, but the ship wasn't taking on water, and we still had the other two sails. I knew next to nothing about sailing, but it seemed the worst impact was on our speed, not our safety. So why was everyone flying about as if the ship were on fire?

"Oh Saints," Kiva breathed.

I followed her gaze to the horizon, where a strip of land grew slowly larger. But that wasn't the problem.

The problem was the line of ships flying blue and gold flags.

Illucian ships.

ELEVEN

I stared at the line of ships, my shoulders falling as the strength dwindled from my body. On the other side of those ships, Trendell waited. I could see land, but we would never reach it before the ships caught us.

We'd been so close.

A smaller ship broke through the line, slowly coming toward us.

Spotting Samra, I cut through the scurrying sailors tying off ropes and preparing for battle. Aroch perched on her shoulder, maintaining his balance with an uncanny precision as the captain turned about, bellowing orders.

Onis beat me to her, shouting at the stern-faced woman over the commotion. "This is her fault, Captain." He gestured at me. "Her and that damned beast. They're bad luck, the both of them."

Res snapped his beak. The sailor edged away half a step.

Samra raised her hand. "Get back to your post, Onis. I'll handle this."

Onis shot me a last dark look before heading for the quarterdeck. I glowered after him, then snapped my attention back to Samra.

As always, her face was as difficult to read as an unfamiliar language. Yet I could guess what she was thinking—I'd put her and her ship in harm's way. We couldn't outrun the Illucian ships, not with a broken mast. And if she was captured, the Ambriellan rebels would be leaderless and her family at Razel's mercy.

Hesitation passed across her face. She didn't know what to do.

I seized the moment. "I have an idea."

"This is going to end badly," Kiva said.

"Thanks for the vote of confidence," I replied, wiping my sweating hands on my pants. We stood alone on the quarterdeck: her, Res, and me. The Illucian ship had already crossed half the distance separating us. We couldn't fight—we'd be annihilated. Which meant we had to run. If we could reach land, we'd be safe.

Anxious energy flooded down the line from Res. I reached for him, and he pressed his head against my hand. Relief swelled through me—until Caylus's panicked call rose over the tumult of voices.

"Thia!"

I glanced up, following his outstretched hand to the fast approaching ship. The blue of its flags was brighter than the others, the design clearer now that it was so close.

A kingfisher.

It was Malkin's ship.

"Captain!" Talon called from the crow's nest. "The Illucian queen is on that ship."

My heart plummeted, and I whirled back to face the ship. Sunlight glinted off gold. A figure stood at the prow, golden hair bound back in a heavy braid streaming behind her in the wind. Even from here, her icy gaze pinned me to the spot.

Razel had come for me herself.

My scarred hand prickled with phantom pain.

"Thia." Kiva blocked my line of sight, forcing my gaze to hers. "This changes nothing. We stick to the plan."

"She's exposed, Kiva," I hissed. "We could end this now."

"If you attack that ship, the whole fleet will bear down on us. Our only chance is escaping."

The thought of running again scraped at me. I wanted to face Razel and put an end to this saga, but Kiva was right.

Res cawed, sending pulses of understanding and comfort, and I seized them, forcing my emotions down.

On the main deck, the crew had readjusted the sails and torn down the rest of the mainsail to keep it from getting in the way. Samra had watched the destruction with a flickering muscle in her jaw.

I'd started to apologize, then stopped. Samra didn't want

apologies; she wanted action. Res and I would fix this. We had to.

I spotted Caylus tying off a rope, his skin flushed and beaded with sweat. He caught my gaze, offering a smile that settled my nerves, despite knowing the turmoil that had to be turning inside him.

Samra joined us on the quarterdeck, Aroch gone from her shoulder. "We're ready."

"All right." I let out a breath and reached down the cord to Res. *Let's go.*

With a flash of his wings, Res leapt onto the back rail of the ship. The sky darkened. Clouds began to form, gray and heavy with impending rain. They materialized from the air and spread outward like a ripple of water. Our bond hummed, a steady beat of magic that danced along my skin like the brush of a charged wind.

The clouds crackled with power. Beside me, Samra muttered a prayer that I couldn't make out over the rising winds, one hand clenching the rope knots at her belt.

Res didn't need the storm to summon wind, but I could feel his familiar comfort with it. It came so much more naturally.

"Funnel the winds into the sails," I told him. They'd been set to drive us straight for the coast, though Samra had warned they likely wouldn't survive the sustained beating of Res's wind. They just had to last long enough to get us to land.

Wind exploded around us. The *Aizel* rocked as the current caught the sails and waves smashed against the hull. Several sailors cursed vehemently. I spread my stance, steadying myself.

Funnel it! Even in my head, my voice sounded anxious. If Res lost control of the storm, he'd send us to the bottom of the ocean instead.

The Illucian sailors seemed to have realized something was happening. People scurried across the deck, adjusting sails and—my breath caught. Two massive harpoon launchers were fastened to the front of the ship, the spears loaded.

Doubt crept onto my shoulders like a hissing snake. This was my plan. My call. If this failed, if Res's storm broke atop us... I caught Kiva's gaze, and the steadiness behind it centered me. There was no time to second-guess myself. This was happening.

The sails caught the wind, and the ship lurched forward. Res let out a shrill cry. His wings lifted slightly, as if eager to catch the draft. I felt my excitement mirrored inside him, felt it sling across the connection between us in a flurry of energy.

Rain began to fall, heavy and full.

Attack the ship! I sent an image of lightning striking the Illucian ship from above. Energy crackled around Res's body. It sparked in the sky, the clouds set alight. Thunder boomed, breaking across the sky like an earthquake.

Our sails strained, but even with the increased speed, we were too close to the Illucian ship. We'd be in range of the spears.

"Res!" I called above the wind.

He cawed back, and a bolt of lightning struck the sea feet from the Illucian ship.

"Again!"

A heavy thud sounded behind me, and I whirled in time to

narrowly avoid the strong arms of Onis. He lunged for me again. I sidestepped him.

Kiva snarled, barreling forward. She drove Sinvarra's hilt into Onis's stomach. He doubled over, gasping for breath.

"Stand down!" Samra ordered, wide-eyed. I'd never seen her surprised.

"She's going to get us all killed!" Onis yelled. He threw a hand at the gathering storm. The clouds had spread, blanketing the sky in darkness. The lightning crackling around Res's body had grown, sparking and gnashing like a pack of vicious hounds.

We were losing control.

Something snapped. A rope came loose below. It whipped through the air, nearly catching Talon around the throat. He stumbled back, avoiding it, but at the same moment, a heavy wave struck the ship, careening over the edge and across the deck.

When it pulled back, he was gone.

"Talon!" I lurched forward. A flash of movement, and then Caylus was there, reaching over the edge, seizing something I couldn't see. He pulled back, and Talon's arm appeared over the edge of the ship. A sharp wind gusted, throwing another wave of water at the ship—right for Talon and Caylus.

"No!" I screamed. Res screamed with me, his cry shrill as screeching metal.

The wave stopped as if it'd struck a wall. Then it lashed backward, collapsing in on itself, just as Caylus pulled Talon over the railing and onto the deck, both soaked and panting. Caylus glanced up at me, green eyes wide, auburn curls plastered to his drenched skin.

This time, I felt the magic threading through me as I felt it course through Res. When I turned, his eyes glowed bright silver.

"Demon!" Onis yelled, drawing a long dagger. "She'll bring the Night Captain down on us all."

Kiva had Sinvarra out faster than I could track, the black gold blade gleaming with salty mist. She parried Onis's attack, and then Samra was there, moving as smoothly as a gliding crow. She disarmed Onis, and his blade clattered to the deck. She kicked it away, twisting his wrist until he cried out, dropping to his knees.

But it was too late.

Another boom sounded, deeper and more resonate than the crack of thunder. Wood splintered as a harpoon spear pierced what remained of the mainmast, sending sharp fragments raining in all directions. *Boom.* A second spear bore through the mizzenmast.

Onis's interference had been enough; the Illucian ship had us.

As the ropes retracted, the wood groaned and the space between the ships closed. The rolling waves tossed us together, turning the *Aizel* so we ran parallel to Malkin's ship. His mercenary crew stood along the topsails. Some held a hooked board to create a walkway. As the board fell, linking us together, and the mercenaries leapt from the sails with rope in hand to swing across the roiling sea, my eyes found one figure among the rest.

Razel stood a mere few feet away. The edges of her moonblades stretched from her shoulders like wings. She met my gaze and smiled.

Then everything erupted into chaos.

The battle spilled across the deck. Illucian soldiers and Malkin's men clashed with Samra's crew as rain poured incessantly. I spotted the copper hair of Malkin among them. His eyes were set on Caylus even as he dueled a sailor.

Something struck wood behind me. The next moment, Kiva threw me to the deck. Another arrow whizzed over my head, lodging in the railing between Res's claws. He screeched and leapt from the railing, taking to the sky just as a third one landed beside the second.

I wrenched my bow off my back. Fighting back to my feet, I used the wheel as a shield. With the archer's attention on Res, I nocked an arrow, stepped to the side, and loosed.

It struck the archer in the shoulder, and he dropped his bow.

At the edge of the ship, Razel had approached the plank, preparing to cross.

Res! The board!

Res swept low, a funnel of wind at his back. It slammed into the board, knocking it free a second before Razel could cross. The smallest relief flickered, and then I saw the smile on her face.

She took a step back, and another. Then she sprinted full force at the ship's edge. She jumped, one foot striking the railing, and leapt. She sailed across the open ocean, clearing the *Aizel*'s railing with ease, and landed in a roll, springing to her feet with the litheness of a jungle cat.

"You've got to be kidding me," Kiva growled, hefting Sinvarra.

Razel grinned. "Hello, Thia dear."

I nocked an arrow and fired. She dove to the side, and the arrow lodged in the deck where she'd been. Back on her feet, she drew her moonblades, the curved, dome-shaped blades glinting. Behind her, Malkin had downed his opponent and now advanced upon Caylus, who backed warily toward the bowsprit.

Indecision rooted me to the spot. Razel wanted me alive; she wouldn't kill me, which granted me an advantage. I was safe. My friends were not.

I sprinted down to the main deck. Nocking an arrow, I drew up short and released it into the nearest Illucian soldier's leg. He cried out and dropped to one knee. Then a flash of red was before him, and Talon drove the butt of his blade into the man's temple. The soldier crumpled.

"Watch out!" I screamed. Talon turned, too slow. Razel was on him, her moonblade swinging in a low arc. It slashed across his thigh. He screamed, his knee buckling, and Razel lifted her other blade to cut his throat.

The snap of my bowstring was all the warning she had. With a twist, she knocked my arrow aside, continuing her momentum through with a swift kick to Talon's head. He sprawled across the deck, unmoving.

"Talon!" I lurched for him, but Razel stepped between us. The wind whipped loose pieces of blond hair around her face, her bright eyes two chips of ice ringed in kohl. The rain tracked black tears down her pale skin. Behind her, Malkin had reached Caylus, who stood frozen as if before a demon, his back pressed against the forecastle.

"You've been busy." Razel shifted, eyes angling toward Caylus and Malkin. "What a delightful enemy you've made. He was quite motivated to hunt you down again."

Malkin held a coiled whip. Caylus's chest rose and fell, his eyes filled with the fear of a trapped animal.

"I promised him he could have your friend in exchange for information." Razel's voice cut through the storm. "You won't believe the story he spun about a crow that can do more than he should. A weapon like that might actually be able to stand against me." She lifted her moonblades. "Why don't you call down your pet?" she hissed.

Malkin unfurled the whip. I seized an arrow, but Razel launched herself at me. I caught her moonblade with the black gold limb of my bow. She swung through with her other blade, knocking the bow from my hands. I stumbled back. Malkin lifted his hand as Caylus slumped to the floor.

"Caylus!" I screamed, but a howling wind carried the word away. The gust flung Malkin aside and pushed Razel back. A piercing screech ripped through the air. Then Res was on the deck, his wings flared wide, the funnel of wind still barreling from his body. It pinned Malkin to the side of the ship and shoved Razel back inch by inch. She raised her hands to protect her face and, through sheer strength, forced a step forward.

I turned for Res and shoved a foot into a stirrup, swinging onto his back.

"Let me show you what Malkin saw," I growled.

Res leapt onto the ship railing, then took off.

The storm swelled around us as if welcoming an old friend.

Res banked hard and came back at Razel's ship, and like a rolling thundercloud, an ocean wave rode with him. It grew and grew, rising above the other ship a moment before it slammed into it.

Several soldiers were thrown overboard into the raging sea, water drenching the deck and pouring off the sides. Those who'd survived yelled orders, frantically trying to recover. I exalted in the rush of power that flooded the link between Res and me, even as part of me recoiled at the destruction.

On the *Aizel*, Malkin had recovered, advancing on Caylus. But something had settled in Caylus's eyes. Something hard that turned their soft green to jade.

Malkin lashed the whip, and Caylus caught it, letting it wrap around his forearm. Then he jerked it. Malkin stumbled toward him, and Caylus caught him by the throat, throwing him back against the ship railing. A wave crested over the top. When it pulled away, Malkin was gone.

Overhead, the storm grew, expanding in a flood as it fed off Res's energy. Lightning snapped down on the blockade ships, shattering wood and sending soldiers screaming over the edge. Flames erupted to life, their hunger fed by Res's power. The rain turned to shards of hail.

I searched the melee for Razel, but she'd vanished from the main deck.

An arrow clipped Res's wing and sliced open my arm.

Res screamed as our pain flooded the link, and he turned erratically. Unprepared, I tumbled out of the saddle, seizing one stirrup at the last moment.

The wind buffeted me as Res tried to pull up, but my weight

pulled him off balance, the line of the stirrup crossing over his wing and impeding his flight.

Razel stood high on the quarterdeck, my bow drawn with the second arrow she'd plucked from the ship's side. Kiva rushed toward her, sword drawn, but she wouldn't be fast enough.

Razel aimed for Res's heart.

I didn't think. I let go.

Res's piercing cry filled the air. I felt his power erupt a moment before I struck the water and everything went dark.

TWELVE

My vision swarmed back in a flash of images. Dark water closing overhead. Snapping, flickering light. A shadow looming over me.

My lungs screamed for air, and I inhaled reflexively, but only water rushed in.

Then a pair of strong arms seized me. Disoriented, I was aware only of the heat and pressure of an embrace and the strange, weightless feeling of being hoisted from the water. But those arms never let go.

Someone rolled me over the railing, and I hit the deck hard. Turning, I coughed up water and tried to choke down air to my burning lungs.

Then the ship pitched, and someone tumbled atop me.

I wheezed at the sudden weight, shoving at the solid form that had pinned me. My fingers curved around a muscled waist, pushing at the same time as the person sat back, his knees on either side of my hips.

Ericen stared back, blue eyes bright with concern. And... was the bastard smiling?

My heart tore in a hundred different directions. A rush of things rose to the tip of my tongue, but before I could pick one, a screech rent the air.

We both looked up.

Perched atop the broken remains of the mainmast at the center of the ship, wings spread wide, was Res. His body crackled with electricity as the storm surged around him, wind spiraling out to catch the debris of the ship, sending splintered wood and discarded blades into a vicious spin.

Below him, the battle had waned. Kiva slid her sword free from the chest of the last Illucian soldier. The rest of the crew ducked for cover from the rising storm as Samra screamed orders over the howling wind, yelling at me to make him stop.

A flash of gold—then Razel was sprinting for the ship's edge. A soldier flung a rope to her, and she grabbed it. With one final, furious glance at me, she swung to the safety of the other ship. The ropes were cut, and the roiling ocean thrust us apart.

One by one, the feathers from the tip of Res's beak to the edge of his tail hardened into metal. The wood began to creak around his claws, pulling up from the deck. The masts bent and groaned, cracking like splintering bones.

At Res's back, a dark mass gathered, swirling like a turning disk.

"Is that—" A crash of thunder cut off the rest of Ericen's words.

I gaped at the forming storm. Estrel had told me stories of storm crows powerful enough to create hurricanes on their own. She'd never said how to make them stop.

"Res!" I yelled, my voice torn away by the wind. I reached for the cord, and emotions hurtled back down, flooding me with Res's fear and panic. He grasped for control but couldn't lock the magic back inside.

I shoved Ericen up, and he rolled aside, but something pulled me back atop him. Scowling, I shoved him down and pried at the rope around my waist. The other end trailed up to the harpoon embedded in the *Aizel*'s mast—the source of the rope he'd used to get me out.

Ericen slid a knife free from his boot and sheared through the rope with a clean *snick*. One of the sailors who'd hoisted us up helped me to my feet, and I stumbled toward the mast, but my legs felt weak and my lungs were still starved of air. My knees buckled and struck the deck.

Res, you have to stop! I called down the line.

Desperation echoed back, beating through my mind—*help help help*. Once, in the quiet of Caylus's workshop, I'd pushed Res's magic free along the cord. Maybe if I could do the reverse, if I could shove it back inside him before it tore us all apart... I closed my eyes and concentrated on the link. I focused on the feel of it strung between us, on the snap of wild energy darting through it. On Res's own fear at not being able to stop and the magic raging through him, as wild as the surrounding storm.

Then I seized it. Pain shot through me, sharp and radiating like a shock. I gasped, unable to grab the cord. Too much magic sizzled through it.

I forced myself back to my feet. The wind buffeted me back, snapping at my skin with debris. I could barely keep my eyes open.

Ericen appeared at my side, sliding under my arm just as my knees gave again. I fought to keep my feet as he towed me forward through the wind, one arm wrapped like a vise about my waist, the hand of the other clasped about my own.

My wounded arm stung viciously, and everything ached from the fall, but I pushed ahead. If I could just reach him— something sharp sliced along my back, and I gasped.

Res! Pain seared through my back and shoulder. A new emotion shot down the cord: horror.

Res let out a shrill, anguished cry, struggling to withdraw the magic. It kept flowing. A piece of shrapnel sliced my cheek. I tore free from Ericen's hold, forcing step after step toward Res. Then I was before him. The cool metal of his armored feathers was hard beneath my touch. I seized him, wrapping my arms about his neck and pulling him close.

I've got you. I clung tighter to him. He shook in my grasp, alternating beats of emotion pounding inside me. Fear. Pain. Confusion. Fear. Pain. *Horror.*

I've got you, Res. Let go.

The cord shuddered, then slackened. The magic zipping

along it slowed, the tornado of wind and wreckage around us dying. Then all at once, it stopped.

Debris clattered to the deck. The wind fell still. Res's feathers turned from metal to silken black, and he collapsed into my arms. I dropped to my knees.

"I've got you," I repeated, clinging to the words, to him, to an ancient, powerful beast too big to hold that shook in my arms like a hatchling. "I've got you."

The storm had pushed us nearly to shore. With the distance between us, Malkin's ravaged ship couldn't catch up, and we coasted into Trendellan waters with the last remnants of our sails.

I hadn't moved from my spot on the deck, Res still clutched in my arms. Echoing emotion like racking sobs trembled down the bond.

In that moment, I understood. Res had blamed himself for my fall, and he'd lost control. When I'd resurfaced, he couldn't rein himself in, and he'd only hurt me more. A dozen nicks and grazes joined the slice of Razel's blade and the cut of the arrow, and my entire body felt weak from the fall, and Res blamed himself for all of it.

"I'm okay," I whispered, but Res could feel my pain as I could his. It spiderwebbed through my heart, filling me as if it were my own. I wanted to soothe it, to take it away, but it was so raw and full of fear. Like if I touched it, he would scream.

Hot tears trailed down my cheeks, and I knew Res felt the

turmoil inside me. He could feel my desperation, my fear, my shame at not being able to help.

Guilt rocked between us, a second, darker link that bound like a chain.

"We're okay," I breathed, the words half prayer.

Footsteps sounded, and I looked up into Samra's grave expression. I expected her to yell, to blame me for her decimated ship, but she only nodded at the presence at my side. The one I'd been ignoring, even as I felt the heat of his gaze searing into me.

"He belong to you?" she asked.

Something like a laugh choked out of me. I looked up into Ericen's concerned face. Only then did I notice Kiva standing to one side of him, Sinvarra leveled at his throat. He'd disregarded the blade's presence as if it were a gnat.

I expected him to quip back at Samra, but he didn't. For some reason, that made my heart skip.

"Why are you here?" Kiva demanded.

"Traitors tend not to be welcome on Illucian ships," he replied.

"Traitor?" Kiva scoffed.

"I do believe that's what they call you when you change sides." One corner of his lips turned up in a familiar smirk, and a spark ignited inside me. I hated when he smiled like that. Like this was all a game.

I knew better.

If he'd truly changed sides, if he was being honest, it meant he'd turned his back on everything he'd once served. This was not a game.

"Why are you here, Ericen?" I forced myself to my feet, Res rising with me. "What do you want?"

"Those are two very different questions." His voice dipped low, and I felt the intent behind his words pulse between us. It sent a thrill coursing through me despite my exhaustion.

One of the crew shifted aside, and Caylus stepped past him. Like Kiva, he had scratches along his forearms and on his face, but he was otherwise unharmed. Completely oblivious to the tension of the moment, he said, "I managed to get Talon below-decks. He's with his sister," he said. "Everyone else's injuries are manageable." He lifted a hand, offering me my bow. Relief washed through me. "Kiva took it back from her," he told me with a smile.

"And nearly got stabbed again for my trouble," Kiva muttered.

I looked toward Malkin's retreating ship, making slowly for the waiting blockade. More than one had been abandoned, destroyed by Res's magic.

I did that. I expected the thought to turn me raw, but I felt only a hollow pit of exhaustion. People were dead because of me, because of Res's power, and yet some part of me had actually *enjoyed* that battle. Unleashing Res's magic, getting revenge on the Illucian soldiers who'd shattered my home—it'd felt *good.*

It'd felt powerful, and that scared me.

"Will they follow us into port?" I asked Ericen.

"No, not without dragging Trendell into this war," he replied, and for the first time, I really looked at him. He wore a simple tunic and black pants, leather vambraces pulled tight at his forearms. The twin swords usually strapped to his back were in a heap at Kiva's feet. He looked exhausted. "My mother's not prepared for that."

"According to you," Kiva said, tilting Sinvarra threateningly. "I'd say the same thing if I wanted my enemy to be unprepared."

"Yes, what a fantastic strategy," Ericen snapped back. "Rescuing my enemy from raging seawaters in the middle of hurricanes. Keeps me fit."

"He did save me," I noted.

"Because Razel doesn't want you dead," Kiva replied.

"So she traded us her son as a bargaining chip?"

Kiva shrugged. "Wouldn't put it past her."

Something sharp flickered through Ericen's gaze, the emotion shut down as quickly as it surfaced. He held out his hands. "Let's skip to the part where you jump to conclusions and go straight to the cuffs, shall we? We're almost in port."

No one protested as exactly that was done. Even I couldn't argue that leaving one of the most highly trained soldiers in Illucia unrestrained wasn't a good idea, even if he had saved my life. Ericen's loyalty had been called into question too many times for me to vouch for him with total confidence.

By the time we docked, a small crowd had gathered on land, murmuring among themselves. They probably wondered what we'd done to incur the blockade's wrath.

Caylus, Kiva, and I gathered our supplies, Caylus tucking a folded bundle into his pack that I didn't recognize. Something about him seemed different, like he stood a little bit taller.

When I pulled him aside to ask how he was, he looked

almost guilty. "Is it wrong that I'm happy he's dead?" he asked.

I didn't know how to answer. Malkin had torn Caylus's life apart. He'd tortured him mentally and physically and murdered his younger sister.

Instead, I squeezed his hand, only to find that it wasn't shaking.

Samra planned to come with us, leaving what remained of the ship under her first mate's command. Onis had been locked in the brig. She'd wanted to turn him over to the Trendellan guard or at the very least strand him in Terin, but I'd convinced her he'd only been afraid. In the end, she ordered the crew to let him go with his money and belongings after we were out of town.

Luan tended to my shoulder and back. The cuts weren't deep; only the one on my shoulder needed stitches, and even then I wasn't sure it was necessary. Once Res recovered, he could heal me.

We gathered together as two crewmen lowered the gangplank, Res moping along beside me like a kicked dog. I brushed my fingers along his neck, wanting to comfort him, but he didn't respond. The moment we had a second of quiet, I'd talk to him.

Kiva had happily volunteered to take first watch of Ericen, one hand settled on Sinvarra. He didn't seem to mind, far more fascinated by the crow towering over him.

When Samra joined us, I did a double take. Perched on her shoulders like a bird sat Aroch.

"You're bringing the cat?" I asked.

Samra lifted a brow, but before she could respond, a

commotion rose from the gathered crowd below. I turned, expecting pointing fingers and awed expressions and instead found the crowd parting for a retinue of soldiers on horseback, led by a small, thin girl clad in elegant green and gold armor.

A thrill of excitement whirled through me. I knew her.

Her short, dark hair had been gathered into thin braids curling along one side of her head, threaded with tiny glass beads. She sat with a rigid, proud posture, her eyes set on us.

Kiva lurched forward a step. "Auma."

She rode with a small group of Jin soldiers, many of their faces bearing intricate designs in subtle colors. Tama, marks that indicated which guilds they'd once belonged to in Jindae. I recognized the rounded, swirling design of the gem guild tattooed on one man's face, but I'd never had the mind for remembering these things. If Caliza were here, she could have named each one and decoded the marks for everyone's rank and specialty.

Auma slowed her horse at the base of the gangplank. Kiva was the first to move, forcing Ericen forward, the rest of us following a second behind. The whispers rose as Res reemerged fully, eliciting several gasps. I expected him to puff out his feathers and lift his head for the praise, but he remained subdued.

"Your Highness," Auma said in a low, smooth tone with a bow. She spoke to me, but her eyes were only for Kiva, who'd gone rigid. The unspoken words leaping between them thickened the air.

"Auma," I replied. "I'm glad to see you're all right, but what are you doing here?" The last we'd seen her, she'd been fighting

Vykryn in Razel's throne room with a group of Trendellan monks so we could escape. It was thanks to her we were free.

Finally, she tore her eyes away from Kiva, who let out a heavy breath. Auma's gaze glided over Samra and Caylus, narrowed briefly on Ericen, then paused on Res before settling at last on me. "Your sister sent word that you'd be coming by ship. With the presence of the blockade, it made sense you'd dock here in Terin." She turned her horse. "You should follow me. Illucia hasn't been foolish enough to step on Trendellan soil yet, but I don't want to tempt them." The soldiers behind her parted, the crowd edging away to grant them room, and we followed.

People muttered to one another as we passed. Most were dressed in layers of sheer, brightly colored clothing, draped over their bodies like flowing robes. Many split in a deep V or hung open like coats, the men bare-chested, the women with elegantly embroidered bands of cloth across their breasts, baring dark skin to the hot sun.

The wooden dock didn't so much as creak beneath the weight. It was so sturdy and well built that Caylus actually paused to investigate the spot where one of the supports met the dock. I grabbed his arm as I passed, hauling him along. If he stopped and investigated every piece of impressive Trendellan engineering we passed, we'd never leave this port.

Ericen's eyes followed my hands to where they clasped Caylus's arm. Reflexively, I let go, then cursed myself. One corner of the prince's lips turned up in a smile.

"Something amusing?" I asked. Two of Auma's soldiers

had taken over guarding him, leaving Kiva free to talk with her. The guards marched at his back, and I fell into line beside him.

"What? Can't I be happy?"

"Happy to be shackled and imprisoned by your enemy?"

"Ex-enemy," he corrected. "And I don't care if you bind me hand and foot, so long as you're the one who does it, that is." A flush tore through my face, and Ericen laughed. "Joking, Thia. But you should have seen your face." He said it with a smile that made me think that, joking or not, he'd also been serious. His voice dropped low. "Admit it, you missed me."

"I've moved on."

"Then why are you still wearing my gloves?" His bright eyes appraised them, somehow managing to make me feel exposed despite my wearing the uniform of one of the most powerful warriors in all six kingdoms.

"I meant what I said in that letter," he added more softly. "I'm on your side. It's the only place I want to be." He held my gaze as if he might press his sincerity into it. I hadn't noticed before, but a little furrow formed between his brows whenever his eyes narrowed.

I wanted to believe him. He'd jumped into a roiling sea to save me, for Saints' sake! But I couldn't forget the betrayal I'd felt that day in the throne room, when he'd stood by and done nothing as his mother tortured my friends.

Now he seemed determined to do everything he could to make up for that. But how could I trust him?

Movement on his other side caught my eye, and I found

Samra watching me disapprovingly. I stepped back, putting space between the prince and myself. Technically, Samra still hadn't sworn to this coalition. What did she think of me talking so openly with a boy who was meant to be our enemy? We may have reached an understanding, but that didn't mean she wasn't still closely evaluating me.

We turned down a broad, open street teeming with life.

Like the clothing its people wore, the town of Terin over-flowed with color. Buildings of deep cobalt blue, bright winter green, sunset orange, and buttermilk yellow stretched as far as I could see. Everywhere I turned, there were archways: arch-ways instead of doors, archways beneath a bridge connecting two buildings, archways standing on their own as art, the pillars carved with delicate flowers and vines. Like in the Ambriels, remnants of the Sellas stood in the shape of statues or spread across buildings in brightly painted murals.

It felt peaceful here. Alive. My chest tightened.

It felt like Aris before Ronoch.

A strange feeling pulled me deeper toward the city, tugging like a rope. I wanted to keep walking, but Auma turned into a narrow side street before drawing her horse to a halt. She dis-mounted, her movements lithe and silent, and an image of her slitting a Vykryn's throat flashed through my mind. I still had no idea who she truly was.

I glanced at Kiva, whose disquieted expression suggested she was thinking the same thing.

"We can lodge here for the night," Auma said. "In the morn-ing, I'll lead you to Eselin. It's about a two-day journey."

A line of tension snapped in my shoulders, and I let out a quiet breath. We'd made it.

We filed into the inn through an arched door, a spacious room stretching out before us. Small, neatly organized bookcases leaned against every available wall space, plush couches gathered around them, half-hidden by burnt-orange and saffron-yellow drapes.

A woman wearing brilliant purple and yellow robes rose from behind a low wooden counter, a smile crossing her full lips. It only faltered for a second when she saw Res, who'd had to squeeze through the broad, arched door. Her eyes switched from him to me and back again, and whatever conclusion she came to, it involved not asking.

"Miss Tyshi." She addressed Auma. "How may I help you?"

Kiva stiffened, and it occurred to me she might not have known Auma's last name. Yet another reminder that the girl she'd come to care for was full of secrets.

"I need rooms," Auma replied.

Well, at least that hadn't changed—she was as blunt with her words as she'd ever been.

The woman ran a finger along a ledger laid out across the counter, then spun about and gathered several keys from hooks hanging at her back. "Follow me," she instructed, coming around the counter and leading us down a hall to our right.

We followed, splitting up into our rooms. Samra went to one, a few of the soldiers splitting off into several others. The last I saw of Kiva and Auma before they disappeared around a corner was the two of them walking side by side, each curving in toward the other, like a pair of roses stretching up toward the sun.

The sight made me pause outside my door. I looked back to where one of the three soldiers left with Ericen unlocked a door.

The urge to say something else rose and died in my throat. There had always been something between us. Something that shifted depending on the light, leaving me constantly unsure of what I saw. He stared back with an open frankness, as if to say "ask of me what you will."

"Good night," I said.

He smiled as a guard opened the door. "Good night."

I stepped into my room, Res shuffling in after me. With a flap of his wings, he leapt up onto the bed and collapsed in a flurry of feathers, promptly taking over the entire thing, his wings draping off the sides.

"Res?"

He emitted a sound akin to a groan. Emotions pulsed through the connection, flickers of shame and apology and fear.

"Oh, Res." He looked ridiculous flopped down like he was, his wings askew and his beak buried in the blanket. The bed creaked with his weight.

I lay down on my side next to him, my wounds protesting. One bright gray eye opened to peer at me, mournful and tired.

"I'm okay," I reminded him. My shoulder and back ached, but they'd heal. "You saved us today. Without you, Razel would have captured our ship and taken me prisoner." I ran my fingers along the ridge of his neck, and he squeezed his eye shut. "We'll learn to control your magic," I promised.

Doubt flooded the bond, underlain by fear, and he shook his head. The beat of emotion resolved like a chant in my head: *no no no no no*.

"You don't want to control it?" I asked a second before understanding settled. "You don't want to use it."

Res looked at me, then shut his eye again, curling in on himself. My hand still rested on his back, the coiled tension running through him hard as stone.

I didn't know what to say.

Without Res's magic, Trendell wouldn't listen to us. A six-foot-tall crow, while impressive, couldn't stop an army. But the steady thrum of pain and fear rushing from Res tore at me, and I knew I couldn't push him. I didn't want him to hurt like this.

"It's okay," I said again, my voice choked. "It's okay."

Res shifted, his head against me. He was far too big to fit in my arms, but I held him as best I could anyway.

"I've got you," I whispered.

THIRTEEN

Some of Auma's soldiers had risen early to collect supplies and additional horses. Thankfully, they'd taken Res into consideration and had an entire chicken's worth of meat for him when we emerged into the common room. I expected him to gobble it down like he always did, but instead I had to coax him into eating every piece.

"Is he all right?" Kiva asked, strapping Sinvarra around her waist.

I shook my head.

A door down the hall opened, and Auma exited, her fingers nimbly tying off a final braid.

I looked from the door to Kiva. "That's the room you came out of this morning."

She smiled sheepishly, and I nearly toppled over. I'd never seen an expression like that on her face.

"Nothing happened," she hissed. "We just talked."

"And slept. Together. In the same bed."

She swatted at me and I laughed, dancing out of her reach. My amusement faded as Ericen and his guards joined us. The prince didn't look to have slept, and an air of tension prickled between him and his guards.

He still flashed me a smirk when he saw me staring. I quickly looked away, reflexively seeking out Samra. Ericen and I needed to talk, but I worried the captain would judge me for it and hold it against me during the alliance meeting. What would the other leaders say if she told them I was friendly with the enemy prince?

We made for a strange group as we set off through Terin's streets. Res coasted on a current above us, though he kept sending hints of questioning annoyance toward me, as if he didn't understand why *he* didn't get a horse too.

That simple flicker of self-indulgent Res-ness made me breathe a little easier.

Ericen had been denied a horse per Kiva's argument that it would make escape far too easy. Instead, she'd secured one end of a long rope to his restraints and the other to the saddle of her horse, looking far too pleased with the arrangement.

At the edge of town, we followed a wide, dirt path into green grassland, sparsely populated with bush-like trees. Bright orange and yellow flowers popped up through the long fingers of grass, swaying in a gentle breeze that chased the worst of the heat from our skin.

Auma had given each of us a thin, light scarf to protect our necks and faces from the sun, and by early afternoon, we'd all lifted them into place.

I thought about asking Res to give us a fog cover, but I could still feel his ever-present fear about his powers, a feeling that was beginning to worry me more and more. I'd hoped time would ease his franticness about what had happened, but I could still feel him coiled tight, as if curled around a wound. There had to be a way to help him.

If I couldn't, this would all be for nothing.

As we rode, that feeling from the day before rose up in me again. A gentle tugging, almost like the cord between Res and me. It would come and go like a breeze, so faint and fickle I was half convinced I was imagining it. More than once, I caught Aroch studying me from Kiva's shoulders when the feeling evaded me, as if he saw something I couldn't.

I broke from the cat's strange gaze by ducking my horse behind Caylus's and pulling up on his other side. He fiddled with something on the horse's back.

"Is that a glass arrow?" I asked, surprised to see the Illucian weapon in his hands.

"I took it from the ship." He turned it over in his hands. The glass shaft had a strange cast to it, as if impure. "They use them so earth and battle crows can't deflect them, right?"

I nodded. "Wind still works, but it's hard for a crow to do when they're being shot at from more than one direction, and it's not as reactive. Not to mention it's hard to control where it goes afterward." I tapped the point. "That's Alorr metal. It's incredibly lightweight and durable, and it's only found in the Alorr Caves in Jindae. It wasn't until Razel conquered them that Illucia introduced the arrows to their arsenal. Like black gold, it's too refined for a crow to manipulate."

"Hmm." Caylus turned the arrow over without looking at it, his eyes rolled up slightly to the side. Recognizing the look, I dropped back to give him space. He'd be lost in his thoughts for a while.

We traveled until the sun began to set, the terrain shifting from rolling grasslands to patches of wide, sparse trees with bushels of leaves. When the trees began to coalesce, forming a thin forest, we found a shaded spot and set up camp.

Res all but collapsed onto his back, his wings spread wide in a dramatic flourish, as the soldiers set about laying out bedrolls.

Ericen hardly seemed bothered from the trek, though he scowled as Kiva tied his bound hands to the exposed root of a tree, forcing him to sit with them lashed behind his back. I wanted to say something, but I could practically feel Samra watching me.

After tending to the horses, we ate and retired to sleep.

Rolling onto my side, I stared through the canopy at the spread of stars. We were a day's ride from Eselin, set to arrive late tomorrow afternoon, the day before Belin's Day. Soon, Trendell would either agree to support Rhodaire against Illucia or leave us to our fate.

What was I supposed to say to them?

Dread crept along my skin like a scurrying insect. The kingdoms' leaders weren't the only people I had to face tomorrow. I touched the empty spot on my wrist where a feathered bracelet had once hung.

Estrel.

She'd been like a mother to me, and I'd thought her dead. All this time, she'd been hiding, abandoning Caliza and me with a failing kingdom.

Tomorrow, I would ask her why, and I wasn't sure I was ready for her answer.

A gentle breeze rustled the leaves. As it settled, I heard something shift, like the scrape of small rocks being ground into dirt.

I rolled onto my back and froze.

Standing above me, the moonlight turning his blue eyes to glittering ice, stood Ericen.

My breath caught in my throat. He was there long enough to meet my gaze, and then he was gone, slipping silently deeper into the forest. I lay there, my heart stuttering back to life in a jagged beat, knowing he meant for me to follow.

As quietly as I could, I laced on my boots, strapped on my bow and quiver, and went after him. The guard who'd been watching him snored softly against the trunk of a tree, and a small knife lay discarded beside the remnants of the rope binding Ericen to the tree. He must have slipped it from one of the guards earlier.

I found the prince standing in a circle of moonlight. The beams flowed like ribbons through the canopy, bathing the forest floor in an ethereal light and creating a dreamlike tableau—the whispering of the leaves, Ericen's broad shadow on the grass, darker than night, the way he looked at me as if he both wanted to close the distance between us and couldn't bear me coming a step closer.

"Well, this is certainly dramatic," I noted.

He smirked. "I try."

A severed rope dangled from the end of his shackles. I searched the dark for the glint of a blade. Despite defending him to Kiva, it still made me uneasy being out here alone with him. Even without the sleek black leather of his Vykryn's uniform, his sharp features and rigid stance whispered of violence. Except I knew there was more to him than that, more than the training, the blood, and the steel that had consumed his life.

"We needed to talk, and you weren't going to do it in front of the others," he said.

"They'll think you tried to escape." Convincing them he wasn't their enemy had already been hard enough.

He almost looked offended. "If I wanted to escape, I'd be gone."

"I said 'they.' I—" I stopped, glancing up. A dark shape circled overhead, and a moment later, Res glided down on silent wings. He dropped something sharp and shining at Ericen's feet: the knife the prince had used to cut his ropes.

I stared at it. "Res, what in the Saints' name are you doing? Now is not the time to be giving out gifts."

Ericen made no move to take the knife. He simply watched me and waited.

"What's your angle?" I asked, my nerves rising. "Befriend the crow and hope he puts a good word in for you?"

Ericen leaned his weight to one side, giving the impression of a lounging jungle cat. "We do have quite a lot in common."

"Such as an incredibly high opinion of yourselves."

"I was going to say we're both handsome and capable."

"Like I said."

He shrugged. "And we both have a habit of rescuing you. Perhaps that's why, unlike everyone else, the crow seems to get that I'm not here to hurt you."

Pulses of agreement thrummed along the bond along with several faint impressions. A storm. A figure falling. The raging sea.

Ericen had saved me when Res couldn't.

"That was one time," I said.

"Only because you ignored my warning the first time." His expression tightened. "You didn't believe me then and you don't believe me now."

"How can I?" I wanted to. Deep down, I could feel that trusting him was right. But I'd rushed headfirst into his friendship last time, and it'd turned around and bit me.

"I'm trying to help you, Thia." He moved toward me, and I stepped back reflexively. He hesitated. "What I said to you in Isair wasn't a lie. The Sellas are still alive. Or at least one of them is. He's been aiding my mother, perhaps since she destroyed the crows. She's made some sort of deal with them. You have to listen—"

A twig snapped. Someone materialized from the shadows beside him, their sword drawn. Kiva held the tip of Sinvarra to Ericen's neck. "Move," she said, "and I'll slit your throat."

Ericen didn't so much as blink. Had he known she was there? He held my gaze a second longer, pleading, before that familiar mask slid into place.

"Shame," he said, sounding bored. "I'd love to see what you could do with that. You might even be a challenge."

"You wouldn't be," Kiva replied.

"Don't hurt him, Kiva." I stepped toward them.

Quick as a wingbeat, Ericen moved. He ducked, going low and snatching up the blade. Kiva drove Sinvarra down, blocking the attack. The sound of metal on metal rang through the clearing, and I flinched. If the rest of the camp woke, if they found Ericen here...

Ericen exploded up from his crouch, knife aimed at Kiva's chest. She deflected the attack, then drove forward, slamming her shoulder into Ericen's chest and sending him stumbling back a step. He grinned. My breath caught at the way it transformed his face.

He looked alive.

"Stop it," I hissed at them. Their movements were quick, powerful, but they lacked the intent to kill. Well, Ericen's did. I had no doubt Kiva would put Sinvarra straight through his heart.

"I'm shooting the next one of you that moves." I lifted my bow.

Kiva scowled. "You can't be serious right now, Thia."

"Just give me a second to think without the two of you trying to kill each other!" I snapped.

Ericen relaxed slightly, lowering his blade but not dropping it. Kiva didn't budge an inch.

"And what, exactly, are you trying to figure out?" asked a new voice.

I groaned, turning as Samra entered the glade. She'd taken

one of the soldier's bows and stood with an arrow nocked and aimed at Ericen's chest.

Talking Kiva down from killing the prince was difficult enough. Samra looked like she wanted to loose that arrow and keep on shooting until long after he was dead.

"Drop your blade," she ordered.

Ericen assessed the situation. He was too far from the trees to seek cover behind one, and Kiva had backed away, ensuring he couldn't use her proximity as a shield.

"Do as she says," I told him. If he wasn't armed, Samra might be more open to listening, but right now, I truly didn't know if she would shoot him. She'd lost so much to Illucia, to Razel. Even if Ericen hadn't been directly responsible for it, he was part of it, a prince. And if I didn't know him, I wouldn't have hesitated to put an arrow through him.

Ericen let his knife fall.

Auma emerged from the shadows at his back, and he flinched almost imperceptibly. He hadn't heard her approach. Neither had I.

"Walk," she ordered.

Ericen obeyed, his eyes set on me as he passed. He brushed so close I caught the scent of horses and leather, his words low enough only I could hear. "We still need to talk."

The commotion had woken the camp, and though they all climbed back into their bedrolls, I had a feeling sleep came easy to no one. Samra lay on her back, a dagger clasped in one hand. Convinced Ericen would murder everyone in their sleep, Kiva had volunteered to stay up the rest of the night and keep watch in addition to the soldier on duty.

I stood at the edge of the clearing with her and Caylus, my frustration rising. "He could have escaped. Instead, he stayed willingly in a camp with at least three extremely well-trained women who want to kill him just so he could give me information."

"You mean lie to you," Kiva said. "He probably planned to kidnap you and drag you back to his psychopath of a mother!"

"After telling me another fairy tale?"

Kiva folded her arms. "You thought he was on your side last time, and he betrayed you, Thia."

I flinched. "You weren't there when I talked to him in Sordell. He was listening to me. He *agreed* with me."

"And then he chose his monster of a mother over you."

"You don't understand."

"I understand just fine," she hissed back. "I understand that you—" She stopped, biting back her words.

"What, Kiva?"

Her jaw set, the turmoil in her eyes resolving into determination. "That you feel like you spent so long doing nothing that now you have to do everything. Train Res, secure the alliance, save Ericen, save the whole damned continent. But you don't, Thia."

Her words drew claws over a raw part of me. She wasn't wrong, not entirely. I did want to prove that I could do this. I wanted to prove myself the leader I'd always wanted to be.

I am more.

"That's not why I'm doing this," I said. "I'm doing it because it's right. You helped me learn not to give up on myself, Kiva. I can do the same for him."

"And she is really good at it."

We both looked at Caylus.

He shrugged at Kiva's disapproving frown. "You know it's true. Thia could befriend a rabid jungle cat."

"That's exactly what she's trying to do," Kiva griped. She glowered at Ericen as Res hopped over to where the prince had been retied to the tree.

A look of mild wonder slackened Ericen's features, an expression that had slipped through more than once back in Rhodaire. Despite the role he'd been playing, he hadn't been able to hide his interest in the crows. They fascinated him. It was that fascination that'd first led me to start trusting him.

"Look," I said. "Even Res likes him."

Kiva snorted. "Right. Let's trust the magical stork's opinion."

"Kiva."

"Fine!" She threw up her hands. "I won't interfere. But I'll be watching him."

FOURTEEN

The next morning, we rode in silence through golden grass-lands and fields thick with wheat. The path we followed was well maintained, nothing but grasslands and scattered trees in all directions, save for the occasional town we passed through.

The vineyards appeared as we grew closer to Eselin, lines of pale, woody vines resembling miniature trees, stretched out in rows like soldiers. They were lush and heavy with grapes, the scent of sugar subtle in the air. Come Belin's Day, everyone who wished to would take the next three days off work to harvest the grapes, ending each day with a grand festival and family feast.

A dark shape formed on the horizon, growing clearer with each passing minute. The ground sloped up into low, rolling hills, which rose higher still, forming the beginning of the highlands that made up the rest of Trendell's territory. And high on the hills sat Eselin.

The city was filled with color.

It unfurled around us like the spreading petals of countless vibrant flowers, the architecture here similar to that of Terin, only on a much grander scale. The arches rose into beautifully painted domes, the paved streets lined with walkways and alive with voices and movement as people prepared for the coming Belin's Day feast.

Auma led us down a broad street where taverns bordered shops selling glassware and flowing robes of iridescent silk. Teams of people strung garlands of flowers across buildings and hung extra lanterns in the streets, moving with a swift efficiency that made me wonder if they were one of the committees Caliza's husband, Kuren, had told me so much about. Trendell was a place of formality and organization, and he'd always said the kingdom never ran smoother than when it was preparing for something.

Voices rose as people spotted Resyries. A child shouted, pointing, and Res puffed out his feathers.

That was the crow I knew and loved. I grinned as he strutted alongside me. Maybe I'd been worried for nothing.

People recognized Auma and her soldiers, parting to grant us passage. We walked unimpeded up the sloping road toward the highest point in the city, where a terraced arrangement of rose-gold buildings waited. A set of low steps led up the middle, buildings bordering each side, interspersed with flat areas brimming with gardens of midnight-green foliage and dots of wildflower color.

At the top sat a wide, two-story building with an open face of columns and arches framed by curtains of brilliant royal purple fluttering in the gathering evening breeze. My stomach twirled along with the curtains as the reality of what waited for me sank in. Somewhere up there sat the Trendellan king and queen, and in their hands, they held the fate of Rhodaire.

Somewhere up there, Estrel waited.

We dismounted at the base of the terraced hill, servants emerging from buildings at the base level to tend to our horses. Kiva untied Ericen's wrists from the horse but kept them bound, Sinvarra drawn and ready at her side. One of the Jin soldiers kept her bow in hand, an arrow in easy reach.

Res fluttered to my side. "No flopping over," I warned him. "We're supposed to impress them, not ply them for dinner."

He straightened as if already beneath the scrutiny of important eyes. He might be lazier than me on a Rhodairen summer day, but he also liked his praise.

By the time we reached the top of the stairs, my breath came a little faster, my skin gleaming with sweat despite the slowly setting sun. As we crested the final stair, stepping into a wide, rectangular terrace of scattered chairs and tables, I froze.

Among a small, gathered group stood Estrel.

She'd been burned. Badly.

Scar tissue covered the left side of her body. Her skin twisted from the newly healed burns starting at the tips of her fingers, stretching up her arm, around her neck, and down her shoulder blade. Her raven hair, cut to right below her ears, stopped at a hard line halfway down the left side of her skull. The style might have looked purposeful if it weren't for the burns marking her scalp.

My insides turned to stone. I knew Estrel had been burned, but this... I swallowed hard against the rising lump in my throat, a slow fury snaking its way up my skin.

Razel had done this.

Estrel wore her flying leathers, the supple material molded

to her muscular frame. The remnants of the gold and black lines of her Corvé tattoo glimmered in the fading light, and my heart panged at the sight of the crow master marking.

Someone across from her spotted us and said something to her. She fell still as a deer caught in the moonlight.

She turned. I lurched forward. She'd barely broken from the group when I careened into her arms, nearly knocking her to the ground. My injuries stung, but I didn't care as her strength enveloped me, the familiar scent of leather and rookeries rising off her. Tears burned, threatening to spill unchecked, and I squeezed her tighter to keep them at bay.

"You're here," Estrel murmured in her familiar, resonating tone. "You made it, Little Peep."

Something broke open inside me at the name. Estrel had trained me to be a rider nearly my entire life, but she always said I excelled most at talking. The nickname threatened to resurrect the ghosts of memories I'd locked away, memories of fire and acrid smoke, of people screaming... I shoved them away, tearing free of her suddenly as the joy of seeing her shuttered into something dark and empty.

"Where have you been?" I demanded.

Her smile slipped. "That's a long story."

"That's not an answer!" The words tore from me with unexpected strength. I'd known I was angry with Estrel for what she'd done, but I hadn't realized how deep that well went. It hurt to know she'd kept so much from me. I wanted to believe she'd had her reasons, but nothing felt like enough.

"Why?" I asked hoarsely.

Why had she left? Why had she let me think she was dead? Her arms enveloped me once more. I went still.

"I owe you so many answers," she said softly. "I promise I'll give them to you when I can."

Feeling cold and suddenly aware of the people around us, I relented with a nod. Now wasn't the time. We had to appear united.

As Estrel pulled back, her eyes widened, finding Res. "Oh, Thia."

He straightened beneath her gaze, and she moved slowly forward, as if approaching something sacred. Res lowered his head in a small bow as Estrel reached out a hand. It hovered just above his brow, fingers trembling. Then she closed it into a fist and pulled away.

For half a second, her composure fractured, and I knew how depthless the despair that threatened to wash over her was. That she couldn't even bring herself to touch Res... Suddenly, I regretted my outburst of anger, though it still simmered inside me.

Estrel straightened, drawing a deep breath and releasing it slowly. Her attention fell on Kiva, whose wry smile broke into a full grin. Estrel let out a familiar, barking laugh, a sound I never thought I'd hear again. They clasped hands.

Estrel glanced at Ericen as she and Kiva released each other. "You picked up a stray. How'd you come by him?"

"Plucked him out of the sea," Kiva replied. "I never did have much luck fishing."

"I'm sure you're far better at it than swordplay." Ericen flashed her a sharp smile, and I nearly knocked him upside the head. I knew what he was doing. Stranded in unfamiliar territory and surrounded by enemies, he'd fallen back into the familiar comfort of playing the arrogant Illucian prince.

"He saved my life," I explained. "It's a *long story*." I couldn't keep the bitterness out of my voice.

"I say we just slit his throat and be done with him." Samra's hand fell to a dagger at her hip.

Estrel smirked. "As pleasant as ever, Castair."

Samra gave her a stony look, and I looked between them. How did they know each other?

"We're not killing him," I said.

"He could be useful in bargaining with Razel," Auma suggested, to which Ericen snorted.

"Good luck with that," he said. "In fact, she might leave Trendell alone if you agree to kill me."

"Family squabbles?" Kiva asked, sounding delighted.

"What part of *traitorous prince* do you not understand?"

"The part where it came out of your mouth."

Estrel folded her arms, her expression considering. "He's not lying. We just learned today there's a price on his head. His own mother wants him dead. The prince truly is a traitor."

Ericen flinched, and that simple slip of emotion tugged at my heart.

"Take him to a cell," Auma ordered. "We'll handle it later."

Two of the Jin soldiers stepped forward, each taking one of Ericen's arms as they led him away. He glanced back, holding my gaze until he disappeared into a columned building.

FIFTEEN

We sat down for dinner at a long, simple table of dark brown wood beneath a high arched pavilion at the front of the uppermost building. Religion was even scarcer here than Rhodaire, but some traditions still persisted. It was customary in Trendell to serve guests an arrival meal after a long journey to ease the body, accompanied by live music to ease the mind, and we'd each lit a candle before sitting, signifying our safe arrival and the completion of our journey.

A flutist played a gentle tune in the corner as servants brought us roasted duck in plum wine sauce, sliced parsnips and carrots with brown sugar and walnuts, and flat, grainy bread to mop up the juices with. Pitchers of ruby-red wine sat scattered on the table alongside different types of juice.

I tossed Res a piece of duck. He gobbled it down, despite having already finished an entire chicken. Though his appetite had returned, he still grew flustered whenever I suggested using his magic, which only made me more nervous about tomorrow's meeting. What if they asked to see his powers?

Tentatively, I sent a questioning pulse down the line. Res eyed me with a tilt of his head. Then he was gone in a flash of feathers, slipping away to go beg from Caylus instead. My stomach sank, but I pushed the doubt away. He'd be back to his scone-loving, mischievous self in no time. He had to be.

Still, the food on my plate suddenly made my stomach turn.

Caylus had no such problem. He'd already gone through two plates and was on a third. He sat to my left, deep in conversation with one of the Jin soldiers who'd traveled with us, discussing something to do with Trendellan dinner ceremonies. Across from me, Kiva sat angled toward Auma, a smile lighting her face.

For so long, I'd been stuck in a strange world and surrounded by people who hated me. Being here, feeling the strength of Estrel beside me and surrounded by people I loved and trusted, I felt safe for the first time in a long time.

Until I felt a burning gaze at my side, where a girl glared at me from the end of the table. She was Jin, a twisting pattern of thin scars curling up the side of her face in place of tama. Her dark eyes burned with a familiar fire as they bore into me.

Hatred.

A thick jade ring, lined in amber and gold, glinted on her left hand. It tugged at a memory.

I leaned into Estrel, drawing her attention from a conversation with Samra. "Who's that?" I asked, nodding discreetly toward the girl.

A wry smile curled Estrel's lips. "That is Elkona Kura."

I stiffened. I might not be as educated in world politics as Caliza, but I knew that name: she was the Jin princess. That explained the ring—everyone in the Jin royal family wore one. Or at least they had. Now there was just Elkona. She was the only survivor of Razel's massacre, and she'd come to hear my proposal.

And for some reason, she looked like she wanted to skin me alive.

"She doesn't look pleased to see me," I muttered.

"I wasn't," Samra remarked. "And she has more reason to hate Rhodaire than I do."

Estrel cast her a flat look, and to my surprise, Samra drew back as if she'd been chastised.

If Caliza were here, she'd know exactly what to say to quell Elkona's fury. Or at least funnel it into something productive. My instinct was to return her glare until one of us had to blink.

Instead, I turned back to Estrel. A thousand words gathered in my throat. I had so many questions, so many things to tell her, that I didn't know where to start. So I began at the beginning, telling her everything that had happened in Illucia. Except as I spoke, Estrel seemed to withdraw, curving away from me. She grew stiffer with each word I spoke, like an injured soldier waiting out the latest wave of pain.

When I reached the discovery of the other eggs, she went incredibly still, as if my words were a spell and even the shallowest breath would break it.

When I told her about Res's other abilities, she nearly dropped the drink she'd been clutching like a lifeline. "All of them?"

"All of them. And it gets weirder." I told her of Ericen's claim about the Sellas. "Maybe it's all connected," I finished. "Res's powers and the Sellas."

"This has nothing to do with the Sellas," Estrel replied sharply.

I'd expected her to deny the ancient creatures' existence, to say they were gone, not confirm Ericen's outlandish claim. From Samra's expression, I had a feeling she'd known too. Ericen hadn't lied to me. Somehow, the Sellas were still here, and for some reason, both Estrel and Samra had known.

It was yet another question, another secret, but I couldn't bring myself to ask just yet. I thought I'd lost Estrel, and now that I had her back, I didn't want to fight with her again. Because I knew I would. The hurt, the anger—they sat inside me like hot coals. There were so many things she'd kept from me, her survival most of all, and I was afraid of what she might say if I asked.

Some of those questions could wait. Others changed everything. So I forced the next words out between clenched teeth. "Ericen told me that Razel is working with the Sellas. Did you know that too?"

Estrel paled, her hand closing around her cup. "It sounds like the prince likes to talk about things he doesn't understand. Ignore him, Thia. He's lying."

"Like you lied?" The words were out before I could bite them back.

Estrel recoiled, her lips pressing in a firm line. I waited, expecting her to explain, but she said nothing. She looked worn. Exhausted. As if the answers to my questions were weights too heavy to carry.

"Estrel's right." Samra cut through the tension between us, forcing the conversation back to Ericen. "Illucians lie. It's what they do."

"Why do you all keep saying that?" I threw up my hands. "He's the only one who told me the truth about their existence. What good does lying about this do him?"

"It gains him your trust," Kiva said, my raised voice having caught her attention. "It gains him you."

Something about the way she said it made me momentarily unsteady. I gripped the edge of the table, centering myself. "And then what? He tricks me into traveling all the way back to Illucia and straight into Razel's open arms? He's a traitor!"

"Or he forces you," Kiva said. "We don't know that bounty isn't a ploy. It's exactly like something the Illucians would do. And if it isn't, then delivering you to his mother would clear his name."

I snorted harshly. "He could have taken me in the forest. He didn't need to make up stories." Stories that were apparently more than stories.

"But Razel has more pieces on this game board than we do, and we can't let our guard down just because you refuse to see the darkness in someone," Estrel said.

"I've seen it just fine," I growled. "But there's more to him than that."

I had to believe that. I had to believe war would not be his legacy, as it would be his mother's.

I had to believe there was hope for peace.

"Perhaps you can put that faith to use." Auma leaned forward from a whispered conversation with a servant. "The prince claims he has important information, but he'll only tell Princess Anthia."

"No," Kiva and Estrel said at the same time.

I stood. "Where is he?"

Auma rose on silent feet. "Follow me."

Kiva insisted on coming. I expected Estrel to do the same, and though she eventually followed us, she'd looked hesitant to do so. I'd never known her to hesitate over anything.

I left Res in Caylus's care, and we set off along a twisting cobblestone path that ended in a squat, rectangular building on a lower terrace. We entered a long hall with several closed iron doors across one face. Along the opposite wall, silent and still as hunting jungle cats, stood hooded Trendellan monks.

Trendell's army wasn't large, but it was incredibly capable. The monks were a small sect, raised as warriors and assassins from a young age. But where Illucians worshipped war and bloodshed, the monks approached mastering their skills as steps toward fulfillment. I'd been fascinated with them for years.

Auma led us to one of the closed doors. I frowned as Kiva crowded after me. "I'll be fine," I said.

Kiva's hand fell on Sinvarra. "I know you'll be fine, because I'm going to be right there to run him through if he tries anything."

"And I'll just cower in the corner while you do that," I replied dryly, earning an annoyed look from her. "Stay here."

Auma nodded to one of the monks. They unlocked the door before returning to their place along the wall with hardly a sound. I pushed the door open.

A single sona lamp hung from the ceiling of the small room, its light consumed by the shadows at the edges. It was enough to illuminate Ericen, who'd been bound to a chair with his hands behind his back. He looked uncomfortable but unharmed.

He smirked. "I don't suppose you brought dinner?"

Rolling my eyes, I closed the door on Kiva's murderous glower and leaned against it, folding my arms. "Drop the act," I ordered. "Or I'm leaving."

The words had my desired effect. Ericen's smirk vanished, the threat behind his eyes evaporating like mist on a hot day. His shoulders caved as he settled deeper into the chair, but the arrogant air didn't entirely dissipate. It never did, but something still seemed off about him. A little…wild.

"I wasn't sure you'd come," he said.

"I followed you into a forest alone at night," I replied. "You think I'm afraid of facing you tied to a chair?"

He shrugged, the action pulling his tunic tight against his broad shoulders. "I wasn't sure they would *let you c*ome," he clarified.

"You should know me better than to think I'd let that stop me."

He grinned. "Oh, I do."

His words reached deeper than I expected, dragging their claws along something inside me.

"What's that supposed to mean?" I asked, settling into the familiar comfort of our back-and-forth.

"Just that I like to think I know you rather well."

"Really. What do you know?"

He leaned back in the chair as much as his restraints would allow, his gaze ensnaring mine. "I know that some part of you, beneath that façade of peace and harmony, wants war." I started to protest, but he pressed on. "Because just stopping Illucia won't be enough for you. Just stopping my mother won't be enough. You want to tear her apart for what she did. You want to make her suffer." He smiled that wolflike smile of his. "You want revenge."

I stared at him, his pale gaze turned hazel in the orange lamplight. My words stuck in my throat, my thoughts tumbling as I struggled to parse my feelings about what he'd said. Yes, I wanted revenge. I'd promised Samra I would make Razel pay for what she'd done, and I meant it.

But would I pursue that at the cost of peace?

The anger inside me was a constant simmer, simply waiting for a breath of fuel to ignite into an inferno so hot, it could consume anything in its path.

And Ericen could see it.

Some part of me knew he was looking for common ground, growing that connection that had always strung between us in hopes of rekindling my trust. But that didn't make what he'd said wrong. I'd ordered Res to destroy those Illucian ships without hesitation, and they wouldn't be the last casualties of this war at my hand.

"What's the point of this?" I asked. "In the forest, you said you had something else to tell me about the Sellas. What's this got to do with any of that?"

"Nothing at all," he replied. "I just don't like seeing you lie to yourself. You have every bit the potential to become a monster as I do."

His words stole my breath. They made me feel raw and exposed, and I was thankful for the shadows the dim light provided.

"What do you want, Ericen?" I asked hoarsely.

He studied me without answering, a look on his face I couldn't decipher. It was careful, considering, as if wondering how much further he could push me until I cracked. As if wondering if he wanted to.

I glowered back at him.

At last, he replied, "You have Sella blood."

"What?"

"One of your ancestors was a Sella," he said. "I think it's why your family's blood is the only thing that can hatch the crows. It might even be related to why Res can use the other abilities. I don't know. All I know is that my mother was supposed to deliver you to the one she's working with after you hatched the crows, and now that you've escaped, she's desperate," Ericen continued. "Desperate enough to attack Trendell."

This was the information he'd promised in exchange for talking to me.

"If they give you up, she'll stay her army," he continued. "But if they don't, it's reason enough for her to finally strike Trendell."

If that was true, it meant my meeting with the king and queen would hold even more weight than before. If I failed to convince them to ally with Rhodaire, would they turn me over to Illucia to protect themselves?

"Could she sustain that?" I asked. "She had to draw troops from Jindae and the Ambriels just to attack Rhodaire. She couldn't fight a second war spread so thin."

"She might not have a choice," Ericen replied. "The Sella she's working with is dangerous, Thia. She still wants you to hatch the crows, so when all this is over, she'll have an army to deal with the Sellas if she needs it. But they want you now. Her deal with him is precarious. You know the stories. They don't like to have their bargains broken."

The stories from *Saints and Sellas* came floating back. Tales of cruelty and power, of spilled blood and broken bones at the hands of a people too old, too inhuman to feel remorse for what they did.

And Razel intended to set one loose against Rhodaire.

I folded my arms. "But if my Sella blood is why I can hatch the crows, and Razel has a Sella working for her, why can't they just hatch the crows for her?"

"That's what I asked," he replied. "Apparently it's a power that was gifted to your family and them alone. I don't know more than that." Concern tightened his brow. "All I know, Thia, is that you're in far more danger than you think."

SIXTEEN

By the time we left the building, the sun had set entirely, but with so many lights still on in the streets below, the darkness blanketing the city felt faded. It reminded me of being on the upper levels of the castle in Rhodaire, looking out over pockets of life during a quiet night. Before we transferred everything downstairs and blocked the levels off after Ronoch.

We made it all of a step before Kiva blocked my path, her expression expectant. I relayed my conversation with Ericen, mostly. I left out how it began, how his words had cut straight through me, and focused instead on what he said about the Sellas, Razel, and the possibility of war.

"He said Razel is desperate enough to attack Trendell," I finished.

"The king and queen won't betray you to Razel," Auma said.

Estrel folded her arms. "You have no idea what they might do if they're desperate to protect their kingdom."

"I've been the king and queen's ambassador for half a decade," Auma replied, calm as ever. "I do."

I rounded on Estrel. "Tell me about the Sellas. Is Ericen right? Do I have Sella blood?"

Estrel averted her gaze. "Just let it go, Thia. Please. It doesn't matter."

"You mean you don't want to tell me," I shot back.

Her mouth opened, then closed, an uncertainty in her dark eyes that I didn't know how to respond to. I'd run through a hundred horrible scenarios of what my reunion with Estrel would be like. I'd imagined finding her blissful and happy, not having spared a thought for Rhodaire or me these last few months. I'd imagined finding her broken beyond repair. What I hadn't expected was this...uncertainty.

Seeing her doubt herself was almost as painful as knowing she'd abandoned me.

"Please, Estrel," I said. "I need to know."

She sighed softly. "A long time ago, a queen of Rhodaire married a Sella defector. It was he who gifted our people the crows and gave your family line the power to hatch them. Infuriated by his betrayal, the Sellas declared war. All six kingdoms united to defeat them and, with the help of the shadow crows' powers, sealed them away."

Just like Darya's story, except the Sellas were locked away, not killed.

"The Order was formed, a group dedicated to keeping the existence of their prison hidden so no one might find it. To that end, past members removed as much knowledge and information about the Sellas from the world as possible. We kept a lot of it, but most of it was destroyed, the remnants passed verbally within families along with membership in the Order. Samra is also a member, as was your mother."

"And you never told me?" I asked. Was this why my mother had closed the Sella temples in Aris? To further hide their existence?

"It's such an old story, Thia. It should never have mattered." She shook her head. "Besides, it wasn't your burden to bear."

Something in her gaze told me she still felt that way. I wanted to tell her she was wrong, but the words felt petulant on my tongue. If she couldn't see that I was not the same girl she'd left behind, then she wasn't going to listen to me when I said it.

"Is this why Res can use all the abilities?" I asked. "Because of my Sella blood?"

"I believe so. Like all traits, it's stronger in some people than others. Res isn't the first crow to bond a royal who ended up being able to access more than one power."

"What?"

"Your heritage is no small secret, Thia," she said with a sigh. "If your family's enemies had known, it wouldn't have taken them long to deduce where the power to hatch the crows came from."

And once they knew, they would have tried to kill us or use us, just like Razel.

"Most crows who exhibited more than one power would

choose one to focus on and ignore the rest to keep up the charade," Estrel continued. "To be honest, we don't fully understand it. Your bond with Res is different from normal riders. Stronger. I've never heard of one being powerful enough to use all eight though. Your family's Sella heritage must be strong in you."

I shivered at the thought. I didn't want to be part of their legacy of cruelty and violence. And yet hadn't I joined it already? Broken ships and screaming soldiers flashed through my mind.

As if sensing my thoughts, Estrel squeezed my shoulder gently. "There's a weight that comes with that sort of legacy, Thia. You aren't one of them though."

I shook her hand off. "How would you know? You've been gone. You have no idea who I am now."

The hurt that flashed in her eyes made me flinch, but I didn't take the words back. She let her hand drop.

Spinning about, I followed the cord between me and Res back to the terrace table.

We were shown rooms on the top floor of the uppermost building. It was by far the grandest, with windows of colored glass imported from Jindae and delicately painted carvings of small foxes ducking in and out of long vines of ivy, drips of color against its rose-gold face.

Garlands of flowers and ribbons bedecked the whole complex for Belin's Day, and bowls of fresh fruit covered every surface, sweet-smelling candles casting soft light through the halls.

My room was spacious and drenched in textures, from the silken sheets and cotton pillows piled high on the massive bowl-shaped bed, to the luxurious softness of the deep blue carpet, to the sheer layers of curtains hanging over a doorway that led to a balcony overlooking the city.

Res cawed merrily beside me, skittering across the floor and launching himself upward in a flurry of feathers. He settled into the cocoon-like bed, draping his head across a pillow, and drifted to sleep without a moment's hesitation.

I could already tell I wouldn't be so lucky.

My skin felt hot, my body jittery and sore from my injuries, and my mind couldn't hold a thought long enough to dissect it. It leapt from mystery to mystery, problem to problem, from the Sellas to Ericen to the looming alliance meeting.

I ended up wandering the gardens. The night air was warm, the walkways lit by hanging lanterns. Soft tendrils of content-ment slipped down the connection from Res, even in his sleep, and I latched on to them, letting them wash over me. I wondered what he dreamed about.

"Food," I muttered.

"Hmm?"

I started, coming to an abrupt halt. A simple wooden bench sat encircled by a head-height hedge, illuminated by a circle of tiny lanterns. On the bench sat Auma, the scent of cinnamon steaming from the cup of tea beside her, a book in her hand.

"Talking to yourself?" she asked.

I smiled sheepishly. "Yes. Unfortunately, myself doesn't seem to have many answers."

Auma marked her page and closed the book, inclining her head in the barest nod to the bench beside her. I hesitated a fraction. Auma's calm, controlled manner always threw me off a little. It felt like addressing an unmovable mountain—as if she were here before I existed and would be long after. Pushing aside the notion, I sat down as she spoke.

"In Trendell, they tell children a story about the Wanderer. If they don't go to sleep, he'll come and spirit them away to his realm in the Wandering Wood, where they'll never be allowed to rest again."

I laughed. "Are you telling me to go to bed?"

"You've been traveling for some time. Before that, you were in a place of immense danger. You deserve some rest."

Maybe I did, but it wouldn't come. Maybe I'd been in a state of unease for so long, my body didn't know what to do now that I'd reached somewhere safe, now that I had pieces of my family back, however broken. It didn't know how to rest.

"Is that why you're awake?" I asked. "You were there much longer than I was."

"This is the only time I can steal a few minutes of peace." Her fingers absently brushed the cover of the book she'd been reading. The simple action seemed to draw years of tension out of her, and she released a quiet breath. "Reading silences my mind."

I waited, feeling as if I was on the edge of being shown something secret, but she said nothing more. Instead, she picked up her cup of tea, swirling a cinnamon stick through it. "What's keeping you up?" she asked.

"Everything," I muttered, gripping the edge of the bench. "Res. The meeting. My apparently horrible habit of trusting people."

She raised an eyebrow. "That sounds like a very good habit."

I thought of Ericen, alone in his cell. "Even when those people are supposed to be my enemy?"

"You mean the prince." I hesitated, and she smiled. "I've seen the way he looks at you."

I had too. Like he was one wrong move away from losing control of himself. Like he couldn't bear to be around me, but leaving would be worse.

She ran a finger along the rim of her teacup. "It is difficult to walk against the wind."

A shiver brushed my skin. I'd once said that very proverb to Ericen.

Auma continued. "You can only do what you think is right."

Somehow, it didn't feel like she was talking about me. Still, her words resonated. No matter what the others said, I believed Ericen was on my side. I understood why they felt the way they did, but they weren't there when he defended me against the cruel Illucian soldiers, or when I caught him with his face pressed peacefully against his horse's in the moonlight, or the day he'd given me the gloves.

They didn't know the troubled prince I knew.

There was a fire that lived inside him, and it lived inside me too.

"Sometimes—" I hesitated, biting my lip. "Sometimes I think he might be more than a friend."

Auma's dark eyes flickered to me. There was no judgment in them.

"I don't know what I feel for the prince," I continued quietly. "But I feel too much of it."

"You cannot be afraid to see what you see," Auma replied. "If you are, you only end up lying to yourself."

Her words prickled at me. What did I see? Did I see the girl I'd been, wounded and crushed? Did I see the girl Ericen had fallen in love with, brave and strong? Or did I see the warrior I was becoming, the leader?

You have every bit the potential to become a monster as I do.

Ericen's words sent a chill quivering down the back of my neck. He wasn't wrong. I did want revenge. I wanted it so badly, I felt as if it would burn me up from the inside out, and that scared me. But I also wanted my people safe.

"You're right," I said. The words settled inside me, a quiet resolution. I let it lie there, not quite ready to face what it meant, and turned my gaze on Auma. There was something about talking to her. It was like emptying your secrets into a peaceful void. I felt as if she would hold them for me so I didn't have to bear the burden alone. I wanted to do the same for her.

"You said the reading silences your thoughts," I began. "Are they that loud?"

Her fingers tightened about her cup. She held it close to her chest as if protecting it—or herself.

"Advice is more easily given than taken," she said. Her normally impassive expression had faltered slightly, and she looked out over the garden as though it'd become suddenly unfamiliar. "Decisions take courage. It's so much easier to just let things happen."

The vagueness of her response wasn't lost on me. Like she was afraid of what might happen if she were to put her thoughts into words. As if speaking them might make them real.

"From what I saw in Illucia, you're one of the bravest people I know," I said. Her grip on the cup loosened, and I added, "The bravest is Kiva, and the fact that she cares for you tells me she thinks so too."

She closed her eyes as if letting my words wash over her, and a small smile tugged at her lips. When she opened them again, the unease in them had settled.

"Are you nervous about the alliance meeting?" she asked.

I stiffened but forced a nod. "If the other kingdoms won't ally with us, Rhodaire will fall."

Illucia's army was too much for one crow.

One of Auma's hands fell from her cup to brush the book again as if seeking its comfort. The gold title glittered in the lamplight: *Stories of Jindae*.

My heart panged. "Razel will come for Trendell eventually," I said quietly. "The only way to stop her is to defeat her armies or destroy her."

"You mean kill her." It wasn't a question.

I gritted my teeth, my body humming with heat and fury, with memories of crows and people screaming, of the acrid smell of burning flesh and the bite of fire sharp as steel. Of Estrel looking like a ghost of herself, second-guessing every decision.

After everything Razel had done, she deserved it. After everything she'd done, she deserved so much worse.

"Is that truly what you want?" Auma asked.

I don't know. I swallowed the words. "Yes. It's the only way to win peace."

She pressed a finger to my chest, just below my collarbone. My heart thudded against it as if trying to beat away her touch. "Even your very heart is armed. It must have peace before you can expect to bring it to others."

She withdrew her hand, but my heart kept pounding.

SEVENTEEN

A heavy silence followed our small group through halls bright with morning light. I'd woken early to wash and oil my flying leathers, running over words in my head that I still hadn't settled on, even as we approached the throne room. Though with Res following a step behind and Kiva on one side and Caylus on the other, the daunting task of the looming alliance meeting didn't feel quite as impossible.

Except Estrel wasn't here.

We waited for her outside the throne room. Everyone else was already inside, and my anxiety rose at the steady murmur of voices.

"I'm sure she's just running late," I said to Kiva's skeptical look, even as an image of the withdrawn, indecisive Estrel I'd seen last night flashed through my mind. She wouldn't leave me to do this on my own…would she?

As the time of the alliance meeting came and went and Estrel still hadn't arrived, I had no choice but to accept she wasn't coming.

Silencing the emotions that came with the knowledge that she had abandoned me again, I faced the throne room, determined.

"You can do this," Caylus said.

"We're here for you," Kiva added.

Res trilled softly in agreement.

I took a breath and stepped inside.

Instead of walls, rows of columned arches surrounded the perimeter, easily large enough for two full-grown crows to pass through abreast and guarded each by a monk. A domed ceiling, painted with amber foxes winding through colorful flowering vines, rose far above our heads.

Queen Luhara and King Galren Rebane sat on plush cushions on a raised dais ahead of us, a circle of similar cushions set in a ring before them. Most of them were already occupied, some by the crown prince and princess and others by the council. One seat remained empty in honor of Kuren. Elkona sat to the side, Samra beside her.

A hushed muttering broke out as we entered, all eyes finding Res. We approached a section of open cushions, each of us bowing in turn to the king and queen before we took our seats. One remained empty. I refused to look at it.

"Welcome, Princess Anthia," said Queen Luhara. "We're

glad you've arrived in Eselin safely." She wore her dark, spiraling curls gathered atop her head, framing a serene, friendly face. Especially compared to the quiet, stony expression of her husband, who simply nodded in greeting.

"Thank you, Your Majesty," I replied. I knew little about Kuren's parents. Every free moment, I'd spent furthering my training to be a rider, neglecting things Caliza could recite in her sleep. Not for the first time, I wished I'd paid more attention in our lessons.

"We're here today to discuss an alliance between the kingdoms of Rhodaire, Trendell, Jindae, and the Ambriel Islands," the queen continued, her voice soft but firm. Her dark gaze scanned the crowd as she spoke, addressing everyone equally. "Everyone who wishes it will be given an opportunity to speak, but we'd like to begin by hearing from Princess Anthia."

Queen Luhara nodded to me, and my heart fluttered. She was yielding the floor. Which meant I needed to stand up and talk.

Saints. I swallowed hard, standing. Caliza had given me a few pointers on the formalities: stay in front of your cushion, don't talk directly to one person but rather address everyone, speak slowly and clearly.

Faced with so many expectant eyes and such great stakes, every last piece of advice fled my mind.

Caliza should be here, not me. This was what she did, what she excelled at. The only words I was good with were the sharp, sarcastic kind. I didn't have Samra's surety and control, Caliza's tact and knowledge, Estrel's strength and experience, or even Ericen's commanding presence.

I had a half-baked plan, a nearly grown crow, and part of a room that hated me, judging by Elkona's burning gaze and Samra's dark skepticism.

With a start, I realized everyone had been waiting for me to speak for an uncomfortably long time. My hands curled into fists reflexively, and I forced them to relax, resisting the urge to brush away the gathering sweat beneath my leathers.

"We have a common enemy," I began, louder than I'd intended. My voice echoed, corralled by the dome and thrown back again. I winced and caught Elkona smirking in a way that made the scars trailing along her face twist. She was enjoying this.

My discomfort. My inevitable failure.

Res recognized it too, the bond thrumming with annoyance. My jaw set, my nostrils flaring. Did she think this was a game? Our lives, our families' lives, the very survival of our kingdoms were at stake, and she found this amusing?

I straightened. Holding out my left hand before me, I removed the fingerless glove, sparing a brief thought for the prince who'd given it to me, and held up my scarred hand.

"I got these scars pulling Estrel out of a burning rookery." This time, my voice came steady and controlled, even as my mentor's absence yawned dark and gaping inside me. "She'd gone in to try and save my mother, who in turn had been trying to save the crow eggs. She failed.

"That day, my mother died, countless numbers of my people were murdered and irreparably scarred, and our way of life was reduced to ashes." I lowered my hand but left my glove off. As

I spoke, I let my gaze rest on each and every face, letting them see the pain.

"Then I found a crow egg in the blackened remains of a rookery." I stepped aside, letting the circle get their first unimpeded view of Res. He rose taller, the sunlight setting the iridescent sheen beneath his dark feathers aglow.

"With Resyries, we have a chance to save our people. Razel will not stop until every citizen in every kingdom is hers. She will continue to kill and burn and tear families apart. She has already destroyed kingdoms, but she will keep destroying until every ounce of fight, of hope, of life that survived is ground into dust."

At this, I looked first at Samra and then Elkona. Despite their kingdoms being conquered, they kept fighting. But Razel would crush them too in the end.

"Rhodaire is not strong enough to stop her alone." I lifted my gaze to the king and queen. "Trendell is not strong enough to stop her alone. What remains of those fighting in Jindae and the Ambriels *cannot stop her alone.*"

Res's shoulders lifted as his wings spread just the slightest, making his already impressive size look all the larger.

"Together, we have the power to end Illucia's reign. Alone, we'll fail." My words echoed through the cavernous room.

Then, "That felt almost like a threat." It was Elkona, risen from her cushion to address the gathering. A defense leapt to my lips, but I swallowed it. The look on her face—I knew it well. I'd seen it a hundred times in Illucia. She was just trying to bait me, to undermine my power. As Trendellan court custom bid, I relinquished my place and retook my seat. Kiva squeezed my arm.

"The princess makes a fine point," Elkona continued, her voice a low rasp. She wore a soldier's uniform of green and gold, the metal lightweight Alorr. It clung to her wiry frame like supple leather, the joints left free for easy movement. "Alone, none of us can defeat Illucia. What remains of my rebel forces is thin, Korovi is isolated as ever, and the Ambriels are half-enamored by their masters."

Beside her, Samra prickled.

Elkona didn't seem to care. "But what I do not understand is why I should ally my forces with the very people who left them to die. People who even now court the enemy." Her eyes flashed to me.

My heart sank. I'd known Ericen would come up eventually, but I hadn't expected it to sound so vicious when it did.

Elkona looked to the king and queen. "Trendell has a long history of avoiding war. It has for ages been a neutral kingdom, and I respect that, even if I do not agree with it. You offered my people aid when they needed it and have since harbored us despite Illucia's looming threat."

Her gaze swung around to me, alight with a dark fire. "But what did Rhodaire do? You turned your backs on us."

I flinched.

"With all your power, all your wealth, all your *magic*, you stood aside and let us die. Let us burn. Why should we not do the same to you?" She had eyes only for me as she spoke. "Tell me why I should ally my people with leaders that dishonorable."

It was the same thing Samra had said to me back in Illucia

under the guise of Diah, and the answer I'd given had been very similar to what I'd said now. Without each other, we would fall.

Elkona was suggesting that if they banded together, even without Rhodaire, they could survive.

She was suggesting they leave us to our fate.

My mouth turned dry. Without Rhodaire, they would die. They didn't have the numbers. The Illucian army was expertly trained from birth for one thing: war. They wouldn't be defeated by a ragtag group of rebels and a peacetime army, no matter how skilled the Trendellan monks were.

I opened my mouth to tell Elkona this, but movement to her side made me pause. Samra had stood. With a final sharp look in my direction, Elkona retook her seat.

Nervous energy rippled along my skin. I stared at Samra, unable to force the shock from my expression. She didn't meet my gaze.

"Rhodaire's failure cost countless lives," she began, and my hope tumbled, disappearing into a familiar void inside me. "While they hid, families were torn apart, cities burned, and children stolen to serve a foreign queen. Our calls for aid went unanswered. No one came."

Each word struck me deeper than the last. The despair Rhodaire had experienced had been felt a hundredfold in the Ambriels and a hundred more in Jindae. What I had lost, so many others had too, and so much more.

Why did I think they would want to fight alongside people who left them to die?

"But Princess Anthia is not her mother."

My head snapped up, and I found Samra's gaze locked with mine. "What she endured to hatch that crow and bring it safely here before us was no small task. It took strength and bravery and sheer, unwavering will on a level I've seen in few people. She is not responsible for the decisions made when she was a child. She's responsible only for her own choices, and she decided to walk into the heart of Illucian territory, stand face-to-face with Razel, and set fire to her carefully laid plans."

My throat tightened as I straightened.

"Over the last couple of weeks, Anthia has proven herself a leader I will follow." Samra lifted her gaze to the king and queen. "The Ambriels will ally with Rhodaire."

Her pronouncement echoed, both in the chamber and inside my head, a heavy refrain: *A leader I will follow.*

Samra sat, not looking at Elkona, whose very skin burned with the ferocity inside her. I knew that kind of hatred like my hands knew the familiar grip of my bow. I held it close to my own heart. There was nothing anyone could say to convince Elkona that I was not her enemy.

Several Trendellan council members rose to speak. They discussed the logistics of supporting a war, the impact on the Trendellan economy and its people. Some asked me questions about Rhodaire, and I gave the information Caliza had provided me, from the numbers in our army, to our food stores, to our access to ships. All the while, the king and queen remained in silent consideration, and I felt Elkona's searing gaze cutting into me.

The Ambriels would not be enough on their own. We needed Trendell.

"Princess Anthia," said a council member. "Could you please describe for us the extent of your crow's powers?"

Reluctantly, I stood to take the floor. Sweat coated my palms, and I wiped them reflexively on my pants. Elkona's sharp eyes missed none of my nervousness.

"Res is a storm crow," I explained. "His abilities are well suited to fighting large numbers. We can damage the Illucian army in a variety of ways with the things he's capable of, from impacting the battlefield to direct, widespread attacks. However—" I hesitated. Telling them about Res's other abilities could secure the alliance, but what if they asked for proof? I couldn't be certain Res would give it to them.

The room waited, all eyes on me. Then—

"Show us." Elkona's voice dropped like a stone through the silence.

"What?" My voice caught in my throat.

She stood, brazenly disregarding the speaking procedures. "If he's so powerful, prove it. Show us what he can do."

I swallowed hard and looked to Res. He cooed softly, shrinking down.

Please, I begged.

"Well?" Elkona asked. "Does he even have magic?"

"Of course he does!" I snapped.

She gestured to the room. "Whenever it pleases you then."

"Come on, you bloody chicken," Kiva hissed under her breath.

Res, please! I couldn't hold back the wave of anxiety that flooded down the line. Res reared back, cawing, but I felt his power surge. Felt him reach for it—and turn away. He stepped back, shaking his head, his gray eyes bright. His fear, his sorrow, his apology—they all surged along our connection in a tumbling mess.

"Princess Anthia?" Queen Luhara's normally steady voice betrayed her confusion.

I whirled back to her, panic rising. "He can do it," I promised. "He's just scared right now."

"Scared?" one of the council members asked. "Of what?"

I started to respond, then stopped. What could I say? That Res feared his own magic? Elkona would laugh in my face.

"We had a run-in with the Illucian blockade on our way here," I said. "He's just a little shaken from his first battle. He just needs a couple of days."

Elkona snorted, folding her arms. "How convenient."

"Watch yourself," Kiva growled, rising to her feet. "Or are you calling Anthia a liar?"

Elkona's brow rose as if to say "so what if I am?"

"Thia isn't a liar," Caylus said, now standing at my other side. "Kiva and I have both seen Res's powers."

"And aren't you just as likely to lie for her?" Elkona snapped back.

I looked helplessly to Samra.

The captain gritted her teeth, then rose to her feet. "I have also seen the crow use his powers. I can vouch that he is a powerful storm crow and also has access to other crow abilities. Without him, we wouldn't have escaped the blockade. He destroyed a good number of their ships with ease."

Relief swept through me, but it was short lived as the same council member asked, "And how was his control of those abilities? He's quite young, isn't he?"

Samra looked to me, an apology in her eyes. She wouldn't lie. "He's still learning," she admitted, and my hope dwindled with every word. "He lost control toward the end of the battle and—"

"Lost control?" Elkona asked. "So what you're saying is he not only refuses to use his powers now, but if he did, he might strike us all with lightning?"

A murmur rippled through the room at that, uncertainty breaking openly on more than one person's face.

"No, he wouldn't," I said hurriedly. "It was only a momentary lapse. He thought I'd been killed and—"

"And promptly started electrocuting everything around him?" Elkona demanded. "So if you fall in battle, what then, Princess? We contend with the Illucian army and a deranged crow?"

If you fall in battle. The words chilled me, even as my frustration mounted.

"You don't understand," I argued.

She flicked a hand in a dismissive gesture. "I understand just fine. Your crow can't control his magic, and now he's afraid of it or of battle or of losing you. In any case, he's useless." She looked to the Trendellan rulers. "Rhodaire has already broken one alliance with my kingdom. Who is to say they won't break another? They are as dangerous as the Illucians they fight. Jindae will not join this alliance, and I advise you do the same, lest you send your soldiers to the slaughter."

I gaped at her, desperately trying to conjure the words that would fix this, stop this alliance from slipping through my fingers like ash.

Queen Luhara evaluated me, her hands folded before her mouth. Then she rose. Everything inside me went still and cold.

"We have heard all arguments regarding the matter of an alliance between our nations," she said. "Based on the evidence that's been provided, I am not prepared to enter Trendell into any such coalition. You have a place of safety here for as long as you need it, Princess Anthia, but Trendell will continue to remain neutral in this war."

Her words echoed through the chamber. Elkona smiled. I staggered, Kiva's quick hands the only thing that kept me upright.

We'd failed.

EIGHTEEN

We'd failed, and I didn't know what to do.

The throne room had emptied long ago, leaving me alone with Kiva, Caylus, Res, and the slow, creeping feeling descending about my shoulders.

We'd failed, and now Rhodaire would fall.

I stared at the empty thrones and heard Elkona's damming words again and again. *Useless useless useless.*

We'd failed, and it was my fault.

"Thia—" Kiva began but stopped when I shook my head.

Res nudged me with his beak, but I couldn't look at him. Caylus hovered nervously at my side. My eyes snagged on the empty cushion where Estrel should have been.

Suddenly, their presence was too much. All of it was too

much. Before any of them could say anything more, I broke for the open doorway. The wide corridors spread before me in a welcome maze, allowing me to lose myself in them.

I remembered another time not so long ago when I ran. When everything inside me felt too sharp to touch. Too broken.

I'd rested all of Rhodaire's hopes on this alliance, and in the end, it was my inability to lead, my failure as a rider, *me*, that brought it tumbling down.

I don't know how I found her room. One moment, the hallways had swallowed me up, and the next, they'd spit me out in a familiar place.

My hand hovered over Estrel's closed door. A wave of emotion rose inside me. Hurt, confusion, and a coiled fury I was afraid to touch, lest it spring to life and consume me. Fueled by more than just my anger at Estrel, it felt a drop away from roiling into an uncontrollable sea.

I slammed my fist into Estrel's door twice. I half hoped she wouldn't be there, that it'd turn out she'd been called away on some urgent business. But after a brief pause, a voice I would know anywhere called, "Who is it?"

"Me."

Silence. Then, "Now isn't a good time, Thia."

I stilled as an unfamiliar coldness descended over me. Not a good time? *Not a good time?* I seized the handle and, finding it unlocked, flung open the door.

The room looked like a wind crow had gone berserk inside. The blankets were thrown to the foot of the bed, a toppled vase lying in pieces at the base of a cabinet. A nightstand beside her bed had been overturned, and pacing a worn path in the floor rug, there was Estrel.

What remained of her hair was a tangled mess, and she had deep purple shadows under her brown eyes. She must have covered them with powder earlier to hide her exhaustion.

Her eyes widened. "Thia."

"It failed," I snarled.

"What?"

"The alliance!" My voice rose. "It failed, *I failed*, and you weren't there!"

She stared back at me, and the fear, the uncertainty that filled her dark gaze, nearly broke me. I couldn't reconcile the woman before me with the one who'd been like a mother to me. The one who'd caught me saddling Iyla in the dead of night and, instead of reprimanding me, had climbed into the saddle at my back and taken me for my very first flight.

I could still feel the bite of the cold wind against my skin, the power of the crow beneath me, the security of Estrel's arms at my sides… She drew a ragged breath, and the memory slipped from my grasp.

"I'm sorry, Thia," she breathed, wrapping her arms about her stomach. "I—I couldn't—" She shook her head and kept on shaking it. It would have killed my mother to see her like this. It killed me.

A slow heat rose under my skin. "You abandoned me again."

Something hardened in her expression. She drew herself up, and for a moment, I saw the strength and presence of Estrel Cade, one of the most formidable riders Rhodaire had ever seen.

"You think this is about you?" she demanded. "Fine, let's make it about you. I still got news out here, you know. Don't talk to me about abandoning people when you hid in your room while Caliza ran the kingdom by herself."

I recoiled but didn't relent. "At least I'm doing something now! You were like a mother to me. I needed you, and you left. I wanted to be your apprentice, to be Corvé after you. I looked up to you. I still do..." I trailed off, breathing heavily.

A mirthless laugh escaped Estrel's lips. "Your mistake, Little Peep. People who put their faith in me only end up getting hurt."

I shook my head, my throat burning. "No. That's not true. I *need* you! I thought I'd lost you along with her. I thought you were dead, but you've been here the entire time. If my mother could see you—"

"But she can't!" Estrel roared. "And it's my fault! So forgive me if I'm not ready to rush headlong into another battle that will only take more people I love away from me."

My jaw worked, but no words came out. Surprise had drowned out my anger like water to a flame. "What are you talking about?"

Estrel swayed, then collapsed onto the edge of the bed behind her, burying her face in her hands. When she pulled them away, my breath caught. She was crying. "She was still alive when I found her," she croaked. "I tried to save her, but the flames were too much."

I stepped slowly forward, not fully trusting my legs to keep me upright. They'd become lead. I dropped onto the bed beside her. "You went after her. Into the rookery."

Estrel wrapped her arms around her stomach, squeezing

tight. "There were three Illucian soldiers in there with her. She'd killed them, but they'd wounded her. There was so much blood, and the flames were everywhere. I couldn't breathe. I made it to her, but—" She stopped, shaking her head. "My clothes caught fire. I couldn't hold on to her. I couldn't stand the burning. I pulled away, and the floor collapsed underneath me. I woke in the infirmary a week later."

I didn't know what to say. This wasn't Estrel's fault, just like it hadn't been mine. But I knew the guilt twisting knots in her face. I knew its heavy swing like a pendulum in the chest. I knew how it waited at the bedpost and watched every movement, filled every word. I'd held it close. So did Estrel.

I am more. I concentrated on the words, on the truth behind them.

"I can't convince you not to blame yourself," I said slowly. "But I don't blame you, and neither would my mother."

Estrel looked up, meeting my gaze tentatively.

"You knew her as well as anybody," I continued. "She'd be furious if she knew we'd wasted a second worrying about what we could have done to stop her, knowing full well she'd have done it anyway."

"That's easy for you to say. You're not reminded of what you did every time you see your reflection." She lifted her left arm, turning it so the burns along the top were fully visible. The last remnants of a tattoo that'd once said *Iyla* shone on her forearm. "You should have seen the way people looked at me. Like my skin was a portrait of Ronoch, a reminder of everything they'd lost. I couldn't take it."

That was why she'd left, why she'd let people forget about her, even going so far as to let them think she'd died. Maybe she'd even spread the rumor herself. I understood, but I didn't accept it.

"You think you're the only one with scars?" I ripped the leather glove off my burned arm.

Estrel's eyes followed it, widening.

"Didn't you ever wonder who pulled you out of the damned fire?" I leapt to my feet. "Didn't you care?"

Estrel's mouth worked, but no words came out. Understanding dawned slowly on her face as I glared at her, my hands balled into fists.

"I heard the stone collapse. I ran, thinking my mother was dying, and found you lying in the rookery entrance. I pulled you out and doused the flames, but not before my sleeve caught fire and I burned along with you!"

She shook her head, and the pain that flooded her expression pulled the anger right out of me. I drew a deep breath, forcing myself to calm down. Kneeling beside her, I gently closed my scarred hand over the twisted skin of her burned wrist. She tensed at first, then slowly relaxed.

"You can't fixate on this," I said. "*We* can't. I understand you want to run away. So did I. Sometimes, I still do."

And I had. Away from the throne room, away from Rhodaire's impending future of blood and death, from Elkona's voice hissing *useless useless useless*.

I swallowed hard. "But we have to move forward, and that means facing the problems we have now, the ones we can still do something about. My mother would have wanted us to fight. Please, Estrel. I don't know how to fix this. I need you."

Estrel held my gaze, unblinking. But in the end, she turned away. "I can't do this right now, Thia. I need to be alone."

My grip slackened on her hand, and she pulled it away. I rose, stumbling back a step, and turned for the door. My blood pounded in my ears as I slid my glove back on.

She wasn't the woman I remembered, the one who'd taught me how to hold a bow or massage a crow's tired wings with careful fingers. That woman had been sharp as talons and twice as strong. She'd been a jungle cat in human form, a storm trapped in a bottle. This Estrel was an impending wreck. All I wanted in that moment was to ease her pain, but I didn't know how. I'd barely learned to help myself.

Even now, as I walked ghostlike through the open corridors, the snake crept along my shoulders, whispering to me to give up. That familiar weight wrapped me tight and held me close. Halfway down the hall, I simply stopped. I don't know when I ended up on the ground, my knees pulled against my chest, my arms wrapped so tight around them, they'd surely bruise.

I don't know how long I stayed there. Only that I wanted to disappear. To sink into a quiet darkness alone, where my own mind could no longer haunt me.

Res found me still sitting with my back against the wall.

His incessant tugs along the bond only made me feel sicker,

and I buried my face in my hands as he nudged me with his beak, a low, concerned trill reverberating in his throat.

Someone slid down along the wall beside me. I didn't have to look to know it was Kiva.

"It's over," I said quietly. "We can't win."

Guilt ground along the bond. I lifted my head, placing a hand on Res's lowered beak. "It's not your fault. You've done so much for us already." So much for me. "I love you, magic or not, alliance or not."

It was I who had failed. I who didn't know how to begin handling this. Without the alliance, Razel would overrun Rhodaire. She would destroy it piece by bloody piece and take what she wanted from the ruins.

Would she try to force Res to serve her, or would she destroy him too?

I swallowed hard. "How do I tell Caliza it's over?"

"You don't." Kiva spoke without hesitation. She rose, turning to face me on one knee. "Because this isn't over. It can't be. We have to keep trying."

I looked away. "I had my chance. I failed. They're never going to listen to me now."

Her voice was uncharacteristically soft when she asked, "Why is it the only thing you ever give up on is yourself?"

My hands tightened into fists, but she pressed on.

"You took a crow egg into Illucian territory and discovered how to hatch it. You organized a summit of kingdoms unlike anything this continent has ever seen. You even befriended the damned Illucian prince, for Saints' sake! You're one of the most stubborn, determined people I know, but when it comes to supporting yourself, you're the first to doubt and the first to give up." Kiva stood. "Well, I'm not giving up, Thia. Not on this alliance, and not on you." She held out her hand. "One step at a time."

I stared at her outstretched hand. A hundred possible failures rose before it.

You only fail if you stop trying.

It was something Estrel had said to me, when I'd missed target after target with my arrows or found myself flat on my back in a sparring match for the tenth time in a row.

Never stop fighting.

I took Kiva's hand.

NINETEEN

One step at a time.

First, I needed to clear my head. The flurry of emotions taking up space inside me left no room to think. I had too many problems to face: Ericen, Elkona, Estrel, Res's magic, the alliance.

I needed space from them, and there was one surefire way to get it.

A chorus of surprised shouts trailed Res and me into the air. I leaned close to his body, eyes closed, focused on the thrum of the bond between us, on his power and strength and the rush of the wind.

I let every weight drop from me, stone after stone, until there was only me, Res, and the endless sky.

We flew for hours. Over Eselin and out across the

countryside, skimming the tops of the Calase Mountains and diving low through valleys thick with golden grass. By the time we circled back to the royal complex, I felt lighter than air.

Spotting a grassy plateau terraced into the base of one of the hills the complex sat on, I directed Res toward it, and we alighted effortlessly, out flight coordination seamless.

Res sent a questioning pulse down the line as I dismounted and removed his saddle, dropping it into the grass.

"I thought we could practice some magic out here," I said tentatively.

He reared back, huffing, a staccato beat of refusal pounding along the cord. An undercurrent of fear punctuated each pulse.

"It's okay, Res." I stepped toward him, but he drew away, his anxiety flaring. He shook his head, an uneasy trill reverberating in his throat. I retreated, and he calmed slightly, enough of an indication that he was still afraid of hurting me, of losing control.

He was afraid of his power, and I didn't know how to help him.

One step at a time.

"You're okay," I said, letting reassurance and comfort flow down the bond. "We'll work on more flying instead. Okay?" His breathing slowed a little, his nerves settling as he lowered his head.

"Shouldn't he be doing that already?" asked a voice. "I would have sworn that's what the wings were for."

My gaze snapped up to find Ericen descending a path that curled around the hill. Two monks from the cells walked at his back, and his hands were bound before him. He looked pale and exhausted but otherwise unharmed.

Seeing my confusion, Ericen nodded back up the path. "Your friend, the Corvé, convinced them to let me out for some exercise."

Estrel.

Was this her way of apologizing?

"Actually, his wings are just for feigning injuries." I gently lifted one of Res's wings and released it. He played along, letting it flop like a discarded cloak to his side. The joking eased the riling anxiety inside him, the bond settling back to a steady hum.

Ericen halted at the edge of the clearing, the two monks second shadows at his back.

I raised an eyebrow at them. "If you give him enough space to breathe, I promise you he won't bite."

"For now, at least." The prince held my gaze as he spoke, and my breath caught. I cleared my throat in an attempt to cover it up, but the amusement in Ericen's eyes said he'd noticed. The two monks exchanged looks but retreated into the shadow of the hill, granting us a little privacy.

Ericen rolled his shoulders, and I winced at thinking how sore they must be from being bound in the same position for so long. "It feels good to move."

"I'm sorry about all this," I replied. "And thank you for telling me the truth."

He looked surprised. "You believe me then?"

"I figured your imagination didn't extend as far as mythical beings and mysterious powers."

He grinned wickedly, his eyes half-lidded like a lazy cat's. "Oh, you'd be surprised what my imagination can come up with."

A flush crept into my cheeks, and I spun about to face Res, only to almost impale myself on his beak. He'd been standing right behind me, peering at Ericen with blatant curiosity. I gestured vaguely at him. "The crow likes you. I figure if we're wrong, he can just fry you with lightning."

Ericen laughed.

I refused to turn back around, the heat in my face unrelenting. He'd always been able to get under my skin, but these weren't the barbed, caustic words that had once made me want to punch him. These set my skin aflame in a very different way, and I had no defense against it.

My conversation with Auma last night crouched in the back of my mind, waiting for me to face it.

Decisions take courage.

I'd decided to trust Ericen, that much I knew. But what that truly meant, I wasn't sure.

"You said something about flying," the prince said. "Can I see?"

"Good question." I stared pointedly at Res, who huffed and flopped his pretend injured wing, clearly having expected a long break after our flight. "I promise chicken after."

He perked up at that, and I rolled my eyes.

I approached the edge of the hill, peering over. The side had been terraced, creating a line of sloping drops and plateaus like the one we stood on. Res could glide straight to the bottom or land and take off several times to practice control. A valley rested at the foot of the farthest terrace, a trickling stream tracing through it, before the hills reared up into the Calase Mountains that protected the city's back.

Ericen appeared at my side, his shoulder brushing mine. Once, I'd refused to even talk to him about the crows. Now, he stood beside me as mine trained.

"What?" Ericen asked.

I blinked, realizing I'd been smiling. "Nothing."

Res snorted in amusement, sensing the lie.

"Shut it," I muttered. "You're a seven-foot-tall pile of feathers." He cawed, and I gestured to the edge of the plateau. "After you."

It felt strange to smile right now. To laugh. But I leaned into it, letting myself take that first step.

Ruffling his feathers in a way that made him look comically inflated rather than intimidating, Res hopped up to the edge. He snapped his wings open, narrowly missing knocking me down the hill—a fact I didn't think was an accident—and leapt.

Res glided down, alighting effortlessly on the ground at the base of the terraced hill.

"Now what?" Ericen asked.

"He comes back up." I sent an image to Res of him using his wings to hop onto the terrace above in one powerful burst. It was a strength exercise he hated. Sure enough, annoyance at the work involved flickered back, which I didn't grace with a response.

With a hard flap of his wings, he leapt over the edge and onto the plateau. He glanced up at us, measured the rest of the effort required to get back to the top, and plopped onto the ground.

Ericen snorted. "Impressive."

I swatted his arm, which was a lot like hitting stone.

He raised an eyebrow. "Now that's not fair. I'm defenseless."

He lifted his bound hands, and I resisted the urge to say he was about as defenseless as a wolf missing a tooth. It would give him far too much satisfaction.

"I can't deal with you and the crow. I don't know whose ego is bigger," I grumbled.

"Well, at least I can back mine up." Ericen's voice rose, floating down to where Res had started picking pieces of grass free with his beak. The crow perked up, indignation flashing down the cord.

With a huff, he snapped his wings out and leapt up to the next terrace, and then the next, not slowing as he ascended level after level. Then, as he landed on the one before us, he beat his wings in a powerful flutter and flew over our heads. He nearly smacked Ericen in the face with his tail, but the prince ducked in time.

Res flapped his wings, catching a draft that carried him up and out. He soared over the valley. An undercurrent of sheer joy hummed along the connection.

I only realized I'd closed my eyes and lifted my arms when I felt the heat of Ericen staring at me.

I peered up at him. "What?"

A smile crinkled his eyes. "You looked...peaceful." He said it almost longingly.

I cringed before it occurred to me that Ericen didn't know what'd happened today. He'd never known about the alliance meeting, and he didn't know that it had fallen apart. It felt good to stand next to someone without that weight.

"Can you feel what he's feeling?" He nodded at Res.

"An echo of it," I replied. "I wish I could show you."

The truth of that statement caught me as off guard as it did Ericen, who stared back at me with parted lips.

A pulse of delight was all the warning I had before Res brushed by us, wings nearly slapping us both in the face. He let out a cackling caw, spiraling up high into the air before letting himself fall. He caught himself a hairsbreadth from the ground, the grass swaying beneath his current.

We both laughed.

"That's incredible," Ericen said.

I grinned back.

We spent a couple of hours sending Res through flight drill after flight drill. His skills were developing at an impressive speed, his control over the wind as effortless as if his magic guided it.

We watched as he glided in lazy circles above the long, thin trees dotting the valley below, the sky slowly darkening into a sea of stormy blues. In that comfortable silence, I finally said the thing that had been nagging at me since we fled Illucia.

"You didn't call the guards," I said softly. "When we were escaping. You could have called the guards on the grounds to stop us, but you let us go."

"Is that why you decided to trust me?" he asked, the weight in his voice pulling my gaze to him. He made for a forlorn figure with the backdrop of the mountains now cast in purple shadows, and it struck me how alone he truly was now. He'd always been somewhat of an outsider in Illucia, but at least then he'd had a purpose, a goal.

I knew what it was to lose those things.

I pushed aside the urge to tease him, the solemn weight in his eyes too heavy to budge with anything so light.

"I trust you for a lot of reasons," I replied. Months ago, I would never have believed I could say those words to him. Now, they felt right.

"You missed the Centerian, didn't you?" I asked.

Razel had made Ericen a deal: if he won the kingdom's bloody sword tournament, she would make him Valix, leader of the elite Vykryn soldiers of Illucia. It was what he had been working toward his entire life.

He shrugged, a wistful smile pulling at his lips. "I thought I'd give someone else the chance to win. We all know no one could have challenged me."

I rolled my eyes. "There's that familiar arrogance. I was starting to think you'd reformed entirely."

He gave me a lazy grin. "Never."

I laughed. "I could use a little bit of that right now."

He frowned, and I hesitated. Telling myself I trusted him was one thing; actually doing it was another. But I had to start somewhere.

I told him about the alliance.

By the time I finished explaining how it'd failed, the little furrow had appeared between his brows.

"How foolish can they be?" he demanded. "Trendell has only remained neutral in this war because my mother has allowed them to. If she takes Rhodaire, she'll come for them next. They're condemning themselves."

"They don't see it that way," I replied. "They think we'll lose even if we fight, so they should protect themselves as much as possible for as long as possible."

Ericen snorted derisively. "Fools," he said again. "They won't have another chance like this."

Something red flashed on the hill at his back. I barely had time to make out Elkona staring down at us, arms crossed and with the expression of a thundercloud, before she turned away.

My stomach swooped, but my fists curled tighter. Maybe I'd gone about this all wrong from the beginning. After all, what did Elkona really know about me besides what my mother had done?

There is a strength to you that lifts others up, and that's what this world needs right now. Not another politician. You.

I'd walked into a room of people and tried to politick my way to an alliance, but I'd never been good at speaking *at* people. I needed to speak *to* them.

One step at a time.

If I could befriend the Illucian prince, a boy born to be my enemy, then I could befriend Elkona too.

TWENTY

E arly the next morning, Res and I joined Kiva and Auma for
breakfast on the pavilion, where they played a game with
painted cards Auma had taught her back in Sordell.

"Have you seen Elkona?" I asked as Auma placed a card with
a silver fox wreathed in thorny vines on the table.

Kiva scowled at the card, but Auma's expression remained
stoic as ever as she looked up at me. She'd make a fantastic dice
player. "There's a training ground down by the cells to the left.
She's there."

As she spoke, Kiva played a card, to which Auma laid down
another from her hand without even looking.

"You've got to be kidding me!" Kiva's curses followed Res
and me down the winding cobblestone path.

A distant, heavy thudding reached my ears. The repetitive cadence was familiar. It was the bite of steel into wood, the solid thud like a second heartbeat. I followed the sound down the curving path.

The thudding dulled as I approached, emanating from a plateau on the opposite side of the hill that mirrored the one Res and I had been working on. It was a small, personal training ground, with several posts for practicing sword fighting and hand-to-hand combat, a circle of packed dirt for sparring, and several targets set up for knife throwing, a favored skill of Trendellan soldiers.

Stripped to the waist save for a midriff-baring wrapped cloth, her hands wrapped to the elbows, stood Elkona Kura. Again and again, she struck one of the wooden posts, which had been padded with feathers and encased in cloth to soften the blows, though the princess didn't seem to care a bit about the pain. She swung with incredible power, her muscles rippling beneath tawny skin that gleamed with sweat.

The long braid of her hair, woven with beads of glass that glinted in the sunlight, bounced against her back with each strike. With a cry of frustration, she spun about, driving her armored boot against one of the pegs on the post, snapping it in two.

She panted, her shoulders rising and falling in quick bursts. The signet jade ring she'd worn on her hand now dangled from a silver chain around her neck.

Slowly, she turned to face me. Her expression was sharp as cut glass.

"Spying, Princess?" she asked.

My first instinct was to snap back at her, but I forced it down. Looking at Elkona was like looking in a mirror. She was angry and hurt and damaged, and she wanted to set the world on fire. Hot words would only fuel the flames.

"That was pretty impressive." I nodded at the broken training post. "You're quite skilled."

"I know." There was no haughtiness in her tone, only hard fact. "That still does not explain why you have come here."

"I heard a familiar sound." My eyes sought the glint of metal at her feet. Lying sheathed at the base of the post were two moonblades, the handles bone white, the curved blades masked. She must have switched to hand-to-hand combat before I'd arrived.

Her gaze followed mine, and she smiled dangerously, as if imagining what she could make those blades do to me.

"Whatever you feel about me, whatever you feel about Rhodaire, standing against this alliance will only hurt you and your people," I said softly.

Her hands curled into fists, her smile turning vicious. "How kind of you to tell me what is best for my people. If only your mother had had such concern for her allies. Perhaps then my family might yet live, and the Kovan Forest might still stand. Perhaps we might have even been friends, you and I."

"We still can be," I said, descending the short flight of stairs to the terrace. Res crooned, ruffling his feathers nervously as I stopped before Elkona. She towered over me, nearly as tall as Kiva, though she was all wiry muscle compared to Kiva's broad frame.

"Friends must trust each other," the princess replied. She had the voice of a snake charmer gone rancid, as if she might have once been able to talk a man out of coin and drink, but something had twisted and rotted.

"I could learn to trust you," I said. "In fact, I've been told I'm rather good at trusting people I shouldn't."

Her dark eyes evaluated me. The fire from before had vanished, replaced by an emptiness that sent a shiver skittering across my skin.

Without warning, she struck out, backhanding me across the face. The blow stung, pain radiating through my cheek and jaw. I tasted blood at my lip.

Res cawed loudly, his wings flaring wide. I threw up a hand, warning him away.

I'm fine, I told him. *Let me handle this.*

Unbothered by Res's response, Elkona considered me with a tilt of her head, as if waiting for me to turn tail and run. I didn't. I faced her, not raising so much as a finger to the spot of growing soreness on my face, and met her gaze.

A challenge sparked in her eyes.

I struck first, but she dodged with a spin, counterstriking. Knocking aside her punch, I barreled inside her guard, forcing her to stumble back. She spun with a kick to my head, but I ducked and stepped to her side, driving a fist into her unprotected ribs. She let out a hiss of pain laced with delight.

We were in the sparring ring now, hard-packed earth beneath our feet. Her hands were quick. Quick to strike, quick to retract, quick to block. All her motions flowed into one another, a steady stream of strikes and counterstrikes, ground given and ground gained.

I recognized early that she was trying to grapple with me. From what I knew, a lot of Jin fighting styles relied on using the enemy's strength against them. Avoiding her grip proved half the battle, knowing that if she got me to the ground, I was done for.

"You're better at this than I expected," she said through heavy breaths as I escaped her near hold.

I grinned. "I know a trick or two."

I made her pay for every missed hold, striking her ribs, her stomach, her back, until something closed around my wrist, jerking me to a halt. In one smooth motion, she had me on the ground, stray rocks digging into my back. My shoulder screamed in protest as her knee found my chest, driving the air from my already laboring lungs, and the hand on my wrist twisted painfully.

I struggled to dislodge her, but she weighed too much, and her position was too sturdy.

"I should snap it," she snarled at me, twisting my wrist harder.

The pain and lack of air made my vision blur and blacken. I felt the frantic thrum of Res's fear skittering along the line between us, and it took all my focus to hold him off.

"Go ahead," I wheezed. For a fraction of a section, surprise splintered through her ferocity. I forced more words out. "If it will help you heal, do it."

She recoiled as if my words had stung, but her grip didn't loosen. "It is no less than you deserve," she growled, and fear prickled in my chest.

Yet despite her words, she twisted no farther. Her grip

slackened just the slightest, and in that moment, I drove my hips upward and twisted, throwing Elkona off me. She let go of my wrist as she went tumbling to the ground.

I sat up, my wrist raw and aching.

She pushed herself to her knees, her chest rising and falling in a mirror of my own. My heart skittered wildly as I fought to regain my breath.

"I don't suppose you'd teach me that move?" I tried for a smile, but it made my cheek hurt.

To my surprise, she grinned.

A servant brought me ice for my bloodied lip, and though several spots of Elkona's exposed skin were turning purple with bruises, she didn't bother to tend to them. We sat at a small patio table, an assortment of fruits and spiced cakes shaped like flowers and leaves on a platter before us. The familiarity of the scene made my chest ache for home and the patio table I'd grown up eating breakfast at every morning.

Elkona sprawled in her chair, her posture lazy and unkempt, ignoring the bits of her braid that had escaped and now dangled in front of her face. She'd returned her ring to her left hand, and she spun it absently around her finger.

I tossed Res a piece of cake, which he gobbled down. Elkona watched him with barely concealed fascination.

"Want to touch him?" I asked.

Her brow rose, but she leaned forward, her hand

outstretched. Res waited until she was a split second from contact before snapping his beak. She hissed, drawing back.

"Res!" I snapped, and he huffed loudly. "I'm so sorry. He's still mad at you for the fight."

Elkona stared at Res for a moment, her lips parted, one hand clutched in the other. Then she tipped her head back and laughed. The sound was so uproarious, I couldn't help joining.

"Guild Mother save me, he is remarkable," she said as her laughter quieted.

"He is," I agreed.

The light faded from the princess's eyes, her mouth forming a firm line. "When Illucia attacked, I looked for them in the skies. Every day, I thought I would see them. I told my parents to wait. I told them Rhodaire would not forget us, that the crows would blanket the skies and our enemies would know only night."

My hand curled into Res's feathers.

"But they never came. Not when Illucia first struck, and not when they burned the Kovan Forest. Not when they landed at Glass Bay, forcing us to fight a war on two fronts. And not when they marched straight into the royal palace at Shalron and butchered my family, burning everything to ash."

An apology rose and died on my tongue. There were no words big enough for this. Jindae had been our closest ally, and my mother had abandoned them.

"I was at Glass Bay when they landed," Elkona continued. She set her forearm on the table, leaning over it. "I'd begged my father to let me fight, but he refused. So I snuck into a company heading west in response to reports of an impending naval attack. It is the only reason I was not killed with my family when they broke through our lines and marched into the capital.

"We were forced to surrender. I was taken as a prisoner of war, one of so many others." Her voice turned rough, but her eyes betrayed nothing of her pain. "They had no idea who I was, or I have no doubt they would have killed me immediately. Instead, they tortured me for information that I refused to give, carving into my skin a mockery of my people's traditions with a hot blade."

Her fingers strayed to the scars on her face and neck, and a gasp escaped before I could stop it. The marks were a crude representation of tama. She'd never gotten hers because she hadn't been sixteen when Illucia attacked.

"I gave them nothing," she said, her voice a stony growl. "With all the focus on Shalron, a group of soldiers from my battalion who knew I had been among them managed to free me." She sank back into her casual posture, her gaze settling on Res, empty once more. "And now here we are, and I have finally seen a crow."

It took effort for me to keep the burning tears at bay. I relished the sting along with the throbbing in my cheek and wrist and back where my shoulder had only begun to heal. They felt well deserved.

Several moments passed before I could respond. "I won't apologize on my mother's behalf, because no apology is enough. I don't know why she didn't send aid, and I'm ashamed to say that I never asked. My whole life, I thought of nothing but becoming a rider. I woke up with my lessons on my lips and went to sleep dreaming of them."

Those days felt so far away, though it had been only months since Ronoch.

"I thought that dream was dead until I found Res's egg," I told her. "Even now, it hangs in the balance, because hidden away inside Razel's castle are more eggs that she stole the night the crows were killed."

Elkona sat up. "There are more?"

I nodded. "I will stop Razel. I will rebuild my people's way of life. And I will do what my mother should have done from the start: I will be there for Jindae and the Ambriels and Trendell if they need it." I leaned across the table. "I cannot give you your life back, Elkona, but together, we can build a new one."

She regarded me silently, her fingers absently tracing the lines of scars on her face. Then a smile spread slowly across her lips, and she said, "My friends call me Elko."

I grinned, and she matched it.

"I like you, crow girl," she began. "But even if the Ambriellans are still interested and Trendell will reconsider, Jindae allying with you is not up to me."

"What?"

She rose, eyes set somewhere over my head. "Come with me."

Having been hoping to stay slumped in my chair for the foreseeable future, I reluctantly tossed my bag of ice on the table and stood. Elko led Res and me up to the main corridor, following it past the massive dining table laden with dinnerware and vases of colorful flowers in preparation for tonight's feast and around the corner to an expansive deck.

Auma and Kiva stood side by side, leaning on the railing and looking out over the city. Kiva said something under her breath that drew a silent laugh from Auma, the only indication the gentle shake of her shoulders.

Confusion warred with curiosity as Elko marched up behind them with as much finesse as a Korovi ice bear. "*Eena*," she said, and I started.

That term. It was an honorific in the Jin language.

Used to address an older sister.

Auma turned, her expression inscrutable. Beside her, Kiva's brow furrowed, uncertainty spreading like a growing fire. Auma said something back in quick, concise Jin too fast for me to follow, to which Elko shrugged and replied, her response hot and rough.

"Auma?" Kiva asked, her gaze jumping from one girl to the other. Mine followed, taking in the similarities I hadn't noticed before. The slim oval faces and the slope of their noses. Their sharp, dark eyes and the way they both stood as if before a mountain they expected to move.

"You're sisters," I breathed.

Elko flashed a grin, but Auma regarded me warily. Beside her, Kiva retreated a step. Auma's expression softened at the disbelief on Kiva's face. "I intended to tell you tonight."

Kiva shook her head. "I—Excuse me." She turned, striding for the nearest door.

Auma started after her, then stopped, as if the action had slipped through her careful control.

"Kiva!" I called, but she was already gone. I wanted to go after her, but I couldn't leave. Not until whatever this was had played itself out. Besides, she needed time. Forcing Kiva to face a problem immediately was a good way to make it explode.

Res? The crow was already moving, disappearing through the arched doorway Kiva had gone through.

Auma drew a slow breath and leveled Elko with an unreadable look.

"What? It is not my fault you had not told her yet," Elko said.

Auma said nothing, but I got the impression she intended to have a long conversation with her sister later.

Saints. *Her sister.*

"What's going on here?" I demanded. "I thought—" I hesitated.

"That my entire family was dead?" Elko asked. "Almost. As the heir, Auma was sent to Trendell at a young age for her protection when our parents began working to quell the civil war. She was raised here."

I stared uncomprehendingly at Auma. At the crown princess of Jindae, who had endangered herself as a spy in the Illucian capital, subjecting herself to the cruelties of the woman who had taken everything from her—her home, her family, her future. I'd barely survived a few weeks with Razel.

Auma had withstood years.

She regarded me with an imperious gaze, as if she could read every conclusion I'd reached by my eyes alone.

"My sister says you've earned her respect," Auma began. "You already had mine, but I agreed not to pledge Jin forces to your alliance unless my sister felt the same."

Elko slung an arm across my shoulders, nearly knocking me off my feet. "You were right. She has spirit."

Auma was silent long enough to make my stomach clench. Then she nodded. "Very well. Jindae will ally with Rhodaire."

TWENTY-ONE

I cradled a new hope inside me as I sought out Res. Auma and Elkona would support me in a second bid to form the alliance. Kiva had been right—this wasn't over yet.

I reached along the bond. It thrummed back reassuringly, leading me back to the pavilion and down toward the plateau Res and I had trained on. I expected Kiva but found a different familiar voice.

A spark of fury cut through my rising mood. I paused just around the bend of the path, pressing into the shadow of the hill.

"It's frightening when things are outside your control," Estrel said softly to Res. Between the strands of long grass reaching down from the hill, I could just make out the curve of the crow's feathers beside the scarred flesh of Estrel's arm. "My life has felt out of my control for months."

My nails dug into my palms. Out of her control? She'd chosen to leave Rhodaire. Chosen to leave me.

"Fear can do that to you." Estrel's voice was heavy. I opened my eyes. "I was afraid that when she saw me, she'd think me broken. And I was. I was supposed to be her strength. To be anything less in a time like that would have only hurt her more."

I imagined the days I'd spent curled beneath my covers. What would I have done if I'd known Estrel was just as shattered, just as ruined? Seeing her the other night had nearly destroyed me. Would it have been the last weight that dragged me down beneath the depths?

Res let out a soft coo and nudged Estrel's shoulder with the side of his beak.

"I know. I didn't want to hurt her either. But I was wrong to leave and wrong to think she couldn't handle it. We have to trust her to take care of herself. We owe her at least that."

I swallowed against the warring emotions gathering in my throat. The pain that fueled my anger refused to fade, but Estrel's voice, so full of guilt and longing, was familiar to me.

Res turned his head, peering at me through the foliage. Of course he knew that I was here. He felt me like I felt him. I felt the pulse of doubt, much weaker than before, and I felt it fade as I stepped out onto the path, meeting his gaze unwaveringly.

Estrel turned with him, her eyes widening a fraction. She stood, her hand on Res's shoulder.

"I'm sorry, Little Peep," she said, and I gritted my teeth at the nickname.

"Did you even care?" My voice broke. "Did you even think about me? About Rhodaire?"

"Every day." She stepped closer with the hesitance of a flighty crow. "I—" She squeezed her eyes shut as if fighting back things she didn't want me to see. Res nudged her arm, and she opened her eyes, peering down at him. She seemed to draw strength from him, her back straightening as she forced out a breath. "I couldn't save her, Thia. I tried. I tried, and I couldn't save her. I couldn't do anything. And afterward—" She lifted her hands, baring the scars that twisted along her skin. "I couldn't face you. I couldn't fail you too."

Every word she spoke wriggled beneath my skin, pooling cold and sharp in my stomach. She wasn't the only one who'd hidden herself away. The only one who couldn't face what remained of the world she'd loved.

"I'm sorry, Little Peep," she whispered again, bowing her head.

"It isn't your fault." The words came out surprisingly steady.

Estrel lifted her gaze, a tentativeness in it I'd never seen before. It made my chest ache, made my heart beat with a fierce, protective fury.

"Feeling that way wasn't your choice." Just like it hadn't been mine or anyone else's who struggled with depression. You couldn't just snap yourself out of it any more than you could mend a broken bone. It was a wound as real as the scars along her skin, and for those, I would make Razel pay. For so many things, I would make her pay.

"It doesn't make you weak or broken or anything less than," I said. "I'm just sorry it took me so long to tell you that."

I closed the distance between us, throwing my arms about Estrel's neck. She clasped me to her, the familiar strength of her embrace breaking down every wall I'd built, every ounce of pain I'd gathered inside myself, and washing them away.

"I'm just so glad you're here," I said softly.

"Me too," she said. "Me too."

A new kind of heat rose inside me, chasing away the last wisps of anger and betrayal.

This was the heat of mending. The heat of reforging.

Because this was real. This was happening. I had hatched a crow, I had helped it discover its powers, and I had brought it to the heart of this alliance, to the person who was always meant to be by my side.

"We'll make a formal request for a second meeting in the morning," Estrel said when I finished telling her about Elkona and Auma. "And I promise this time, I'll be there for you."

For the rest of the afternoon, Estrel helped me train with Res. She corrected his form, gave him pointers on techniques to try, and even reminded him that in addition to wings, he had this wonderful thing called a tail that was quite effective at providing direction.

There was a moment, as the sunlight glinted off the backs of his dark feathers, the sheer breadth and strength of his wings stealing my breath, where I felt outside myself. Like a spectator in someone else's dream. Except this was *my* dream. One I'd worked toward for a lifetime.

At last, I stood beside Estrel, training a crow I called my own.

I only wished Iyla were there to snap Res into shape each time he started to beg for a snack.

He appeared before us, claws outstretched, wings thrown back like a tapestry caught in the wind. He was no less majestic, no less artful in the way he landed. As he tucked his wings in tight, a flurry of adrenaline-laced excitement skittering down the bond, I grinned.

"You're perfect," I told him.

"What do you say to giving a little magic a try?" Estrel asked him. A flicker of unease crept down the cord, and Res shifted uncomfortably, digging his talons into the dirt. "I know. But with training, you'll learn to control it, and your fear." She reached out a hand, hesitating. Then she laid it on Res's beak. "Trust her," she said softly.

I laid my hand atop hers.

Res leaned into our touch, still for a single, peaceful moment. Then he stepped back, and the pulse of power rose beneath our hands. Energy roared to life around the bond as his wings lifted. The clear sky grew thick with mist that coalesced into heavy clouds, and the wind swept up to pull at my clothes and hair. Lightning crackled, splitting the sky with echoing booms of thunder.

Beside me, Estrel laughed. She spread her arms as the rain began to fall. I joined her, turning my face to the churning sky, relishing the rush of power undulating between Res and me and the feel of each cold, shocking droplet like a call to life.

Res released a piercing caw. A voice rose above the wind,

and then another. A crowd had begun to gather on the edge of the plateau above. They pointed at Res and gestured up at the sky, leaning close to be heard over the storm.

An idea struck me, and in an instant, I was on Res's bare back. He moved immediately, knowing what I wanted without me needing to ask. With a stroke of his wings, we were airborne. The storm unfurled around us as we rose.

More people gathered at the plateau's edge. I saw Caylus and Kiva, Auma and Elkona, Samra and—there. Queen Luhara emerged from one of the nearby corridors, her normally impassive face slack with wonder.

You are a tempest of lightning and thunder. You give me strength, and you will do the same for them.

I leaned close to Res, "Show them what you can do."

The storm erupted. Wind spiraled around us in a cyclone. The rain fell still, the droplets hanging midair. They turned first to ice, then mist. An inky shadow rose, swirling dark ribbons into the wind before dispersing, only to be replaced by tongues of fire. I could feel Res's concentration, his struggle for control as he reached out for one power and then the next. But he didn't falter.

He let the flames go and the shadows settle, let the rain fall and the wind quiet. Then he alighted effortlessly behind the growing crowd beside where Estrel had just arrived.

Queen Luhara stepped forward. "What is the meaning of this?"

"Your Majesty." I inclined my head. "I intended to submit a formal request in the morning for another meeting to discuss our kingdoms' alliance, but I never have been very good at political conversation. You were concerned about Res's abilities; it seemed more fitting to show you."

Res screeched again, flaring his wings to their full impressive width. Even in the dim light of the storm, they cast a shadow over the gasping crowd.

"The Ambriels are with Rhodaire," Estrel said with a nod to Samra, who returned it. "As is, recently, Jindae."

Queen Luhara looked to Elkona and Auma, who bowed their heads.

"I've learned from my mother's mistakes," I said. "She tried to close Rhodaire to the world, thinking that would keep it safe. But in the end, it only made us weaker. I want to be better than her. I want to *do* better. Let me show you that I can. Ally with us. Help us defeat Illucia."

The snap of Res's energy faded as he let the storm dissipate, his eyes returning to their normal gray as the sky outside thinned, blooming cobalt once more.

In the resounding silence, the air felt alive.

The queen surveyed us with scrutinizing eyes. Then she lifted her head, her strong voice carrying across the courtyard. "Trendell has been a nation at peace for as long as our history remembers. We have striven hard to remain neutral, to be a place of learning and growth, not destruction."

I stilled.

She inclined her head. "But we recognize that a change is upon the world. If we do not act, we will be acted on. Trendell will ally with Rhodaire."

I felt like a cloth someone had wrung dry, every ounce of emo-tion spent and gone. It left me feeling strangely light, as if a gentle breeze could carry me away. I'd be half-inclined to let it. After the queen had pledged Trendell to the alliance, we'd agreed to meet again the next morning to begin planning our defense. In the meantime, messenger birds were sent to Rhodaire as well as the soldiers waiting in the Ambriels and Jindae. One was even sent to Korovi in a plea for them to reconsider their position.

Then the courtyard emptied, leaving me alone with Kiva, Estrel, Caylus, and Res. I sprawled out in the grass, releasing a breath it felt I'd been holding for a lifetime.

"I can't believe it worked." My lips twitched, spreading into a grin. The feeling was infectious, matching smiles filling Estrel's and Kiva's faces.

"Well done, Little Peep," Estrel said, and my heart swelled.

TWENTY-TWO

I'd never seen such an amazing feast.

The long corridor table had been laden with food and drink for the second of the three Belin's Day feasts, from roasted lamb in a blackberry glaze to vegetables marinated in rosemary and oil and platters of fresh cheese and grapes. A three-tiered stand held everything from dark chocolate cake to creamy fruit tarts sprinkled with cocoa, and pitchers of wine sat beside jars of Rhodairen talcé. Vines of purple and white flowers wound up the table legs and draped across its surface, glowing in the light of hanging lanterns.

A deep, sonorous string instrument intertwined with a lively drumbeat from out in the courtyard, and the chatter of people hummed in the air. Res scurried from person to person, gobbling down treats and scraps and dropped morsels.

Caylus arrived late, his auburn curls tossed askew, his golden skin flushed as if he'd run up the compound's many stairs. He dropped into the empty seat across from me.

"Been out at more lectures?" I asked. He'd spent nearly all the time since our arrival down at the city's university.

"They're amazing," he replied, slightly breathless. His tunic pockets practically overflowed with trinkets. "I've been attending some on man-made materials, like the glass arrows the Illucians use. Did you know that different types of glass shatter with different sounds? They called it a resonant frequency, and—" He paused, realizing he'd begun to ramble, and I bit my lip to hold back a laugh. He smiled sheepishly. "Anyway, I'm working on a project I want to show you later."

"I'd love to see it," I replied, relishing in this familiarity in everything around me. The sights, the smells, the sounds—they washed over me like a wave of sunlight, warm and full. Weeks ago, this moment had seemed incredibly far away. This morning, it had seemed impossible. Now it didn't feel real.

I'd made it to Trendell. I'd forged an alliance with the other kingdoms. I had a crow whose power transcended any I'd ever seen before.

Now, I had a chance of protecting Rhodaire.

Tomorrow, we would begin planning. Tonight, I relished in the simple feeling of being alive.

I sat beside Elko, who was in the process of regaling me with a tale of how she'd once stolen the sword of a Korovi Miska warrior who'd come with a visiting ambassador. She was several cups of wine in, and her boisterousness had only grown.

"She found me in the palace courtyard cutting down moon-berry stalks," she exclaimed. "She was so angry, she challenged me to a duel. Apparently touching a Miska's sword is punishable by death."

I smirked, thinking of Kiva's run-in with Shearen back in Seahalla. She'd wanted to run him through for stealing Sinvarra.

Reflexively, I scanned the courtyard for her, but she still hadn't arrived. Auma was also missing. Caylus sat across from us, his head buried in an ancient-looking tome on glass working, and Estrel was deep in conversation with Samra, Aroch lounging across her shoulders.

"Anyway," Elko continued, "I thought my parents would talk my way out of it, but they made me fight."

"Did you win?" I asked.

She laughed. "I was soundly thrashed. I think I still have a scar on my ribs." She touched a spot on her side, looking far too wistful for someone describing an injury from a near-death experience.

A flurry of sharp whispers preceded Auma and Kiva stepping into the corridor. Though I couldn't make out a word they said, it was clear from Auma's mollifying gestures that she was trying to get Kiva to listen, and Kiva wouldn't even stop walking.

"The least your friend can do is hear my sister out." Elko's voice had settled into an uncharacteristic graveness. "Auma had her reasons."

I sighed. "And Kiva has hers."

She snorted, her lips curling wryly. "Is that not how it always goes?" She shook her head. "It is too easy to forget how to talk to one another."

"You're assuming she ever knew how," I muttered as Kiva broke away from Auma, leaving the princess behind. I set my talcé glass on the table, but it was as if Kiva could feel my intentions. She met my gaze from the far end of the table and shook her head. She didn't want to talk.

Spotting her, Aroch leapt down and scurried over to her.

All our lives, Kiva had put duty before all else. She'd spent years pursuing her mother's respect, honing herself into the weapon Captain Mirkova wanted—a shrewd, loyal, honorable weapon. Now she'd finally found something else she loved as much as being a guard, only to discover she'd been lied to.

It made my heart hurt.

Elko leaned forward, voice low. "Talking to people seems to be something you are good at. You seem to actually be friends with the murderous prince."

"Son of a murderer prince," I corrected, then winced. I didn't actually know if that was true. All I knew was that Ericen hadn't been involved with Ronoch or the demise of Jindae or the Ambriels.

Elko waved a hand, dismissing the distinction. "And what do you plan to do when you face the Illucian queen on a battlefield? Talk her into forgetting that your crows tore her family apart? Forgive her and convince her to be friends?"

"No." My hand closed around my glass. I could never forgive her. Not after what she'd done. "I intend to make her pay."

"How?" Elko pressed, leaning closer.

"What do you mean?"

"She killed my parents. My brothers. My friends. She burned my kingdom down and stole children from the ashes, turning them against their families, their nation. And still she strangles what little life remains. The effects of her actions will be felt for generations." A dark fire glinted in the princess's eyes. "She deserves to suffer as we have suffered. She deserves to die. Slowly."

That quiet, burning heat in my veins stirred in response to Elko's words. It riled and rose, and I closed my eyes against the memories of blood and fire that came with it, letting the familiar pain wash over me.

You want revenge, Ericen had said. *You have every bit the potential to become a monster as I do.*

A chill prickled at the back of my neck. Was that the Sella side of me that wanted that? Estrel had said I wasn't one of them, but that thought did little to comfort me. If my thirst for blood and revenge didn't come from my Sella side, then that only meant it was me.

I heard Elko lean back in her chair and opened my eyes to find her downing her wine. She slammed the empty cup on the table. "If I get the chance, I will extract every drop of blood owed from her body before I kill her. She will regret ever stepping foot in Jindae."

Those words were a promise, and I believed them.

So much death. So much destruction.

And only more to come.

After dinner, I left Res asleep beside Caylus as he stroked the crow's head and followed the winding stone path down to the cells, a slice of chocolate cake in hand. My conversations with Elko and Auma turned over in my head as I spiraled back through memories in Illucia. Memories of Ericen fighting Razel in my place, of him letting me fill a box with pastries to the brim, of him standing in the stables, his forehead pressed against the night-black face of his stallion, Callo.

Whatever everyone else believed, Ericen was not my enemy. I was sure of it.

And now, surrounded by my allies in celebration, I'd felt like something was missing. Someone. I wanted Ericen on my side, *by* my side, in moments like these and through whatever we faced next.

I'd just reached the plateau below and started for the cells when a searing orange light washed over the courtyard. Someone screamed, and I whirled, dropping the plate as my hand went for my belt knife.

Atop the highest plateau beside the main complex, fire cut across the grass, eating its way through plants and wood and stone alike with an unnatural ferocity.

I felt Res come alive in a panic. Fear thundered through our bond as he sought me.

Armor up! I screamed down the cord even as I sprinted back up the stairs. Monks swarmed alongside me as council members and dinner guests rushed past us away from the fire.

The flames licked along the outermost building, the stone crumbling like paper into ash. It was the same as the fire that'd burned Cardail, the same that'd torn through Aris on Ronoch.

The dining corridor was in chaos. Whoever had started

the fire hadn't come alone. Elkona and Samra dueled some-one, Auma engaged with another alongside Kiva. Estrel and Res fought beside each other, his metal wings flashing like knives as they cut and slammed into bodies. Two monks rushed the king and queen inside.

I recognized these people. They had kingfisher tattoos on their arms.

These were Malkin's mercenaries.

Rain, Res. We needed those fires out.

Res dove forward, slamming his head into a mercenary and knocking him hard into a pillar at his back. His head came away bloody as he crumpled to the ground. The crow was beside me the next moment as clouds swallowed the starlight.

Rain fell in a downpour over the flames, hissing as it struck. Then something flashed at the corner of my eye. The scream had no sooner formed in my throat than it died as the arrow plunked harmlessly off Res's armored body. The archer who'd fired it gaped at the uninjured crow. Then I was beside her, drawing a line up the side of her arm with my knife. She dropped the bow with a yell, stumbling back—and straight into Elko's incoming attack.

The archer dropped, and for an instant, I stared at the blood blooming at her side where Elko's moonblade had slashed deep, at the yawning emptiness in her green eyes. Then someone jos-tled me from behind. I lurched forward, seizing the bow from the ground and a handful of arrows, and came up beside Elko.

"Have you seen Caylus?" I asked.

She deflected a knife strike. Then a metal wing curled

around us, blocking a sword a second before Res slammed the mercenary back.

"Toward the fire!" Elko yelled. Then she was at Auma's side.

Res and I pushed toward the edge of the corridor where the flames had been reduced to wisps. A man stumbled back, clutching his jaw. Behind him, Caylus spun, driving his elbow into a second attacker's sternum.

Then something snapped through the air. It struck Caylus in the back, sending him to his knees with a cry. A line of red traced down his exposed skin.

Malkin stepped forward. I nearly stumbled as I stopped running. He couldn't be alive—I'd seen the ocean take him.

The copper-haired crime lord grinned down at Caylus with all the menace of a rabid wolf. He raised his whip.

In a breath, the scene played out before me: the opening between Caylus and one of the men as I nocked my arrow; the choice between putting an arrow in Malkin's leg or in his chest; the reminder that my mercy was what had brought Malkin here. What had caused this battle to begin with.

I would not make that mistake again.

I loosed. The arrow slammed into Malkin's chest. He dropped to the ground, his men turning too late to help him. Caylus drove his fist into one's nose, breaking it. Then two monks were there, detaining them, and the last of the fire flickered and died.

Caylus stood panting like a wild animal, his hands closed tight into fists. Res rushed to him, cooing as his armor faded back to feathers and he nudged Caylus with his beak. I slid past them to Malkin, who clutched at the arrow in his chest, blood flecking his lips as he coughed for air he couldn't get.

Even dying, he grinned at me. Blood coated his teeth. "Razel didn't—" He coughed again. "Didn't think you had it in you."

"That's what she doesn't understand," I told him. "I'll do anything to protect the people I care about."

He laughed, a wet, wheezing sound. "And you almost succeeded."

The words came out with a final breath, and Malkin fell still.

Almost? I looked to Caylus, but his jade-like eyes were only for Malkin. I spun, taking in Res, then Estrel, Samra, Kiva, Auma, even Elko, who'd cornered the last of the mercenaries. All here, all okay.

My eyes went toward the prison cells down below. "No."

I bolted across the courtyard and down the stairs. The monks outside the building had gone to help in the fight, but two had remained behind inside. They lifted weapons as I bounded inside.

"Open the prince's cell!" I ordered.

They didn't hesitate. One slammed a key into the lock, wrenching the door open. My bow dropped to the ground with a clatter.

The cell was empty. A smoking hole gaped in the back wall. Malkin's attack had been a distraction.

Ericen was gone.

Pandemonium flooded the grounds. Small groups of soldiers traversed every path, and monks slipped by in the shadows, searching every inch of the hill. They poured down into the city, lights filling the night sky like fireflies as they knocked on every door.

I left it all behind. Singed grass crunched underfoot as I curved around the edge of the outer building with Res at my side, the note I'd found in Ericen's cell clutched in my hand. Its words replayed in my mind.

> *Thia dear,*
>
> *I have a theory. Do you want to know what it is?*
>
> *I think you care about my son.*
>
> *I've witnessed what you're willing to do for the ones you care for. Follow the instructions contained in this letter. Do it now. If you don't, Ericen will die at sunrise.*
>
> *I told you caring is a weakness.*
>
> *Queen Razel*

Armed with my black gold bow and arrows, Res and I made for the back of the palace compound. We slowed before a small, ornately gilded shrine, its walls painted a muted spring green. It rested in the center of a ring of stones that each weighed more than me and cast long shadows across the blackened garden surrounding them.

Razel had said this would be here.

Carved into the building's dark wood door was a symbol I recognized from *Saints and Sellas*: two straight, ridged horns, like notched spears, connected by a curve.

An aizel's horns.

"Sellador," I breathed. The lost Sella kingdom's name felt like magic on my tongue.

I brushed my fingers over the carving. The world lurched. The shadowy greens and blues of the moonlit night flared into bright tones of emerald and sapphire beneath a noonday sun. Voices echoed, sharp and heated and familiar.

I turned, my head spinning, and the world teetered and blurred. Res was gone. In his place stood Estrel and my mother, so much younger than I remembered. They passed without seeing me, stopping before the shrine. The edges of their Corvé tattoos gleamed against their brown skin in the bright sunlight.

They were arguing about something, though their voices sounded like someone talking underwater. The vision shuddered as my mother's fingers brushed the Sella symbol on the wood. Her fingers curled into a fist.

In a burst of light, the vision came apart at the seams. I stumbled, and Res let out a low cry as he appeared at my side, holding me steady. Air rushed into my lungs as I breathed quick and deep, trying to clear the last of the receding fuzziness from my head.

The vision had felt so real, just like the one I'd had the day I left

Rhodaire, when I'd touched my mother's headstone. Were they a result of the magic line we'd shared? Was our power connected?

"My mother," I said breathlessly to Res. "She was here."

Res rustled his wings, a thrum of reassurance pulsing down the bond, followed by a sense of urgency. I drew a sharp breath, straightening. He was right. Ericen was in danger. Still, I hesitated at the doorway, knowing I risked myself by doing this. Going after him was a gamble, but leaving him felt like letting Razel win. The only reason Ericen was in this mess was because he'd wanted to help me. If I left him behind, what kind of leader was I?

My mother.

My hands curled into fists at the thought. If I left him behind, I would be no better than her—abandoning the people who trusted her. I would not do the same.

"Let's go." I pushed open the door, entering the shrine. The inside was bare, save for a replica of the front door on the far side.

That strange connection that'd tugged at me in Terin materialized again, as if it'd just been waiting for me to remember it. It felt like a rope pulling at the center of my chest, demanding that I follow.

I tried the handle of the door, but it wouldn't turn. What had Razel told me to do? Above the door, the same symbols had been carved into the wood. I pressed two fingers to the Sella symbol and, feeling foolish, commanded the door open.

The symbol began to glow like trapped moonlight fighting to escape. I stepped back. Then the symbol flashed, the door rocking in its hinges, before fading back to wood.

The door clicked open.

The meaning behind that small sound struck me like a blow. Razel's letter had said only a Sella could open the door. She'd claimed it would lead me to a road. A lost road that only one with Sella blood could find.

Hearing Ericen say it had been one thing. Seeing the truth of it for myself was another.

Taking a slow, calming breath, I stepped through.

TWENTY-THREE

R azel had said the door would lead to a road. She hadn't said it would look like this.

It was like I was still stuck in the vision, the world warping around me as if I were looking at it from underwater. Colors shifted in undefined shapes, occasionally sharpening into something recognizable: a soldier knocking on a door; a group of revelers staggering by, their laughter warped; a tall, dark-leafed tree.

I looked down at the path and immediately wished I hadn't. What felt like hard stone beneath my feet was nothing but solidified air, like a wind current woven into a walkway barely wide enough for me to cross. And below it, the world twisted and turned, flashing bits of color and images.

Res made a soft sound behind me, and I felt the brush of his beak against my back. This was magic unlike anything I'd ever seen, and yet I knew it. Shadow crows could bend space in ways we didn't fully understand. It was how they blended into shadows, sliding through them to travel from one location to the next in an instant. The most powerful of them could take their riders along, and Lady Kerova had once described the disorienting rush of images and sound that accompanied the journey.

But she hadn't mentioned a road.

Was this how Malkin and his mercenaries had reached Eselin?

A door identical to the one back in the shrine waited ahead on a ledge of packed earth. I let out a relieved breath when I reached it and pressed my hand against the Sella symbol, demanding it open. Like before, it came alight, the door shuddering and releasing.

I pushed it open and stepped through.

My apprehension plummeted as the door revealed another small, empty shrine, every bit the same as the one I'd left. The only difference was the temperature, the air here crisper, colder, and...fuller? It felt charged, like the shifting air above a crackling fire.

I shut the door behind Res and approached the one on the far side of the shrine. Pushing it open, I stepped into lush green grass up to my knees. To my right, the field extended to the horizon. To my left—my breath caught, and I fell still.

The Wandering Wood sat before me.

The colorful forest spilled like dye across the gently sloping hills. A full moon hung heavy in the starlit sky, shining as bright as a gemstone to illuminate my way. A breeze whispered through the grass, the sound of the rustling stalks soft as the slide of smooth silk. I ran my hand through the grass—it felt like brushing air.

"It's real," I breathed. "I think—Res, I think we're in Sellador."

That passage had been a true Sella road, connecting two locations. And somewhere in the forest before me, Razel held Ericen hostage. Still, I hesitated. According to the stories, I had only until dawn to escape the wood, or I'd be trapped until the next full moon.

I stepped into the wood.

A howl went up, a ghostly sound carried by the wind that sent a shiver running through me. An answering howl followed, nearer than I would have liked.

Res pressed up beside me, tense as marble. He didn't like this any more than I did.

"This way," I said, following the pull. The place of light and color that I'd read of was not what lay before me. The pure dark brown of the thick, proud trees in *Saints and Sellas* looked gray and thin in real life, the leaves crunching underfoot like delicate bones. The air felt stiller and thicker than a humid Rhodairen summer day, yet drier than the desert.

This was a washed-out version of the dreamland I'd seen in the tome.

It felt like it was dying.

Res trilled quietly, the sound a soft rasp yet somehow still too loud for the silent forest.

"I'm aware it's creepy," I grumbled back, and the wood swallowed my voice. The uneasy atmosphere made my skin crawl and my muscles tense. Part of me wanted to turn and run. I pressed on.

Finally, the tree line broke, granting me entrance into a large glade. The air here felt thickest of all, each breath an effort to draw in and push out. Fog blanketed the clearing, hanging low and heavy as overripe fruit.

The mist drew together in a shudder, and then all at once, it dispersed, scurrying like shadows before the sun. It revealed a circular pond on the far side. The water was a pale gold, as if lit from below by a thousand candles. At the center sat a small island connected by several thin land bridges, a single tree standing at its center.

Bright silver and gold leaves hung heavy on branches thicker than my torso. Gnarled roots lifted and fell through the earth like the body of a snake, reaching out of the edges of the island into the glow of the lake.

At the base of the tree sat a bound figure, his head drooped. Ericen.

Shearen stood with a sword to his once friend's throat.

Razel stepped up to the edge of the island, flanked by five Vykryn in black leather. The queen's own uniform was lined in gold, her hair woven back in a tight braid. A simple, gilded circlet sat over her brow, the edges of her moonblades reaching up over her shoulders.

Her smile was a sharp knife. "Hello, Thia dear."

Twin emotions stampeded through my veins: a vicious fury

entwined with icy hate. Lightning snapped from Res's beak, striking the earth a foot from where Razel stood and sending up a shower of dirt. She didn't so much as blink. Thunder echoed overhead, drowning the hard beating of my heart.

Razel laughed. "Oh, you want to play with magic?"

Figures moved in the shadows of the trees. Tall, lean, and hooded, they emerged from behind the drooping branches all around the clearing, surrounding us.

One stepped up beside Razel, lowering its hood.

Unnatural golden eyes stared out from a gaunt, angular face too sharp and hard to be human, and a strange glow emanated from beneath his pale skin as if moonlight were trapped beneath it. An immeasurable sense of age surrounded him like a cloak.

A Sella.

He lifted one long-fingered hand. A flame ignited in his palm.

"No." The word fell useless from my lips. This was the figure I'd seen on Malkin's retreating ship. The one who had truly set those strange, all-consuming fires.

Ericen's words came flooding back.

The Sellas are still alive. Or at least one of them is. He's been aiding my mother, perhaps since she destroyed the crows.

This was the Sella who had set fire to Aris on Ronoch.

Even with the traitors who had aided Razel, even with the elite Illucian archers and limited targets, Ronoch had still seemed impossible.

Now it made sense.

This was how the fires had erupted into infernos all at once. This was how they'd burned through stone and metal and bone.

Razel had been working with him from the beginning, and now somehow, there were more of them.

The queen spread her hands in a magnanimous gesture. "Allow me to introduce my friend, Valis. I'm sorry to say he wants you and your family dead every bit as much as I do."

For the war. For locking them away. Everything Estrel had said was true.

"The prison your family trapped them in has been weakening. At first, only Valis was strong enough to emerge, but it's weak enough now that others have joined him. This is only the beginning." Razel turned to the strange tree. It pulsed with an unnatural golden light that filled the air with power, making it difficult to breathe. The world swayed, and a dark figure moved in the light.

The tree was the prison. This was where the other Sellas had come from—and there were still more emerging.

"My, how terrified you look," Razel mused. "I'd almost forgotten how much I enjoyed it."

My throat had gone dry, my hand seeking my bow. The clearing was big enough for Res to take flight, but escaping would mean leaving Ericen behind to die.

I looked at the prince, his dark hair casting shadows along his face. In sleep, he looked peaceful in a way he never did when he was awake. As if this were the only time he could bring himself to let down his guard.

In sleep and around me.

Ericen was my friend. With the way my heart beat wildly against the idea of leaving him behind, I knew he might be more.

Even without that, we needed him. He had vital information on Illucian battle tactics and insights into his mother's mind the rest of us didn't.

I wouldn't leave him.

"You really do have a bad habit of trusting people you shouldn't," Razel said with a smile.

I shivered. I'd forgotten how cold that smile could make me feel. How much I hated it.

She looked as comfortable as a queen at court, as if she already owned these woods and the people in it. As if she already owned me.

Her eyes alighted on Res, a hungry, possessive look filling them. "You want to save everyone, and in the end, it's what will get you killed." She stepped aside, revealing a ragged-looking man, a scowl on his cracked lips.

Onis.

I stared at the crewman, my mind turning and turning and turning. We'd left him on Samra's ship. How—?

"That rebel filth's crew is dead." Razel's words struck my thoughts still. "All save this one, who told me a very interesting story."

Everything inside me went cold. "No," I whispered, as if that simple word could change the past. They were gone, all of them. Talon, with his joyous laugh. Darya, whose warm voice wove worlds. Luan, who'd saved Kiva's life.

"I've known about the Jin forces gathering outside of Shalron for weeks, but I was content to let them play at rebellion for now. Until Onis told me about the alliance forming against me."

Indignation hardened her words, as if the idea of her conquered people turning against her offended her as much as it infuriated her. She smiled her knifelike smile. "By now, the contingent of soldiers I sent to Ira should have killed every last rebel."

Pure horror twisted my gut, and I backed into Res's chest, the urge to run from what she'd said, from what was happening nearly overwhelming me. This couldn't be true. The Jin forces dead?

"And the most interesting story of all?" The queen ran a finger along the length of one moonblade handle. "That rather than turn my traitorous son aside, rather than kill him as you should have, you kept him with you. You advocated for him. You even seemed to care about him."

"You promised me a reward," Onis growled, laying his hand on the queen's shoulder.

She stilled. My warning died in my throat as Razel spun, freeing a moonblade from her back and slashing it across Onis's throat in one smooth movement.

He gaped, hands clutching at his neck, trying to stem the flow of blood. But it ran through his fingers in rivulets of red, streaming down his chest and arms and staining the grass a dark, muddy brown. The gurgling noises scratching from his ravaged throat made me gag, and I turned my face away as he collapsed into the earth.

"I won't come with you," I said.

She laughed, the sound as cutting as I remembered. "Tell me, what progress have you made with your crow? How fast can his winds push aside a glass arrow?"

One of her archers aimed a translucent arrow at Res's chest.

"I can make more of him. All I need is you."

On reflex, my bow was in my hand, an arrow nocked and aimed at the archer's chest. "Move, and I'll put an arrow in your heart," I warned. But it was pointless. The archer didn't even blink. She would die if it was required of her, and Razel would let her. And that still left the second one.

Be ready to armor up, I warned Res.

"She is meant to be ours," Valis said in a low voice.

The humor turned to ice in Razel's eyes. "And she will be, when I'm finished with her. We had a deal."

"Our deal had an expiration."

Razel shifted, her bloodied fingers curling tighter about the moonblade. Was that fear in her eyes?

"Let me handle this," she hissed.

Res let out a low call. Images of lightning and hail flickered through my mind. We'd practiced enough with wind that he might be able to turn the arrow aside fast enough.

My fingers tightened about my bow, the string digging into the leather of my gloves.

Beneath the tree, Ericen stirred. He blinked slowly as he woke. I stepped toward him, then forced myself still.

Razel's eyes widened with delight at my concern. "Or I can kill the prince."

"What?" Shearen lurched forward. "You said you'd pardon him. You can't—" He fell silent at a look from Razel, her expression dangerous.

Ericen had gone still, assessing the situation carefully. "You don't have to do this, Shearen," he said carefully. "I know you.

I know what you've done in pursuit of becoming Valix, and I know it was never what you wanted. Your father's approval, my mother's respect—it's not worth this! I'm not the only one who thinks so. Illucia is tired of this fight. It's gone too far."

"Too far?" The words bubbled out of Razel in a laugh. "Oh, Eri. I knew you were weak, but not like this. You've betrayed your people, and now you seek to bring them down with you?"

Ericen pulled against the ropes. "You've lost your mind," he snarled. "You've thrown our kingdom's future into this point-less war for what? Revenge?"

"Yes!" The queen rounded on him. "Is that not a good enough reason for you? You think I should let them live happily and peacefully after what they did to me? To my family?"

"You've already taken enough from them!"

Razel laughed. "It will never be enough!"

"Mother—"

"Enough!" she screamed. The wood swallowed the word, drowning the air in silence. Razel's chest heaved, her hands drawn into tight fists. "You weren't there! You didn't see their bodies torn to bloodied ribbons. You weren't forced to watch!" Her pale skin had turned white as ash. "You didn't have to listen to the people you loved beg for their lives."

I thought of the dead mercenary in the dining corridor. Of her quiet, lifeless eyes and the blood on Malkin's lips. My stomach turned.

"Eri," Shearen began, but Razel cut him off.

"You aren't worthy of the Illucian crown," she said, voice

utterly void of emotion. "You never were." She didn't look at Shearen as she spoke. "Kill him."

"No!" I lurched forward.

Valis lifted his hand, spreading the fire between his palms like a string.

Thunder boomed, and the sky split open.

Lightning erupted in the clearing. It struck one of the Vykryn and sent the others scurrying for cover. Where it singed the grass, flames leapt to life in its wake, casting the glade in a deathly orange glow.

My arrow struck the rope binding Ericen to the tree. It snapped, and he leapt to his feet. One of the Vykryn released an arrow, but Res's wind lashed it away even as his feathers turned metallic. Ericen seized an arrow from the second archer's quiver and drove it through her neck. He seized her bow, nocking an arrow and aiming at Razel.

"You've gone too far." Razel's voice trickled out from the darkness. "You've betrayed your kingdom."

Ericen's face was a cold, rigid mask, the light of the full moon casting sharp shadows across it. "I'm going to save my kingdom. From you."

Razel's snarl mixed with the ring of metal as she drew her moonblades. "You've let this foolish girl corrupt your mind."

I expected Ericen to snap back, to defend himself as he always did. Instead, he turned away, his bright gaze falling on me, and his eyes widened. "Thia, behind you!"

I whirled. At Res's back, a hooded Sella had emerged, daggers of ice in his hands. I caught his first attack with the limb of my bow, dodging the second. As I spun out of the way, Res released a bolt of electricity at the Sella.

A wall of earth rose before him in defense, exploding as the lightning made contact. A second Sella stepped up beside the first.

My mind raced.

Shroud us, Res.

The tree's shadows enveloped us. I'd meant for him just to conceal us, but I felt the ground ripped away beneath my feet. The world turned, blurring to black. A second later, it re-formed. Except we were no longer at the edge of the wood.

Res had teleported us to the glowing tree.

The portal's light had changed, growing darker, forming shapes with heads and arms and legs. It was the doorway between our world and the prison—and it was opening. It brightened in a burst of light. Then a hand reached out.

"Destroy it, Res!" I yelled, lifting my bow to catch the blow of a Vykryn's sword. Wind funneled past me, striking the soldier in the chest and sending him flying into the pond. I turned, nocked an arrow, and released it at Valis. He discharged a flame that incinerated the bolt in a flash, then moved to Razel's side, defending her.

Confusion pulsed down the cord. Res didn't know what he was doing any more than I did. But Estrel had said that the shadow crow's power had created that prison. Maybe Res's could reseal it.

The flames sparked by Res's lightning licked around the far side of the island.

When we teleported, it felt like space opening, I told him. *Try closing the space in the tree.*

Resolve pulsed through the bond. I fell back, bow lifted to defend him. Ericen moved to my side. He'd taken down the remaining Vykryn, leaving only Shearen and Razel among the Sellas.

"Stop them," Razel ordered.

Shearen didn't move. He was staring at Ericen as if he'd never seen him before. But Valis stepped forward, the other Sellas around the edge of the clearing closing in.

Power burst free of Res, lightning erupting in the sky. Valis's fire snuffed out like a candle flame. Something pulled at me along the cord, Res's power tugging at me as he consumed massive amounts of it.

The tree's light flickered.

"No!" Razel screamed. The air shifted, as if space were collapsing in on itself. The island shivered and fell still.

The light went out as the prison doorway closed.

I seized Ericen's hand, pulling him close to Res. Exhaustion echoed through our bond.

"I know, I know," I whispered. "But you can do this."

The shadows curled around us. Razel lurched. Then the darkness whisked us away.

We tumbled out of the shadows just beyond the forest's edge. Res stumbled, letting out a weak caw. This was as far as he could take us.

Ahead, the shrine sat bathed in a pool of moonlight, the door wide open.

"This way!" I yelled. We sprinted for the shrine. Inside, the second door was already open, the strange road visible beyond.

I shoved Ericen in after it. "Don't look down. Don't step off the path."

"What path?"

"Go!"

Ericen lurched forward, Res and I on his tail. The same disorienting feeling as last time threatened my senses, but I pushed forward, and we burst into the Eselin shrine. I paused, turning back.

"I know you're tired," I told Res, "but we can't let them follow us. Can you collapse this like you did the prison opening?"

Res trilled softly. I backed away, feeling his power surge. Exhaustion pulled along the cord, then something else. I lurched slightly, gasping, and Ericen reached out to steady me.

It felt like the opposite of that day in Caylus's workshop when I'd pushed the magic free of Res. This felt like he was pulling *from me*.

Beyond the road and through the open door, the Sellador shrine began to shudder. The air shifted. The ground churned, the stone of the building crumbling. Then it collapsed.

The road dissolved in a flash of light. When my vision cleared, only stone filled the doorway we'd come through.

I fought to catch my breath, a new tiredness rolling through me that mirrored Res's own.

"We can't rest," I said. "We have to warn everyone about Razel."

Outside, voices echoed from the upper corridors. How long had we been gone? They would still be searching for Ericen, sure the prince had escaped for some nefarious purpose.

I stepped forward and nearly stumbled, but Ericen was there. A Jin soldier spotted us, calling for help. Another soldier jogged down the hill, but a second form shot past them both.

I caught Kiva before she could knock me to the ground, barely registering her touch before she'd pulled back, demanding, "Where in the Saints' name have you—" She stopped, having noticed Ericen.

His gaze landed on Kiva, and he smirked. I barely had enough time to step in front of her, digging in my heels to keep her from shoving past.

"What are you doing here?" she demanded of him, then to me, "What is he doing here?" Her voice was wild, her eyes alight like the glint of flame against steel.

"Not now, Kiva," I said, my voice dead. "I need to talk to everyone. Now."

Kiva shook her head and kept shaking it, and it was only then that I realized how pale she was, how tired looking.

Unease crept up the back of my neck, my gaze lifting to the compound at my back. It was deathly quiet.

"Kiva, what's going on?"

Her lips parted to respond, then snapped shut. She was still shaking her head.

There was something sprinkled across her uniform. Pinpricks of red, like bloody mist.

I swallowed hard. "Kiva?"

"One of the mercenaries escaped," Kiva said, her voice hoarse. "He attacked Elkona."

TWENTY-FOUR

The world turned. I stared at Kiva, not really seeing her, a single word resounding in my head like a funeral drumbeat. *Dead dead dead dead dead dead.*

My jaw worked, but I didn't have the breath to form words.

Distantly, I heard Ericen ask, "What happened?"

"Don't pretend you don't know," Kiva snarled. She lurched forward.

The motion snapped me from my daze. I slipped reflexively between them, barely aware of my body moving. Kiva's heat, her fury, pressed against me, suffocating. I felt dizzy.

"He's been with me the entire night," I said.

"That doesn't mean he wasn't involved in the attack," Kiva said. "Couldn't you tell during the fight, Thia? They were *targeting* her. He probably fed them information! How else did they know who she was, that she was here? He's the reason she's barely holding on!"

"Right. And then I stuck around to take the blame in hopes of being executed."

Ericen's flippant tone sparked something inside me. I shoved him back a step, surprise flitting across his face. "This isn't a joke! I don't know how to convince them you weren't involved."

"Are you so sure I wasn't?" he sneered. "It is, after all, in my blood. To lie and trick and betray."

"You were trapped in a prison cell and then with me the entire night. I know you weren't involved. I—" I stopped, facing Kiva. "Did you say barely holding on? Is Elko still alive?"

"For now," she replied grimly.

The mercenary had missed Elkona's heart, but only just.

We'd joined Auma in the apothecary's quarters, where she sat beside her sister's bed, grim-faced and with all the coalesced tension of a storm ready to break. Her shirt was stained red with the mercenary's blood. Apparently, she'd cut him down a second too late.

Elko was pale, her face wrought with pain even in her sleep.

Kiva rubbed Auma's back, the motions gentle. Whatever distance had grown between them when she'd learned of Auma's deception, it was gone now.

Ericen had stayed under guard, though I'd convinced them

to put him in a spare bedroom rather than back in the cells. Or rather, I'd ordered them to, and, surprisingly, they'd listened.

"Can you heal her?" Auma asked hoarsely.

"I don't know," I said. "Res's sun crow powers aren't as strong as his others. He should be able to help, but he won't be able to restore her entirely."

A soft golden light rose from Res's feathers. It flickered as he struggled to maintain the power. He bowed his head over Elko's wound, letting the light wash over her.

When he stepped back, Auma adjusted the bandages carefully on Elko's shoulder, revealing a wound that looked days old. A more experienced sun crow would be able to restore Elko's lost blood and knit muscle and blood vessels back together, but with Res's help, she'd live.

I shook my head, standing so quickly, I knocked my chair back. "I'm sorry. This is all my fault."

"What are you talking about?" Kiva stood too, her expression clouding.

"Onis betrayed us," I told her. "He told Razel about the alliance, and now the rebels in Ira are dead."

Auma's head snapped up.

I kept talking, knowing if I stopped, I'd never say the words. "He must have told her the Jin princess was in Eselin too. And the mercenaries, they came through the road."

"Slow down, Thia." Kiva placed a hand on my shoulder. "What in the Saints' name are you talking about? What road?"

Taking a deep breath, I told them everything.

By the time I'd finished explaining, Auma's expression had grown so grim, Kiva suggested I give her some space. I immediately sent a message to Queen Luhara and King Galren asking for an audience. Everyone needed to know what had happened.

Then I found my way back to my bed and climbed under the covers, shutting the world out. Res lay down beside the bed, one wing draped over me in comfort and protection, and in the darkness of my cocoon, I wept.

Samra's crew was gone. The Jin rebels were dead or captured. The murderous Sellas were free, and they were working with Razel to destroy my family, to destroy Res.

After all the work I'd done, after all the alliances I'd forged, none of it mattered.

We were hopelessly outmatched.

We could not win this war.

A dark cloud enveloped me, that familiar weight hanging a chain across my shoulders and about my neck, drawing tighter with each breath.

When my bedroom door opened, I didn't know how much time had passed since it'd closed. I recognized Kiva's steady stride and the clap of Sinvarra against her hip, but I didn't want to face her.

Res trilled softly, and then the covers were jerked off, flooding my eyes with light. I peered up at Kiva, her face a hard, pained mask.

"You're mad," I croaked.

"You're short," she replied. I blinked, and her brow rose. "Sorry, I thought we were stating the obvious."

I winced but clung to the opening she gave me. "I'm not short. You're just tall. And mad."

"And hungry. But there's a short, girl-shaped problem between me and the kitchen."

"I play this game with Res. Be better than the crow, Kiva." Res nipped at my fingers, and I snatched my hand away, sitting up.

Kiva half smiled, but it quickly died. "At least the pigeon doesn't lie."

"Omit occasional information," I corrected halfheartedly.

"Lie."

"Forget vital facts?" I tried, my guilt sinking deeper and deeper inside me.

Kiva raised an eyebrow, looking about as impressed as Estrel the first time I'd fired a bow.

I sighed. "I'm sorry, Kiva. I should have told you when I found the note. I knew what'd you say and—" I hesitated.

"And you didn't want to hear it," Kiva finished. "Because you knew I'd be right."

"I didn't know that," I snapped. "Ericen isn't a danger to me. He's—" I stopped, on the brink of saying something I wasn't quite sure I was ready to put into words.

Her expression darkened with each word until she looked ready to knock me upside the head. "He's dangerous, Thia!" She threw up her hands in frustration. "You trust too easily."

"And you don't trust at all! You didn't trust Caylus either.

And Ericen, he… Ugh, that's not what this is about! I'm trying to apologize."

Kiva drew a sharp, deep breath and let it out slowly. "Why do you think I'm here, Thia?" she asked through gritted teeth.

I deflated, the answer coming immediately. "For me."

"For you," she agreed. "So *let me* be here for you. You don't have to do this all alone."

"I know," I said softly, burying my face in my hands. "I ruined everything, Kiva. So many people are dead because of me, and now more will die."

She dropped onto the side of the bed, wrapping me in her arms. I leaned into her. "It isn't your fault," she said. "What Onis did is his responsibility, not yours. You can't let your guilt destroy you. You've worked too hard to get where you are, and I need you too much."

I held my breath, the familiar words I'd once spoken to her slowly working away at the coiled tension in my chest.

"You're my family, Thia, and I'll always be here for you," she said, and I held her tight. Res hopped to our side, his massive wings enfolding us in warmth and silk, and for a moment, I let myself believe that everything would be okay.

"You're my family too," I told her, lifting my head. "Which is why I need you to trust me. I know you don't like Ericen, but you also don't really know him. I do. Trust *me*, Kiva, even if you can't trust him."

She let out a heavy breath. "Fine. But if he so much as looks at you funny, I'm skewering him."

I grinned.

A message arrived from Queen Luhara that she'd convened a council meeting in an hour, and I tried to prepare myself to face my friends and all the people who'd placed their faith in me and tell them that it was all for nothing.

Kiva had gone back to sit with Elko and Auma, only after I'd promised her I wouldn't go back to sleep. Res, however, had made no such promises and promptly sprawled across the entire bed in a heap of slumbering feathers.

Feeling aimless and dreading the coming meeting, I followed the corridor around to Ericen's guarded room. He called me in when I knocked, ignoring the looks the guards gave me as I entered.

The prince stood by a row of arched windows on the far wall, looking out over the expanse of vineyards that blanketed the rolling hills at the back of the compound before they jutted sharply into the Calase Mountains.

"I never thanked you." He turned at the sound of my footsteps, his expression solemn. "Thank you for coming for me."

"Of course. I don't leave my friends behind."

He stepped toward me, and suddenly, it wasn't the looming meeting and threat of war that made my stomach flutter and my heart beat erratically. A gentle breeze tugged at my hair through an open window, soothing my hot skin. I tried to focus on its cool touch, but all I could think of was the disappearing distance between us.

When the prince slowed less than a hand's width away, I found my throat too dry to speak. A depthless intensity shone in his gaze, strong enough to hold me aloft if the floor dropped out beneath me.

The thought struck me still. I'd come after Ericen because he was my friend, because I'd abandoned him once before and I refused to do it again. But I'd known all along that wasn't the whole truth.

You cannot be afraid to see what you see.

There was a question in Ericen's blue eyes. Blue as the ocean bathed in sunlight, blue as the sky on a clear Rhodairen summer day—a sky I wanted so badly to fall into.

So I did.

My lips found his, soft and questioning at first. But when he tilted his head down to meet me, and I felt the urgency behind his touch, I let go and fell.

My hands were in his hair and at his neck, and I pressed up onto my toes to reach him. The rough calluses, earned from years of blood and steel, brushed across my face and along my neck with a quiet tenderness. I felt his fingers tangling in my curls, felt them tracing lines of fire across my skin. I lost all sense of time and place, of the loss and fear and pain, and of the future that likely held more of them all.

Then a gentle tug, like someone shaking me awake. Res pulled again along the cord, questioning where I was, what I was doing. A slight flush filled Ericen's pale skin as I pulled back, his fingers brushing mine.

I sent a reassuring wave back to Res, my cheeks burning.

Ericen smiled. "I've wanted to do that for a long time."

"Pretty sure I did it and you just followed along," I replied. His smile quirked into that one-sided smirk. I brushed the edge of his hand. "We're convening to discuss our next moves an hour from now. I want you to come with me."

That little furrow appeared in his brow. "Why?"

"Because if you can give the alliance helpful information, they might believe you're on our side." And maybe, just maybe, he could help salvage our situation. Whatever insider information he could provide on Illucian battle tactics and plans for their attack on Rhodaire might help us.

Ericen was silent. He returned to his spot at the window, eyes set on the landscape beyond. He'd broken from his mother's hold, and he'd turned his back on Illucia to help me, but he hadn't gone so far as to give up secrets and information that would work against them.

I stepped up beside him, waiting.

"I've spent so long trying to be who she wanted. Someone who would make her proud." He closed his eyes, letting out a slow breath. When he opened them again, he looked resolved. "It's time I did what's best for myself and for my people."

I squeezed his hand. "I'll be right here."

He clasped it back. "I know. Do you have a plan?"

I leaned forward against the window, focusing on the cool touch of the glass. "I think I've done enough damage," I replied. "Someone else will have a plan."

"I thought you didn't concede?" he asked, and the words pulled at the weight inside me. I'd said them to him the first time we'd sparred in Sordell; it'd been the first night I'd really begun to trust him.

"Stealing my lines is a cheap move," I murmured against the glass.

"You're not worth more effort in this state."

A smile tugged at my lips, the familiar banter filling me like the heat of a fire. I pulled back from the glass to look at him, and he stared back with an easy smile, the one that never failed to make me really, truly *see* him.

He was right. I couldn't walk away from this. I'd begun this fight, and now I needed to end it.

"You and Kiva have more in common than either of you know," I said.

He shrugged one shoulder. "I'm still better with a sword."

I laughed. Part of me would love to see if that was true; the other didn't want Kiva stabbing the boy I liked.

The boy I liked.

My cheeks flushed at the thought, and Ericen's sharp eyes didn't miss it, but he was mercifully quiet. I ordered tea, and we spent the rest of the time before the meeting just talking in a way we'd never done before. He told me about missing Callo, the stallion he'd left behind in Sordell, and how the horse had loved to go galloping in the rain. I talked about Caliza and what I'd give just to argue with her over something trivial if it meant being there with her.

When at last the meeting time arrived, I felt thawed, like my layers of guilt and grief had been sheared away by Kiva's tender strength, Ericen's stories, and Res's quiet contentment slipping down the line in soft waves.

After Ronoch, I'd been afraid to talk to people about the coiling snake and its unbearable weight. But in time, I'd shared with Kiva, and then Caliza and Caylus, and I'd walked myself out of the darkness that had engulfed me.

It was those relationships, those people, who made me strong, and they would do the same for this alliance. Razel might have magic on her side now, but we had four kingdoms united against her, inside information from Ericen, and a crow whose magic transcended any seen before.

I prayed it would be enough.

TWENTY-FIVE

Rather than meet in the throne room, we'd convened in the war room. A circular table surrounded a round platform in the center that bore an incredibly detailed map of the six kingdoms. The dark wood walls were lined with monks, one beside Kiva at Ericen's back to my left.

Estrel sat on my other side. After everything I'd learned, I'd expected to feel a rush of emotions. I didn't. I was just tired and a little hurt and far more unmoored than I'd ever felt. Like all the strings that had once held me fast to this world had been cut, and the place I found myself in now was something altogether new.

My world had changed so much the last few weeks.

When I reached the part in my story about Samra's crew and Onis's betrayal, the captain collapsed back into her chair, stunned.

Aroch, who perched on her shoulder, nudged her head with his, but she didn't respond. My throat began to close, and I held back the urge to break down into tears as I explained that the Jin rebels were lost, fighting my way through the rest of the story.

"Res and I closed the doorway, but Razel has six Sellas on her side," I concluded hoarsely, addressing Queen Luhara.

Her dark eyes were thoughtful, her fingers splayed across her mouth in contemplation.

Samra stood, Aroch clinging to her shoulder. Her good eye was rimmed red, but whatever tears she'd shed were gone. "So what you're saying is that we're hopelessly outmatched now?"

I flinched. With the loss of the Jin rebels and the addition of the Sellas to Razel's ranks, her strength rivaled ours. Even with Res, fighting this war would be a risk. These kingdoms had already lost so much; could they really be asked to lose more?

The captain's normally stony expression turned wary with doubt, and I knew she was thinking of her family back in Seahalla. She had already lost her crew; she wouldn't lose her family too.

My eyes unintentionally found Auma, who sat still and silent as a shadow. She'd missed cleaning a few flecks of blood from her jaw, and her dark eyes looked haunted.

"We can still win this fight." Estrel stood. "Now that Razel knows about the alliance, she'll have to gather more troops to counter us. It'll take time, and we can use that time to hone Res's magic."

"What good will one crow do us against an army of magical beings?" one of the council members asked.

"One crow with the power of eight," I said.

Samra crossed her arms like a soldier barring entry. "Even if Razel's attack is delayed, it won't be for long. And when it finally comes, one crow isn't enough, no matter how many abilities he has."

"You're underestimating Res's power," Ericen cut in, and I felt Res puff up, bolstered. "Illucia has faced the crows before. There's a reason my mother destroyed them before attacking Rhodaire."

"Why are you even in here?" Samra snapped back. "He shouldn't be witness to any of this."

I looked to Ericen, who hesitated. Would he fully turn against his kingdom?

He stepped forward, the monk stiffening behind him and Kiva's hand going to Sinvarra. But I moved aside to allow him next to me.

"I'm here to help you," he said. "I'll provide you with whatever information I can regarding my mother's armies and strategy in exchange for amnesty."

It wasn't enough. I could see the reluctance on everyone's faces. They'd spent too long with Illucia as an enemy to crush their desire to lock Ericen in the deepest, darkest cell they could find.

I might not be able to get them to let go of their past, but maybe I could get them to see a different future.

"There's an additional advantage to granting Ericen's request." I paused, looking to him. He hesitated but nodded. "You must remember he'll inherit the throne after Razel." A murmur spread through the room, and I spoke over it. "In ensuring his safety and accepting him into this alliance, we ensure that when this war is over, Illucia doesn't remain our enemy. Razel already disavowed him as a traitor. She was willing to kill him in the wood, and he's done nothing but help me since before I left Sordell. We can trust him."

Auma stood as if rising against a heavy burden. "During my time in Illucia, I was always struck by the prince's sense of honor and morality in a kingdom that tried to strip it from him. Like so many of us, he is not responsible for the sins of his parents. I believe we can trust him." She met my gaze with a nod. Then whatever surge of emotion had pushed her to her feet deflated, and she collapsed back into her chair.

Kiva was at her side in an instant, abandoning her post behind Ericen in a move that left me staring. Kiva's mother had trained her to leave no room for love, only duty. Looking at her now as she wrapped her arms around Auma, I had no doubt the princess had broken through that armor. Kiva had learned to bend without breaking, something her mother could never do.

The silence hung like a funeral shroud across the room until at last, Queen Luhara stood. "I'm inclined to withdraw Trendell from this alliance," she said in a voice of stone.

"And I the Ambriels," Samra said. A murmur rippled through the gathering.

My throat went dry. I looked at Estrel, who stared back wide-eyed. This couldn't be happening. Without them, Rhodaire wouldn't survive.

Standing, I met Queen Luhara's eye across the room, and she called for silence. By the time everyone had quieted, my nerves had settled.

"I'll be the first to admit that when it comes to politics, I'm still learning," I said. "That was always my sister's calling, not mine. But it is also Razel's." As I spoke, I met the gaze of each person in turn, hoping they could see my sincerity. "She knows exactly what she's doing. The attack on Samra's crew? The strike against the Jin rebels? Infiltrating Trendell? They were coordinated, targeted moves meant to hurt each of you and make you think twice about this alliance."

"Thia's right," said Ericen. "She did this because she's afraid. From the beginning, her plans have always relied on you being isolated and alone. She doesn't know how to face a united front. She's scared to face you together."

I nodded. "Dissolving this alliance is exactly what she wants."

"So we're playing straight into her hands," one of the council members said. "What does it matter if we know that? Even if we band together, can we defeat her?"

"Ira wasn't our only stronghold," Auma said. "There are rebel forces scattered throughout Jindae. We're not out of this fight."

Relief swept through me, even as I realized that Auma hadn't originally intended to share this information. She'd meant to let us think she had nothing to offer in order to protect what remained of her forces. Did this mean she'd changed her mind?

"We may have an edge on Razel too," Estrel said. "That shrine wasn't the only one of its kind, was it, Your Majesty?"

Queen Luhara frowned. "That's correct. There are several others on the grounds. Are you suggesting they possess the same power as the other?"

"They will once Thia activates them," Estrel replied. "These roads once connected all the major cities in each kingdom. It'll take a few days, but we can use the roads to Jindae and the Ambriels to gather the remaining troops."

Of course she knew about the roads. It was probably another piece of information the Order had kept for themselves.

Estrel looked to Auma and Samra. "Do you both have ships?" The two nodded, and she pressed on. "You can both sail to a higher point in Rhodaire and flank the Illucian army. Razel is too confident and didn't plan for an attack from behind. Her failure to anticipate this alliance leaves her military focused at the front, on Rhodaire." She looked to the queen. "Thia can funnel the Trendellan forces through Aris and bolster the Rhodairen army from the front. Razel won't expect our ranks to swell so quickly. With the element of surprise, we can take the fight to her."

"That might actually work," Samra admittedly grudgingly.

I seized the upward turn of the conversation, leaning my hands on the table. "We've all seen what Razel is capable of. What she's willing to do. None of our kingdoms are safe, and alone, none of us will survive." I looked to Res, whose eyes glowed a soft silver as his magic awakened. Lightning sparked along his beak and through his feathers. "What she doesn't know is what we're capable of. We can still win this battle."

Queen Luhara exchanged looks with her husband, and they spoke in hushed tones. Samra regarded me gravely, as if she might see the future in my eyes.

But it was Auma who spoke.

"Jindae stands with you." She rose from her chair. "I too do not abandon my friends."

I met her gaze, bowing my head.

"You have my rebels as well," Samra said with a nod.

"And the Trendellan army will honor its pledge," said the queen.

Relief flooded through me in a cool wave, only to hit the simmering anger inside me and steam. We had the other kingdoms' support. With their help, we would reach Rhodaire in time to defend it, and we'd have the strength to win.

Heat flared through my skin, my nails digging into my palms. I could feel that familiar darkness pressing in the back of my mind, that need to give in, to give up after everything that'd gone wrong. But something hotter pushed back. Something rash and full of talons.

My heart raced with the rising fire in my veins.

Even your very heart is armed, Auma had said. *It must have peace before you can expect to bring it to others.*

But I didn't want peace right now.

I wanted war.

TWENTY-SIX

I was going home.

I couldn't believe it. Even as I packed what little I had, even as I gathered with everyone outside the Trendellan shrine, it didn't feel real. Standing beside Ericen, knowing he was returning to Aris with me, that I *wanted* him to, only made it stranger.

They'd given him his swords back, and he stood rigid as a statue beside me, his attention lost somewhere in his thoughts.

Auma and Samra had already crossed their Sella roads to rally their surviving forces, though Samra had left behind a gift for Kiva. Aroch now perched on her shoulders.

I rose onto my toes, searching the commotion of passing servants and nearby guards. A flash of auburn caught my eye, and then Caylus appeared in the corridor. He nearly walked straight into a woman carrying fresh loaves of bread, but she managed to dodge him without him even noticing. I met him halfway.

"You're leaving?" he asked.

"I have to," I replied. "This battle has already begun."

"I heard. I have something for you." At his back, three young boys each wheeled a small contraption forward. They looked like horns with a crank for a handle.

That familiar excitement filled Caylus's eyes as he held up the glass Illucian arrow. "I discovered this glass was actually a composite. That means they melt it down and mix it with something else, in this case Alorr. The sound these produce will shatter the glass arrows, but you have to be in range of them, and I can't guarantee they won't break anything else of the same composite. Also—"

I flung my arms around him in a tight embrace. He went quiet, then enfolded me in his arms.

"Thank you," I whispered.

"Be careful," he said quietly.

I snorted, pulling back. "Not really my style."

A faint smile tugged at his lips.

I squeezed his hand. "Are you okay?" I hadn't seen him since Malkin's true demise.

"I am," he replied. "I'm going to stay here and attend the university. The king and queen agreed to sponsor me for a term." This time, his smile filled his whole face. "For once, I know what I'm looking for." He offered me a folded paper. "I also made you this."

When I flattened it, I found a familiar image staring back. Me dressed in my flying leathers, Res a hovering shadow at my back. He'd redrawn the image he'd made for me that day in his workshop. The one Razel had burned to ash.

It was a quiet reminder of strength. Of *my* strength.

I nodded to him, folding the drawing up and tucking it safely away. Then I joined the others, and together we crossed through the shrine.

We emerged in the castle graveyard.

The mausoleum was coated in dust and cobwebs, and Ericen had to throw his shoulder into the door to force it open. We stepped out of the dim building and back into Rhodaire.

The scent of ripened fruit filled the air, sweet and heavy. The long grass swayed about my ankles, brushing against the headstones in gentle whispers. Above, the sky was a familiar, clouded blue, just like the one I'd spent so many days staring up at, dreaming of soaring through on the back of a crow.

My heart swelled, filling my chest, my throat. I stepped slowly back onto familiar soil, soft and moist beneath my boots. Not frosted with cold or rocky from the sea or coarse and dry— soft, warm earth. I wanted to sink into it and never rise.

Res trilled softly. I laid a hand on his shoulder, his head too far above me now. "Welcome home." The bond thrummed with contentment, and he leaned into me.

"Halt!" a voice called. Two Rhodairen soldiers appeared at

the fence line, hands on their swords. They were half-drawn before they saw me. Disbelief dawned slowly on their faces as they took in Estrel, presumed dead, and Ericen, the Illucian prince. By the time they spotted Res, they were gaping.

I grinned, and Kiva stepped past me. "Lyris, Seair!"

The sound of her voice snapped both guards to attention, though their eyes kept flitting back to Res.

"L-Lieutenant Mirkova," Lyris stuttered. "Wh-what's going on?"

"Where's the queen?" I asked.

"In her office," the soldier answered. "How in the Saints' name—" Her words failed her, and she simply pointed at Res.

I grinned. "Caliza will explain everything soon."

We followed Lyris and Seair up the hill to the castle. They kept looking between Estrel, to whom they bowed their heads each time, and Ericen, the distrust evident in their faces, and Res, for whom no emotion seemed large enough.

We passed other guards and servants, gasps of surprise and excited murmurs preceding us as people went running to spread the news. We'd barely stepped into the entrance hall when someone came sprinting around the corner.

I caught Caliza in a viselike hug. It may have only been a few days since we'd seen each other, but so much had happened since then.

She pulled back, smiling broadly. "The alliance?"

I nodded, and her eyes widened. "I'll tell you everything in a bit. But first, I brought you a few surprises."

The others had kept back a respectful distance, but now

Estrel stepped forward, enveloping Caliza in a strong hug. She muttered something in Caliza's ear that earned a smile from my sister before moving aside.

Kiva remained at Ericen's side, her hand resting on Sinvarra. The intimidation of her pose was slightly lessened by the presence of Aroch on her shoulder. "Dungeons or Belgrave?" she asked, referring to the city's prison.

Caliza's expression grew serious as she took in Ericen. "Come. Let's go into my office."

Estrel didn't join us. Though she'd claimed she wanted to see to her old rooms, I knew the truth: she didn't want to enter my mother's office. I let her go. Readjusting to being in Rhodaire would be difficult; she had a lot of ghosts to face, but she'd be there for us when we needed her. I'd find her afterward and update her.

There was another familiar face waiting in Caliza's office though. With broad shoulders and a kind face, Caliza's husband, Kuren, had dark eyes that seemed to be constantly waiting for you to confess all your innermost feelings. I'd done it more than once. A thin scar along the hard line of his jaw stood out starkly against his dark skin, a souvenir from the first crow he'd ever met. Apparently, he'd tried to pet it from behind.

I launched myself into his open arms. "It's so good to see you!"

A deep laugh rumbled in his chest. "And you. I hear you've been quite busy."

"I can't imagine what you mean." I pulled back.

He smiled, and the warmth of it made me relax. His smile always had that effect. It was as if the simple motion released some power inside him that sucked all the stress out of anyone within ten feet of him.

We took our seats. A half hour later, Caliza and Kuren had updated us on Rhodaire's situation, from supplies, to soldiers, to the battle itself, and I'd told them about the alliance, the Sellas, and our current plan to flank Razel's army.

Like we'd predicted, we'd had to give ground since Rosstair, falling back to Elaris. With Lesiar Lake at its back, the walled city would make a good defensible position.

"The house leaders and I agreed that if you secured the alliance of the other kingdoms, we'd meet her forces there," Caliza said. "The town has been evacuated of everyone not contributing to the fight and sent south. It's under a day's ride from Aris."

"This won't be a typical battle," I warned them. "The Sellas I faced in the wood could use similar magic to Res. At least fire, water, and earth. I don't know what the others can do."

Kuren leaned back against Caliza's desk, arms folded in an easy posture. "We should meet with Lady Kerova and Lady Turren later to discuss battle tactics. We'll need to adjust. I'm particularly concerned about facing an opponent wielding earth magic. Zellen Arkos wrote a really fascinating essay on wall sieges that I think is in your library here."

Caliza scoffed. "Arkos? He wouldn't know siege warfare if it built a wall around him."

"Viden then?"

"If you want to fall asleep after the second word."

"Pretty sure that's all books," I muttered.

They both rounded on me, Kuren's eyes wide with shock,

Caliza's narrowed in condemnation. I slapped a hand over my mouth to silence a laugh.

Ericen chuckled softly. "Alternatively, I can help?" All eyes turned to him, but it only seemed to make him more comfortable. "You've only ever had to think of how to use these powers, not how to defend against them. Illucia, on the other hand, has volumes dedicated to crow warfare."

"Like those arrows," I said, remembering the souvenir Caylus had plucked from the *Aizel*. What else did Illucia have developed to counteract the crows? "Speaking of, I have a gift for you," I said to Kuren, withdrawing a set of blueprints. I'd found them tucked into the side of one of the horns Caylus had made for us, clearly drawn by someone else's steady hand. Kuren took them from me, unfolding them in his lap. "It's the design for those horns I brought back with me. We should produce as many of them as quickly as we can and ship them out to Elaris."

Kuren's eyes flitted across the page, absorbing information at an inhuman rate. It was too bad he and Caylus hadn't gotten the chance to meet.

"We planned for me to open the Sella road two hours after my arrival to let the first wave of Trendellan soldiers through," I continued. "We can send them to Elaris straight away." With the use of the road, they'd be fresh and rested, with a short march ahead of them. "We'll do the same again tomorrow at the same time and the day after to move the army through in sections."

"If you can give me the details of Elaris's defenses, I can try to predict what my mother will do," Ericen said. He stood behind my chair, his hands on the back of it. I could feel the warmth of his fingers pressing into my back.

Kiva snorted from where she leaned against the wall, one finger toying with Aroch's paw. "So you can walk them straight to her? No thanks."

"Sooner or later, you're going to have to accept that I'm here to help you," Ericen said.

"Or I could just stab you."

I rolled my eyes. Ericen might not be able to see it, but something had changed in Kiva's countenance toward him. Her quips had turned joking—mostly. She might not fully trust him, but I could see her making an effort.

Caliza shot Kiva a stern look. "Your mother hasn't returned from Korovi. That means you're in charge of the castle guard."

Kiva's face darkened. "Have you heard from her?"

"Her last letter came a week ago. She was still trying to convince them to aid us," Caliza replied. "For now, I want you to work with Prince Ericen to train the other lieutenants on basic Illucian sword techniques and weak spots in their armor. They'll ride out tomorrow and distribute that information to the soldiers already in Elaris."

Kiva clenched her jaw, her reflex to retort no doubt battling with her desire to follow orders. Though I couldn't see his face, I had a feeling Ericen looked somewhere between amused and smug.

Caliza turned back to Ericen. "What else can you tell us?"

The prince crossed his arms. "The most important thing to note is that Illucians treat crow warfare like a knife fight: the first step is always to control the knife. They'll do the same with Res. If they can draw him out and kill him early, they can drastically change their strategy."

He talked for nearly half an hour, giving us everything he could. From the knowledge that their warhorses' footing was weak to the advice that arrows were highly effective against thin Vykryn uniforms. Normal soldiers wore metal-reinforced armor, but the Vykryn believed that a worthy warrior didn't require it, and if they died, they did so willingly in the service of their god.

With his help, we made plans to plow the fields outside the walls of Elaris, making the land uneven and dangerous for the Illucian horses. Messenger birds left with instructions for archers to target Vykryn, the knowledge that normal Illucian armor was weak beneath the arms, and details on Res's abilities.

By the time Ericen finished, Kiva looked slightly less like she wanted to stab him, and something like hope shone in my sister's eyes.

"Thank you," she said.

Ericen bowed his head.

Kuren finished writing down the last of Ericen's information. "I'll have copies of this sent to Lady Kerova and Lady Turren. We'll meet with them tomorrow to discuss final plans."

"Great," I said, letting out a breath. "Now I could really use some fresh Rhodairen air."

As the others filed out of the room, Caliza caught my arm, holding me back. She pulled me wordlessly into another hug, and for a moment, we simply stood there in silence, each memorizing the feel of the other's arms.

"You did it," she whispered, holding tighter.

"And you held the kingdom together while I did."

As we pulled back, Caliza slipped the silver bracelet of feathers off her wrist. "You should have this back."

I smiled, lifting my hand so she could slide it over onto my wrist. I ran my fingers along the metal, still warm from her skin. It'd belonged to Estrel once, a gift from my mother. They might not have been related by blood, but they'd still been sisters. The matching piece, a feather circlet, sat poised on Caliza's brow.

"Mother would be proud of us," she said.

I snorted, waving a hand. "Forget Mother. *I'm* proud of us."

A quiet laugh leapt from her lips, and she hugged me again. "Me too."

The smell of the royal training grounds was painfully familiar. It made my heart ache with longing for a time when Estrel and I would rise before most of the castle, training for hours first by torchlight and then beneath the pale pink sky of dawn.

Although simple, the courtyard had more than enough for my purposes. A small sparring ring, a few well-used dummies, and a view of the clouded sky. I leaned my head back, staring up at the darkening clouds. The air smelled thick with rain, a promise of a coming storm. I couldn't wait to feel the warm rain against my skin.

I hadn't realized how much I'd needed home.

"Care for a partner?" a low voice asked from behind.

I smiled over my shoulder at Ericen, nodding to where Res had settled down in the corner to sleep. "I already have one of those."

"A less lazy partner then." He returned my smile, stepping into the yard.

Res lifted his head, cawing indignantly.

I snorted. "Well, you are lazy," I said, and he laid his head back down with a huff. "How about a rematch?" I suggested, drifting toward the sparring ring. With everything I'd learned recently, I felt alive with energy. Nerves, excitement, fear—they flashed through my veins like lightning, making me jittery.

Thunder boomed in the sky above, matching my nerves.

Ericen followed me into the ring, his lips pulled up in that one-sided smirk that never failed to irk me. "First one to tap out?"

I lifted my hands, shifting into a stance as the sky broke and warm rain fell. "I'm not holding back," I warned him.

His smile widened, his fingers slipping under the hem of his shirt. In a fluid motion, he had it over his head and was tossing it aside into the damp dirt. "Neither am I."

I had barely had time to feel the heat flushing my face when he struck. Cursing, I dodged him and backed to the other side of the ring.

"You did that on purpose," I growled.

He laughed. "A soldier should use all the assets at their disposal."

"I wouldn't say assets," I muttered.

Ericen raised a doubtful brow, that stupid smirk spreading

once more. Lightning split the sky. I sprang forward, swiping for his jaw. He leapt away, laughing.

Back and forth we went as the rain drummed around us. Water dripped from strands of his black hair and in rivulets down his chest, and my clothes grew heavy, clinging fast to my body. Unlike last time, I didn't shy from landing my own blows, and with each spin and step that took me out of the prince's reach, the furrow between his brows grew.

I caught him in the ribs, then in the stomach with a kick. He stepped back, as sturdy as ever. I needed to get him unbalanced.

As Ericen struck, I knocked aside his blow, spun inside his guard, and threw my elbow into his gut. He wheezed, stumbling back.

I tackled him.

We tumbled to the wet ground, his back hitting hard. I landed atop him, one knee in his chest, the other foot braced against the earth, a fist raised to strike. He fell still, a look of surprise on his face I'd never seen before. For a moment of long, thick silence, I was all too aware of the heavy rise and fall of his chest, of the heat of his skin burning through two layers of cloth.

Then Ericen laughed and ran a hand through his rain-soaked hair, pushing it out of his eyes. It'd escaped its soldier's cut in the last few weeks, the ends curling like beckoning fingers. "You stole my move," he rasped, still breathless.

I smirked. "Getting slow in your old age."

"I'm barely a year older than you are."

"And yet you move like Res after breakfast."

The crow let out a low caw of agreement, and we both laughed. The sound echoed through the courtyard, a reminder we were alone. The rain drummed a steady beat on the stone. Only a flurry of feathers told me Res had taken to the sky.

Ericen's eyes searched mine. One hand cupped my face, his calloused fingers gentle against my skin.

I leaned down and kissed him.

Ericen surged up, catching me in his arms and holding me close. My legs hooked around his waist, my hands finding his feather-soft hair, his lean neck, the bare skin of his corded back. Pressed between the power of the storm and the prince's strength, my body came alive.

I kissed him until we were both breathless and the storm fell apart around us, the rain softening to a quiet drizzle and the thunder fading. A light shone through the darkened clouds, washing the courtyard in gold.

And still, we held on.

TWENTY-SEVEN

I n the end, Kiva found us.

We practically sprang apart when her raucous laugh filled the courtyard. Whereas my cheeks flushed red as fire, Ericen glowered at Kiva with a dark menace that would have once made me nervous. Now I knew when he was all bark and no bite.

Kiva dragged Ericen away to start training the lieutenants, and I returned to the mausoleum to activate the Sella road. Estrel joined me, and we chatted to pass the time. It took almost an hour for all the soldiers to pass through, as the road was narrow and only allowed for one through at a time. Estrel organized them with their captains and sent them toward Elaris.

A tall Jin soldier passed through, followed by a familiar face. "Elko!"

She grinned, slapping me on the back hard enough to make me stumble. "Crow girl! Which way to Elaris?"

I blinked at her. "You're going to fight? Does Auma know that?"

"My sister is not my keeper. Besides, I'm healed." Elko pounded her first on her chest, then blanched. "Or at least I will be soon."

Estrel leaned toward me. "I've got this." She slung an arm around Elko's shoulders, leading her a short distance away and speaking quietly to her. Elko cracked her knuckles, a grin curling her lips, before she clasped hands with Estrel and struck out toward the castle.

I raised an eyebrow when Estrel returned.

She shrugged. "I told her someone needed to stay behind and protect Caliza."

With the last of the soldiers through for the day, we returned to the castle together, everything inside me light as a feather. It slowly faded as we rounded the castle and the graveyard appeared. The pale blue light of dusk filtered through the stone mausoleums and intricately carved headstones, glinting off the black metal gate.

I slowed, thinking of the headstone deep inside, presided over by the carving of a single crow, beneath which my mother slept. Estrel paused, looking back at me.

"Why didn't you ever tell me?" I asked.

Her face made it clear she knew I meant the Sellas. "It was your mother's decision." And loyal friend that she was, Estrel had kept her secret. I understood that.

"Why though?"

"She didn't want to burden you with it," she replied. "Your mother, she never wanted the responsibility of being queen. She was wild as a youth. Even you'd be impressed at the amount of trouble she caused."

I raised a doubtful brow. The woman I'd known had been hard and unyielding as stone.

Estrel grinned. "I'm serious. Did you know Larisa once caught her sneaking out through the balcony of a visiting noble's room, the same day your father had come with his family to discuss their engagement?"

I gaped. "*No.*"

"Oh yes. Larisa was furious. I don't think your father ever knew. Larisa covered up the whole thing." She smiled wistfully. "She was always cleaning up after your mother and me."

I grinned, imagining my mother scaling the castle walls, dressed in nothing but her nightgown, and Kiva's mother shouting at her to get down.

Estrel's own smile faded. "She was crowned young, like Caliza. The responsibility, the demand—it weighed on her, wore her down. Though your parents loved each other, your father was more concerned with war than running a kingdom. Then he was killed in that battle with Illucia, and suddenly your mother was alone with two children, a kingdom, and a war."

Once, Ericen had told me a similar story about Razel. She'd wanted to breed horses. But when Lord Turren and a group of his soldiers attacked Illucia, they murdered Razel's husband along with her older sister and mother. Her father died shortly after, and she was made queen younger than even my mother.

The story the Rhodairen people knew was that Lord Turren had retaliated for my father's death of his own volition. After, he was banished, his complicit soldiers were stripped of their crows. Then Razel had used the anger and humiliation that had festered in their hearts to turn them against Rhodaire. They'd betrayed us, helping her accomplish Ronoch.

Then she'd executed them.

"Did she order the attack on Razel's family?" I asked, my chest tightening at the memory of the night in the throne room, when Razel had stood with a blade pressed to Kiva's throat and told me that my mother was not as innocent as I believed.

Estrel let out a quiet breath. "I don't know," she said. "She was so broken, so angry after your father's death. She—" Estrel hesitated, shaking her head. "I don't know."

I nodded. Maybe I would never know.

Who would Razel have been if she hadn't had her family ripped away from her? Who would my mother have been without an army of responsibilities slowly draining her dry?

Perhaps the two of them hadn't been so different, as Ericen and I weren't so different.

I'd told Kiva once that the cycle of revenge between our kingdoms needed to end, but I wasn't sure I could be the one to break it.

I wasn't sure I could forgive the woman who'd taken everything from me.

TWENTY-EIGHT

I t took a lot of prodding and more than one handful of chicken to get Res up the next morning, but a short time later, we stood on one of the four landing platforms at the top of the castle.

Ericen eyed the edge of the platform with unease. "Is this where you execute people?"

I adjusted the saddle on Res's back. "Only the ones I really don't like."

"I take it I'm safe then."

I rolled my eyes as Ericen peered uneasily at the edge.

"This is incredibly high up."

A smile pulled at my lips. "Don't tell me the great Illucian prince is afraid of heights."

The pale shade of Ericen's skin contrasted with the indignant scowl that filled his face. "Of course not."

Res snorted, and if ever the crow had made a more mocking sound, I'd never heard it.

Ericen glowered at him, and I laughed even as my heart stuttered a drumbeat in my chest. It'd been months since I'd flown from one of the landing platforms. Another of the many things I never thought I'd do again, just like I thought I'd never fly out over Aris with my own crow.

The platform door opened, and Kiva stepped out, Aroch trotting alongside her. "I heard you were jumping off the castle. Has Res flown this high with you before? I prefer you unsquished."

I rolled my eyes again. "I'm not going to die."

"You can get squished and not die."

"She'll be fine." Ericen's words steadied the beat inside me. He crossed his arms, meeting my gaze with a reassuring smile. "If there's one thing I've learned about Thia, it's not to underestimate her. She gets too much satisfaction out of proving you wrong."

"You would know," I said.

"Unless we're talking about flirting. That she can't do to save her life."

"At least I'm not afraid of heights," I shot back.

"Afraid of heights?" Kiva asked, looking delighted. "Did you know we're over a hundred and fifty feet in the air?"

"I didn't," Ericen replied with an edge. "Shall I push you over to confirm it?"

"I would say Thia would catch me, but I'm still not convinced she won't be flattened herself in the next minute."

"You two almost sound like friends," I noted, and Kiva blanched.

I laughed as I swung onto Res's back. Leaning down, I whispered, "Let's show them all what we can do."

Rearing back, Res released a piercing call.

Then he leapt.

My half scream, half cry of joy was lost to the wind as Res dove. I'd expected him to soar straight out, to take the easy route. I should have known. After all, he had a flair for the dramatic.

Wind screamed past my ears, my eyes watering against the pressure. On reflex, I counted.

Fifteen, sixteen, seventeen...

Now! I squeezed my knees, and Res's wings snapped open, catching an updraft that sent us sailing upward. He screeched, and I felt his joy intermix with wild abandon as the wind carried us higher.

We rose faster, his wings taut against the draft. In a burst of speed, we shot past the platform to Kiva's whooping cheer.

Stay focused, I told Res, even as the desire to lose myself to the feel of the wind coursed wild.

With the pressure of the thermal sending us upward, Res would have to fight the wind to stay level. *Wings down*, I reminded him. He pitched them at a downward angle, straining against the current, and we leveled out. A moment later, we'd broken free of the rising air and were gliding back around in a wide circle, a grin on my lips, a call echoing from Res's throat.

Caliza had asked me to take Res out above the city, knowing

the sight of a full-grown crow and rider would help lift Aris's falling spirits.

Even forty feet up, the failing state of the capital was clear. Tents had been pitched in courtyards for refugees fleeing the northern towns, makeshift neighborhoods of their own. The once opulent and lush foliage that blanketed Aris had started to wither and die. We passed more than one closed shop that'd still been open when I left for Sordell.

With the images of the dying city heavy in my heart, I spent longer than planned out with Res, praying as Caliza did that his presence would give our people hope. When they cheered as we coasted above them, children chasing our shadow through the streets in hopes of catching a stray feather, it was they who gave me hope.

We returned only to funnel more Trendellan troops through the shrine, then set out again. This was our last day of freedom in the skies, for come tomorrow, we'd set out for Elaris, and war.

That night, I stayed sitting at the patio table long after dinner had ended. I lounged back with my feet up on the railing, surveying the quiet garden beyond and replaying the tactics meeting that'd just ended. We had a solid plan—hit Razel first before she could finish fielding more troops, led by Rhodaire and Trendell from the front and supported by Jindae and the Ambriels from behind.

Razel thought she'd destroyed the Jin rebels and broken the Ambriels, making their approach from behind key to our plans. Two days from now, we'd know if it was enough.

I adjusted the plate of orange cakes resting in my lap. Already I felt a little sick, my stomach full to bursting, but I ate another.

Res groaned from beside me. He perched hunkered down, his wings spread, powdered sugar dotting his black feathers.

"We're finishing this plate," I informed him. He groaned again.

"I can help you with that." Ericen's footsteps were light on the patio, the shadows cast by the sona lamps sharpening his features. He dragged a chair over to my other side and dropped down, propping his boots up on the railing. I offered him the plate, and he took a cake.

The silence between us was comfortable, and for a little while, I simply breathed in the scent of fruit trees and listened to the crickets chirp.

"Have you ever fought in a war?" I asked when the cakes were gone.

Ericen dusted the powdered sugar off his hands. "I haven't."

"I...think I'm scared," I said softly. "I'm afraid of losing more people I love."

The prince was quiet for a moment, and I closed my eyes against the rising panic. What if Kiva was hurt? Or Res? I couldn't go through that again.

"My mother always said having people you love is a weakness," Ericen said at last. "She loved people, and they were taken from her, and she was powerless to stop it. She never wanted to be weak again."

Was that why Razel had treated him so horribly? Because she hadn't wanted to love him, lest she lose him too?

"But she was wrong," he said, a note of finality in his voice. "Love doesn't make you weak." He looked at me, his piercing eyes pinning me to the spot. "It makes you stronger."

My breath caught, a gentle chill prickling along my skin despite the warm night. Ericen's gaze lingered. I took his hand in mine, powdered sugar and all, and held it. He squeezed my fingers gently, his sword calluses rough against those from my bow. When our grips slackened, our fingertips remained intertwined.

He leaned his head back against the chair, staring up at the clouded sky. Without a word, I tossed him one of the remaining two orange cakes. He caught it with his free hand, and we ate in silence.

War had broken both our families. Its echoes still haunted us.

But we could be better than our parents' legacies. Their mistakes didn't have to be our own.

Come tomorrow, we would march to battle. But for tonight, I was content to sit beside a boy who had once been my enemy, cocooned in the sort of silence that sometimes knitted broken things back together.

TWENTY-NINE

We set out for Elaris in the afternoon.

After letting the last contingent of Trendellan soldiers through the Sella road, we gathered our supplies and prepared to leave. With Res's help, Estrel had seen to the creation of several new black gold weapons, including a whole quiver of arrows for me. The refined metal was near impossible for crows to bend, and we were relying on the same being true for the Sellas.

I refused to say goodbye to Caliza, the action feeling uncomfortably final, and instead simply hugged her as hard as I could.

Then Ericen, Kiva, Estrel, Res, and I left.

Elaris was less than a day's ride from Aris, a trip that Res and I could have made even faster. Instead, he napped in the back of an open wagon. Conserving his strength would be key to this fight; as the battle in the wood had proven, his magic was limited. He hadn't complained.

The rest of us rode horses as we passed through the Kessel Woods, though we kept pace with the marching army, not wanting to tire the beasts. Many of the horses had come through Trendell from Jindae, but with our reliance on the crows, Rhodaire had never fielded a large cavalry, and many of our recent additions hadn't been training for more than six months.

We passed out of the wood's dense foliage by late afternoon, the trail winding through valleys of long-fingered grass and patches of broad-leafed trees. Only a few weeks ago, I'd made this same trip, a prisoner in Ericen's carriage, all too aware of what waited for me at the end. This time, I enjoyed the familiar scenery, the feel of the waning afternoon sun and the gentle wind, and the company of my friends, even knowing what we rode toward.

Until we rose from a deep valley and reached the crest of a hill, Elaris spread out before us in the next basin, and my heart stopped.

The city was already under attack.

The clang of distant metal merged with the screams of the dying.

Row upon row of Illucian soldiers stretched out toward the northern border, pinning Elaris between Lesiar Lake and a tide of soldiers in blue. Arrows flew at the wall from a small force that had broken off from the larger army, protected from easy return fire by a small, broad-topped tower on wheels.

Ericen had spoken of the top towers. Larger versions of them reached up from the Illucian ranks every few yards, providing canopy-like protection from the skies. The top towers were a favorite defense of Illucia against the crows, allowing them to create pockets of archers that could fire and then quickly retreat below protection. They were incredibly effective against battle crows, and while less so against Res, it would take a lot of magic for him to destroy all of them, and it would make him an easy target.

A narrow stone bridge connected the shore and the back entrance to the city, and it was for it that we rode with all haste.

Res shot awake in the back of his wagon, but I warned him to keep down and lifted the hood of my cloak to hide my face. Estrel, Ericen, and Kiva did the same. Razel likely had scouts looking to report when the crow arrived, and I'd rather them think we were just another contingent of ground reinforcements.

The soldiers at the back gate let us through, and we rode through ranks of Trendellan and Rhodairen forces to the front of the city.

Our horse's hooves clattered across the cobblestones as we entered a broad courtyard. Lady Kerova met us at the base of the wall. A lithe, graceful warrior, she had Auma's calm bearing and Kiva's fierce gaze, and it showed as she dealt out orders to passing soldiers.

I dismounted, making for her. "Status report?" I asked.

"Your Highness," she greeted with a swift bob of her head. "This is the third strike Razel's forces have made in as many hours. So far, they've only been testing our defenses, but based on your intelligence regarding the Sellas in her employ, I fear they may only be a distraction to lull us into a sense of security with a false pattern. When their true attack comes, it won't be led by archers."

A Rhodairen soldier descended a nearby set of steps and saluted Lady Kerova. "The enemy has retreated. We have two wounded to report and seven confirmed dead on the Illucian side. Also, there's a disturbance in the Illucian forces. It appears someone is making their way to the front lines from the command tents."

"Show us," Estrel ordered.

We followed the soldier to the top of the wall. I stilled at the edge of the battlement as the true scope of the army's size unfurled before me. Hearing troop numbers from Caliza was one thing. Facing them spread along the basin, knowing each of them was here to kill Res, to kill my friends and my family, was something else entirely.

The rows broke about two-thirds of the way back to make room for a line of royal-blue tents. It was from there that a ripple of motion rolled through the army, soldiers separating to allow through a group of four hooded figures on foot.

The Sellas had come.

"Razel must have decided against waiting for additional troops," Ericen said. "She probably thinks the Sellas are enough to turn the tide."

"I only see four," I said. "There were six in the glade." Where were the other two?

"What do we do with these ones?" Kiva's hand curled around Sinvarra.

Lady Kerova looked suddenly uneasy. "The Ambriellan and Jin reinforcements aren't set to reach us until near nightfall. Somehow, we must last until then."

Ericen stepped up to the wall, surveying the ranks below. A dark swath of earth cut a line between the wall and the soldiers beyond, the ground uneven and loose to impede the cavalry's approach. "They'll start by trying to create an opening in this wall, probably hoping to draw Res out into those archers in the meantime," the prince said. "Then they'll use cavalry to overpower your infantry that rushes to plug the gaps."

"And they have an earth Sella that can tear holes in it like paper." I watched the approaching group with rising dread. Questioning beats pulsed down the line from Res.

Not yet, I sent back.

"If this wall falls, the city will fall," Lady Kerova said. "We don't have the numbers to match them without the Jin and Ambriellan forces for long."

"So we hold the wall," I said. "No matter what."

The waiting was torture.

We had no choice but to watch as a solitary top tower trundled toward us at an agonizingly slow pace, pushed by soldiers from behind. Our goal had gone from initiating this battle ourselves to prolonging its start for as long as possible, leaving us all but immobile until Razel's forces made their first move. But every second we waited was a second closer our reinforcements came to reaching us.

I searched the command tent line, looking for a flash of gold, but if Razel was here, she was safely sequestered inside.

The top tower paused at the edge of the strip of overturned earth outside our archer's range. One of the hooded figures lifted a hand. With a wave of their fingers, a wide swath of dirt flattened into solid earth. Immediately, the Illucian cavalry began lining up behind the swath, the loose ground no longer an impediment to their massive horses.

"He's going to start tearing down pieces of the wall," I said. My fingers curled anxiously around the string of my bow. At our backs, our soldiers readjusted into ranks accordingly, trying to position for where the Illucians would enter. "Res and I can re-form them, but only for so long. His magic isn't endless."

"All right. So then we need to take that earth creep down first," Kiva said. Then a smile curled across her lips. "I have an idea."

No one disagreed as she laid out her plan, though I wanted to more than anything. Everyone here had come to fight for Rhodaire, for their family and friends and people. It wasn't my place to ask Kiva not to do this. But that didn't stop me from wrapping her in a stranglehold of a hug before rushing off to my position.

As I swung onto Res's back, the ground shook.

Stone cracked, a piece of the wall shifting. Smaller pieces started to crumble from it, sending soldiers scrambling left and right to escape the deteriorating section.

Power surged along the bond, and Res's eyes glowed silver. The shaking stopped, the wall's cracks sealing, leaving it slightly sunken but still whole. A moment of heavy silence fell with the settling dust. Then another crack rent the air, and another, and another. The wall splintered, and Res struggled to keep pace, sealing piece after piece.

We wouldn't be able to keep this up for long. Eventually, part of the wall would crumble. Sealing the cracks was one thing, but re-forming a wall out of stone might be beyond Res's earth crow skills, and it would drain his power.

We darted left and right along the flight path that lined the base of the wall, enabling crows to travel at the speed of flight while still benefiting from the protection of the wall.

I hated this. Battling an unseen enemy, being put in a reactive position. We'd just begun, and yet already this fight was out of our control.

A shout went up, then a hail of arrows rained down from above.

Res's magic flared, deflecting the wooden bolts with ease and sending them careening into the stone wall.

"Saints, pull back!" I yelled. Res circled around just as another wave of arrows fell where he'd been flying.

They'd been tracking his movements based on where the wall resealed. Had the Sella even been *trying* to take down the wall, or had that all just been a trap for Res?

The Sella's attack changed directions, striking along the wall back the way we'd come. Res and I held back, taking signals from the wall guards. They laid down cover fire, pinning the Illucian archers while Res and I fixed the wall, but our timing wasn't perfect. We could only begin to seal a crack before another one opened, forcing us to leave imperfect fixes behind.

We reached the central courtyard just as Kiva bounded down the stairs.

"Caylus's horns are in place," she said. "I'm ready."

The urge to argue rose, but I swallowed it down. We couldn't spend the rest of Res's strength playing tug-of-war over the wall. Still, my stomach turned as I gave Res the order.

A perfect replica of him formed from the shadows of a nearby building. Kiva threw up her hood and leapt onto the shadow crow's back.

"Send me toward where the forest meets the lake!" she called.

The fake crow lifted into the air and shot out along the wall under Res's control. Immediately, Rhodairen soldiers started cranking the horns, emitting a high-pitched keening sound, and just in time too. A wave of glass arrows shattered midflight, the Illucian archers having switched ammunition upon confirmation of a crow.

"Now, Thia!" Ericen's call came from the battlement above.

Res took flight.

As we soared high into the air, I quickly assessed the result of our ploy. Ericen had been right. The Illucian troops were trained to prioritize the crows. The moment Kiva appeared on the fake crow, all the archers' attention had followed her.

Leaving the earth Sella undefended.

Three top towers spread before the wall now, protecting

pockets of archers. Below the center one sat the Sella on horseback. His hand was raised, his focus on a new swath of wall, likely thinking Res and I occupied. Someone yelled, pointing at us, but I'd already nocked an arrow.

As Res angled downward, granting me a clear shot beneath the high top of the tower, I drew and loosed.

The Sella lifted a hand to knock the arrow aside, but the black gold was too refined a material to bend. His eyes widened a fraction before the bolt took him in the heart.

He crumpled to the ground.

Res rushed for the wall as the archers' attention swiveled back to us. Bowstrings snapped. Glass shattered midair from the cry of the horns.

An arrow skimmed my arm.

I cried out, and Res banked hard, simultaneously brushing aside another wave of wooden arrows. The last thing I saw before Res dove beyond the wall was the empty sky where the shadow crow had been.

Kiva was gone.

THIRTY

R es dove behind the wall even as I screamed at him to pull up. He alighted on a low perch that'd been built for easy crow landing, images of flying arrows mixing with pulsing questions along the link. I leapt off his back, bolting up the stairs to the battlement.

Ericen met me at the top. "She fell when that arrow skimmed you. Res lost control of the shadow crow."

I barreled past him to the edge, but he seized me, pulling me back behind the wall as arrows crested the ridge. One pierced a Rhodairen soldier through the neck; another took a Trendellan in the arm. I stared at the blood that coated them.

"She was flying low when she fell," Ericen said swiftly. "We can't see what's happening, but a squad of soldiers went after her."

"I have to go after her." I pushed off the wall.

He stepped in front of me. "And do what? Fly Res over an army of archers? You'll both get killed. Kiva wouldn't want you to go after her now and you know it!"

"I can't just leave her!" I screamed. She could be injured or—*No!* The thought threatened to tear me open. If only we could neutralize the archers. Then I could get Res into the sky safely and find Kiva.

Ericen's expression hardened. "How many people can Res conceal?"

"Two, maybe three? And I don't know for how long." I watched the sea of soldiers, hoping for a glimpse of Kiva. "But there might be another way to hide more. What are you thinking?"

The prince freed his swords from his back. "I'm going to get you your opening."

Clinging to the hope of Ericen's plan, I flew down the stairs to the base of the wall where I sent a runner with orders to open the main gate on my mark. Then I called Res.

He landed beside me, head nudging mine as concern thundered down the cord. "We're going to get her back," I told him as I swung into the saddle.

For now, let's give them a storm unlike anything they've ever seen.

Res cawed as power surged along the cord. Dark clouds veined with lightning began to materialize in the sky, rain bursting forth in a heavy downpour, but it was all only a distraction for the gathering fog. Res coalesced it above the edge of the battlement atop the gate, then slammed it down like a second wall. At the same moment, Rhodairen archers laid down cover against the cavalry.

Res took off.

With the cover of the fog wall, Ericen and a small team consisting of two Trendellan monks, Lady Kerova, and two Rhodairen soldiers slipped out the front gate.

I heard the Illucian archers dying before I saw them.

We rose above Res's fog wall just as Ericen and Lady Kerova reached the first tower. The archers' guards were ill prepared for the head-on assault, and they fell to a flash of steel. The Trendellan monks hit the second tower, the Rhodairen soldiers the third.

Seeing the posts under attack, the front line of cavalry struck forward. But the rain had already puddled on the hard ground formed by the Sella, and Res's power seized it. It thrust upward in a wave of spikes, spearing the legs of the front line of warhorses. Bestial screams filled the air at the animals' pain, turning my stomach, but the effect was immediate—the following lines of cavalry couldn't move forward with the front line collapsed before them.

It wouldn't take them long to circle around, but the earth Sella hadn't solidified the entire area, and the uneven rocky ground would slow them down. By the time they made it through, Ericen and his team would already be retreating. Even now, they struck down the final archers, freeing the skies for Res and me.

Then an earsplitting crack rent the air.

Res wheeled about in midair. A huge section of the wall had crumbled. Two Sellas stood before the opening, the water they'd slammed into the weakened wall like a battering ram pooling around their ankles.

The city was exposed.

The Illucian cavalry charged, led by a hooded Sella.

Ericen and the others retreated behind the closing gate as arrows flew at the charging force. The Sella deflected them all with a flick of his hand.

"He's a battle Sella," I breathed.

The cavalry splashed past the water Sellas and through the opening in a rush of hooves and yells.

"Strike the water!" I yelled to Res.

Lightning snapped, hitting the shallow pool as a wave of soldiers shot through it. Horses and people screamed as they were electrocuted, arrows striking the stunned soldiers the shock didn't kill. The current caught one of the water Sellas, stunning her, then an arrow took her in the heart. Bodies dropped in a natural barrier against a second charge, but several of the soldiers made it through, including the battle Sella.

He deflected the sword of the first soldier who came for him with a sweep of his hand. With another, he turned it against its wielder, sending it through the soldier's neck and through the necks of several soldiers behind them. His strength was incredible.

The Sella advanced on a fallen soldier. A column of silver torcs lining his upper arm turned liquid, melding into each other and sloughing down his arm into a sharpened blade. He pulled it back.

Then Estrel was there, a black gold blade in hand. It didn't respond to the Sella's attempts to control it, and she landed a strike across his bicep before he realized.

It took everything inside me to turn away from that fight. In the aftermath of the lightning strike, the first pang of fatigue had slid down the bond from Res. Constantly resealing the wall had drained his magic, which was probably exactly what they'd wanted. In fact, this whole battle seemed an exercise in drawing out Res's magic.

Why not attack with the earth and water Sellas at once? Where was Valis to burn through stone? Instead, they took turns, letting Res waste his magic against one before turning out another, all with the steady, controlled pace that indicated they knew they had the upper hand.

Something was wrong, but without an idea of what, I had to play their game.

It would take time and a lot of energy to fix that large an area of the wall, and with one water Sella still alive, they'd only tear it down again, so in the end, I left the infantry to hold the opening, choosing instead to deal with the Sella first.

Ripping my bow free, I nocked an arrow and directed Res down to the battlement. Leaping from his back, I raced along the wall as he caught an updraft, soaring high into the air and disappearing into the cloud cover.

The water Sella had erected a shield of ice to protect itself from arrows, and though Res had tried to take control of it, the Sella's power was stronger than his, and he couldn't budge its control.

Which meant we had to break it another way.

At the edge of my vision, the remainder of the Illucian army prepared to rush the opening once it was free of bodies, black warhorses rearing and frothing at the bit.

I felt a flash of exaltation from Res before he dove.

The clouds tore free of the sky, swirling around him in a dark tornado ablaze with lightning. It glinted off the gleaming metal of Res's armored feathers as he barreled through the water Sella's ice wall, shattering it.

I loosed my arrow a split second later.

It pierced the Sella through the eye.

Res tried to pull up, but he misjudged the speed with his armored body and slammed into the front line of cavalry. I screamed for him, flinging myself at the wall, but hands pulled me back. Panic resounded along the cord between us as I clawed at the people restraining me.

Swords flashed, striking the spot where Res had been consumed by the warhorses. It was as if a dark sea had swallowed him. I could feel his fear, his pain. He struggled to right himself, to find which way was up and escape.

Hold the armor! I screamed down the cord, praying he could maintain control. Only fear echoed back. Swords flashed, and more soldiers joined the fray.

Then a spray of silver exploded upward. Horses reared back, sending riders tumbling to the ground, where their fellows trampled them. The earth surged beneath Res. It rolled up like a wave to toss him into the air, his metal armor fading as his wings spread wide.

A sword caught the side of his leg. Res's pain hit me like a blow to the chest. I stumbled back, the hands going from holding me back to holding me up. Another sharp wave coursed through me as something nicked his wing, and then my bow was in my hands and I was firing arrow after arrow after arrow into the crowd of soldiers, the other archers stepping up alongside me.

Bolstered by a powerful wind, Res spiraled high into the sky, then dove fast for the ground on the far side of the wall.

I tore from the battlement to meet him. He pulled up from his dive, wings flaring wide, but a flash of pain blazed from him. He cringed inward, feathers flickering silver a second before he hit the ground like a falling star.

Then I was at his side, my hands searching his body, unable to do anything but strangle my panic into silence as I sought his mind. "You're okay, you're okay. Tell me you're okay." The words poured out of me even as I struggled to send reassurances along the cord, to grant the peace and comfort he needed to heal.

Res cawed weakly, slowly shifting his wings out from under him, trying to pull back onto his feet.

I forced a hard breath out, then in again, willing myself into a calm that felt so impossibly remote. I pictured my fear and anxiety as a snake, imagining it slithering off my shoulders and far, far away from me. Then I projected that serenity to Res.

He seized hold of it. A moment later, a soft golden light rose from his feathers. It flickered, fading out, then back in, and with every spurt of it, his exhaustion echoed, but slowly, his body healed.

Then the Illucian cavalry flooded the city.

THIRTY-ONE

E ricen appeared before me, his face sprayed with red—someone else's blood. "Can he move?"

"I don't know." The words were half sob as he pulled me to my feet.

"Come on, you bloody chicken!" he snapped. "You don't see me lying around."

Res cawed, his power surging alongside a flash of indignation. The golden light flared, and he wrenched himself to his feet.

"There you go," the prince said with a smirk. "How injured is he? We need him to close that opening."

"He doesn't even have enough strength to heal," I said. "I don't think he can close it." Even if Res had been at full strength, forming something that large out of the earth alone would have been a true test of his earth crow powers.

The Rhodairen and Trendellan cavalry had lined up at the opening and now engaged the incoming flood of Illucian soldiers. Horses slammed together. Soldiers fell screaming. Thunder beat the sky alongside their cries.

Eventually, our cavalry would be overrun, and our infantry wouldn't be able to stop the tide of warhorses.

Someone broke free of the fighting, heading toward us. I had an arrow nocked before I recognized Estrel.

Her left arm was stained red, and she cradled it close to her body. She readjusted her grip on her blade. "I lost track of the Sella I was fighting. How many of the damn things are left?"

"That's the last one," I said with a small flicker of relief. "If the other two are here, I haven't seen them. We just have to last until the reinforcements arrive or Res has enough energy to re-form that wall."

Estrel grunted. "Easier said than done."

As if in recognition of her words, our line broke.

Illucian infantry flooded through the wall gap on the heels of the cavalry line. Rhodairen and Trendellan soldiers rushed to meet them, but their organization had failed, and we could only last so long against the sheer Illucian numbers.

A contingent of soldiers broke off, rushing for our group. Ericen and Estrel turned to meet them. I nocked an arrow, laying down cover for them as they fought, and we formed a protective arch around Res.

Time slowed. My muscles burned. I thought only of the next arrow, the next swing. Of the forward and backward momentum of Estrel's and Ericen's strikes. Attack, step back, arrow. Attack, step back, arrow. Breathe.

Soldiers fell.

My thundering heart filled my ears. I became aware of every breath, every movement. The world fell away as blood splattered my pants, my hands, my bow.

A Trendellan monk and two Rhodairen soldiers had joined Ericen and Estrel, but Res was too noticeable of a target. More and more Illucians broke off, making straight for us. Our line was wearing down, and my open shots were few and far between. Every time we fell back deeper into the city, they pursued us, Res limping just ahead of us.

We couldn't hold out much longer.

"Fall back!" Lady Kerova's voice sounded above the tumult. "To the lake!"

The lake. It was a death trap. With only the thin strip of stone across it, our troops would bottleneck and be slaughtered.

But they were already being slaughtered.

We fought and ran and struck and fell back. Ericen killed two Illucian soldiers in a row. Estrel took down a third. Six more took their place.

Somehow, we reached the far end of the town, drained and bleeding and with muscles burning. The city was overrun. A tide of black and blue slid inevitably toward us.

A Rhodairen soldier stumbled back beside me, her dark eyes wide. "It's gone."

I seized her shoulder. "What's gone?"

"The path."

I spun. Over the heads of the backed-up infantry, I could see through the arch leading out to the lake.

The earth Sella had destroyed the stone pathway.

They'd cut off our retreat.

A sword caught the monk in the stomach, the tip piercing through his back. Another cut across Estrel's leg, sending her to the ground.

The battle Sella grinned down at us.

Ericen stepped in front of Estrel, downing a Vykryn as he moved. I put an arrow in the one coming for his back. But there were too many. The battle Sella's makeshift sword caught Ericen along the side of his arm, then he slit the throat of a Rhodairen soldier. She fell, a sickening wheeze cutting through the thunder in my ears.

My fingers sought another arrow—and found only air.

The battle Sella stepped back and threw something wide over our heads. A net fell over Res. He let out a piercing screech and flared his wings, but they only tangled in the ropes. Two Vykryn moved in, tugging him down. A third lifted a sword.

A scream tore through me as I threw myself at the Vykryn. My shoulder rammed into his chest, knocking him back. I swung through with my bow, catching him across the face with its sharpened edge. The other Vykryn closed in on me, and I backed away, panting hard.

Over their shoulder, I met Ericen's gaze. Saw him fighting viciously to get to me. Saw the tide of soldiers swallow him up and knew that it was over, that we'd lost.

The battle Sella raised his sword over Estrel's exposed neck.

Then a black gold blade pierced through his chest.

He dropped, the Vykryn turning too slowly. Kiva killed them before they realized what she'd done.

Relief nearly sent me to my knees as Kiva, bloody and scratched and bearing a wild grin, said, "I brought some friends."

Over her shoulder, a ripple went through the Illucian soldiers. One by one, they turned, forced to face something charging through their ranks from behind.

Our reinforcements had arrived.

The Jin and Ambriellan forces flooded across the field.

Unlike Rhodaire's, Jindae's cavalry had been second only to Illucia. That might showed in the line of horses rushing the exposed infantry's backs. Soldiers turned too slowly as horses barreled through them, blades flashing.

Ericen broke between two soldiers, shoving his way to Kiva's side as Estrel and I tore the net away from Res. He let out a low caw, tugging at me along the line. He wanted to fight.

I swung back around and into the saddle. He straightened, his leg finally healed.

"Get those ranks formed back up!" I shouted to Kiva. "And stay out of Res's way!"

Then we shot into the sky.

Magic stuttered down the bond, then flared to life. He coasted out along the sea of Illucian soldiers.

Then lightning began to rain.

Soldiers screamed and ran for cover beneath the towers, but there weren't enough to shelter them. Res's storm tore through their ranks.

This was the true power of the crows. For all Illucia had done to counteract them, when their tricks and weaponry failed, they had no response to the crows' magic.

Between the rallying forces inside the city, the reinforcements flanking from behind, and us wreaking havoc down the center, the army broke.

Soldiers fled. Lines splintered. Bodies fell.

Res and I swept back along the wall, the power of the storm flooding our veins. It was like Res drew strength from it as power undulated along the bond.

We alighted atop the battlement, surveying the battle inside the city, looking for places to help, but our forces were already driving the Illucians out.

Then I saw a familiar figure picking its way toward Ericen's exposed back, sword drawn.

Shearen.

My arrow caught him in the leg.

He screamed as he dropped to his knees. Res landed before

him, and Ericen spun, sword raised. I leapt off Res's back, another arrow nocked, but Shearen threw up a hand.

"Stop!" His voice tore with pain. "I didn't come to fight."

I drew back my bowstring.

"Please!" he cried, letting his sword drop and holding up his hands. "I'm on your side."

Ericen's hand stayed mine. Reluctantly, I lowered my bow.

"Explain," the prince ordered.

Shearen stared up at him, dark blue eyes exhausted and pained. "I came to warn you. This entire battle has been a distraction."

My stomach dropped. "What?"

His eyes met mine. "Razel is attacking Aris."

Sounds blurred in my ears, and I forced myself to breathe even as I surged forward, seizing Shearen by the throat. "What do you mean?" My fingers dug in sharply. "Tell me what you mean!"

Ericen grabbed my wrist, pulling my hand back. "He will, Thia." The steel in his voice calmed me as Shearen coughed, hand going to his throat.

"One of the Sellas she freed rebuilt the road to Aris," he said hoarsely. "Or at least he was rebuilding it when I left. They said it would take a few days, but if this battle has begun, then the road must have almost been finished before they attacked."

"Liar," I hissed. "You just want Res and me out of the battle."

Ericen leveled his sword at Shearen's throat. "Give me one

reason to believe you." The second meaning of his words was clear—*give me one reason not to kill you.*

Shearen lifted his head, exposing his throat openly to Ericen's blade. "Because you were right." He swallowed hard. "Back in the wood, you were right. This has gone too far. Razel has lost control. Her need for revenge has taken over. She's not doing what's best for Illucia. Maybe she never was. I'm not the only one who thinks it either. There have been protests in the streets. Civilians who are tired of this war. Vykryn too."

He held Ericen's gaze unwaveringly. "I'm so sorry, Eri. I made so many mistakes, and by the time I understood what I'd done, I'd already driven you away. I thought earning her respect would regain me yours, and perhaps, in time, your friendship. But that night in the wood, I realized that serving her was only going to lose me you for good. Any leader willing to sacrifice her own family isn't someone I want to follow." He bowed his head. "You are."

I looked to Ericen, his face slack with shock. Indecision riled through me. Every instinct told me not to trust Shearen, to stay and fight, but I couldn't ignore the fear that Aris was truly in danger.

Caliza. My heart panged.

My hand closed around Ericen's. "It's your call," I said. "I trust you."

His fingers tightened on mine, and his gaze lifted to Res. "Let's go."

We sent word to the others of our departure and orders to accept Shearen's and any other willing Illucian's surrender rather than kill them. Then Ericen climbed onto Res's back behind me, and we took off.

What boost of energy Res had gotten from the storm, he funneled into the wind, propelling us even faster across valleys and forests, rolling hills and lakes dark with the setting sun. The prince held fast to me, his arms around my waist as we soared along the racing current.

Every second felt a lifetime long, every minute an eternity. Even with the boost of the wind, Aris felt so far away.

When at last we sailed over the Kessel Woods and Aris rose before us in the night's distance, I knew immediately that we were too late.

The castle was on fire.

THIRTY-TWO

I t was Ronoch all over again.

Flames ate their way through the gardens. They climbed over stone and tore through trees. Smoke cloaked the grounds, obscuring the movement of shadowy dueling figures. I caught glimpses of Vykryn dueling Rhodairen soldiers guarding the main gate and outside the abandoned rookery.

"Saints," I breathed.

"The landing platforms," Ericen said over my shoulder. "We can assess everything safely from there."

I nudged Res, and we alighted upon the nearest platform a moment later. Up here, the sky was clear, the air free of cloying smoke.

Below, a battle raged.

Soldiers emerged from the mausoleum beside the one to

Trendell. Their progress was slow due to the narrow confines of the road, but enough had gotten through to give our castle guard a fight.

"We have to put the flames out first," I said. "Then destroy the road."

Ericen slid off Res's back. "You deal with the fire, I'll make sure the castle is secure and pass on the message about the road."

I leaned down, kissing him swiftly. "Be careful."

His hand squeezed mine. "You too."

Then he was gone, and Res and I were airborne again, circling the grounds. Magic snapped between us along the cord, wild and rich with the need to be used, even as I felt it scraping at the last of his strength. The safe flight had rejuvenated his magic, but he still wasn't at full strength.

Res's eyes began to glow. Clouds gathered, slowly darkening as the storm grew until the sky was black with shadows. The wind rose, howling past my ears and tearing at my braid.

Thanks to the smoke cover below, no one would see the storm coming.

Rain, I told Res.

Thunder boomed, the only warning of what was coming before the storm broke and flooded the world below.

Rain fell so thick, it drenched me almost instantly, blurring my vision. The fire below flickered and waned, spots of it dying in a snap of light as the downpour continued.

We circled lower, targeting the more resilient patches with Res's fire magic until the last of them had withered and died.

We have to blow away the smoke. Once it was clear, our forces would be able to mount a counterattack to reach the Sella road and collapse the mausoleum.

The bond pulsed again as the wind began to gather. *Push it down and away.*

With a flap of his wings, Res sent a wave of wind barreling down through the grounds, and then another, and another. With each stroke, the smoke thinned, carried away by the growing current. The beats became a steady rhythm, funneling into a stream of air that dispersed the last of the smoke and grew still.

The first arrow nearly took Res in the wing. The second one split my cheek, sharp enough that I didn't even feel it. Only the hot rush of blood along my skin told me what'd happened.

My heart faltered. I gripped tighter with my knees as Res beat his wings in a powerful flurry, driving us higher and out of range. We swept over the landing platform, landing slightly off-kilter, both of us breathing hard.

"Saints," I breathed. Not thinking, I touched my cheek. Pain seared and I winced. Soft golden light wisped off Res in response. "No," I said quickly. "It's not bad. Save your strength."

The shouts of soldiers echoed from below. I peered over the side. With the fire out and the smoke cleared, our soldiers poured out the main door, meeting Razel's forces in a clang of metal. With Valis in her ranks—and I had no doubt the flames were his doing—we didn't have the luxury of battening down the castle and waiting them out. We had to defeat her strike force and end this before too many soldiers came through the road.

I turned Res toward the other side of the platform. Soldiers poured out one by one from the Sella road inside the mausoleum.

A lean figure stood before them, his hands wreathed in flames. Valis. Which meant the shadow Sella was inside holding the road open.

"We have to stop them and destroy the road," I said. Res trilled softly. Because it was made of black gold, he wouldn't be able to bend it with earth crow powers.

I scouted the air path from here to the graveyard, noting a pair of archers guarding either side of the mausoleum. Their bows were nocked with glass arrows, aimed at where we'd landed. Waiting.

If we leapt from here, they'd shoot us down.

"How do you feel about being a shadow crow for a while?" I asked.

Res lifted his wings, power thrumming through the cord. Shadows coalesced around us in an inky cloak until we peered out at the world through a haze.

Go.

Res leapt, wings snapping out to catch us. He circled around behind the mausoleum, banking hard to drive us down.

Attack.

Lightning exploded from Res's beak. It struck the side of the mausoleum, crumbling and melting its side. Soldiers yelled. They turned, bows raised, but couldn't find the source of the attack.

A ball of flame narrowly missed my shoulder. Res cut sharply to the side, letting out a piercing cry. He turned his wings down, forcing us along an updraft and back toward the landing plat-form. I glanced back. Valis regarded us with hooded yellow eyes.

He could sense us.

Another fireball whizzed past my ear. I leaned low to Res's

body, shrinking his target. Res beat his wings, driving for the platform and safety. An archer released an arrow, guided by Valis, and the others followed suit. Res flung back a wind, knocking the rush of arrows aside. But they were coming from too many angles. He'd no sooner sent one scattering than another barely missed his flank.

Then suddenly, a shrill, piercing sound erupted through the grounds. Soldiers clapped their hands to their ears, their faces twisting in pain.

Crack, crack, crack! The sound of breaking glass split the night like shattering ice. Res reared up and over the side of the landing platform, shaking his head as if to toss away the horrible noise.

The next moment, one of the archers shouted, throwing aside his quiver. The other followed suit, his hand coming back stained red.

I stared, uncomprehending, as a chorus of shouts echoed among the breaking glass. Then I remembered.

"Caylus," I breathed. Leaning over the edge, I spotted Ericen near the base of the castle. He tore his hand free from the crank, drawing a sword with the same motion and meeting the blade of another Vykryn. No sooner had he than another Vykryn intercepted the fight on the prince's behalf, protecting him. Two more joined, fending off the attacker.

Shearen had said he wasn't the only Vykryn on Ericen's side. He'd been able to organize ranks so that some of them joined Razel's personal guard, but he didn't think they'd act unless they had a reason to. It seemed Ericen had given them that reason.

I leaned close to Resyries, eyes set on the mausoleum. "Go!" He leapt.

THIRTY-THREE

W e dove.

Wind bit at my skin and snapped at my hair, barreling past quicker and quicker. As the earth grew closer, I squeezed my knees, and Res's wings shot out, carrying us fast along the ground.

The soldiers had yet to recover from the sudden sound. The exploding glass had cut them and Valis, who held his side. He pulled his bloody hand free, and a rush of fire enveloped it. Shouts rose, swords being drawn. Lightning gathered at the tip of Res's open beak.

Bring it down.

The bolt struck the mausoleum, folding it in on itself. A third strike collapsed it in a rush of molten metal. As we circled back around for a final assault, Res formed more lightning, his exhaustion thundering alongside it. He was scraping the wells of his power. This was all he had left.

We dove low. Res prepared to strike. Then, between one breath and the next, something thudded into him.

His wings snapped into his body and we plummeted.

My stomach dropped, the world twisting and flipping. Then pain, resounding through me like a quake. We slid across the earth, stone tearing at my skin, and rolled to a stop.

I lay still. Every inch of my body radiated pain. My head pounded, shattering each coherent thought I tried to process.

We'd fallen.

We'd *fallen.*

"Res." I barely heard my own voice through the pounding in my head.

He didn't respond.

I lashed out along the cord, pulling sharply. What came flooding back was wild and hot, an avalanche of fear and pain and unbridled fury. I gasped, bolting upright, and found Res struggling to right himself.

An arrow shaft stuck out of his leg.

"No!" I screamed, clawing at dirt and rocks, scrambling to his side. He forced himself to his feet, his injured leg pulled tight to his body.

I was at his side in a heartbeat, my scrapes and bruises forgotten. Res crooned, the sound ragged with pain.

"You're okay," I told him, hands hovering uselessly over the protruding shaft. I traced the line of his leg, seeking the tendons and muscles I'd once memorized, and let out a heavy breath.

The arrow had missed tendon, artery, and bone. It was a flesh wound.

"Thank the Saints," I breathed even as I questioned where the arrow had come from. Caylus's machine had destroyed the glass arrows... I stopped as my eyes took in the plain wood of the shaft. It was a normal arrow. We'd been too focused on the glass.

I gave Res no warning before I snapped the shaft, sliding both ends free.

He screamed, the sound shattering my eardrums and my heart in one.

"I'm sorry." I forced back the tears that burned at my eyes. *I'm sorry, I'm sorry.*

Res panted heavily and tried to move his leg, but contracting the muscle sent a shuddering ripple through him. Fear trembled along the bond, and I sent back reassuring pulse after reassuring pulse.

"Can you heal it?" I asked, though I knew the answer.

Golden light wisped around him, then flickered and died. My heart went with it. He was too weak—his magic had run dry.

A twig snapped. I froze. We'd crashed in a small copse of trees off the edge of the forest, something the Illucian soldiers weren't likely to have missed. But when I unslung my bow and nocked an arrow, ducking around Res's side, it wasn't a Vykryn I found coming for me.

It was Valis.

I loosed the arrow before I could think. He incinerated it with a flick of his hand.

I'd nocked another before he even lowered it, but he lashed out. A whip of flame shot from his hand. I dove, rolling aside as it struck the ground inches from where I'd been. The wet ground smoked and hissed.

Another fire had started on the grounds. Between it and the nearly full moon, I could see Valis clearly as he advanced, languid and unhurried as a jungle cat approaching its kill.

He was beautiful, in a cruel way. With white-gold hair and amber eyes like a lion's, he prowled ever closer, his movements lithe in a predatory way. With the flames at his back setting his tawny skin aglow, it was easy to see how people had once worshipped his kind as gods.

A graceful smile spread across his lips. "Little crow queen," he said in a voice of warm honey.

Res let out a shrill cry and tried to move in front of me. Pain flared down the line between us, and I sucked in a breath, placing a hand against his chest. *Stay still. I've got this.*

Valis's golden eyes washed over Res, his smile unfaltering. There was something slightly unhinged about the look, about the way that smile didn't break.

"I've waited a very long time for this," he hissed. "For what your family did to me." He drew a sword from his back. It erupted with pale orange flame. "I'm going to enjoy watching you burn."

He lunged. I shot forward, swinging low and dragging my hand through the earth. I came up with a handful of dirt and thrust it into his eyes. He snarled, swinging wildly, but I slid beneath it and came up behind him, striking for his kidneys with the limb of my bow.

He moved faster than I thought possible. He turned, sword coming down in a swift arc. It never struck. The next moment, Valis hit the ground hard from the impact of Res's body, his blade skittering out of reach. Valis rolled, springing lithely to his feet. Res cawed, wings flaring as lightning crackled around his body. It faltered, then died.

Valis thrust out a hand, and fire gathered at his palm. I loosed an arrow, stealing his attention as he was forced to burn it. Then I was on him, my knife in one hand, my bow in the other. He moved so fast. It was everything I could do to match pace with him as my attack quickly turned to defense.

Then all at once, his body erupted with flames.

I stumbled back with a cry, tripping over a root in my haste to escape the fire. Valis drove his flaming sword down—and straight into another blade.

Elkona deflected the sword with a slash of her moonblade. Quick as a wingbeat, she'd drawn a red line across Valis's stomach. He reared back, but her blade came around, slicing clean through his right wrist.

Valis screamed, his flames extinguishing.

I found my feet, nocking an arrow. The bowstring snapped. The arrow took Valis in the chest. He fell back a step, snarling, and then Elko was there, cutting a deep wound across his thigh.

As she leapt away, I took her place, my dagger biting into his stomach.

Then with a final turn, Elko slashed her blade through his throat.

Valis coughed, blood coating his lips. He fell back against a tree as Elko pulled her blade free, slick with crimson.

I stared at the Sella's lifeless body a moment, breathing hard. Then I looked to Elko. Blood speckled her face, turning the grin she gave me almost vicious. She held out her hand, and I took it.

"Let's end this," she said.

THIRTY-FOUR

The battle sprawled across the castle grounds.

Illucian soldiers pried at the mausoleum with their blades, trying to reopen the collapsed entrance, but it would be useless—they had no Sella to operate it. Our forces had pushed through and were rushing them. Elko shot past me with a whoop of delight, intercepting a Vykryn coming for a Rhodairen soldier's back.

A flash of blue caught my eye, two fighting soldiers parting to reveal a sight that stilled my breath.

Ericen was dueling Razel.

She struck in a wild frenzy, her moonblades flashes of silver in the light. Ericen had lost one of his swords, barely parrying her attacks with the remaining one. The sleeves of his shirt had been scorched away, his skin red and raw where the flames must have caught him.

Ericen ducked a blow, and another figure stepped forward, taking Razel's follow-up strike—another Vykryn. But even between the two of them, they couldn't take her down, even as they sliced her arms and legs and side. Razel fought with a wild fury, and the other Vykryn was favoring an injured leg.

Then in one swift move, she drove her sword through the Vykryn's leg. Her other hand came up, a dagger clasped in her fingers. She drove it through the Vykryn's neck.

He toppled to the ground as she ripped her weapons free.

"Stay here," I ordered Res. I forced myself forward even as my body struggled.

Res lurched after me, screeching.

Stay! I screamed down the line.

A Vykryn met me as I emerged from the tree line. I caught his sword on my bow, deflecting the blade and ducking low. Then Res was there, his claws tearing through flesh.

"I told you to stay, you bloody chicken!"

He cawed back, limping after me on his injured leg. He fought with beak and talons, rending flesh as I struck out with my bow, taking out knees and slicing along ribs with the sharpened edge, even as my energy fled me bit by bit.

When at last we broke through the flood, my heart stopped.

Ericen fought Razel one-handed, his other arm hanging limp at his side, coated in blood. He favored his right leg, barely able to put weight on it, and a wound on his forehead leaked blood into his eyes.

The queen dove inside his guard, catching him in the jaw with an elbow. He fell back against the castle, his sword dragging along the earth.

Razel drove her moonblade down.

My arrow struck the blade from her hand. She whirled, but I already had another arrow nocked and loosed. It skinned her wrist, and she released her other blade with a snarl. Behind her, Ericen collapsed against the wall, sliding to the ground.

A dangerous fire burned in Razel's eyes. "I wondered when you'd find me, Thia dear."

I leveled an arrow at her. Never had I been so aware of the tension in the string, of the power coiled inside. Here, among the flames and the dying, the acrid scent of smoke breaking loose memories I'd locked deep, deep inside, my hands quivered. Not from exhaustion, and not from fear, but from the desire to simply let go. To let my arrow find her heart.

It was no less than she deserved.

Razel must have seen the battle playing out on my face, because she grinned like a salivating wolf. She stood tall, imperious in her gilded armor, and stepped toward me.

I stepped back, lifting my arrow. "It's over," I rasped. "The Sellas are dead. You have no weapons. Surrender."

Razel laughed. "You're too weak to kill me." She stepped forward, and then again.

I held my ground, my hands trembling.

She deserves to suffer, as we have suffered. Elko's words were a thunderstorm in my head. *She deserves to die.*

My mother. The crows. My people. Jindae. The Ambriels. She'd killed so many.

So why couldn't I kill her?

How many had died at my hand already, at the whim of Res's power? What made this any different?

Why am I so weak? I'd spent countless hours lying in bed, asking myself that question. It had taken facing Razel, facing my past as well as my future, for me to understand I wasn't weak at all. I never had been.

I caught Ericen's gaze behind her. He nodded.

Survival took strength, and I had survived. Moving forward took strength, and I had forged a new path.

Forgiveness took strength, and I would not let Razel take that from me.

I would not become her.

"You're right." I lowered my bow.

Razel's smile sharpened.

"But I won't let you go either."

I shot her in the foot. She snarled, the sound more fury than pain. Without batting an eye, she ripped the arrow from her foot and clung to it like a knife. Then she lunged, slashing.

I deflected the arrow with my bow. A piercing cry followed as Res struck, biting through the shaft and sending the arrowhead tumbling into the earth. He curled his body before me like a shield as Razel leapt back into a crouch, remnant lightning sparking through the crow's feathers.

Razel rose with Ericen's discarded sword in her hand.

I clutched my bow, fingers swiping for an arrow—and found

none. My heart stuttered. Then Razel was upon me, a tempest of fury and steel.

I forced her aside, away from Res. She struck again and again. I deflected her blade, retreating with every step. Res's anxious energy flooded the cord, but I warned him back. Razel struck with reckless abandon, her normal grace gone in the face of her rage. Out of the corner of my eye, I saw Ericen struggling to his feet.

I lashed out with the sharpened edge of my bow, slicing Razel across the arm. She hissed, thrusting her blade while my guard was open and catching me along the ribs. White-hot pain flared along my side, and I spun away to give myself space.

She advanced, but then Res was there, forcing her back with a flare of his metal-tipped wing, the most his faded magic could muster. My strength ebbed, and the world began to darken. Between fighting the Sella and my wounds, my body couldn't take much more. Res fell back, ready to support me.

"I will tear you apart," Razel snarled. "I will destroy what remains of your pathetic kingdom. And when this world is mine, then I will at last have peace."

"Haven't you figured it out yet?" I rasped, clutching my side. Blood seeped through my fingers. "No matter how many people you kill, they're never coming back."

Razel straightened sharply, her nostrils flaring. "You think I don't know that? You think I care? Family is weakness. Love is weakness. Let me show you."

For an instant, everything was still. Something like regret passed through Razel's face before her expression hardened to steel.

She spun and drove her blade through Ericen's stomach.

I screamed, and the sky screamed with me.

Power erupted down the cord as Res rose tall behind me. I could feel his magic feeding on me, feel my energy running down the bond the same way it had when I'd pulled it free of him in Caylus's workshop. This was my strength, my magic— and Res was drawing on it.

Thunder boomed, shuddering through the sky in an earthquake of shattering sound. The wind howled, snapping my hair against my skin, but I didn't feel the sting nor the tattoo of the pouring rain.

Razel withdrew the sword. Ericen gasped, blood spurting from his lips. As he slid to the ground, a crimson smear trailed along the castle wall in his wake.

I screamed again. The rain hardened into ice, falling like stones as Res's magic erupted. At my back, Res let out a piercing call, snapping open his wings to protect me from the buffet of the wind and the bite of the hail.

Lightning struck a pace away from Razel. She stumbled to the side, fumbling to raise her sword in the heavy winds. I pushed harder on the link, willing my strength to Res.

The hail struck like arrows. Ribbons of red appeared on Razel's face and neck, hands and arms. Like the countless lines she'd sliced into her own skin in sacrifice to her god, so the ice cut more and more. She raised her hands to protect her face, but it was no use. The ice grew larger, turning from pebbles to sharpened fragments of glass. They drove into her body like knives.

With a scream, she lifted her sword and lunged for me. Lightning struck the ground right before her, throwing her back. She hit the ground hard, her own blade cutting into her leg. Blood stained her golden uniform, her hair, and her body until her skin looked raw.

She struggled to her knees, shards of ice rising from her skin in spikes. Her chest heaved, and she coughed blood, her skin paler than snow.

Res cawed again, the sound melding with the thunder.

Then the queen of Illucia fell.

THIRTY-FIVE

B lood puddled beneath Razel's body, running in rivulets through the earth as the rain chased it away. For a moment, all I could do was watch the tiny rivers move, as if with each drop of life they carried away, they took a piece of me with them.

A piece of my anger, a piece of my fear. A piece of my pain, and a piece of my shame.

Then the ground grew too flooded to see them any longer, and Res released his hold on the storm.

The rain stopped, the wind quieting as the last peal of thunder boomed. The cloud cover thinned, and rays of moonlight reached low over the tops of the trees.

Across the castle grounds, the sounds of battle gasped and faded. The fires had been put out by the rain. The surviving

Vykryn were outnumbered, the remains of the mausoleum surrounded.

I swayed, and then my fuzzy mind snapped back into place.

"Ericen," I breathed, lurching forward. He clutched his stomach, his breath coming in ragged bursts. It took several blinks before my vision focused enough to see the wound. Then my stomach churned. I ripped off a piece of my shirt beneath my leathers. Gathering it up, I pressed it against his stomach.

He hissed and yet somehow still managed to smirk at me. "You almost look concerned," he rasped, and I choked on my voice.

"I can fix this," I said, the words half prayer. The ground felt far away beneath me, even as I knew I sat upon it. Blood soaked through the cloth quickly. Too quickly. I pushed harder.

Res gathered over us, cooing softly. The cord between us felt fragile and frayed, like a rope worn from rubbing against stone.

With what little strength remained, I pushed hard on my magic, willing it to Res so he could heal the prince.

Nothing happened.

I pushed harder, but it was like scraping the bottom of a dry well. A shudder reverberated through me, and I sucked in a deep breath, trying again and again and again.

Ericen's hand fell over mine. "Thia."

"No." I shook my head. "No, no, no. I can do this. I can do this!"

I ripped at the place where the energy had once resided inside me but found nothing.

It was empty.

"No," I breathed.

My strength was fleeing my body like a river breaking its dam. Res wobbled, then dropped to his knees, exhausted from his burst of power. My vision blackened at the edges. Distantly, I was aware of the shadows encroaching. They enveloped me like a blanket.

As the last of my strength fled me, Ericen's hand loosened on mine, and darkness claimed me.

I woke with a face full of feathers.

Shoving Res's wing off my face, I let out a low groan and sat up. Pain lanced through my side, and I clutched reflexively at my injured ribs. The crow didn't move, his breaths coming in heavy, snore-like rumbles. I blinked as my vision solidified.

I was in my room.

Sunlight poured in through massive windows, making Res's feathers glimmer with iridescent light. It was quiet, the sort of silence that settled after a storm, after the rain had washed everything away.

My muscles felt like stone, my throat rough as sand. I lifted my shirt to reveal angry red skin and a thick, scabbed line bordered by dark purple bruising. Everything else ached right along with it.

Last night came tumbling back in flashes. The blood and gore of the battle. Razel's pale skin lined with red. Ericen's lips coated in blood.

My heart lurched. I struggled out from beneath Res, who

lay draped across the bed like a blanket. My body protested as I swung my legs out, stumbling as my knees threatened to buckle. Using the wall as a guide, I struggled across my room to the door.

I'd barely reached it when it flew open. Kiva filled the door frame. For a split second, all I could think of was how clean she looked. Bandaged, washed of blood, her hair braided neatly. How long had I been asleep?

"What in the Sain—" she began. My legs gave. She caught me before I hit the ground.

"The battle," I breathed. "The others."

"You need to get back in bed." Kiva slid her arms under me, hoisting me against her chest.

My head swam. The next moment, I felt the bed beneath me, and I fought to keep myself from going under. I barely caught her muttering something about Res being a useless guard chicken.

"The others," I said again, but if she responded, I didn't hear it.

The next time I woke, someone sat in a chair beside my bed.

At first, my vision blurred. Then relief burst through me in a fierce, heady rush.

Ericen's feet were propped on the bed, one of Res's wings draped over him as he massaged the joint with one hand. Res cooed softly, like a cat's quiet purr.

He was *alive*.

I choked on a sob of joy. Ericen leapt to his feet at the sound, Res following. He let out a low caw, the bond thrumming, and laid his head on my lap. Deliberately, he shuffled to the side, trying to crowd Ericen out. The prince refused to move, giving the bird a flat look.

I ignored their silent battle, laying a hand on Res's head. Silence pooled between us, comfortable and familiar. I let it linger, if only for a moment. One moment of peace before responsibility came rushing back.

"How're you feeling?" Ericen asked at last, handing me a glass of water from my nightstand.

I drank greedily. "Like I got hit by a crow," I replied once I'd finished, earning an indignant trill from Res. "What happened? Is everyone all right?"

A smile curved Ericen's lips. "We won."

My breath released in a rush, and I swallowed hard as a knot unraveled in my chest. It was over.

"Your friends and family are fine," he said. "Res has been taking care of the wounded. He healed the worst of your wounds too."

Res puffed up as I patted him.

"How did you survive?" I asked. My voice was hoarse, my throat raw. "At the end, I couldn't—" Even the memory hurt to touch.

"You," he said quietly. "Right before you passed out. Res's body practically exploded with light. I think he thought you were dying." A smile tugged at his lips. "I was just lucky you fell on me. Apparently, even when you're fainting, you can't resist me."

I snorted harshly, seizing a pillow and walloping him with it. In true Ericen fashion, he caught it in a viselike embrace and used it to pull me close.

Then he kissed me.

When at last he pulled back, I felt steady again.

"Now what?" he asked.

I smiled, my fingers curving over his. "Now we move forward."

I filed out of Caliza's office alongside Kiva. The last few weeks had been a whirlwind of meetings and bureaucracy that'd left my head spinning, but I was proud of what we'd accomplished.

Kiva had recounted for me how Res's shadow crow had been flying over the lake when it'd dispersed. By the time she'd swum out, Illucian soldiers were bearing down on her. She'd led them into the woods, picking them off one by one. That was when she'd stumbled across our reinforcements clashing with the Illucian rear guard. They'd overpowered them and gone straight for Elaris.

After Ericen and I left, our forces had broken through the last of Razel's lines and subdued the rest of her army. Some chose to fight to the end, but many surrendered when faced with three armies. They'd been escorted back to Illucia under Rhodairen guard as a sign of good faith to the empire's new king.

Ericen's transition hadn't been easy. A small contingent of the surviving Vykryn had already pledged to him, led by Shearen, who Razel had apparently made Valix before his betrayal. With one of the kingdom's most influential leaders pledged to Ericen, the rest of the military quickly fell in line. It didn't hurt that by Illucian customs, Ericen was the rightful king. Tradition was a powerful force in Illucia.

It'd only been a few weeks, but I already missed him.

What would become of our relationship now that he was king had been a thought I'd refused to ruminate on for long. I knew I wanted to be with him, but our circumstances seemed designed to keep us apart. He had a kingdom to reign in and rule; I had one to rebuild. But the idea of losing him threatened to open a hole inside me.

Rhodaire had pledged what support it could to the other kingdoms, though Caliza wasn't particularly happy when I explained I owed Samra a new ship, especially with so much work to be done in Rhodaire itself. She spent a good hour lamenting over the one-of-a-kind stained glass windows Caylus's horn had broken. Apparently, they'd been a gift from a long-ago queen of Jindae, made of the same composite as the glass arrows.

Caylus had sent me a letter from Eselin, saying he intended to stay there and become a scholar. He'd already gotten a job at a local bakery, where he'd started selling his inventions, including a teapot that retained heat better. He'd sent one along with his letter, painted meticulously with a delicate crow design.

Estrel appeared in the doorway as Kiva and I entered the foyer, a grin on her lips. "I have something to show you guys."

I glanced at Kiva, who shrugged. Caliza joined us as we followed Estrel out into the garden and around the castle to where the royal rookery was nearly fully repaired. The foundation of the structure had gone undamaged in Ronoch; all we'd had to do was clear away the wreckage and rebuild the inside.

Estrel led us toward it, then paused with one hand on the door. She flashed a last smile before she pushed it open.

I froze in the doorway as Caliza gasped.

Scattered across a bed of hay, their shells bright in the noonday light, sat the remaining crow eggs. I gaped, covering my mouth with both hands, and simply stared. And then slowly, I began to laugh. A deep, shuddering, half-sobbing laugh of delight.

Beside me, Kiva grinned uncontrollably, her shoulders shaking with growing laughter.

Then I saw Ericen standing at the edge of the nest, a gleam in his blue eyes.

I launched myself at him. He caught me, spinning me about and setting me back on my feet. Then his lips were on mine, and I lost myself to the feel of his fingers in my hair and his body against mine.

Someone cleared their throat.

I pulled free with a sheepish smile. Ignoring Kiva's smirk, I dropped to my knees beside a pale gold sun crow egg, running my fingers along the silken shell. A quiet humming greeted me, the prickle of magic flowing through me.

Caliza knelt beside me, something uncertain in her face. Tentatively, she brushed her fingers along an earth crow shell. "I can feel something," she said. "It feels...alive."

A slow smile split across my face. "You can feel its magic."

Her eyes widened, and she pressed her hand flat against the

egg. For a moment, she simply sat like that. Not as the queen of a struggling kingdom, with a bloody past behind her and an uncertain future before her. Nor as the daughter who'd never been enough for a woman who asked too much.

She was just a girl, enraptured by a dream.

Then she let out a slow, heavy breath, and the weight of years went with it. Her free hand went to mine, squeezing it gently. I squeezed it back, then stood, leaving her to her new-found power.

As I rose, Kiva let out a whoop and darted across the room, catching me in her arms. Her grin was infectious. I laughed and smiled up at Estrel, whose face was wet with tears. She laid a hand on my shoulder.

"We can bring them back," I told her. The words broke something open inside me. But it was a good sort of breaking. It was like the hatching of an egg, giving way to something beautiful.

Something new.

A gentle breeze tousled my braid. It slipped against my skin and tugged at my clothes as if begging me to come and play with it. The sunlight glinted off my feathered bracelet, a familiar, comfortable weight once more.

Res stood beside me on the landing platform, his wing slightly lifted to give me better access to the saddle I was securing. He tugged incessantly at the cord, demanding we fly.

As I did the last tie and stepped back, Ericen stepped onto

the landing platform, looking about as comfortable with his decision as a man balancing on a cliff edge.

He'd told us how he'd put in motion the steps necessary to establish a ruling council in Illucia. Never again would a single person wield the power Razel had once held. But the transition would take time, and he wouldn't be able to visit me until it was complete.

Good thing I had a magical road that could transport me between kingdoms. Once we rebuilt it, of course.

Since Caliza and I were the only ones who could operate them, we'd adhered to each kingdom's wishes regarding their use. Trendell, Jindae, and the Ambriels had all agreed to leave them functioning, as it made transporting supplies and support their way a lot easier, but they were in the process of creating guidelines for their operation.

Ericen smiled, pulling me from my thoughts. He stopped a short way away. "This feels higher than last time," he remarked.

I raised an eyebrow. "These platforms do have a nasty habit of shifting places."

He snorted sharply, focusing on me rather than the sheer drop on either side of him. "Kiva said you'd be here."

I blinked. Kiva had willingly told him where I was?

I stepped toward him, my smile growing as I asked in a low voice, "Well, now that you've found me, what do you want with me?"

His face flushed, and I warmed at the sight. "The same thing I've always wanted," he said softly, and suddenly, I felt three times my size. Ericen had a way of making me feel that way, as if I were so much larger than myself.

It'd taken me a while to realize that the same fire that lived in him lived in me. Now, all I wanted was to let it burn.

"I see." I closed the last of the distance between us. The scarlet in his cheeks deepened. "And exactly how far will you go to get what you want?" I leaned closer and felt more than heard his intake of breath.

His fingers brushed my face. "Anywhere."

My lips brushed his, and then I leaned back, grinning. "Over here?" I asked, stepping toward the edge.

He lurched, as if my presence had been holding him upright, but moved after me.

I stepped back again. "What about here?"

He followed. I stepped again, and he tensed, eyeing the edge nervously. "This isn't funny, Thia."

"Now who can't flirt?" I asked.

"Threatening to jump off a hundred-foot-high platform isn't flirting."

I took another step. The strain in Ericen's face grew tauter. "Thia."

I stepped back again.

"You said you'd follow me anywhere," I said with a grin.

"Don't you dare."

I stepped off the edge.

"Thia!" His scream followed me as I plummeted through the air. The bond between Res and me came alive, and the next moment, he was above me, his wings tucked tight in a perfect dive.

I spread out my arms, slowing my fall, and he shot past me in a blur of feathers. Then he was beneath me, and I rolled, seizing the edge of the saddle. With a heave, I pulled myself in, sliding my feet into the stirrups.

Res's wings snapped open. He cut sharply upward, pumping his wings harder and harder until he caught a rising wind.

We spiraled upward, past the landing platform, past Ericen grinning up at us, and up through the clouds.

Up and up and up.

Together, we rose.

EPILOGUE

I was a storm.

It was a feeling I'd chased my entire life. From as far back as I could remember, I longed for the brush of the wind in my hair and the rush of the sky splitting open before me.

Not long ago, I'd thought it would never be possible again.

Today, a new future waited.

Res tilted into a broad bank, swinging back around toward the rising sun. I leaned close and we dove, spiraling through the morning clouds with wild abandon. When we pulled up, Res's wings flared wide, and we fell in alongside Ericen and his shadow crow, Zara.

Ericen might ride a horse like he'd been born to it, but even with five months in the sky, he still clung to Zara's back as if she might flip upside down at any moment.

We soared low over sprawling streets thick with vines and trees laden with fruit. The Rynthene Canal traced a glimmering line through a city slowly waking, early preparations for the evening's festivities already underway. Those few awake waved up to us as we passed.

The whole scene felt like an afterimage, left behind in the wake of a lightning bolt's flash. Slowly, it melded with a new reality.

We passed Jenara and her crow, Sen, setting out to water the expansive fields that had been reseeded. She flew alongside Esos, the earth crow rider who'd trained Res on our way to Trendell. Near the center of the city, smoke rose from the central forge, lit once more by a fire crow's power. Laz had been hard at work in it for weeks crafting new black gold weapons. Apparently, they'd been the blacksmith who made Sinvarra and my bow.

At my prompting, the riders who'd aided me had returned to Aris to fill the vacant Corvé positions. We'd hatched one crow of each type, which was the most the restored levels of the royal rookery could handle. The rest had had to wait until the remaining rookeries could be repaired—a process that had been completed only days ago.

Just in time for Negnoch.

Already, the reopened Kalestel riding school had been flooded with applications from old riding families and new alike. Rhodaire had come together, ready to rebuild what had been lost. Soon, they would have their chance.

Res and I led Ericen and Zara back to the castle, where we alighted on one of the landing platforms. Auma, Kiva, and Elko were waiting for us. As we dismounted, we shook hands with Auma before Elko pulled each of us into a massive bear hug. My arms curled awkwardly around the moonblades at her back. They'd once belonged to her mother, and she'd recovered them from Razel after the battle.

When she released me, I realized delicate gold and green lines covered the scars on her face and neck, marking her as the new queen of Jindae, a position she'd filled when her sister abdicated. Auma loved her kingdom, enough so that she recognized the people knew and loved Elko, not the distant princess who'd spent her life in foreign places. She was content knowing what she'd done for them.

"Your tama!" I exclaimed.

She grinned, brushing them with her fingers. "I hear you're due for a new design yourself."

"You mean late for a new design," Kiva remarked, arms folded. "We've been up here for twenty minutes! It's cold!"

"It's going to be way colder in Korovi, you know," I replied with a roll of my eyes. A few weeks ago, Kiva's mother had stopped answering her letters. When the third one didn't receive a response, she'd decided to seek her mother in Korovi herself. She left tomorrow.

Auma leaned into Kiva. "Kiva's temper will keep her warm," she said.

Kiva wrapped an arm around her. "I thought that's what I had you for."

A faint blush rose in Auma's cheeks, and Elko let out a bark of laughter.

"I thought you were late?" Ericen asked, his tone close to disapproving. Punctuality was yet another thing he and Kiva agreed on. They'd started keeping track, making a game of it. Whichever one agreed with the other had to buy them a drink.

"I'm going, I'm going!" I waved to Res, who nipped at Zara's wing teasingly, then leapt into the sky before the other crow could retaliate. She took off after him, the two quickly turning to shadows in the sky.

The others followed me inside where the upper levels of the castle were slowly being restored. They walked me to a room at the far end of the hall where a quiet murmur of voices trickled out.

Elko clapped me on the shoulder. "Good luck, crow queen. It'll only hurt a lot."

I glowered at her, earning a snicker from Kiva.

Ericen stepped between us, filling my vision with only him. "You'll be fine."

"Come with me?" I asked him.

His eyes brightened, and I slipped my hand into his, tugging him toward the open door. I slammed it in Kiva's laughing face.

Inside, Estrel waited with Lady Kerova. A long table with a thin sheet sat before the house leader, a chair and small table beside it, laden with needles and ink. I shivered, and Ericen squeezed my hand.

"You know it's against tradition for anyone but the abdicating Corvé and the inker to be present for this," Estrel grumbled. She sat on a small couch, a cup of tea in a saucer resting in her lap. It was a special blend Caylus had sent me from Trendell.

"Then we shouldn't be too surprised that Thia is dispensing with it," Lady Kerova said in her serene tone.

Estrel rolled her eyes. "Whatever. You, turn around." She gestured for Ericen to face the wall. Only she would speak to the king of Illucia like that.

I chose not to tell her it wouldn't be the first time Ericen had seen me undressed.

Ericen obeyed with a smirk. I removed my flying leathers and the shirt I wore underneath before lying facedown on the bed. As Lady Kerova sat down beside the small table, a second chair slid up beside me. I heard the shifting of the needles, the slosh of ink, and then Ericen's hand slid back into my own.

I closed my eyes and held on.

Several hours later, the Corvé tattoo was done.

I felt the wings stretching down my back, every inch of skin sensitive and raw. Before I dressed, Gavilan's sun crow healed the worst of it, progressing the tattoo to several days old and enabling me to slide my shirt back on with ease once he and his crow had left. No sooner had I than I was hiking it back up, trying to see the gold and black lines that now covered my back in the full-length mirror on the wall.

Something clicked into place inside me at the sight of it. I let my shirt drop, feeling tears threaten.

I'd made it.

Through fire and blood and war, I'd made it.

I'd become the next royal Corvé.

When I faced the room again, Estrel stepped up before me, enveloping me in a tea-scented hug. It was so different from the leather and crow scent of her I was used to. Different, but still her.

"Congratulations, Little Peep," she whispered. "Now, you have some crows to hatch."

I stood side by side with my sister in the royal rookery, surrounded by crow eggs.

Their shells shimmered in the rays of moonlight trickling in through the open windows. T-shaped perches ringed the edges, one occupied by Res, the other by Zara. A level below, the newest crop of riders waited to claim their eggs, their excited whispers echoing to our room above.

Ericen, Kiva, Auma, Elko, Estrel, Kuren, and Samra stood around us in a ring. The Trendellan queen and king had been invited too and gracefully declined, sending their congratulations.

Once, this had been one of the most closely kept secrets in all of Rhodaire.

Now, we shared it freely with our friends.

Magic was a tool, but it was also a burden and sometimes a weapon. Just like the crows. With the hatching of these new crows, one day, Rhodaire would have its strength again. Its power. And it was my responsibility to use it better than my mother did, to share it instead of hoard it.

Caliza stepped up beside me, a small knife in her hand. I

held its twin, and together, we each cut a thin line on the back of our forearms.

Together, we blooded the shells of each egg.

Together, we stepped back and watched as the eggs began to glow, and the humming grew like a rising wind.

Outside, the piercing call of a crow cut through the night. Res cawed back, then Zara, their calls echoing in the rookery. Res's eyes began to glow, and thunder boomed.

Before us, the first egg cracked open.

THE WORLD OF THE
STORM CROW

WINGS OF ARIS

THE THEREAL WING

SAINT: Edair Thereal

CROW: wind crow

EGG: creamy white

HEAD OF HOUSE: Lady Dovelin Thereal

INDUSTRY: entertainment, such as theater, music, and art-work. Wind crows protected crops from storms, helped facilitate flight paths throughout Aris for other crows, provided favorable winds for sailors, and helped with city maintenance, such as sweeping up feathers.

THE KEROVA WING

SAINT: Harla Kerova

CROW: shadow crow

SHELL COLOR: matte black

HEAD OF HOUSE: Lady Kumia Kerova

INDUSTRY: highly involved in the military, with a focus on espionage. Shadow crows helped conceal spies from both sight and sound, and also made up a large percentage of the military crows.

THE TURREN WING

SAINT: Royceir Turren
CROW: battle crow
SHELL COLOR: dark metallic gray
HEAD OF HOUSE: Lady Ryna Turren (previous head, Lord Zeir Turren, banished for treason)
INDUSTRY: weapons production, most famously black gold weapons, made from the feathers of battle crows. Aside from producing feathers for black gold, battle crows also made up the bulk of the military crows, helping with patrols, and also with transportation of heavy materials with their increased strength.

THE RYNTHENE WING

SAINT: Selka Rynthene
CROW: water crow
SHELL COLOR: deep ocean blue
HEAD OF HOUSE: Lord Relel Rynthene
INDUSTRY: highly involved in the navy, as well as trade and transport of goods, with a focus on production of ship and fishing supplies. Crows helped purify water, water crops, and manipulate the ocean for easy sailing and fishing.

THE BRYNTH WING

SAINT: Shaldra Brynth
CROW: earth crow
SHELL COLOR: forest green
HEAD OF HOUSE: Lord Culveir Brynth
INDUSTRY: architecture and city infrastructure, as well as the heart of Rhodairen knowledge pursuit. Known for crafting stone and woodworks. Crows helped with construction of new buildings and manipulation of farmland and tended to city landscaping.

THE GARIEN WING

SAINT: Azrel Garien
CROW: storm crow
SHELL COLOR: shiny black with specks of color
HEAD OF HOUSE: Lady Idrel Garien
INDUSTRY: produced the majority of crow provisions, from riding leathers to saddles. Storm crows helped with weather control, particularly for agriculture, and also marked time for important events through thunder.

THE CYRO WING

SAINT: Ciaran Cyro
CROW: fire crow
SHELL COLOR: bright red
HEAD OF HOUSE: Lord Ressen Cyro
INDUSTRY: food production and distribution, from restaurants to shops. Fire crows maintained the central forge, used by Turren smiths and Brynth crafters alike.

THE CARAVEL WING

SAINT: Adeliza Caravel
CROW: sun crow
SHELL COLOR: pale gold
HEAD OF HOUSE: Lady Rasara Caravel
INDUSTRY: healers, production of herbs, tonics, and poultices. Sun crows worked with healers, healing the sick and injured.

KINGDOMS

RHODAIRE

CAPITAL: Aris

RULED BY:

Queen Caliza Cerralté

King Kuren Rebane

Crown Princess Anthia Cerralté

Queen Alandra Cerralté—deceased (killed on Ronoch)

King Caros Cerralté—deceased (killed during the Last Crow War)

ENVIRONMENT:

Located in the Southwest

Hot, humid weather with frequent storms and high rainfall

Dense foliage in tropical landscape

RELIGION:

Rhodairens pray to the Saints, eight legendary crow riders said to have established Aris with the help of the Sellas, but religion isn't highly ingrained in society

ECONOMY:

Once centered around the crows

Large exporter of raw materials, grains, fruit, and other foods

Known for their black gold, a steel-like material made from battle crow feathers

Leaders in architectural and agricultural studies

CULTURE:
Very open, straightforward, and trusting

Family-focused with an emphasis on sharing

ILLUCIA

CAPITAL: Sordell

RULED BY:

Queen Razel Rulcet

Crown Prince Ericen Rulcet

King Gavilan Rulcet—deceased (killed in the Last Crow War)

Queen Ranielle Rulcet—deceased (killed in the Last Crow War)

Princess Kashel Rulcet—deceased (killed in the Last Crow War)

Prince Consort Celin Inastra—deceased (killed in the Last Crow War)

ENVIRONMENT:

Located in the West

Cold, cloudy weather, with winter snowfall and frequent rain

Vast green grasslands and rolling hills with numerous lakes and small rivers

RELIGION:

Illucians pray to Rhett, a god they worship through bloodshed and war, which is heavily ingrained into society

Many willingly give their blood during prayer as a sacrifice to Rhett

ECONOMY:

Supported by conquered nations (Jindae and the Ambriels) which provide food and raw materials and are highly taxed

Once exported weapons, armor, fine horses, wool products, and meat, but no longer trades with other kingdoms

CULTURE:

Conniving, manipulative, and power-hungry

Very militaristic and focused on honor, status, and strength

THE AMBRIEL ISLANDS

CAPITAL: Seahalla

RULED BY:

Illucia

Previously ruled by the high council, which consisted of representatives elected from the noble houses

The leader of the council, Kovan Castair, remains a figurehead

Part of Seahalla is also under the influence of the Drexel crime family

ENVIRONMENT:

Located off the western Illucian and Rhodairen coasts

Mild weather with frequent fog and occasional high winds

Surrounded by dormant sea volcanoes

RELIGION:

Ambriellans pray to Duren, the god who rules the sea by

day, attending temple whenever they choose, often
to pray for safe travels on the sea for themselves or
family

They also believe in Duren's sister, the goddess known as
Diah, the Night Captain, who rules the sea at night

More superstitious than religious when it comes to daily
practice, for example carrying rope tied in different
knots for luck, or happiness, or safety

ECONOMY:

Exports large amounts of seafood, ships, products made
from the coral surrounding the islands, whiskey, oil, and
sona lamps

CULTURE:

Very giving, with a focus on community and sharing food
and belongings

Easygoing and peaceful

KOROVI

CAPITAL: Vashka

RULED BY:

An elected government of only noblewomen, led by Vokana Mirkova

ENVIRONMENT:

Located in the North

Covered in snow almost year-round, save for the thaw during the summer months

Lots of mountains and thick pine forests

RELIGION:

The Korovi pray to the goddess Lokane, who is served by her priestesses, which are made up of the noblewomen, believed to be daughters of the goddess

The right to lead the Korovi government is considered goddess-granted

ECONOMY:

Korovi trades very little with other kingdoms

Occasionally exports animal products, work animals, and is rumored to have recently discovered oil in their mountains

CULTURE:

Extremely isolationist

Straightforward, unforgiving, and orderly

JINDAE

CAPITAL: Shalron

RULED BY:

Illucia

King Kycyra Kura—deceased (killed when Illucia invaded)

Queen Seyfyer Kura—deceased (killed when Illucia invaded)

Crown Princess Elkona Kura—rumored to have survived assassination

Heavily influenced by the leaders of each Guild prior to Illucian invasion

ENVIRONMENT:

Located east of the Ardrahan Sea

Vast golden grasslands and forested valleys

Four distinct seasons, tending toward dry and warm

RELIGION:

The Jin believe art and religion are one; they worship creation of new, beautiful, and creative things

ECONOMY:

Divided into several guilds, such as artist, gem, hunter, agriculture

Large exporter of precious stones, jewelry, metal, wood, and glass, as well as seafood and grain

CULTURE:

Extremely resilient, hardworking, people who are very good at dedicating themselves to something and mastering it

TRENDELL

CAPITAL: Eselin

RULED BY:

King Calren Rebane

Queen Luhara Rebane

Crown Prince Seren Rebane

Prince Kuren Rebane

Princess Kashna Rebane

ENVIRONMENT:

Located in the Southeast

Hot, dry, with golden hills and scattered woods

RELIGION:

While the Trendellans have a vast array of myths, including many lost legends regarding the Sellas, religion plays little role in their day-to-day lives, with their focus on science and knowledge

ECONOMY:

Large exporter of wine, chocolate, and new technology, as well as rare spices, ingredients, and historical information

CULTURE:

Very intelligent, wise, and learned

Peaceful, curious, kind

CONTINUE READING FOR
TWO BONUS STORIES SET
IN THE WORLD OF THE

STORM
CROW

ERICEN

E ricen couldn't feel the rain.

It slid down his face and pooled in the crevices of his armor, a second skin, and still he didn't move. Anthia and her friends had long since vanished into the mist. Vykryn had been summoned. Horses saddled. Hooves beat wet earth as they took off after the fleeing princess. He should be with them, should be leading the hunt. Instead, he did nothing but watch from the castle doorway as everything fell to pieces.

He'd been deluding himself for weeks. He'd told himself he could have everything: his mother's approval, the respect of his people, Thia. How foolish he'd been. The tightrope he'd been balancing on had finally snapped: it was time to choose.

He turned back into the shadows of the castle. Ever since he was a child, the castle had always reminded him of the carcass of some ancient beast. Its halls were hollow bones, its spires jagged teeth. Whatever life had once filled it had been scavenged, leaving behind something so empty it felt transient.

Now, it felt like the scaffolding beneath an executioner's block. Stepping inside meant risking his mother's wrath. Risking his mother's wrath meant risking your life. There'd been a time when he'd dismissed thoughts like that. Not anymore. His mother's fury had become a finely wrought blade these last few months. Ever since she'd destroyed the crows. She'd always been dangerous, always been cruel. But now she was unsteady. Unmoored. Whatever tethers had anchored her in her pain and anger had come undone. She was lost, and he had no idea what she might do next.

The throne room door slammed behind him. He almost flinched, caught between the mask he wore for his mother and the true face Anthia had stripped bare.

"You're empty-handed." His mother's voice was the graze of sharp claws, pricking just below the surface of his skin. At her side, a hooded figure stood impossibly still, only a swath of golden skin visible in the shadows.

Ericen gave himself a breath. Just one. Then he faced his mother. Shoulders back, hands clasped behind, eyes forward— the perfect soldier.

The fake smile that slid across his lips felt as natural as a sword in his hand. "For now. We have her trail. She's heading west for Port Maranock."

His mother sat on her gilded throne as if she were a part of the gold-and-black stone, surveying him with sharp eyes. He knew that look. She was deciding where to cut first.

"Each time I give you a task, you fail me," she said. "I thought you wanted to prove yourself."

Beneath the weight of her words and the force of her gaze, Ericen felt himself weaken. He felt his rigid posture crumple, his facade fade. But he said nothing. He knew better than to fight. Unlike Anthia. She'd never stopped fighting, even when everything had been stacked against her. His mother had underestimated her, had thought she could break her with her past, her mistakes, her fear of fire.

She'd never realized that Thia was the flame.

His mother's silence unsettled him. She was looking at him like she knew his thoughts. Then she let out a quiet sigh in a sound like ice settling. "I expect her at my feet before the Centerian. Bring her to me, or you will be barred from entering."

Illucia's tournament of champions. The one she'd promised him that if he won, she would name him Valix, leader of the Vykryn, his people's elite military unit. There was no higher honor, no more respected position. Every breath, every cut of his sword, every drop of blood he'd spilled—it had all been with this singular goal in mind.

Now he had it within arm's reach, and for the first time, he wanted something else more.

That realization nearly broke him.

He'd thought if he wasn't an active player in his mother's game that he wouldn't be complicit in her actions. That her crimes were not his own. But that only went so far. He was not responsible for his mother's darkness, but every time he stepped aside, he gathered a little of his own. How long before his shadows were as deep as hers?

"Ericen?"

His head snapped up. Had that been...uncertainty in his mother's voice? He studied her narrow face, her mask that he'd learned to mimic from the day he'd understood that just by existing he caused her pain.

She stared back, every inch the Illucian queen. He sought that uncertainty. That same shred of emotion he'd coveted for years. But that was the trick, he realized. She'd strung him along with promises and possibilities. If only he did this, if only he proved that, one day, it would be enough.

But love was not conditional. He understood that now.

You can make another choice. Thia's words. She'd given him another option, another path, and he'd been too afraid to take it.

He wouldn't be this time.

Ericen bowed, his mask firmly in place. "I will find her."

And when he did, he would do whatever it took to help her stop his mother.

KIVA

K iva *hated* traveling.

The monotony, the stale bread, the incessant *clomp clomp clomp* of a horse's hooves. Not to mention they'd long ago left behind anything resembling decent weather and were now trudging through two feet of snow in a forest of pines so tall and dark, they blotted the gray sunlight into dappled shadows. If it hadn't been all crows on deck in Rhodaire, she'd have complained a little more earnestly about the lack of bird-shaped transportation, but as it was, she'd only lamented the absence of spontaneous rain clouds and stray feathers in her hair instead.

Thia had known what she'd meant, because Thia always knew what she meant and had sardonically offered Ericen's shadow crow to teleport them the first leg of their journey to

Korovi, which Kiva had promptly declined. Or rather laughed at. Now, she was sorely regretting that decision.

"I think if you glower a little harder, we'll get there faster," said a quiet voice to her right.

Kiva groaned as Auma pulled her horse into step alongside her. "I've been in five different kingdoms in the last two months. I just want to sit by a fire and eat all of Thia's pastries when she's not looking. Is that too much to ask for?"

"I do believe it was your idea to embark on this journey," Auma replied with a smile. She'd done her short hair in an array of thin braids Kiva longed to twirl around her finger and wore a thick, fur-lined coat that nearly swallowed her small frame. "I was more than happy to never see this…*stuff* again." She shook a hand, dislodging several flakes of settled snow. "I've had more than enough of it in Illucia."

"Oh, come on, it's not that bad." Kiva ran a finger along the dusting of snow on her saddle. "Think of all the good things that come with snow. Fluffy clothes, hot tea, body heat—"

"Kiva!"

"Just saying, I'm *really* good at keeping people warm."

Auma swatted her shoulder, hiding a small smile behind one hand. Kiva returned it, catching Auma's hand before she could pull away and wrapping her gloved fingers around it.

The movement jostled the sleeping shape inside Kiva's jacket, and Aroch popped his head up from the collar. The addition of the little white cat to the trip had seemed far less absurd in the comfort of her room in Aris, but in the midst of the snow and pines, it tipped past ludicrous. But something about the little creature steadied Kiva's nerves. Plus, the cat had made it quite clear he would not be left behind when he'd all but packed himself in her bag.

She scratched him behind the ear with a sigh. "Let's just blame my mother instead. She's the one not answering my letters."

Which was why several weeks and far too much time on a horse later, Kiva, Auma, and the four royal guards Caliza had lent her were now a few hours' travel outside Vashka, the Korovi capital. Her mother wasn't the type to drop communication unwarranted. Something was wrong.

Auma squeezed her hand. "We'll find her, Kiva. If she is anything like her daughter, I'm sure she is just fine."

Kiva forced a smile in return. "That's exactly what I'm afraid of."

The transition from forest to town was gradual. A small cabin here, a snow-laden barn there. With the constant snows, Korovi farmers grew little, relying heavily on keeping herds of reindeer and breeding frost rabbits. Her mother told her once that one of the things she missed most about Korovi was the traditional frost rabbit stew they made each year for Koscanya, the yearly weeklong celebration of the goddess Lokane.

The single buildings turned to settlements, which turned to organized rows of slant-roofed homes, the snow pressed flat along the streets by teams of reindeer-led sleighs dragging rectangular blocks of stone. Glistening gold ornaments tied with sprigs of pine hung in doorways, marking them as homes that had been blessed by the priestesses. Each year, the priestesses visited every home in Vashka, granting them the goddess's protection.

Kiva knew all this from the books she read about Korovi as a child. When they'd only made her feel more separated from her homeland, she'd sworn off reading altogether. Thunking her sword into things was far more satisfying anyway.

Seeing it all now made her wish she'd never stopped reading.

She wanted to know what the two-pronged candelabras in each home's window meant, longed to understand the significance of the red ribbons she saw in some girls' hair. This world felt at once foreign and familiar, hers and not at all.

You belong here, she told herself. *You belong.*

Heads turned and eyes followed as they traversed the neat, orderly streets, making for the Sacred Palace at the heart of the city, where Kiva intended to ask the high priestess very nicely where her mother was. Visitors were as common in Vashka as the sun, so it was no surprise when whispers followed them all the way to the Hallowed Square, where the Sacred Palace waited in all its stiff elegance.

Aroch squirmed the whole way inside her jacket, as if sensing that they'd reached their destination at last. Or perhaps aware of the fact that the Korovi were as kind to strangers as rabid wolves. Though they had an official letter from Caliza stating they were there under her protection, the Korovi were known to have a stab-first-and-ask-questions-later sort of policy, and Kiva wasn't exactly great at official decorum.

The only structure built of stone in all the city, the Sacred Palace was pure white trimmed in gold paint, the whole of it made of curves and rounded arches, circular platforms and cylindrical towers. All save the square base, which had four sets of stairs, one leading down in each direction as a symbol of the palace's accessibility to all the city. While a nice gesture, Kiva knew from her mother that practice was much different, though she could have surmised that from the presence of the two Miska warriors at the foot of each staircase.

A massive fire ringed by a delicate metalwork fence sat at the base of each staircase: the Goddess's Flames, kept burning year-round. They cast strange shadows against the building's face and those of the female warriors watching them approach.

"I see my sister's stories of the Miska were not exaggerated," Auma said as they slowed their horses in the square. "They look formidable."

Each warrior was dressed in white leather, their forearms and waists wrapped in dark-blue-and-silver cloth. A longsword hung at each one's hip, and they stood with the bearing of stone, which would have been intimidating enough. Toss in that each of them had a foot of height and shoulder breadth on Kiva, and the Rhodairen guards suddenly looked very uncomfortable.

"Well," Kiva said with a sigh. "Here's to not getting executed."

They were made to wait. And wait. And wait.

The room they'd been put in was circular, as was everything

inside it. The couch. The table. The hanging glass sona lamps. The swirling ice-blue designs on the white stone floor. The entirety of it had been draped in gold ribbons in honor of Koscanya.

It felt very much like they'd been swallowed by some snowy creature and now resided in its stomach, which, Kiva supposed, wasn't that far off. It was said the Sacred Palace had been built to mimic the sleeping form of an Aizel, the great-horned snow cats known for their connection to the Sellas.

In most of the world, they were dark omens, but to the priestesses of Lokane, they were goddess-blessed, symbols of the honor-chosen, Lokane's favored servants. It was said in the time of the Sellas that the Aizel would arrive to choose the next high priestess.

The Rhodairen guards had sat down to a meal of hard cheese and dried meat, the extent of Korovi hospitality. Kiva, whose stomach resembled a series of jumbled knots, opted to pace in front of the door while Auma watched concernedly from the couch, Aroch perched on her shoulder and batting at one dangling braid.

"Saints, if someone doesn't open that damn door in the next five minutes—" Kiva's threat was silenced by the groan of said door opening. She whirled to face the arrival, a not-so-pleasant remark already on her lips and froze.

The woman standing in the doorway was a near reflection of her mother.

Broad, sturdy shoulders, a square face with a sharp, hawk-like nose, and shrewd blue eyes. Even the way she carried herself—as if there were a stick very far up an unsavory place—was like her mother down to the way she clenched one fist as she surveyed the room, as if measuring how many of them she could fight at once. She wore a flowing silver dress with billowing blue-trimmed sleeves, a white leather corset hugging her strong frame, and the handle of a bone knife rested at her hip.

Vokana Mirkova—her grandmother, and high priestess.

All the fire left Kiva in a breath and reflex seized hold. She straightened, bringing her boots together and throwing her shoulders back. She'd nearly saluted before she realized what she was doing and promptly trapped her hand against her thigh to keep from moving it.

Vokana's cold eyes settled on her last. "Sakiva," she said. Her Korovi accent was thick, but it was the downward twist of her lips that shaped the way she said her granddaughter's name. She all but spit on it.

Her grandmother lifted the letter Caliza had sent, which had been confiscated from them upon their arrival. "Your queen writes pretty words, but she says little. Tell me why you are here."

Kiva winced at the chosen words. *Your queen* practically screamed *You are not one of us.*

"Grandmother." She bowed stiffly at the waist. All her practiced words had left her. She hadn't expected to deal with her directly. In fact, she'd hoped to be greeted by her mother, safe and well and having lost track of time, even if Larissa Mirkova was more likely to lose track of her left hand.

Someone moved beside her, and Kiva straightened to find

Auma at her side. She'd shed her coat, revealing the dark-jade silk vest and leather pants she wore beneath. "May the goddess's grace warm you, My Lady," she greeted with a small bow. "My name is Auma Kura, Princess of Jindae. We seek information, if you'd be so gracious as to grant it."

Relief swept through Kiva. At least one of them knew how to do this correctly.

Vokana's lips twisted into another frown. "More pretty words. They waste my time, and a waste of my time is a waste of the goddess's time. Speak your purpose."

"We're here to see my mother," Kiva replied, perhaps a bit more hotly than she should have, but she didn't care for the way her grandmother was speaking to Auma. Forget the fact that they were of equal rank. No one spoke to her like that unless they wanted to see the other end of Kiva's sword.

"Your mother is not here," Vokana replied.

Kiva blinked. She must have misheard. "But she came to discuss the alliance—"

"And left when she was denied." Vokana folded her wiry arms behind her back. "If that is all, I have duties to return to."

Kiva lurched forward. "Wait—"

"You will be given rooms to spend the evening, but I expect you to depart with the first light."

"Grandmother—"

But she was already gone, the door swinging shut in her wake.

Kiva stared at the closed door for one, two, three heartbeats, and then she was tearing it open, all too ready to corner her grandmother and demand a better answer. Two Miska stepped into her path, swords half-drawn.

"You will remain here until your rooms are prepared," said one, their voice deep and smooth. Despite their words, their eyes practically begged Kiva to resist, their hand curling around their sword pommel.

"But—"

"You heard them," said the other. She put a hand to the door. "Inside."

Auma placed a hand on her shoulder, and Kiva allowed herself to be led back inside. The doors closed behind them, resolute in their rejection.

"I—I don't understand." Kiva ran a hand along her hair, fingers tangling in her braid. "If she left, then why isn't she home?"

"Simple," Auma said, gathering Aroch from her shoulders. "Because your grandmother is lying."

The rooms they were given were plain and bare, nothing like the comfortable suites the Trendellan king and queen had hosted them in. Kiva was half-convinced the mattress was made of stones, and despite there being no windows, there seemed to be a perpetual draft. The only decoration was a limp cut of gold ribbon. Apparently, even these rooms couldn't escape Koscanya's light.

She couldn't sleep, and not only because she and Auma intended to make their move as soon as the night was deepest.

At night, the sounds came creeping back. The clash of metal, the screams of dying soldiers. The final battle against Illucia had long since passed, but sometimes Kiva still woke up screaming. Some nights, she was falling from the shadow-made crow; some nights she was too late to save Thia from the Sella that had nearly killed her. But most nights, she just stood in an endless battlefield and remembered.

Auma helped. Her very presence soothed. But tonight, their plan relied on them having separate rooms.

Kiva waited by the door, Sinvarra strapped across her back. It was nearly time. Then—a crash, followed by a scream. The heavy footfalls of her guards fell away. Kiva cracked open the door, peering out into the hall. She was alone, the guards drawn to Auma's screams.

Slipping out, she shot down the hall in the opposite direction of Auma's room, her nerves like crackling ice. Their plan had only gone so far as getting Kiva out of her room. She knew nothing of the Sacred Palace's layout and had absolutely no idea where to begin looking.

All she knew was that Vokana had lied—which meant that her mother was still here, somewhere, and Kiva was going to find her.

She followed the curving corridor to a small atrium they'd passed through on their way in. When they'd first arrived, she'd seen a group of Miska emerging from a hall, practice swords in hands, and beside the highly capable warriors seemed like a good place for a prison.

She'd just reached the atrium when something darted

past her. Cursing, she had Sinvarra half-drawn before her eyes adjusted to the moonlit dark well enough to recognize what it was.

"What in the Saints' name? *Aroch?*" She gaped at the tiny white cat. "How did you even...? Never mind. Go back. Go." She pointed behind her, but Aroch merely lifted his nose to the air and sniffed. Then he took off down a hall to the right—*not* in the direction Kiva had been going.

"Aroch!" she hissed, hesitating. If she followed him, she'd waste time she didn't have. But her grandmother had seen the cat with them, and her guards had left him safely in Kiva's room. If they found him, they'd know she was out.

Muttering a string of Korovi curses, she sprinted after him.

Aroch ran down hallway after hallway draped in gold ribbons, completely ignoring her attempts to coax him back. More than once, he reacted to another presence coming the other way before Kiva and darted into a nearby hall, taking her out of harm's way until the danger had passed. Somehow, and she had absolutely no idea how, the cat seemed to be leading her somewhere.

At last, the hall took a final turn, emptying them into a corridor that dead-ended at a door.

And it was guarded by a Miska.

It was the warrior from outside the door earlier—the one who'd seemed ready to fight. They leapt from their chair, freeing their sword in the same motion.

Kiva held up her hands. "I don't suppose you'll just let me pass?" she asked hopefully.

The warrior lowered into a stance. "Submit peacefully and I will not hurt you."

"Right." Kiva drew Sinvarra. "Just watch out for the cat." Then she struck.

The Miska parried with ease, and just like that, they were dancing around each other, the broad hall accommodating their sweep and strikes.

It took Kiva all of a few seconds to realize she was outmatched.

The Miska was faster and stronger. It was all Kiva could do to block the blows ringing through her muscles. Memory coated each move she made, flashing unwanted images: torn limbs and ravaged flesh, blood and smoke and bile. Thoughts that had pulled at her ever since the final battle. They made her doubt herself. Made her think too much.

She could not win this fight. Not like this. But maybe she didn't have to.

Strength comes in many forms. It was something Auma had said to Thia, all those months ago in the dark Illucian castle, and it was something Kiva had striven to remember ever since. She didn't have to outfight this person—she had only to win.

For this room, like all the others, was hung with ribbon.

Catching another of the Miska's blows, Kiva shoved her sword down and threw her shoulder forward, driving them back. Then she dropped Sinvarra and threw her boot against the low windowsill, using it to leap. Her fingers closed around the ribbon, and she tore it off as she landed, pulling a knife from her hip sheathe and shearing one end free. She'd just cut the far end loose when the Miska barreled down on her with a cry.

Kiva caught their wrist with the ribbon.

The Miska blinked at her, the moment of surprise all it took for Kiva to wrench the warrior's sword free and swing their wrist behind their back, just like Auma had shown her—perhaps a little too enthusiastically—so many times before. Off guard, the Miska tried to turn with her, just as Kiva knew they would. With one well-placed heel, Kiva tripped them, sending them to their knees. Then she snatched their other wrist, tying them tight.

"Sorry," she said and slammed the dagger hilt into their head. They crumpled, unmoving but still breathing.

"Come on," Kiva said to Aroch, who'd been waiting by the door. "That won't last long."

Snatching up and sheathing Sinvarra, she took the keys from the Miska's belt and unlocked the door. It'd no sooner swung open than someone descended upon her with a cry. Kiva yelped, throwing up the arm to block their weapon. It thudded hard into her forearm and she stumbled back, scrambling for Sinvarra before she realized what she'd just been struck with: a chair leg.

The wielder raised it for another blow, then stopped as their gaze settled. The chair leg clattered to the floor. "Sakiva!" her mother rasped.

Kiva threw her arms around her mother's neck. Her mother stiffened, but she didn't tell her to let go, which was practically an *I love you* coming from her.

She pulled back, her excitement waning as she took in

her mother's weary state. She looked healthy but tired, dark smudges underlining her eyes.

"Thank the Saints you're all right," Kiva said.

"Your Saints have no power here," said a voice from behind. Kiva whirled, drawing Sinvarra, and came face-to-face with her grandmother. Five Miska stood at her back, the one she'd knocked out already coming to. Another warrior leaned down to untie them, and they glowered darkly at Kiva as they stood.

"How dare you instigate violence in the house of the goddess," Vokana intoned. "You will be punished for this, royal protection or not."

"Mother, please." Larissa stepped past her, and Kiva nearly balked at her pleading tone. She'd never heard her mother speak like that. "She acted only to protect me. Do not punish her for my mistakes."

Vokana lifted her chin. "She has disobeyed a direct order and attacked me in my home. Clearly, your rebellious nature did not end with you. Your daughter is every bit as dishonorable as you."

"That's rich, coming from a woman who banished her own daughter and holed up in her palace while the world burned," Kiva said, stepping up beside her mother. "What do you know of honor?"

"Sakiva," her mother hissed, but Kiva didn't listen.

"You ignored our alliance's pleas for help, imprisoned a woman under Rhodairen royal protection, and lied to my face when I came looking for her. You are a hypocrite who only cares about honor so long as it fits her uses."

Silence descended in the wake of her words. Her grandmother's face remained unchanged, only the slow open-close, open-close of her fist revealing her displeasure.

Then she said simply, "Take her."

A Miska stepped forward, and Kiva hefted Sinvarra. Vokana held up a hand, and the Miska paused. Then the others shifted aside, revealing Auma. She'd been bound and gagged, a bruise blossoming around one eye.

Everything in Kiva stilled into a killing calm, and for one, endless moment, she nearly lost herself to the rising fury. Then, with every ounce of self-control she possessed, she lowered her sword. Slowly, she sheathed it. Then she stepped forward, straight for her grandmother. A Miska moved to intercept her, but Vokana waved them off.

Kiva stopped before her grandmother. She pressed a single finger to the bone-hilt of Vokana's blade. Touching another Miska's blade was a grave insult, and it meant only one thing: a duel.

Whispers chorused through the hall. Kiva held her grandmother's cold gaze. "If I win, we go free."

Vokana's hand tightened into a fist. "When you lose, you both accept your fate."

The dueling arena was no simple sparring ground.

Set in one of the cylindrical towers, the room was as ornate as the rest of the castle, and sadly free of gold ribbons. She wouldn't be repeating that trick again.

Besides, she had a feeling it wouldn't work on her grandmother, who might have been in her early sixties but was still lean with muscle and power.

The Miska from the hall had accompanied them, along with her mother and Auma, who, it turned out, had freed herself of her restraints long before they'd even found Kiva and had been all too prepared to strike from behind had Kiva tried to fight her way out.

They'd been left alone with her mother at one end of the room to prepare.

"It may not be too late to reverse this, Sakiva," her mother said. "If I submit to my mother's will, she may let you go unharmed."

"I'm not leaving you here." Kiva drew Sinvarra, hefting the blade's familiar weight. "What happened to you anyway?"

Her mother drew a quiet breath. "I did not react well to her refusal to help. My banishment meant that should I return here, I would forfeit my life. Only Queen Caliza's writ of royal protection kept me safe. I broke that when I struck my mother."

Kiva let out a low whistle. "Nice."

"Kiva," Auma said.

"What? Vokana is out of line." Kiva laid the flat of Sinvarra against her shoulder. "She's more stubborn than Thia and Res combined."

"She is set in her ways like a river into stone," her mother said. "There is no changing her."

"Rivers bend," Kiva said quietly, thinking of the prince she'd left behind with her best friend. "They forge new paths."

She knew her grandmother despised her, all because her mother had married a man from beyond the Cut when marriage was forbidden to a noblewoman, whose service was meant only for Lokane. But the Korovi had clung to old ways for generations. Never growing, never changing. She'd seen what that did to people in Illucia, seen what isolation did to the world when Rhodaire refused to send aid.

The similarities she saw in the snow kingdom scared her.

"She'll listen when I win." Kiva turned to face the other side of the room, where a Miska was handing her grandmother a beautiful white-handled sword.

Auma squeezed her shoulder. "Be careful." She leaned in, placing a soft kiss on Kiva's cheek that sent a flush raging across her pale skin.

"And good luck," her mother said.

Aroch nudged her leg with his head, as if to echo them. Was it her, or did the cat look a little bigger and a little...whiter? As if he were glowing, just faintly. She shook her head. The moonlight coming in through the high windows was playing tricks on her.

Taking a deep breath, Kiva approached the circle in the center of the room. The dueling rules were simple: first blood drawn or to force their opponent from the sparring circle won. It was an exercise her mother had put her through a thousand times, and now, she realized, that her mother's mother must have put her through.

A Miska stepped to the edge of the circle, hand raised. Kiva hefted Sinvarra, and her grandmother lifted her own blade. The Miska brought down her hand. "Begin!"

Vokana struck first. Kiva parried easily, countering with a strike to Vokana's ribs that her grandmother danced away from. She was light on her feet despite her long, broad frame. Quicker than Kiva, but perhaps not as strong. With each traded blow, Kiva tested her theory and found it held. She struggled to match Vokana's speed, but when she caught her blow and turned it to a test of strength, her grandmother strained against her.

"You are unworthy of this battle," Vokana hissed as their blades ground against each other.

"My mother taught me"—Kiva heaved a breath—"that if you can talk while you fight, you aren't fighting hard enough." She shoved with all her might, sending her grandmother stumbling to the edge of the circle. Vokana caught herself at the last moment, her foot just inside the bound.

Then they were trading blows again, steel against black gold. Kiva felt herself tiring as keeping up with Vokana's strikes became more difficult. Then her grandmother feigned, and Kiva realized too late. On the wrong foot and unbalanced, it was all she could do to throw herself backward fast enough to avoid the tip of Vokana's sword.

She stumbled, dropping to one knee, and her grandmother raised her blade.

A flash of white. Aroch leapt toward the circle. Then he *changed*.

One moment he was a flying white cat; the next, he'd landed a massive creature, his head easily as high as Vokana's chest. Horns longer than Kiva's arms and ridged like a ram's reached straight back from between the cat's tufted ears, its fur white as fresh powder tipped in silver. Its coat flowed, coiling like mist. No, *emitting* mist. She couldn't tell where the creature's fur ended and the wisps of fog began.

An aizel.

Kiva surged to her feet with a cry, snapping Vokana out of her dazed stare. She swung, and her grandmother caught the blow, but she was already moving. She shoved Vokana back a step, then brought her blade down in a two-handed arc.

Vokana's sword caught the blow—then snapped.

Kiva's strike came down with a *zing*, the tip cutting a thin line in her grandmother's cheek. Blood welled, then dripped down her pale skin.

Panting, exhausted, and very, very confused, Kiva let out a small laugh.

"Kiva!" Auma was at her side, one hand on her arm, completely unconcerned by the massive cat of fog standing right beside them. "Are you all right?"

"I'm fine," Kiva said. "I think. You can see that, too, can't you?" She gestured at Aroch.

"We can all see him, Sakiva." Her mother had joined them too. "Where did he come from?"

"A bakery," Kiva replied.

Her mother stared at her, but the energy necessary to explain more had fled her long ago. She leaned heavily on Auma, who fit perfectly below her arm.

None of the Miska had moved, and her grandmother had not looked away from the aizel. As they watched, Aroch nudged Kiva's head with his own.

"Horns! Horns!" Kiva groaned, and Aroch licked her face.

"I—" Vokana started but fell silent, at a loss for words.

The urge to throw Aroch's presence in her face rose, but Kiva shoved it away for later. This wasn't the time. As much as she disagreed with a lot of Korovi's practices, she understood them, and she respected the tradition they came from. She knew how hard it was to accept you were wrong about someone, especially someone you didn't want to like.

It took more than words. It took honor.

Vokana touched two fingers to the blood on her cheek and peered at the crimson staining her fingers.

Aroch stepped forward, and her grandmother straightened, shoulders back. Then the aizel bowed, and Vokana bowed back.

When she rose, her face was resolute. "You have won, Sakiva. You and your mother are free to go. But—" Vokana hesitated, and her mother stiffened. "But I ask that you remain with us a little while longer."

Kiva blinked. That wasn't what she'd been expecting. "Why?"

She looked to the Miska warrior who Kiva had fought in the hall. "You have defeated me, and you bested Enik, our greatest warrior." Enik grimaced, and Vokana continued, "I come from a very long, proud tradition of priestesses and Miska, and never in my life have I seen an aizel in the flesh, nor my ancestors in theirs. This is a sign from the goddess that perhaps it is time to revisit those traditions."

Auma sighed quietly. "Is this what passes for a family reunion in this kingdom?"

Kiva couldn't help it—she laughed. The sound echoed in the high tower, until even her mother cracked some resemblance of a smile.

"I guess we could stay for a little while," Kiva said, patting Aroch on the back. "I do have some questions. Like why in the world you waited until *now* to transform. We really could have used a giant magical cat, oh, I don't know, *during the war!*"

"That's simple." Enik stepped forward. "Aizel's can only change when their magic has been recharged. Likely this one has been away from a strong magical force for some time and was only able to transform after being here for some time. Vashka is well known to be a well of magic, not unlike the Wandering Wood of the Sellas. Do you know nothing of our people's myths?"

"I know that I beat you in single combat," Kiva replied.

"Next time, I will defeat you," Enik snarled. "In a fair fight. Korovi do not fight with tricks."

Kiva crooked a grin, slinging one arm over Auma's shoulder and the other over Enik's. "I am not only Korovi."

ACKNOWLEDGMENTS

I can't believe I'm here again.

Getting to write and publish a book has been an incredible experience, made better by all the support from my family and friends, but there's something particularly special about finishing a sequel. Thia's story is very close to my heart, and I'm so thankful for everyone who helped bring it into existence.

As always, to my Guillotine Queens. Brittney Singleton, your mind for marketing and design is amazing, and your early help on this was equally so. Jennifer Gruenke, thank you for all the man buns and for not making me carry a balloon around YALLFest alone. To Sam Farkas, for teaching me to ride the subway (trains are hard!), and Kat Enright, for always having everything a person could need at a festival. Thank you to

Alyssa Colman, Jessica James, and Tracy Badua, for helping fix my wild plot early on. To Ashley Northrup and Bibi Cooper, whose jokes and humor give me life, and to Amy Stewart (we miss you!). Our Friday chats and screams into the void kept me steady. I couldn't have come this far without you all and your stories inspire me every day.

To my incredible agent, Carrie Pestritto. I'm so lucky to have you in my corner, and I'm so excited for a future of working with you. Thank you for all the time and energy you've dedicated to this journey.

To my editor, Annie Berger, who once again helped me find the heart of my story while juggling a bazillion emails from me. Thank you for helping to bring this story to life.

Publishing a book really is a group effort, and I've been so lucky to have such amazing support from my family and friends, most incredibly my roommates and best friends. Maliena, whose excitement and support for this story has meant the world to me. I'll catch a spider for you any day. To Alex, who read my early drafts overnight and listened to me complain about writing for way too long (I think you know more about publishing than me now). Brock, for being an encyclopedia of random facts and scientific knowledge, and for plotting out that final battle scene with me. I appreciate all the LOTR examples. And to Lauren, for constantly lending her phone's much nicer camera for all my ridiculous book pictures and for supplying the occasional much-needed glass of wine.

Thank you to Rosiee Thor for fielding all my publishing panic and always knowing more than me about it. To Alexandra

Overy and Amber Duell, whose own stories I've been so lucky to read and whose friendship means everything.

Once again, thank you to Tran Nguyen and Nicole Hower for my amazing cover. I will never be able to stop staring at it. To the Sourcebooks Fire team: Sarah Kasman, Cassie Gutman, Travis Hasenour, Sabrina Baskey, and everyone else involved, thank you!

Lastly, thank you to all of my readers, and to the bloggers, bookstagrammers, librarians, and booksellers who helped promote and support these little birb books.

And, as always, to my mom and dad: I love you.

ABOUT THE AUTHOR

Kalyn Josephson is a fantasy writer living in the California Bay Area. She loves books, cats, books with cats, and making up other worlds to live in for a while. Visit her at kalynjosephson.com.

FIREreads

────────── ⑤ *#getbooklit* ──────────

Your hub for the hottest young adult books!

Visit us online and sign up for our
newsletter at FIREreads.com

 @sourcebooksfire

 sourcebooksfire

 firereads.tumblr.com